CHARLES McCARRY established an international reputation as a novelist with the publication of his worldwide bestseller, *The Tears of Autumn*. He is the author of eleven other critically acclaimed novels (*The Miernik Dossier, The Secret Lovers, The Better Angels, The Last Supper, The Bride of the Wilderness, Second Sight, Shelley's Heart, Old Boys, Christopher's Ghosts, Lucky Bastard* and *Ark*) that have been translated into more than twenty languages. His nine non-fiction books include *Citizen Nader*, the authoritative first biography of Ralph Nader. He is the former Editor at Large of *National Geographic* and has contributed dozens of articles, short stories and poems to leading national magazines. His op-ed pieces and other essays have appeared in *The New York Times, The Wall Street Journal* and *The Washington Post*. During the 1990s and 2000s, McCarry served for a decade under deep cover as a CIA operations officer in Europe, Africa and Asia.

Novels by Charles McCarry

Ark

Christopher's Ghosts

Old Boys

Lucky Bastard

Shelley's Heart

Second Sight

The Bride of the Wilderness

The Last Supper

The Better Angels

The Secret Lovers

The Tears of Autumn

The Miernik Dossier

CHARLES McCARRY
THE LAST SUPPER

DUCKWORTH OVERLOOK

This edition first published in UK in 2015 by
Duckworth Overlook

LONDON
30 Calvin Street
London E1 6NW
Tel: 020 7490 7300
Fax: 020 7490 0080
E: info@duckworth-publishers.co.uk
www.ducknet.co.uk

NEW YORK
141 Woostr Street, New York, NY 10012

A catalogue record for this book is available
from the British Library.

ISBN 978 0 7156 4737 0

Printed and bound in the UK

To Rod MacLeish

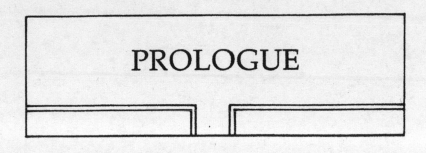

PROLOGUE

Molly

In his dream, Paul Christopher, thirteen years old, wore a thick woolen sweater with three bone buttons on the left shoulder. His father's yawl *Mahican* was sailing before the wind, her port rail awash in the swelling waters of the Baltic Sea. The weak northern sun was just rising astern, behind the mist that hid the coast of Germany: not the mainland, but the island of Rügen, whose white chalk cliffs rise four hundred feet above the sea. Aboard the yawl, the man the Christophers called the Dandy scampered, quick as a rat, down the ladder into the cabin. Paul's mother was alarmed. "Our guest is hiding in the picnic basket," she said. *"Ssshhh,* every time a secret is told, an angel falls."

Paul went below and opened the wicker picnic basket. The Dandy crouched inside among the fitted plates and food boxes and thermos bottles. He was striking their guest on the kidneys with a rubber baton and forcing him to eat the buttons from Paul's sweater. The Dandy wore a Gestapo badge. The guest was dressed as a rabbi; he smelled of the dust of books and of strange food. The Dandy made a sympathetic face to show Paul that he too was disgusted by this alien stench. Then he fed the rabbi another button.

A storm came up. Paul's father shouted, "Paul, take the helm!" The jib broke loose and they struggled with it; the canvas billowed and snapped in the howling wind. Paul's mother fell overboard. He dove after her. In the pewter light at the bottom of the shallow sea, among rocks bearded with seaweed, he found his mother's body with buttons sewn to its eyes.

In a chilly room in Paris, Paul Christopher's lover, a girl named Molly, kissed his fluttering eyelids. He woke from his dream. Molly sat up in bed. She had beautiful breasts, with large aureoles that were the same color as her unpainted lips. Though it was January and the window was open, she sat for a long moment in the cold draft, looking into Christopher's eyes, before she pulled the quilt to her chin.

"You spoke in your sleep, in German," Molly said. "What did you dream? You have such amazing dreams."

"I was sailing with my parents."

"Sailing? In Germany?"

"In the Baltic. My mother was drowning."

"Oh, dear. Did you save her?"

Beneath the covers, Molly shivered. Her skin was cold to the touch. Christopher got out of bed and closed the window. It had begun to rain, the gray cold rain of northern Europe wetting the gray stones of the city.

Molly wrapped herself in the quilt and came to the window. She put her chin on Christopher's shoulder and spoke into his ear. She was an Australian who had been taught in an English boarding school to speak like an Englishwoman; when she was sleepy, as she was now, her native accent was just discernible, like a thready scar concealed in a wrinkle by a plastic surgeon.

"*Did* you save her?" Molly asked.

Christopher nodded.

"Good. I was worried that I'd waked you at the wrong moment."

"At the wrong moment?" Christopher smiled at Molly's reflection in the windowpane. She dug the point of her chin into the muscle of his shoulder.

"You don't know that dreams go on after we wake up?" Molly said. "Why should they stop just because they're interrupted? We can only see the people in our dreams when we're asleep, but that doesn't mean they aren't always there. Perhaps they can see *us* when we're awake."

Molly saw that Christopher wasn't listening to what she said. He was staring into the street below. Molly followed his gaze. There was little to see: the rain falling through the dim streetlight onto the shiny cobbles, the stubby branches of a plane tree pruned for the winter. The brake lights blinked on a parked Citroën.

"Is that Tom Webster's man in that car?" Molly asked.

"Yes."

"Is he really going to guard me all the time you're gone?"

"It won't always be the same car or the same man, but the car will always be in that parking place. They'll blink the brake lights on the hour and the half hour to let you know they're there."

"Wonderful Tom. That will buck me up tremendously."

Molly opened the quilt and put her arms around Christopher from behind, enclosing him in the folds of the coverlet. Her skin was warm now. She stroked his naked back with the length of her own body.

"You have such a sweet body," she said.

Christopher turned inside the quilt and put his arms around her.

Later, in bed, Molly got to her knees and turned on the lamp. The Japanese, when they paint on silk, sometimes mix pulverized gold into the pigment, so that the depths of the painting will gather light and magnify it. Molly's auburn hair had this quality. Christopher touched her and smiled. Seeing the male pleasure in his eyes, she shook her head, impatient with her own beauty.

"No," she said. "Just this once, don't look at me. Listen."

"It's difficult," Christopher said. The bedroom walls were mirrored and everywhere he looked he saw the reflection of Molly. The whole apartment, borrowed as a hiding place, was mirrored. It was furnished with glass tables and cubical black leather chairs. The vast bed in which Molly and Christopher now lay was circular, like a bed in a movie about a movie star, and the quilt Molly had wrapped around their bodies was a reproduction of a playing card, the jack of hearts. All these images and especially Molly's nudity, were reflected from mirror to mirror.

"Your plane leaves in three hours," Molly said. "I don't want to send you off in a sad mood, but really, Paul, I'm filled with dread."

She was very pale. The lamplight shone directly on her face. Christopher had lived with Molly for nearly two years but he had never until this moment seen the faint constellation of freckles on her cheekbones;

[5]

always before, the surrounding skin had had enough color to conceal them.

"It isn't just being left alone," Molly said. "I'm used to that, you're always going up in smoke right in the middle of things, I *hate* it." Molly shuddered and pulled the quilt around her body. *"Why* does it always have to be so cold in France, so damp?" she asked. "Why is there never any light? It's like a tomb."

She heard herself speaking and for a moment the light of amusement came back into her face. She hated melancholia.

"It's not France, it's not being left alone," she explained. "I'll tell you what it is, Paul. I'm eaten up by suspicion. I suspect *you* of something."

Christopher sat up and began to speak.

"Don't say anything," Molly said. "Let me finish. I'm going to make a charge against you. If what I suspect is true, I want you to admit it to me. It's the least you can do."

Molly cried easily, but usually from happiness. Her eyes were dry now.

"What I suspect is this," she said. "I think you're going to go out and get on an airplane in three hours' time and fly out to bloody Saigon and I'll never see you again. You have no notion of coming back. You're going to let them kill you so that they won't kill me."

Molly examined Christopher's face. He would not look into her eyes, so she gazed at him in the mirror.

"All right," she said. "Don't answer; I knew you wouldn't. But if you leave me in that way, with such cruelty, I'll never forgive you. I won't, Paul, not even in death."

She turned off the lamp and drew close to him. In the darkness he could smell her skin, soap and the forest odor of lovemaking. They had just come back from the mountains and the scent of woodsmoke lingered in her hair; there had been a fireplace in their room; Molly loved all sorts of friendly flames: candles, burning logs.

"It isn't true," Christopher said, now that it was dark.

"Then don't leave without saying good-bye," Molly said. "Don't *do* that again. Paul, don't vanish. I mean it. Really I mean it."

She turned on the lamp again so that he could see how serious she was. Christopher kissed her eyes; she was crying now. Molly lifted his arm and wrapped it around her body. Her muscles were tense. He knew that she meant to stay awake until it was time for him to go. But soon the warmth of the bed relaxed her and she fell asleep.

At midnight, Christopher slipped out of bed and put on his clothes. There was very little light in the room, just the reflection of a streetlamp, but he had been lying awake in the dark and his eyes had adjusted. He could see Molly quite plainly. Her face was buried in the pillow. She was dreaming. She pushed a long bare leg out of the bed, muttered a few words, and resumed her soft breathing. Her left hand turned on the sheet; she was wearing all the rings Christopher had ever given her: emerald, topaz, scarab, opal, one on each finger. He always brought her a ring when he came home from a journey; she never took them off.

Molly spoke again in her sleep. Christopher could not make out the words. He knelt beside the bed and slipped his hand beneath the covers, but he could not bring himself to wake her. He stood up. Molly had left her purse on the dressing table. He took an envelope out of his coat pocket and crossed the room, walking softly over the thick white carpet. Molly moved in the bed. In the mirror, Christopher could see her sleeping face. He opened her purse and placed the envelope inside. He paused in the doorway and looked once more at Molly's sleeping faces, dozens of them, reflected in the mirrors.

Then he went into the living room. A fur coat lay in a heap by the door where Molly had left it. He picked it up and draped it over a chair. Then, just as Molly had feared, he left without saying good-bye, locking the door behind him.

The sound of the key in the lock woke Molly. Naked, she ran into the living room. The elevator whined in its shaft. She tried to open the door, but the complicated locks defeated her; she broke a nail, twisting the bolt. Sucking the wound, she went to the window. In the street below, Christopher was talking to the man in the Citroën. He had got out of the car and the two of them stood in the rain, chatting. They looked up at Molly's window, but it was at the top of the house and they didn't see her, a pale stripe of flesh against the darkness of the room.

Christopher finished talking and walked away. He had an American walk; he did not hold himself in any particular way as Europeans did, he simply walked as if it didn't matter to him what class strangers thought he belonged to.

"Damn you," Molly said, watching him.

Her eye fell on the fur coat. She put it on, meaning to follow Christopher into the street, and struggled with the locks again. She could not get them open.

Molly ran back to the window. Christopher had vanished, but the man in the Citroën was still out in the open. He looked upward at the window. Molly stepped back into the dark. The man searched in his pocket for something, found it, looked up and down the street, then hurried away.

Molly knew what he had had in his pocket: a telephone token. He was going to use the public telephone at the Métro station, around the corner on the Boulevard Beauséjour, to report Christopher's departure. He would be out of sight for ten minutes: Molly had timed him earlier in the day, when he had made another phone call.

"Damn you," Molly said again, speaking to Christopher.

She turned and walked rapidly out of the room, dropping the fur coat to the floor. It wasn't hers; it was a borrowed coat—rabbit pelts, she thought, dyed to resemble some more elegant dead animal. In the bedroom, she put on a skirt and sweater, ran a comb through her hair, and pulled on a pair of boots. She opened her purse, looking for French money for a taxi, and found the envelope Christopher had left.

She tore it open. There was no note inside, just a thick sheaf of hundred-dollar bills, thousands of dollars in American currency. Molly looked helplessly at the money; it seemed insane to carry such a sum into the street. She dropped the envelope onto the unmade bed and pulled the sheet over it.

Struggling with the locks again, Molly turned the knobs the other way. The bolts slid open at last.

At the airport, Christopher presented his ticket at the baggage room and claimed his battered leather suitcase, then carried it through the deserted terminal and into the men's toilet. In a cubicle, he opened the bag. It was exactly as he had left it: two tropical suits, a set of rough clothes with boots, shirts, toilet articles. The lining was undisturbed. He closed the brass locks, flushed the toilet, and opened the door of the cubicle.

Tom Webster stood at the sink, combing his cropped hair. In the mirror, Webster turned his earnest, bespectacled face toward Christopher. "I thought I'd see you off," he said. He held up a soothing hand, as if he expected Christopher to be angry or frightened by his presence. "It's all right," he said. "I checked all the crappers. We're alone in here."

Christopher put his suitcase on the floor and leaned against the tiled wall, watching the entrance.

Webster spoke in a husky whisper. "It's not too late to change your mind," he said.

The loudspeaker system chimed and Christopher's flight was called in French and Vietnamese.

"I checked the passenger list. Kim is on the plane with you," Webster said. "They're waiting for you out there. You can still turn around."

Christopher shook his head and picked up his suitcase.

"I'll help you, we'll all help you, fuck Headquarters," Webster said. "Take Molly and get lost. Enough is enough."

Christopher started to speak to his friend. At that moment, a man carrying a rolled newspaper came into the brightly lighted room. He gave the two Americans an incurious glance, then went to the urinal. Christopher walked swiftly out the door. They were calling his flight again.

Webster remained at the sink, washing his hands, until the man with the newspaper finished at the urinal. Then, wiping his wet hands on his raincoat, Webster followed him.

Still clutching his newspaper, the man hurried out the doors leading to the roadway in front of the terminal.

Webster followed him outside. The man was behaving exactly like the French businessman he appeared to be, brusque and self-important. But Webster was curious about him. At two o'clock in the morning, his suit was perfectly pressed; had he been returning from one of the long flights from Africa and Asia that arrived in Paris at this time of night, his clothes would have been rumpled. He would have had a growth of beard, but he was clean-shaven.

When the man with the newspaper got outside, he didn't hail a taxi. He stood patiently on the curb, holding his newspaper like a baton, waiting.

A taxi stopped on the wrong side of the roadway. The passenger was a girl. She paid the driver and didn't wait for her change. The taxi door on the traffic side was flung open and she got out, her skirt riding up as she slid across the seat. Her legs were long and extremely beautiful. When he saw them, the man with the newspaper pushed out his lips in a little pouting kiss of lust.

Now the girl was walking rapidly across the roadway, the heels of her boots clattering on the pavement, her bright heavy hair moving around her face. Webster, who had begun to watch her because of her legs, saw that the girl was Molly. He lifted a hand. Molly saw him and her mouth opened in its frank smile. Her eyes were sleepy and her face was still a little puffy from bed.

Webster stepped off the curb, holding out his hand to Molly. Out of the corner of his eye, he saw the Frenchman raise his rolled newspaper, as if to signal a taxi. A car that had been parked across the roadway sped away from the curb, tires shrieking and gears changing. Its lights were off. It was a dark green Peugeot. Webster saw all that, and saw the man drop his newspaper and walk rapidly away.

When the Peugeot hit her, Molly was still smiling. Her eyes were looking directly into Webster's. Her hair opened as if she had fallen into deep water and like a swimmer she floated for a long moment in the air, her back deeply arched, before she struck the pavement.

As the Peugeot sped away, fragments of smashed chrome fell off it and rang on the concrete. A policeman blew his whistle. Down the roadway more whistles sounded, shrill and thin. Overhead, Christopher's jet climbed steeply, losing the lights of Paris as it passed through a layer of clouds.

When Webster, running clumsily, reached Molly, he saw that she had lost her boots; a porter, standing thirty feet away, picked one up, as if to return it to her.

A shaft of white bone, jagged at the end, had punctured the skin of Molly's thigh. She lay on her face, her hair thrown forward, her neck bare. The blood ran out of her body in a long thick ribbon, meandering among the cobbles of the gutter and collecting in a pool against the curb.

She wore a ring on every finger of her outflung hand, Christopher's gifts.

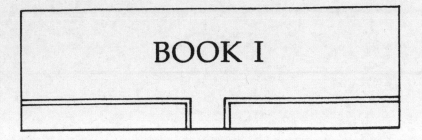

BOOK I

Hubbard

One

The first link in the chain of events that led to the murder of Molly Benson, an innocent young woman who happened to love Paul Christopher, was forged on an August afternoon in 1923, on the island of Rügen, before either of the lovers was born. On that day, a young American named Hubbard Christopher, Paul's father, walked up a steep path toward Berwick, the home of a Prussian family called Buecheler. Hubbard Christopher, then twenty-one years old, intended to pay a courtesy call on Colonel Baron Paulus von Buecheler, the current occupant of Berwick. Forty years before, Buecheler had been at school in Bonn with Hubbard Christopher's father, and the two men, both soldiers, had kept up a lifelong friendship.

As Hubbard approached Berwick, tramping through a forest of ancient beeches, he felt a peaceful delight in the natural beauty of the island. There was a leafy scent in the air, the sea was a deep painterly blue. For the past six months, Hubbard had been living in Berlin, but he had grown up in the Berkshire Hills of Massachusetts and he was happiest in country places. He attracted a certain amount of attention. Hubbard was six feet four inches tall, a great height in those days even for an American, and according to the German idea, he was not dressed for exercise. He wore a blazer and flannels, white buckskin shoes, and a straw hat. The Germans he encountered on the path were more suitably attired in hiking boots, short leather pants, and open shirts. All possessed rustic walking sticks with sharp metal points, and the path, riddled by these implements, looked as if a myriad of birds had hopped along it, leaving innumerable tracks. Many of the Germans bore rucksacks. Hubbard's only burden was a parcel tied with gold string. The Germans strode purposefully among the beeches, chests heaving as they did breathing exercises. Hubbard sauntered, an expression of good humor suffusing his long, horsey face.

When Berwick came into view, Hubbard recognized it at once; he had seen the house often in photographs. Nevertheless, he was surprised by its appearance. It was smaller than he had imagined, a simple square structure in the Italian Renaissance style. Though he admired its chaste beauty, Hubbard would not have called it a castle; it seemed smaller than many Massachusetts houses. The Buechelers did not call it a castle, either; they always referred to it simply as Berwick; it was the local people who called it Schloss Berwick: nobility lived within, and life was more orderly if there was a castle with a noble in residence, a badge of rank against which everyone else's position could be measured.

Hubbard had been invited for coffee at five o'clock. He was precisely on time. The front door of Berwick was flung open and Paulus von Buecheler came out to greet him. Pebbles crunched beneath his brogans as he marched down the gravel path. Paulus was a shiny man: bald head, shaved cheeks, polished old shoes, one watchful intelligent blue eye, a glittering monocle covering the other eye.

"Christopher?"

His hand, gripping Hubbard's, was rough and strong.

"Yes," Hubbard said. "I'm delighted to meet you, Herr Colonel Baron."

" 'Herr Colonel Baron'? After all those birthday presents I sent you?"

"Uncle Paulus, then."

"That's better." Paulus von Buecheler pumped Hubbard's hand again and gazed upward into his face. Paulus's belted tweed jacket fitted like a military tunic, and he had a loud soldierly voice. He was clearly pleased by Hubbard's punctuality. Gripping Hubbard's elbow, he set off for the house.

"You speak like a Prussian," he said. "You can't have learned German from your father. He had a *terrible* Rhinelander accent."

"I had a Prussian tutor."

"Very wise of your father. Now you must meet my wife and my niece."

Paulus stood aside, gesturing for Hubbard to go through the open door. Once inside, Hubbard saw that Berwick was larger than it appeared to be from the outside, and this camouflage pleased his Yankee soul. The entrance hall, thirty feet square, rose to the roof. Hubbard paused in the middle of a frayed Persian carpet and looked around him. Boars' heads and suits of armor decorated the walls. A large Flemish tapestry, bathed in sunlight, hung on the landing of a double staircase. Hubbard gazed at it, transfixed.

"Would you like to go up?" Paulus asked.

"Yes, if you don't mind."

On the landing, Hubbard examined the tapestry more closely. A unicorn, its horn in profile, gazed over its shoulder into the room. Behind the unicorn, elephants, giraffes, leopards, and barnyard animals all grazed together in a field of wildflowers. Hubbard smiled in pleasure at the childlike innocence of the dead weaver who had made the picture.

A female voice said, in English, "Do you like the tapestry?"

Hubbard looked up and saw a gloriously pretty girl of eighteen descending the stairs. She was small, with delicate feet and ankles. She had auburn hair and a face that only a German girl could have: utterly smooth creamy skin, unblemished and unwrinkled, with the nose, the mouth, the perfect line of the jaw fresh from the sculptor.

"It's wonderful," Hubbard replied.

"My niece, Baronesse Hannelore von Buecheler," Paulus said.

"Lori, in the family," the girl said, extending her hand.

Hubbard had never met such impetuously informal Prussians. The skin on Lori's palm felt the way the skin on her neck looked: fresh, firm, untouched. She had very large gray eyes, heavily lashed. These looked gravely into Hubbard's face.

"Do you know about tapestries?" Lori asked, continuing to speak English. She did so with a slight Scottish intonation; Hubbard supposed that she had learned the language from a nanny. Perhaps the nanny had come from Edinburgh. He imagined the poor woman, happy enough with the Buechelers, caring for this lovely child, then caught in Ger-

[15]

many by the war: Hubbard often reconstructed whole biographies from the single toe bone of such fossil hints; he was a writer.

"You learned English from a Scot?" Hubbard asked.

"From my mother, who was a Scot. We were discussing the tapestry."

"I know very little about tapestries," Hubbard said.

"This one is from Arras, sixteenth century."

"A mille fleurs? Not late fifteenth?"

Lori gave him a sharper look. "Perhaps so. My grandfather brought it home after Sedan in 1870; he wasn't an art expert."

"Hubbard speaks German," Paulus said.

Lori changed languages. "You live in Berlin, I hear," she said. "Why?"

"It's a good place to work."

"What sort of work are you doing in Berlin?"

"I am trying to write."

Lori von Buecheler smiled for the first time, eyes shining, lips pressed together. "To *write?*" she said.

In the library, Paulus's wife put cream and sugar into Hubbard's coffee and offered him a plate of pastries. Hubbard had brought the pastries from Horcher's restaurant in Berlin, wrapped in the elegant package he had carried through the beech forest.

"All the way from Berlin! How clever of you to get Horcher's to give you these wonderful pastries," said Hilde von Buecheler. "However did you persuade them?"

"I have an account at Horcher's," he said.

The uncomfortable chair, upholstered in horsehair, on which Hubbard was sitting was too small for him. He squirmed. Lori's amused eyes registered his discomfort. Paulus took an éclair.

"An account at a restaurant?" he said. "Amazing."

"Is that unusual?" Hubbard asked. "A man I met, a Russian, advised me to make a deposit of twenty dollars on account. It was a very good investment; I eat at Horcher's every day and never seem to get to the bottom of that twenty-dollar bill."

Paulus laughed. "You're not likely to get to the bottom of your twenty dollars, either," he said.

The summer of 1923 was the time of the great inflation in Germany. The Reichsmark, before the war, had been exchanged at four to one American dollar. Now, nine years later, one dollar was worth two trillion Reichsmarks. An egg, which had sold for eight pfennigs in 1914,

[16]

cost eighty billion marks. The price of a single match was 900 million marks.

Paulus cut a plum tart with knife and fork and ate it all up in a matter of seconds, like a soldier in the field wolfing his rations between sorties. "Your father's pocket money, if we had it today, would probably buy Horcher's," Paulus said. "Kitchen, dining rooms, silverware, secret recipes, pastry. He had two dollars a week, in 1885. The wealth of the Indies."

Hilde von Buecheler blinked. Talk of the inflation made her nervous; beneath her marcelled steel-gray hair, the baroness had the profile of a falcon, but she was a timid woman who had lost three sons in the war and feared to lose what was left of her family. This year the Buechelers had come to Rügen from Berlin even before the start of the summer, in order to escape the madness that had seized the city. People, friends of the family, not strangers, were selling everything—paintings, sculpture, jewels, even their houses—for a handful of American dollars. Families lived and, Hilde supposed, died by the *valuta,* the hour-by-hour, minute-by-minute rise and fall of the exchange rate against the dollar. Near the Potsdamer Platz, Hilde had seen a working-class woman with a laundry basket filled with money, billion-mark notes, going into a bakery to buy one day's bread. The woman was distracted by some sort of commotion in the street and put down the basket to watch. Thieves stole the basket, dumping the money onto the sidewalk. It was a windy day; the money fluttered along the pavement and nobody bothered to pick it up. That night Hilde dreamed of banknotes blowing in the wind along the Unter den Linden during a parade, drifting against the boots of the soldiers like snow, whispering. Before her husband could finish his pastry and take up anew the topic of inflation, she changed the subject.

To Hubbard, who had just taken a mouthful of éclair, she said, "Your father fell in battle?"

Hubbard chewed rapidly and swallowed his morsel of crust and custard.

"Not exactly," he said, getting out the words just as Paulus put down his knife and fork, making the china plate ring. "My father went out with a cavalry patrol in Mexico, was captured by Pancho Villa's men, and executed by a firing squad. He was wearing civilian clothes. The Mexicans thought he was a spy."

"Yes. Unfortunate," said Paulus. "Tell me, Hubbard, have you finished university?"

"I left a bit early."

"And why have you come to Berlin? Is it such a good place to be a writer?"

"Berlin is a very cheap place to live," Hubbard said.

"That's your only reason for being there?"

"No, not the only reason," Hubbard replied. "Also, I'm interested in disorder."

Paulus snorted with laughter. "You will find a great deal to interest you in Berlin, then," he said. "Our money is worth nothing, our victories have been erased from the pages of history, and the country is being run by a pack of Socialists."

"It's all very sad," said Hilde.

"On the contrary, it is an *excellent* thing," said Paulus. "You will not find many people in Berlin who will tell you the truth. Five years ago, all the people who now believe in nothing believed in the Prussian orthodoxy. That orthodoxy evaporated in 1918. A new orthodoxy will arise; human beings cannot live without an orthodoxy."

Hilde took her husband's plate from his hand. She smiled nervously at Hubbard. "If you are interested in art, you must look at the pictures," she said. "Perhaps Lori would like to show you."

"If he is interested in art," Lori said, "he certainly doesn't want to see a lot of portraits of old men in uniform. We'll go for a walk instead."

"Excellent," Paulus said. "Where are your bags?"

"I left them at the station."

"We'll send for them. You've brought walking clothes? Do you sail? You must stay for several days."

"That's very kind of you, but I must go back to Berlin. . . ."

"Berlin in August? Nonsense. You'll be company for Lori. She hardly ever sees a man who has all his parts. Only Americans have them, it seems."

Paulus, erect in his tweed suit, threw his old shoulders back a fraction of an inch farther, a suggestion to Hubbard to stand a bit straighter. Americans did not teach their children to command the muscles of their own bodies; they permitted them to slouch.

"Lori is also interested in disorder," Paulus said. "You will have a great deal to agree upon." He smiled fondly at the girl. "Lori is an example of the adventurous new woman," he said. "Fortunately, she's pretty enough to be able to say whatever comes into her head and be forgiven for it. That's in her genes—the frankness, not the forgiveness."

[18]

Hilde had been waiting her turn to speak. "We'd be very happy if you'd stay through the weekend," she said. "The weather will be fine. Young people should be outdoors. Lori is taking the train back to Berlin on Monday. Perhaps you could travel with her."

Hubbard looked once again into Lori's huge gray eyes. "I'd be very glad to accept," he said.

— 2 —

Walking swiftly, swinging her arms, inhaling and exhaling deeply so as to derive maximum benefit from her exercise, Lori led Hubbard through the forest. Diagonal shafts of watery seaside light fell through the lacy branches of the beech trees. Had Lori been less pretty, Hubbard would have been amused by her energy, so solemn and Prussian, but instead he found her endearing, a maiden in uniform. Like the other Germans, she was properly equipped. Before leaving Berwick, she had put on walking boots and thick woolen knee socks and a leather jacket. Hubbard, in his tea-party clothes, ambled along beside her, stealing glances at her profile. He had spent his childhood playing in the steep Berkshire woods, full of thorns and wild berries and wild game. By comparison, this forest—trees planted at intervals of thirty feet, rank on rank—was like a park. Nothing at home was so well kept outside of cemeteries.

"Does anything live in these woods?" Hubbard asked.

"Stags," Lori said, marching along. "Wild boar. My father used to bring me on boar hunts when I was a child. They speared them, you know. It was tremendously exciting."

"You don't go on hunts now?"

"Not since I was twelve."

"Why?"

"It's dangerous for everyone after a female reaches puberty. There is always the possibility that one's flow will start unexpectedly. The boar scents the blood and charges at the wrong moment."

Hubbard lost step for an instant. He had never before discussed menstruation with a woman; it had never occurred to him that such a conversation was possible. Fortunately, Lori displayed no desire to pursue this mysterious subject. She had stopped doing her breathing exercises, but still she strode along, straight into the forest. She seemed to have an objective in mind.

[19]

"Your father is also dead?" Hubbard said. He did not know why he had asked such a question; maybe the bluntness of his hosts was contagious. Lori was not startled.

"Yes, dead," she said. "Since 1918. Like your father, he was murdered by fools. A gang of Bolsheviks beat him to death in the Tiergarten. He was out for a Sunday walk. They tore off his epaulets, broke his sword, trampled on his decorations, the entire ritual."

"Why?"

"They were killing officers that day. It's said that he laughed at them. It's the curse of the Buechelers, blurting out the truth and laughing at the wrong time."

They had arrived at the shore of an unruffled pond, deep in the wood.

"Here is the Borg, as it's called," Lori said. "We can sit down for a moment and look at the water."

Old stones lay scattered near the edge of the dark water. Lori sat on one of them and waited for Hubbard to take his place on another. As he settled his bony body on a stone, Lori grinned at him.

"Is this more comfortable than the horsehair chair?" she asked.

"Considerably," said Hubbard.

"There is a reason why the furniture at Berwick is so uncomfortable," Lori said. "For forty years there were not many visitors. In the summer of 1860, Bartholomäus von Buecheler, the son of the builder of Berwick, invited Otto von Bismarck to dinner. Bartholomäus adored Bismarck's wife, Johanna, because she was a woman who had absolutely no sense of humor and was therefore indecently amusing. He sat himself next to her and got her onto the subject of adultery. Bartholomäus had heard that Bismarck wrote letters to his wife about his love affairs, and he wanted to confirm the existence of these dispatches from the field. After an illuminating conversation, during which a lot of champagne was drunk, Bartholomäus called a question down the table to Bismarck. 'Prince, your wife has just been telling me that in your letters from France you wrote her every detail of your love affair in Biarritz last summer with that Russian woman, Ekaterina Orlova,' he bellowed. 'An excellent principle. Now that you are back in your wife's bed, do you write to Orlova as well, describing your conjugal exertions?' Bismarck was an egomaniac, as you may know; insults drove him into fits of hysteria. He mistook Bartholomäus's joke for an insult and threw one of his tantrums. Without taking another sip of wine, he rose from the table and dashed out of the house. On the way, he tipped over all the suits of armor in the hall; you can see the dents in some of them still. Thereafter, the Buechelers dined alone at Berwick until official mourning for Bismarck ended."

Hubbard laughed. Lori, seated on her broken stone, seemed to be pleased that she had made him do so. In the dim atmosphere of the forest, her prettiness, intensified by the amusement in her face, gave off a kind of light.

"Your ancestor wasn't a very good politician," Hubbard said.

"Not a very good *politician?* What a commentary."

"You don't believe in politics?"

"No. Don't tell me you do."

"I don't," Hubbard said. "You're quite safe with me. What are these stones?"

"In olden times, this was a temple to a pagan goddess called Hertha. Waldemar, the king of Denmark, scattered the stones when he conquered Rügen in 1169 A.D. Waldemar was a Christian. Hertha is mentioned by Tacitus."

Lori leaped to her feet and strode off among the beeches once again. Hubbard fell behind, so as to gaze without embarrassment at her moving body. He had no lustful motive. Hubbard loved—had always loved —the prettiness of women and their gracefulness. He hadn't the knack of imagining them naked when they were clothed; the sight of Lori in her tweed skirt and leather jacket, russet hair bouncing and opening like a fan at every firm step, was pleasure enough for him.

They walked on. The forest grew thinner. Lori, a few steps ahead, passed out of the trees and stopped. Her skirt billowed in the wind. Beyond the edge of the wood, Hubbard glimpsed the sea, frothy with whitecaps in the fading light. It was the same color as the bark on the beeches. He lengthened his stride and, lost in the beauty of this observation, walked out of the forest. He saw where he was just in time to keep from plunging over the edge of a towering chalk cliff.

Lori pointed downward. "One hundred twenty-eight meters," she said, the wind thinning her voice.

Large flakes of chalk had broken off the cliff; Lori picked up two or three and scaled them over the edge. The wind blew them back over her head like kites. She lifted her arm above her head and let it go limp. The wind moved it. She turned her solemn face toward Hubbard.

"I think the wind is strong enough," she said.

"Strong enough for what?" Hubbard asked.

"Watch."

Standing at the very edge of the cliff, Lori spread her arms, closed her eyes, and leaned forward into the wind. It filled her clothes, spread her hair, and suspended her slight body, as if she were soaring, more than four hundred feet above the stony beach below.

Hubbard seized Lori's outflung arm and pulled her back to safety. Her eyes flew open. They were filled with anger.

"Why did you do that?"

"You were going to fall."

"Why should I fall? Take your hand off my arm. Do you think I'm so stupid that I would fall off a cliff into the sea?"

Hubbard let go of her. "Well?" she said.

"I was just trying to protect you," Hubbard said.

"Protect me? Protect me?" Lori spun on her heel, put a hand on the turf, and sprang over the edge of the cliff. Hubbard leaped forward, hand outstretched, but she was gone. He looked down. Her skirt swinging, Lori was already fifty feet below, clambering down the precipice, the toes of her boots creating little clouds of dust as she slammed them into the soft chalk.

Hubbard went after her. The cliff was not perfectly vertical and there were plenty of places to hold on. Over the centuries, the copious rain that fell on Rügen had carved furrows in the chalk, so that climbing was fairly easy.

Hubbard was at the bottom in less than five minutes. Lori waited for him, her hand to her mouth, sucking a cut she had got on the chalk. When she took her hand away, the chalk dust left a white mustache on her upper lip.

"Let me tell you something," she said. "No other person, above all no man, will make rules for me or take precautions on my behalf. I will dispose of myself as I judge best."

Hubbard held up his hand, palm outward, the universal gesture of peace. Lori had never seen such a tremendously tall young man, or one who was so little interested in hiding his thoughts. She turned and walked away. The beach was a carpet of smooth round stones. They rolled under Lori's boots and she lost her balance and fell heavily, uttering a shriek.

Hubbard seemed to think that this was funny. He laughed loudly. Then, giving Lori a delighted smile, he walked on by, leaving her sprawled on the shingle. Lori was furious. A German boy would have given her first aid. Hubbard picked up a flat stone and skipped it across the water. Lying on the stone beach, rubbing her bruised hip with her wounded hand, she opened her mouth to call out for help, but then she remembered herself and struggled to her feet alone.

Watching Hubbard as he sauntered away, such a tall careless figure, so ridiculously strange, Lori began to smile. She was angry at herself. Why was she smiling? It was inexplicable, but she could not stop. She limped after him, floundering, unable to control whatever it was that caused her to grin like a fool.

—— 3 ——

On the train to Berlin, Lori bombarded Hubbard with questions about his work.

"Whose work does your writing resemble?" she asked.

"Why should it resemble anyone else's writing?"

"You must have a model. Only geniuses are original at twenty-one. Stephen Crane, *The Red Badge of Courage*, Herman Melville, *Typee, a Peep at Polynesian Life*."

"Melville was older than twenty-one when he wrote that."

"Twenty-seven. But he was captured by cannibals at twenty-two. Surely that was a form of writing. Experience *is* art; copying it down is just the last stage."

"Then I have the cart before the horse, writing before being captured by cannibals."

"Don't be so sure. Berlin is full of cannibals—like your Russian who knows how to eat forever at Horcher's on one twenty-dollar bill."

In her prim traveling clothes, Lori looked like a schoolgirl, but she had completed her formal education. She was Teutonically at home in the country of facts and figures. Like most German girls of her class and generation, she knew the history and literature of her own country by heart. Also, she was fluent in French, English, and Latin and was familiar with the literature written in those languages. Literature was her passion, especially poetry.

"Do you write poetry?" she asked as the train passed among the blue lakes of the Mecklenburg plain.

"I haven't yet fallen in love," Hubbard said.

"Ah," said Lori, with a laugh. Hubbard had never before met a girl who thought that love was a subject for mirth.

Back in Berlin, Hubbard commenced a summery courtship. He took

Lori to galleries and concerts and plays. They rode in the Tiergarten, boated on the lakes and canals, drank tea and danced in the afternoon at Kempinsky's Hotel, dined at Horcher's, lunched at outdoor restaurants.

One Saturday noontime at the Swedischer Pavillon by the Wannsee, Hubbard watched Lori's hands, deft and tanned with scrubbed unpainted nails, as she slit a smoked trout along its spine, butterflied it, removed the bones, picked up the first mouthful on her fork, and touched the pinkish flesh with creamed horseradish. She lifted her eyes, but not to look at Hubbard. After two weeks in his company she was used to having him stare at her and she no longer paid much attention.

Voices were singing in the Grunewald, a great many voices. The music grew louder as the singers approached. Hubbard could not place the tune.

"Is that the 'Marseillaise'?" Hubbard asked. "In Berlin?"

Lori put down her fork and composed herself. Her eyes were fixed on the edge of the woods, which ran down nearly to the edge of the lake.

"No, not the 'Marseillaise,' " she said.

Out of the trees marched a straggling line of young people. They were carrying flowing red banners and when he saw these, Hubbard recognized the tune. The marchers were singing the "Internationale." They wore broad red bands on their left arms and carried a thicket of placards demanding justice for the workers. They were not themselves workers: they had the pale skin, the long hair, the haunted defiant faces of intellectuals. Young women pushing baby carriages trudged along beside their men, singing too; their faces were radiant with righteousness, like the exalted countenances of members of an evangelical sect singing a particularly rousing hymn.

"The Red Front," Lori said. "I don't want to see this." She kicked Hubbard under the table and he took his eyes off the marchers. "Look straight at me until they're gone," Lori said.

She smiled a bright artificial smile, as if she were making conversation with a stranger at a dinner party.

The singing stopped and the sound of angry shouting buffeted the air. The waiters ran to the railing overlooking the lake in order to watch whatever was happening on the beaches. Hubbard's eyes wandered.

"No," Lori said, rapping on the table; "keep looking at me."

But Lori's own eyes lifted and she frowned. Someone had come up behind Hubbard; he could feel the presence of another person at his back. A jovial hand fell on his shoulder.

"Really, Hubbard, you must come and see this," a male voice said in easy but accented German.

Hubbard stood up. "Otto," he said. "Baronesse von Buecheler, may I present Mr. Rothchild."

Rothchild, a wiry man impeccably dressed in an unwrinkled linen suit, inclined his head. He had the posture of a fencer.

"You must be Hubbard's Russian," Lori said. "The twenty-dollar deposit at Horcher's."

By the shore of the lake, a woman was screaming, one long piercing shriek after another.

"Forgive me," Rothchild said, "but you're missing a rehearsal for the next war. The Stahlhelms have ambushed the Communists. Come."

Rothchild took Hubbard's arm and pushed him toward the railing. He crooked his arm for Lori and gave her an inviting smile.

Lori remained where she was, her back to the commotion. Rothchild bowed and joined Hubbard at the railing. He threw an arm around Hubbard's waist.

"Look," he said, "what luck."

Men wearing steel helmets were fighting with the Red Front marchers. The screaming woman was holding with furious strength to the handle of a baby carriage. One of the Steel Helmets gave it a kick and the baby flew into the air and fell into the milling crowd. The woman, shrieking in terror, crawled among the stamping feet of the fighting men, reaching for her baby, who tumbled over the fine brown forest dirt like a football. Finally she seized the child and curled her body around it. Sweating and cursing and howling in pain and anger, the brawlers trampled on the woman. She stopped screaming. The fight moved away from her and down into the shallow edge of the lake. Men wrestled each other into the water. A Steel Helmet, wearing two Iron Crosses on his civilian jacket, darted into the lake, making a row of explosive splashes as his boots punched the water, and seized the weedy young man who had been at the head of the Red Front parade. He wrestled the weaker man down and held his head under the surface of the lake. Every ten seconds or so, he would pull the man up and let him breathe, shouting furiously into his face. Then he would push him under the water again. The woman lay quiet on the beach. She wore a bright green polka-dot dress; the skirt had been thrown up so that her lacy black drawers were exposed.

"Look, black underwear," Rothchild said. "The flag of free love."

The woman lay so still that Hubbard thought that she must be dead. Abruptly, the fight stopped. The Steel Helmets climbed onto the beach, fell into platoon formation, and marched off into the Grunewald, singing "Die Wacht am Rhein." The Red Front crawled out of the lake. The woman in the green polka-dot dress sat up. Her baby uttered a series of loud shrieks. The woman took out one of her breasts and fed the child as her comrades threw themselves down on the ground, groaning and cursing, among their fallen posters and red banners.

"*Lovely* sight," Rothchild said.

Lori had disappeared. Her smoked trout lay on her plate as she had left it, the first bite still impaled on the fork.

Hubbard found her in the car, her arms wound around her lifted knees, her face pressed against her skirt. He put a hand on her hair. She didn't move.

Hubbard stroked her hair. Lori lifted her face—filled, he knew, with the memory of her father's murder. A tear ran down her cheek.

"Those people, one side or the other, are going to kill any child I have," Lori said. "I know it."

— 4 —

Within a month, Lori and Hubbard were lovers. It was Lori who managed the seduction.

She began her assault in a nightclub called Kaminskys Telephonbar. Each table was equipped with a telephone, so that clients and prostitutes of both sexes could call one another up. A very tall Negro with a painted face sang in English; he was naked except for a woman's fur coat. When he lifted his arms at the end of a song, the coat opened and a slender erect penis emerged like an inquisitive brown snake.

Hubbard blushed in deep embarrassment. "Look," he said, "I think we'd better go. I didn't know."

But Lori was delighted by the atmosphere of clownish sexuality. "It's wonderful here," she said. "Let's dance."

On the dance floor, Lori put both arms around Hubbard's neck. Actual dancing was impossible. In a space not much larger than a round dinner table, twenty couples swayed to an American song. Because Hubbard was so much taller than Lori, her body clung to his. He felt her breasts against his stomach and the warmth of her flesh through the thin cloth of her skirt. Lori knew what he felt. Laughing as she had laughed on the train, she kissed him, a sweet virginal kiss at first, but as he drew away she pulled his head back and ran her tongue over his lips, a slow warm animal lick that started at one corner of his mouth, ran over his upper lip, and then back across the lower. Grinning mischievously, she gave his lip a little nip with her white teeth, like a period.

They stayed until dawn, dancing and drinking sparkling Mosel. As Hubbard drove her home through the empty streets, Lori, kneeling in the passenger seat, licked his ear. Hubbard tried thinking about football; it didn't work. He tried to push her away, but she resisted and went on licking his ear. When he tried to slow down, she put her own foot on the accelerator. As they entered the Potsdamer Platz at fifty miles an hour, a taxi pulled out of the rank in front of the railroad station, into the path of their car. Hubbard slammed on the brakes. The car, rocking crazily, skidded along the streetcar tracks and spun completely around twice before Hubbard brought it under control again.

"Really, Lori," Hubbard said, "I think you'd better sit down."

Lori slid into the seat, put her knees primly together, looked into Hubbard's face with her cat's smile, and began speaking about his work again. The kiss in the nightclub, the tongue in Hubbard's ear, the wild ride in the open car might never have happened. She was a scholar again. She ran her hands over her hair, which had blown wildly around her face moments before, restoring it to perfect order.

"Are you actually writing," she asked, "or are you merely trying to make yourself interesting?"

Hubbard was stung by this accusation. "I've written a novel," he said.

"Good. You must read it to me."

Read you my manuscript?

"What else? You need an opinion, intelligent criticism. You must read your book to me tomorrow. I'll come to your rooms."

— 5 —

Hubbard had taken a furnished flat in Charlottenburg, on a fashionable street. The furniture, left behind by the owners, was a mixture of uncomfortable Bauhaus and tattered Louis XV. Very good Persian carpets were spread over the floor. The walls were hung with new German painting, brutal caricatures of bourgeois life, abstractions in primary colors.

"Not a very Bohemian flat," Lori said, "except for the pictures. Surely they didn't come with the place? Nobody in this neighborhood knows about this sort of German painting."

"Otto Rothchild helped me to find them."

"Ah, the valuta again. Do your friendships generally last?"

"Yes."

"I thought so. Pity. I'll never like this Russian."

Hubbard had arranged his manuscript in a neat stack on the table and placed two chairs opposite one another. He indicated the chair in which Lori was to sit. Instead, she sat on the floor, curling her legs beneath her.

Hubbard began to read. At seven o'clock the maid brought them a cold supper. Hubbard put down the manuscript.

"No," Lori said. "Read on to the end. Food later."

"But I'm hungry."

"Later."

"Now. I'm also thirsty. My throat is giving out."

The maid had placed beer on the table, a brown liter bottle with a porcelain stopper on a bail. Lori scrambled to her feet. Limping a little on cramped muscles, she went to the table and poured a full glass for Hubbard and a quarter of a glass for herself. Hubbard drank the beer.

Hubbard filled two plates with cold ham and sour potato salad and refilled the beer glasses. Lori demolished the food. She went to the table, spread two pieces of black bread with pale butter, and put thin slices of cheese on top. Hubbard ate his with his fingers; Lori used a knife and fork.

"Is that the way Americans eat cheese?"

"Yes."

"You must have very dirty napkins. Is that the way Americans *are* —the way you have written about them?"

"How exactly did you imagine them?"

"Not like the ones in your book," she said. "Read."

It was past ten o'clock when Hubbard read the last word. By then he was so tired and so hungry, and so far into the region of his own imagination, that he had half forgotten that Lori had been listening to him. She rolled over onto her stomach, put her chin on the pillow, and stared into the ashes of the fire. She said absolutely nothing. Hubbard was puzzled by her silence, and took it as a sign that she was trying to

find a way to tell him that she did not like his work, or did not understand it, or found it too complicated—the usual complaints people made
about what he wrote.

"Who exactly are the people in the book?" she asked at last.

"They're imaginary."

"That evil old man with his mills is not imaginary. Neither are the
Irish and German children going to work in the darkness and coming
home in the darkness and dying of tuberculosis."

"The old man is evil? He's like my grandfather in some ways. There
are children in his mills who go to work when they are eight years old
and die of tuberculosis before they're twenty."

"And the boys, the inseparable brothers?"

"The good one is like a cousin of mine."

"And the bad one is you. You're going to publish this novel?"

"If a publisher will take it."

"How will your family take it?"

Hubbard shrugged. "It's all true."

"Precisely. You don't fear your family?"

Hubbard shook his head.

"They're going to hate you," Lori said.

Hubbard fetched the beer bottle, opened the top, and offered it to
Lori. She was on her face again, staring into the fire.

"I hadn't expected this," she said. "You're a genius."

Hubbard, his mouth full of tepid beer, paused for a moment, then
swallowed. The bitter taste of the beer ran up into his nose. Lori's
intense gray eyes looked directly into his.

"You won't answer me? Then I will answer for you. You *are* a
genius. I'll insist on that, and not only to you. To the world."

Lori kissed Hubbard on the mouth. She looked as if she had
remembered a delicious secret. She turned down the lamps and drew
him to the floor. It was utterly plain to him what she expected.

Two

When Lori was in the eighth month of her pregnancy, Paulus von Buecheler came to call on her in Hubbard's flat in Charlottenburg. Hands folded on the knob of his walking stick, Paulus sat on a chair made of steel tubes and leather straps.

"What medicinal furniture," he said. "Even the arts and crafts of the Socialists are designed to correct the flaws in humanity. This is like sitting on an artificial limb."

It was eight-thirty in the morning, late in the day for Paulus, who had been reading out orders at dawn all his life, to be discussing matters of importance. He had refused a cup of coffee, a signal of stern intentions.

"Hubbard should be back soon," Lori said. "He's meeting the train from Paris; his cousin is visiting us."

Lori had not seen Paulus for six months, not since she had moved in with Hubbard. She had not mentioned her pregnancy when she left Berwick; her intention to live in concubinage had been enough of a shock to Hilde. If Paulus was surprised by Lori's condition, as he sat in his Bauhaus chair, he gave no sign. Lori folded her hands on her kicking baby and waited for her uncle to say what he had come to say.

"Pregnancy seems to agree with you," he said, by way of addressing his subject. "Your Aunt Hilde thinks you ought to be in Rügen. The sea air is full of iodine. Hilde always went to Berwick when she was pregnant in order to breathe it in; her doctor believed that it strengthened the fetus."

Paulus had been staring into space as he spoke. Now he turned his face to Lori, monocle glittering in one eye socket, moisture in the other.

"We are quite alone at Berwick, you know," he said.

Paulus stopped talking and Lori said nothing to fill the silence. She knew how alone her uncle and aunt were. The first of their sons had been killed in 1914 at Tannenberg, the second had fallen in 1916 at Verdun, and the third, a pilot, had been shot down in 1918 by an American aviator. The American, a member of a naval flight called the First Yale Unit, had written to Paulus and Hilde, describing what he termed the "sportsmanship" of their son: evidently, Bartholomäus had saluted the American just as his ship burst into flames. It seemed queer to Paulus that his youngest son, the most gifted of his children, should have been added to the total of 1,773,000 Germans killed in the Great War, dying at the hand of an amateur American sailor who, to judge by his letter, looked on the war as a university prank. After Paulus, inasmuch as Lori's father had been murdered, there were no more Buechelers in the male line.

"You do not, I suppose, have any idea of going to America to have the baby?" Paulus asked his niece.

"I doubt that I'd complete the voyage. Besides, Hubbard is not very welcome at home because of his book."

"Oh? Has he insulted somebody?"

"Nearly everyone; it's about his mother's family. But it is a brilliant novel."

"No doubt. Do you plan to marry this extraordinary novelist?"

"Yes. I didn't suppose that you wanted an illegitimate great-nephew named after you."

"Named after *me?*"

"Who else would I name him after?"

"Your father."

"Children shouldn't be named for the dead. I'm tired of the dead. He'll be an American; Americans don't seem to die young for stupid reasons, like the rest of us."

Paulus looked around the room at the primitive lines and the raw colors of Hubbard's growing collection of revolutionary works of art. His eyes rested on a naturalistic drawing of Lori, smiling her chatoyant smile, standing easily with her feet together and her hands hanging loose, nude and pregnant.

"That is quite beautiful," he said.

"I'm glad you think so. The maid quit when I hung it."

They heard the key in the lock and stopped speaking. Two male voices spoke English in the hall; suitcases thudded to the floor. Hubbard, enormously tall, came into the sitting room. When he saw Paulus, his face lighted up with his guileless grin. Paulus stood up and gazed with amazement at the young man who followed Hubbard into the room.

He, too, was a gigantic, smiling American. He looked exactly like Hubbard. Lori, who had begun to rise from her chair, sank back in astonishment. Where Hubbard was fair, this fellow was dark. Otherwise they might have been twins.

"My cousin Elliott," Hubbard said. "Paulus, what a pleasant surprise. Colonel Baron von Buecheler, may I present my cousin, Elliott Hubbard."

Hubbard spoke German. Elliott, who did not understand this language, said nothing, but shook hands vigorously with Paulus. Then he turned to Lori. "I'm Elliott," he said in English.

Lori gripped his hand. "The good brother," she said. "This is indecent. You're replicas. Hubbard, why did you leave this secret out of your novel?"

"It's the only thing he did leave out," Elliott said.

Hubbard, grinning in pleasure over the success of his surprise, explained to Paulus. "Elliott's father and my mother were twins," he said. "They did everything together. It was a double wedding, and Elliott and I were born a year later, a month apart."

"Who is older?"

"Elliott."

"If your name is Hubbard Christopher," Lori said, "why is his name not Christopher Hubbard?"

"Things are bad enough as they are, Lori," Elliott said.

An exact duplicate of Hubbard's grin lit up Elliott's long bony face. Lori rang for the new maid and ordered midmorning coffee. The servant, a red-faced cheerful fat girl from Rügen, burst into laughter and clapped her hand over her mouth when she saw Hubbard and Elliott, side by side.

This time Paulus took coffee when it was offered, and ate a plum tart. When he had finished, he addressed Elliott, speaking English as swiftly as he had chewed his pastry.

"Any special reason for your journey?"

"You didn't know? I've come to be best man at the wedding of my cousin and your niece."

"Excellent," said Paulus. "It looks as if you'll have a chance to be a godfather as well."

— 2 —

In the event, both Elliott and Paulus von Buecheler were godfathers to the son of Hubbard and Lori Christopher. The child was born at Berwick on June 14, 1924, a date celebrated in the United States as Flag Day. The midwife who, nineteen years earlier, had delivered Lori was in attendance, and the birth took place in the same room in which Lori's father, uncle, and more remote ancestors had been born.

"All those spirits will be with me," Lori said, "but I want Hubbard here, by my bed, in the flesh."

"A *man*, in the birth chamber?" barked the midwife.

Lori insisted. The labor lasted for hours. Hubbard sat through the night beside Lori, timing her contractions. These became stronger and more rhythmic.

"Think of the sea," the midwife said. "Row, row for the shore."

"My God," Lori said, "it's worse than the sea. This is taking away my will. It's taken over my body. It's doing what it wants to me."

The crown of the baby's head appeared, then his flattened ears and his glistening unawakened face. Lori's body opened to release him and the petals of her flesh and the baby's skin were the same hues of pink, as if Hubbard's child were undoubling from a rose.

"Here is the prow of the little ship," the midwife said.

"I have no control over this, Hubbard!" Lori said. "No one *told* me!"

Hubbard gripped her hands. Lori seized his huge curved thumbs in her tiny fists and dislocated them both. The baby slid free. The midwife turned him over and squeezed his penis. The baby opened his eyes and turned his head. He had his mother's deep gray eyes.

"A little baron!" the midwife cried.

Paul Christopher was a quiet child. Born into a family of talkers, he was a listener. Even as a very young child he never interrupted. Years afterward, he might ask a question about a story he had heard at the age of four; he seemed never to forget anything.

"He is writing," Lori would say, watching his alert face as he sat on the floor at coffee time, listening to adults, puzzling over jokes. She wanted him to be a poet, but she feared that his genes would compel him to be a soldier.

In the morning, Paul would stand beside his parents' bed in his nightclothes, watching and waiting until one of them woke. Lori opened her eyes morning after morning to find herself gazing into the eyes of her son that were so much like her own eyes. As soon as she woke, he told her what he had dreamed the night before. He dreamed about Massachusetts long before he ever went there: Hubbard's stories about their family, about the woods and the American animals, so truly wild, gripped his imagination. Paul had his mother's face as well as her eyes, but an American body, strong and loose and made for sport. He had inherited his father's temperament, joyful and forgiving. He walked at ten months and his first connected words were in English, though Lori always spoke to him in German.

For three seasons of the year, in Berlin, Hubbard wrote every day from six in the morning until noon. He published his books, novels and poems, in the United States, and as they were never translated into German he was unknown to the Berlin intelligentsia. He was little better known to most of his own countrymen. "They tell me you're a writer, Mr. Christopher?" American women would say to Hubbard at the Fourth of July party at the Embassy. "How interesting. What sort of things do you write?" With his instinctive good manners, Hubbard would begin to reply. Lori would interrupt. "Not the sort of things you read, obviously," she would say in withering tones. She never stopped believing that Hubbard was a genius.

The Christophers spent summers at Berwick. Exercise and conversation were the family pastimes. By the time he was six, Paul could climb any cliff on Rügen. He was a strong swimmer who knew the treacherous island tides. He woke every morning at five-thirty, drank a cup of hot milk and ate a piece of black bread, and went for a two-mile walk through the beech forest with Paulus. Before the boy learned to read, Paulus told him about Rügen, its flora and fauna and history.

Others had told him about Paulus, heroic tales. Paulus had commanded a regiment of lancers at the Battle of Tannenberg. When the

Russian center broke, at about six in the evening on August 28, 1914, Paulus had pursued the flying rabble of the Russian 15th Corps through the forest of Grünfliess, putting two hundred enemy to the spear in a brisk skirmish on the shores of a lake and setting their bivouac on fire. During a saber fight with a Russian officer, conducted from the backs of heaving chargers, Paulus had severed the right hand of his enemy. Incredibly, the maimed Russian had turned his horse and galloped into the lake, shouting to rally his routed troops. Paulus, seeing his wounded foe fall from the saddle, spurred into the water and rescued him. Dragging the unconscious Russian into the burning camp, he thrust the spurting stump of his wrist into a fire, cauterizing the wound. The Russian, treated by Paulus's regimental surgeon, survived.

"Did Uncle Paulus meet the Russian again, after the war?" Paul asked Hilde.

"He invited him to Berwick, but he never came. He must have been slaughtered by the Bolsheviks, like your grandfather."

Paul received little Christian instruction from Paulus, his German godfather. "Bismarck was a Christian, he was very vocal about it," Paulus said, "and a greater bastard never lived. Memorize the Sermon on the Mount; I advise you to live by it even if you don't have a single spark of religious faith."

Conversation was an addiction of the Buechelers. During their long banishment under Bismarck, the family learned to get along without outsiders. To avoid turning into a family of bores, they had kept their minds fresh by learning new facts, new languages, new skills. Even now, guests were a rarity at Berwick. Anecdotes were forbidden. Stories withered the mind, Paulus said; new talk had to be invented every day. This required a great deal of reading, and there were hundreds of books in the house. The hours between lunch and dinner were set aside for reading; at the beginning of June, twenty books were placed in Paul's room, and he was expected to read them all by the end of August.

"Admirable," said Hubbard, "but Paul ought to get in more sailing."

Hubbard was a great believer in sailing. With the meager royalties from his writings, he bought a white-hulled yawl and named it *Mahican*, after the tribe of Indians that had lived on his family's land in the Berkshires. In this vessel, Paul and his parents sailed in all weathers in the shallow, heaving Baltic. Lori packed delicious lunches in a wicker picnic basket that Paul's American godfather, Elliott Hubbard, had bought at Abercrombie & Fitch. This hamper glistened with varnish and its broad riveted straps smelled of good leather. Thermos bottles, food boxes, plates, glasses, and cutlery fitted inside, also fastened by leather straps. All his life, Paul remembered the picnic basket as the most beautiful object of his childhood.

It was a nine-hour sail to their favorite destination, a Danish island called Falster. They would cast off in the dark, on the tide, arriving at Falster at midmorning, then sail back to Rügen the following midnight. Falster was a windy, peaceful island of low grassy dunes, with a wooded cliff along the northeastern shore. They would anchor under the cliff, load the picnic basket and a blanket into the dinghy, and row ashore. Here, the rules of Berwick did not apply, and Hubbard would tell stories.

The stories always had to do with Paul's paternal ancestors. Fifty years before the American Revolution, a twenty-year-old youth named Aaron Hubbard (always called "the first Aaron" by the Hubbards) drove a herd of spotted pigs up the Housatonic Valley from Connecticut into the Berkshire Hills of Massachusetts, to fatten them on beech nuts. In the eighteenth century, the Berkshires were still a Mohawk hunting ground—wild, stony, mountainous country. No one lived there except for a few Mahican Indians who had been driven out of the Hudson Valley, farther to the west beyond the mountains, by the fiercer Mohawks. Aaron did not run into any Indians. He spent the summer alone with his pigs, wandering through the woods, sleeping in the open, falling in love with the country.

"There was an October blizzard that year," said Hubbard Christopher, telling the story on the beach at Falster, "and Aaron and his pigs were caught in it. He was driving them through the woods, trying to find a cave or something for shelter, when he saw, of all things, a light among the trees. It was a Mahican encampment. The Indians took Aaron in. He stayed all winter as there was no way to get out through the snow, slaughtering the pigs one by one and sharing them with the Mahicans. The Indians took a fancy to pork. Aaron had already taken a fancy to the land.

"In the spring, Aaron made an agreement with the Mahicans. In return for one pound sterling, a barrel of molasses, and ten spotted pigs, the Hubbards could have all the land they could fence in a single day. Aaron went back to Connecticut and fetched his nine brothers. Between sunup and sundown, the Hubbard boys nailed rails to trees and fenced twenty square miles.

"On the highest hill at the western edge of their land, the Hubbards put up a house. At first it was just one room, a kitchen with a sleeping loft above it, made out of whipsawed planks and hand-hewn maple beams, fastened together with wooden pegs. When the wind blew, it creaked like a sailing ship; it still does. They were the first Hubbards to own land and that gave them the feeling that they'd come into port after a tremendous stormy voyage. They called the house the Harbor.

"A family of Mahicans lived on the place until one summer when they died of measles, all but one. The survivor was a ten-year-old boy named Joe. He came to live at the Harbor. The second Aaron, your great-great-grandfather, was about the same age as Joe. He and Joe had always been inseparable friends. In the family they were called Damon and Pythias. Outsiders called the Mahican boy Indian Joe, but to the Hubbards, he was—well, I've always imagined that he was pretty much what *I* was, growing up at the Harbor two hundred years later: not exactly a son, but more than a nephew.

"One day, when Joe and Aaron were about eighteen years old," Hubbard continued, "Joe went out hunting by himself. It was early December. The ground was frozen but there was no snow. Joe was a great hunter. He always got something. But this time he came back empty-handed. He told the family he'd fired his shotgun at two crows and brought them down with a single charge of buckshot. He'd looked for the dead crows but couldn't find them. It was almost dark when Joe got back.

"Just as he was finishing his supper and getting ready to clean his gun, the town constable came to the door with some terrible news. A young man named John Parker, a schoolmate of Aaron and Joe, had been found lying in the woods, shot dead. A farmer, an older man called Eleazer Stickles, had seen Joe follow the victim into the woods, and shortly afterward, he'd heard a shot. The constable smelled Joe's gun barrel. 'Recently fired,' he said. 'What load were you using?' Joe said he'd been using buckshot. 'To hunt crows?' the constable said. Joe said he'd been hunting deer; he'd just happened to shoot the crows after it became obvious to him that he wasn't going to see any deer; conditions were wrong. 'Where are the crows?' asked the constable. Joe said he hadn't been able to find them. 'John Parker had buckshot in his heart,' the constable said. He arrested Joe and charged him with murder.

"John Parker had been a popular young fellow, good-looking and from a prosperous family. The town was convinced that Indian Joe had killed John Parker. Nobody would believe the story about the crows. They put Joe in chains. Aaron protested, but the constable said Joe

[37]

might escape before they could hang him. Aaron went into the woods, looking for the dead crows. Joe had described the spot where he'd shot the crows, but Aaron could never find them. It was below zero for twenty straight days. Aaron went out at first light and came back after dark on every one of those days. He caught pneumonia, went into a delirium, and when he woke up a week later, they told him that they'd hanged Joe.

"The Hubbards buried Joe in the family graveyard, with a boulder for a headstone. Aaron, when he got better, went up there in the snow and carved Joe's name on the stone and the word *Misjudged*. Aaron refused to go to church. He said the people praying in the church had murdered Joe. That remark was not easily forgiven, and it was never forgotten.

"In April, it began to thaw during the day while it froze at night, so they could sugar. They were setting the buckets—drilling holes in the trees so that they could pound in spouts and hang the buckets to collect the dripping sap. And as Aaron turned the drill stalk into one old double maple tree, he looked up and saw something black in the fork where the tree grew apart. He climbed up, and there, lying together, caught in a grapevine growing on the maple, were Joe's two crows, full of buck-shot. Aaron took them to the constable.

"The constable wouldn't look at the crows. 'First Joe had such fine eyesight that he could shoot two crows on the wing,' he said. 'But then he couldn't find them. Now you bring me these carcasses and tell me that both birds fell out of the sky into the same maple tree, lodged in the same grapevine, and stayed there all winter without an owl or a wildcat or a raccoon touching them. Aaron, I know that you and Joe were friends. But go on back to your own house and stop bothering me.'

"Aaron put the dead crows in a box and took them to church on Sunday. He got there before the stove was lit, and waited, blowing out his breath in the freezing air, bundled up in his winter coat, sitting in a straight chair in the choir stall, his face to the pews, holding the box with the crows in it in his lap. He wasn't dressed for the Sabbath, but wore his work clothes. Aaron's lips didn't move during the opening hymn and the Lord's Prayer. While the others sang, Aaron's eyes moved from face to face, and when they opened their eyes after the prayer they found him staring at them again. As the minister started to read the lesson, Aaron stood up and interrupted.

" 'I've got something to say to you,' he said. Aaron opened the box and displayed the dead crows. He explained where he'd found the crows. He didn't see a flicker of belief on any face in the congregation. Aaron realized that these people, many of them relations, all of them men and women he'd known all his life, could not possibly believe him. To believe that these were the crows that Joe had shot was to believe that Joe was innocent of the murder of John Parker. And to believe in Joe's innocence was to confess that the town had hanged the Indian by mistake—or perhaps by something worse than a mistake. They ignored Aaron and went on with their service.

"The next Sunday, Aaron was back, sitting in his straight chair at the front of the church, wearing his barn clothes and his dirty boots, silent and accusing, staring at the worshippers in the pews. He came back the following Sunday, and every Sunday after that for twenty years. After a while, only visitors and children asked who Aaron was, sitting up there with his eyes glittering. The older people would tell the story, and that served to keep alive the memory of the hanging of Joe. That seemed to be enough for Aaron, though he never really made another friend in Mahican.

"A quarter of a century passed. Aaron took a wife, had children, grew gray. One January day, around dinner time, there came a knock at the door of the Harbor. Melody Stickles, Eleazer Stickles's wife, stood on the threshold. Aaron didn't know her at first. He hadn't seen her since she was a girl. She'd been the town beauty, and every boy in school, including Aaron, had been in love with her when she was fourteen. But her family had been poor; her father had more or less sold her in marriage to Eleazer Stickles, a much older man. It was remembered in the town that Melody had cried at her own wedding, walking down the aisle on the arm of her father—he'd worn a dirty shirt, buttoned at the neck, and wide galluses with a red rose stuck in the buckle; no one ever left out that detail in telling the story, or how the tears flowed down Melody's cheeks. She sobbed while speaking her marriage vows. After the wedding, Melody's father went right out and bought a pair of fast coach horses, and she went home with Eleazer.

"On the day she called on Aaron at the Harbor, he hardly recognized her. He hadn't seen her—no one had seen her, really—for twenty-five years. 'Aaron,' Melody said, standing in the open door, 'Eleazer wants you to come to the house. He's on his deathbed.'

"Eleazer Stickles's ancestor had built a bigger house than was needful. Aaron had never been inside. What he saw when he did go through the door amazed him. Every room was stacked to the ceiling with fifty years' accumulation of junk. Boxes, newspapers, magazines, old horse collars, jars, bottles—Eleazer was a miser. In all his life, he'd never thrown a thing away. He burned fallen twigs in the kitchen stove. Cats slept on the stove; it was lighted only to cook supper, and then not for very long.

"Melody led Aaron along a footpath among these mountains of trash, and let him into a room where Eleazer lay in bed. He was covered with blankets, with a tanned horsehide thrown over the top, hair side down. Still Eleazer shivered in his bed. It was below zero inside the house; the January wind howled in the eaves and bellowed down the cold chimneys. On the outside of the door of this room, Aaron had noticed a heavy iron bolt, extending all the way across the panels. It was like a dungeon lock. There were iron bars on every window.

"Eleazer, shuddering under his covers, peered at Aaron as he took in these details. 'Curious, Aaron?' he said.

" 'About what, Eleazer?'

" 'About them iron bars on the windows.'

"Eleazer looked around for Melody, but she had left the men alone in the barred room.

" 'I put the bars on this room the day that Indian Joe shot the crows,' Eleazer said.

" 'The day he shot the crows?' Aaron said.

" 'That's right,' Eleazer said. 'I was out cutting timber that day. I broke a chain hauling out a big log and came on down to the house to fetch another chain, leaving the oxen in the woodlot. That's when I heard Joe's shot and saw the crows fall. Joe was standing in the clearing, reloading his gun. He never saw me. Joe was the best shot around in those days, wouldn't you say?'

" 'Yes,' said Aaron, 'I'd say that about Joe.'

" 'Joe wasn't sure where the birds fell, and he was still looking for them when I lost sight of him. I played a little trick on Joe on the way down the mountain, but I'll come back to that. I kept my spare chains in the tool shed; the door to that shed is right beside the window to this room. As I put my hand on the door, I heard a bumping sound: bump, bump-bump, bump-bump-bump-bump. Like that. Couldn't place the sound. Melody was new then, we'd only been married a year or two, and I didn't know her habits the way I do now. I thought she might be doing something I could tease her about, so I sneaked up to that window.' Eleazer pointed to one of the barred windows.

" 'There was a good bit of sun that day,' Eleazer said, 'so I couldn't see into the room without shading my eyes. I took off my hat to block out the sun and looked in. What I saw, Aaron, was Melody on the bed.

She had her legs around a man. He had his boots against the footboard so that he could push at her better. The sound I'd heard was the headboard banging against the wall. I could tell by the way Melody was acting that this wasn't the first time she and this fellow had banged that headboard against the wall. I watched till it was over and the fellow rolled over on his back. It was John Parker; Melody had always been sweet on him, though when I'd ask her she'd say no, no, she was never sweet on anybody. As soon as he got off her, she got on top of him. He was still wearing his boots. Neither one of them saw me.'

"Eleazer stopped speaking. Under that mound of covers, he looked small and wasted, but there was a feverish light in his eyes, as if the memory of his wife with another man gave him something to live for.

" 'What did you do then?' Aaron asked.

" 'I got a shotgun, came right into the kitchen next door and took it off the wall. Them two never heard me over the banging of the headboard. Then I went up and waited on the cow path where it goes into the maples. It was two hours or more before John came up the path. When he did, I killed him. Then I came down and hitched Melody to the bed with a cow chain and a couple of padlocks and put the bars on the windows. Took me all night and most of the morning, but I got it done. This is Melody's room. Until today, when I sent her over to the Harbor to fetch you, she never went out of it again except to cook for me in the kitchen, and you can be damn sure nobody else ever got in. That's the story of the iron bars on the windows, Aaron.'

"Ten thousand times, Aaron had imagined learning the truth, and he'd always thought that when he did he would feel some overwhelming emotion. But for long moments, as he stood in silence, staring down at Eleazer on his deathbed, he felt nothing. The truth had been lying here all these years, while Aaron glared at the congregation on Sunday, and now he'd found it the way he'd found Joe's crows— by accident.

" 'Eleazer,' Aaron said, 'what was the trick you played on Joe? Do you call killing John Parker a trick?'

"Eleazer said no, that wasn't it. 'The trick,' said Eleazer, 'was what I did to his crows. I found them, lying in a couple of juniper bushes. They'd fallen about twenty feet apart. I picked up the crows and tossed them up into an old double maple tree, just to tease Joe. That tree was way over on the edge of your land, Aaron, and I never could find it again. I didn't hide the crows to trap Joe. When you found the crows I thought I was done for, I thought they'd ask how they got into the tree; it couldn't be natural; somebody had to have slung them up into that maple. But the question never occurred to them. I figured they'd know who'd killed John—his body was on my land, Melody was chained to this bed, behind bars. I thought somebody would ask why I'd done that to her. I figured to hang for John Parker. And I would have, Aaron, if there'd been enough snow for John to have left tracks in and out of Melody's bedroom.'

" 'You let Joe hang for you.'

" 'That's right,' said Eleazer. 'You see how it was, Aaron. I wanted time with Melody, to teach her a lesson. That was the reason. I've had the time; I've got a lot to thank Joe for.'

" 'Are you going to tell this story to anybody else?' Aaron asked.

"Eleazer stared at him. For an instant, the light came back into his dying eyes. 'What story?' Eleazer said. 'You're the closest kin I've got, second cousin once removed, Aaron, and if anybody wants to know why I called you over here, it was just to tell you good-bye.'

"Aaron never told anyone Eleazer's story, either. He went back to the Harbor and wrote it all down in his account book. Then he climbed up to the cemetery on the mountain and carved the word *Vindicated* on Joe's gravestone. He would never explain what he meant by that, and it wasn't until somebody read his account book, fifty years after he died, that the truth was known. Aaron never set foot inside the church after he came home from the Stickles place. That told the town everything he wanted them to know."

Above Falster, the northern lights had faded, and the punctual summer dawn began to bleach the horizon. "We'd better sail," he said.

Mahican was pulling hard against her anchor cable in the moving tide. Paul helped his father put up the mainsail and take in the anchor. Away from land, there was a brisk wind, and the sea was rough. It was a long, hard beat back to Rügen with much tacking, and on the voyage home there was no time for talk.

Just before noon, the chalk cliffs of Rügen came into view, white in the gray weather. Paul took the tiller as they tacked into the harbor. Hubbard loosed the sheets as Paul put the helm over. As the boom swung over the cockpit, Lori and Paul ducked. Their faces were very close together and Lori kissed Paul on the cheek. The wind took the mainsail and it shuddered and snapped.

"Promise me something," Lori said. "As you live your life, don't be like Aaron. Don't be silent. Don't wait for the truth to wake up like some sleeping beauty. Make them *listen* to the truth."

"All right."

"No. This is important. Promise."

"I promise, Mutti," Paul said.

Lori nodded gravely, as if she had been relieved of a great worry. She went forward and stood beside Hubbard in the bow as the yawl approached its anchorage through flocks of raucous gulls. They wore matching yellow foul-weather jackets and when Hubbard put his arm around Lori, her slight body seemed to merge with his so that for a moment they formed a single figure. A drifting mist, low on the water, added to this illusion. Long after he had grown up, Paul remembered his parents as they were that morning.

— 3 —

That summer, life at Berwick changed. The Nazis had been in power for three years and they had had time to put their own people into the police and the local government even in a remote place like Rügen. The Buechelers were hardly aware of this: they had no contact with the police and the rest of officialdom. After the drab fallow season of the Weimar Republic, Germany under the new regime had blossomed out in uniforms and banners. Once again, the Germans were happy; the whole country seemed to exist in a daze of patriotic joy. In the beech forests on Rügen, youths marched under party banners, shattering the quiet with their singing. On weekends, the full-throated sound of them came through the open windows at Berwick.

"Government by operetta," Lori said; "the Germans have a weakness for it."

It was a minor annoyance. Just as they cared nothing for society, the Buechelers cared nothing for politics. They never read the newspapers. There was no radio at Berwick; Paulus and Hilde and Lori may have been the only people in Germany who, in 1936, had never heard Adolf Hitler's voice.

There was nothing political in what Lori did on the terrace of the Kursaal Café in Putbus, the town on Rügen nearest to Berwick. She and Paul had gone into town to do some business, and afterward they had stopped at the café, a favorite place of theirs. It was midafternoon; the café was fairly full. When the waiter brought Lori's coffee and Paul's chocolate, he murmured something to Lori.

Swabbing his napkin over the spotless table, the waiter flicked a glance toward a pimply youth with a dead white face who sat alone a few tables away.

"Gestapo," he whispered.

"A secret policeman?" Lori said. "Then why is he dressed like an actor?"

Except for a flowing white aviator's scarf, the Gestapo man was dressed entirely in black: a closely fitted black leather coat, a black felt hat, black kid gloves. For some reason he wore riding breeches and black leather knee boots. He was drinking coffee with his gloves on and reading a dossier that he had extracted from a bulging, brand-new pigskin briefcase.

"He's the new Gestapo chief for Rügen," the waiter said. "He belongs to the new type."

At this moment, a milk cart, loaded with rattling cans, came into sight. Under cover of its noise, the waiter let Lori in on Rügen's new joke.

"His name," the waiter said in a stronger voice, "is"—he grinned broadly and shielded his mouth with his napkin as he spoke—"Stutzer."

"Stutzer?" Lori said. "That's his *real* name—'dandy'?"

Stutzer's eyes were fixed on the milk cart. It was drawn by a dog and a peasant woman. It was a common sight in Rügen, and elsewhere in rural Germany, to see peasant women harnessed with a dog to a cart or yoked with an ox or a cow to a plow. This woman had heavy bare legs, chapped bright red. She was leaning into the harness, pulling hard to haul the load up a slight hill. Her husband, smoking a curved pipe, walked along ahead of the cart.

Stutzer wasn't looking at the woman. He was gazing instead at a drunk who staggered along behind the cart, clowning. Everyone in Rügen knew the drunk; his name was Heinz and he had lost his mind in the war. In the buttonhole of his ragged coat he wore the ribbon of the Iron Cross, first class. Heinz came to the café every afternoon at coffee time to steal cream. The coffee came with little porcelain pitchers filled with cream. Heinz crouched on the pavement, watching the tables. As soon as a coffee drinker had taken as much cream as he wanted and put his pitcher down, Heinz would dart to the table, snatch the pitcher, and drink the teaspoonful of cream that was left. He made a kind of music-hall act out of his raid: watching for his chance with exaggerated craftiness, pouncing quickly, looking to left and right before he drank, then scuttling away to await another victim.

Stutzer the Dandy beckoned the waiter and ordered a second cup of coffee. While he waited for it to arrive, he went back to reading his dossiers; it seemed that he had lost interest in Heinz. Meanwhile, Heinz stole cream from two or three tables. As the Dandy's coffee was served, he watched, licking his lips.

The Dandy poured cream into his cup, put down the pitcher, and lifted the coffee to his lips in a gloved hand. Heinz darted to the Dandy's table, seized the tiny pitcher, and tossed off the cream. The Dandy watched him drink. Then, holding his cup in one hand and the saucer in the other, he stood up in his Gestapo costume and swung back his right leg in its polished boot. As he took a sip of coffee, he drove the toe of his boot into Heinz's head. It made a sound like two blocks of wood being struck together.

The whole café had been watching this comedy. The sound of the Dandy's boot striking Heinz's skull extinguished every smile. As if on a signal, everyone except Lori and Paul stared into space, as if neither the Gestapo man nor his victim existed.

Lori put down her own coffee cup, rose to her feet, and strode to the fallen drunk. Blood ran from Heinz's nose and mouth. Lori knelt beside him and felt for his pulse.

"Napkin," she said.

The waiter, standing behind Lori, put a napkin into her hand. Lori wiped Heinz's face and turned him on his side so that he would not strangle on the blood that was filling his mouth. Paul took off his jacket and covered him.

The Dandy took a new document out of his briefcase and read from it, absorbed, as he sipped his coffee.

Lori moved Heinz's slack jaw. "Fractured," she said. "Perhaps the skull also. Put him in the back of the car."

Paul and the waiter carried Heinz to the car. Blood dripped from Heinz's mouth, leaving a spotty trail on the cobbles. The Dandy took no interest in these activities. He went on reading his documents and sipping coffee.

"Stutzer," Lori said.

The Dandy lifted his eyes momentarily at the sound of his name, but did not respond. He turned a page, lifted a gloved finger, and with eyes fixed to the next page, took another sip of coffee.

"Stand up," Lori said, in her clear voice.

The Dandy stood up. He was perhaps twenty-five, a sallow man with soft pink lips and a triangular face. He put a hand, the hand of an equal, on Lori's sleeve. He began to smile. After all, what had he done to Heinz that any German officer would not have done to a commoner who had insulted him and his class?

Lori did not bother to remove the Dandy's hand from her sleeve. She raised her own gloved hand and struck the Gestapo chief of Rügen on the face, a tremendous blow with the back of her fist, like a saber cut. The Dandy's black fedora flew off his head and scaled across the room, spilling a cup of coffee on another table.

Lori turned on her heel, got into the car, and took the wheel. "Sit in back with that man, Paul," she said. "Hold his head in your lap. Mind he doesn't choke."

As Lori turned the car around, reversing in one precise arc, changing gears and going forward in another, the Dandy, still hatless, was standing where she had left him. The wind lifted a lock of his brilliantined hair so that it stood up like a feather.

Twenty people sat in the café, but Paul's eyes were the only ones looking at Stutzer the Dandy.

Thereafter, nobody on the island of Rügen would look Lori or any of her family in the face. The waiters at the café would bring coffee, the butcher would cut meat, the baker would deliver bread, they would all say thank you and run to open the door of their shops, but they did all this with averted eyes.

According to the doctor who treated him, Heinz, the drunk, recovered. But it was decided by the medical authorities that he required institutional care. He disappeared.

— 4 —

This happened in 1936, the summer that Paul was twelve. One night, toward the end of the summer, Paul, unable to sleep, looked out his window and saw a boat standing offshore. She was signaling with a light. Then she sailed around the point. Paul put on his clothes and went outside, thinking that he could run through the beech forest and see the boat again. It would be something to tell his parents the next day.

It was a moonless night and the wood was very dark, but Paul knew the way perfectly. In part, he was guided by a sense of smell: approaching the Borg, he could scent the cold mist rising from its dark surface.

Then, to his surprise, he heard a man and a woman speaking in low tones. They were standing among the stones of the old temple. Drawing closer, Paul recognized his mother's voice. He expected to hear Hubbard's voice next, as his parents were always together, but the man with Lori spoke in a tenor, not in Hubbard's deep baritone, and he had white hair, visible as a patch of movement in the darkness. Paul realized that the man with Lori was Zaentz, the artist who had made the nude drawing of Lori that hung in their sitting room in Berlin. Paul wondered what he was doing in Rügen: the Christophers' Berlin friends never came to the island.

"We must climb down the cliff in the dark," Lori's voice said. "It's not difficult. The cliff is white, so you'll be able to see, and there are plenty of places to hold on."

As Paul had seen her do dozens of times before, Lori led the way to the cliff, swung over, and clambered to the bottom. Zaentz, after giving a short, nervous laugh, went over the edge, too. Paul followed them down. Below him, he could hear the brisk sound of his mother's boots, kicking into the brittle face of the cliff, and Zaentz's heavy breathing. From time to time, Lori spoke to Zaentz, telling him where to put his feet.

The grown-ups did not hear or see Paul; he had learned about stealth from Hubbard's tales of Mahican woodcraft. On the beach, Lori and Zaentz took off their clothes and hid them in a crevice in the chalk. They were wearing bathing suits. From the boat that Paul had seen from his window, a light flashed once, from a point about a half-mile off the headland. Paul realized that the boat was *Mahican.*

As soon as she saw the light, Lori plunged into the sea and started to swim with her strong crawl toward the light, which blinked regularly on a count of ten. Zaentz, swimming less well, followed her, his white hair gleaming.

Paul took off his clothes and hid them in the crevice with the others'. Then he, too, began to swim for the boat, lifting his head every twenty strokes to locate the light. A strong tide was running out, and he moved swiftly with the frigid water. As he got farther from shore, the swell grew higher, so that sometimes he had to wait to be carried to a crest before he could see the light flashing from *Mahican;* rolling onto his back to rest, he could see the chalk cliffs, phosphorescent in the black night, far behind him.

Mahican's white hull was only ten feet away when Paul saw it at last. He gripped the rudder and, hidden in the darkness, looked upward at his father, who was holding Lori's hand as she climbed up the ladder.

She was shuddering with cold. Hubbard threw a blanket around her and wrapped her in his long arms.

Zaentz, water pouring from his stout body, heaved himself aboard. Hubbard reached out and shook hands with him. Lori's head was pillowed against her husband's chest. Paul swam silently to the ladder and, still undetected, climbed aboard too. For a long moment, he stood close to his parents, naked, wet, and shivering.

Suddenly, as if she felt his presence, Lori's eyes opened. She wore an expression that Paul had never before seen on her face: for the first time in his life, his mother was not glad to see him. There was fear in her eyes. It lasted only a moment. Then, as if he were standing by her bedside and she had just awakened, Lori smiled and said, "Paul. I didn't know you were joining us."

"Where are we going?"

"For a sail with Zaentz," Lori said. She felt his skin. "You're freezing. Go below and get dry. Put on warm clothes from the locker."

When Paul came on deck again, *Mahican* was running on the tide without lights, sailing due west. Paul knew then that their destination was Falster. He joined his parents in the cockpit. Hubbard gave him the tiller. There was very little wind. In the still night their woolen clothes smelled of lanolin. Lori opened the wicker picnic basket and poured a hot drink from a thermos. It was coffee instead of the usual chocolate, as Paul had not been expected. When Paul had finished his drink, Lori sent him below with food and a hot drink for Zaentz. He sat on a bunk, a blanket wrapped around his bare torso. The hair on his chest and shoulders was white, too, and as thick as his spade beard.

"You're quite a swimmer," Zaentz said, sipping coffee and eating bread and sausage. "Weren't you afraid, swimming out to the boat?"

The question surprised Paul. He had known that he could swim to the boat. He had also known that, if he missed the boat, he would never be found. "Control, control," Paulus was always saying. "Do only what you know you *can* do. When you're afraid, it's because you have gone beyond your capabilities." Swimming to the boat, Paul had had the flashing light and the cliffs to guide him, and he swam as naturally as he walked. Even at the age of twelve, Paul knew that it was useless to explain oneself. He had never been afraid. He smiled at Zaentz. The artist, who had always liked him, pulled off Paul's knitted cap and ruffled his hair.

Mahican dropped anchor off Falster just as dawn was beginning to show. Zaentz came on deck for the first time since they had sailed from Rügen.

"I heard the anchor go down," he said. "Is this Denmark?"

"It is," Lori said.

Zaentz had always been full of jokes. But now he was weeping behind the tinted lenses of his round steel spectacles.

Just before the Christophers had left Berlin for Rügen that summer, Zaentz had come to the apartment in Charlottenburg, bringing all his pictures with him. When Paul woke in the morning, Zaentz's pictures, dozens of them, were strewn around the apartment, propped up on the furniture, leaning against the walls. Except for the drawing of Lori during her pregnancy, the pictures were brutal caricatures of German faces twisted by greed or lust or hatred.

"Why is the one of Mutti so much like her?" Paul had asked.

"The others are like themselves also," Zaentz replied. "I draw what I see."

Aboard *Mahican*, he hugged Lori long and hard and kissed her repeatedly.

"I'll never forget," he said.

Lori patted his bearded face. "It will be over soon," she said.

Zaentz shook his head. The gesture was like a shudder.

Hubbard brought the dinghy alongside and Zaentz climbed in. Hubbard pulled the cord on the dinghy's motor and headed for shore. It was low tide, and Paul watched through the boat's binoculars as Zaentz walked over the wet sandy beach, strewn with kelp, and then climbed the dunes and disappeared. He was wearing a rucksack. At the crest of the dunes, he turned and waved, first at Hubbard, who waited in the bobbing dinghy just offshore, and then to Lori and Paul aboard *Mahican*.

Lori, standing behind Paul, wrapped her arms around him. The morning star was bright above the sun.

"Put down the glasses," she said. "Look at the morning star."

The east grew brighter. Lori put her cheek next to Paul's. "Paul," she said, "you know that Zaentz is a secret, don't you?"

Paul nodded. He looked toward shore again; the footprints Zaentz had left as he walked over the wet beach were clearly visible.

"Good," Lori said. She kissed his ear and turned his face toward the rising sun; she hadn't done such a thing since he was a small child.

The first crescent of the sun was pushing above the tundra. The morning star grew dimmer. Then it vanished. Lori tightened her embrace.

"An angel has died," she said. "That's what my mother used to tell me when the morning star went out."

When they returned to Berwick, Paulus was waiting for them.

"The Dandy has been here," he said. "He brought these."

The clothes Lori and Zaentz and Paul had left on the beach, hidden in the crevice in the cliff, lay on a table in the hall.

"I told him you often swam from the cliffs," Paulus said. "He asked if you swam with a friend. These clothes obviously don't belong to Hubbard."

Paulus held up the shirt Zaentz had been wearing. It was an old shirt, one he had worn while working in his studio, and it was smeared with paint.

"The Dandy held this shirt up to his nose," Paulus said. " 'Do you know,' he said to me, 'that Jews smear themselves with goose grease at the beginning of winter, and then their women sew them up in their underwear, not removing it until spring? Even turpentine won't kill that smell,' the Dandy said; 'it penetrates the skin and squeezes out through the sweat glands.' "

— 5 —

Paul spent the following summer in the Berkshires. His American godfather, Elliott Hubbard, met him in New York and drove him in a yellow Chrysler convertible to the Harbor, 150 miles to the north. Elliott never drove at less than sixty miles an hour, leaving a huge plume of dust behind as they roared over the dirt roads that led to the Berkshires.

They arrived at midnight. In the morning, Paul asked Alice Hubbard, Elliott's new wife, to show him Indian Joe's grave. They climbed together through the pasture above the Harbor to the Hubbard burial ground, a mossy plot surrounded by a tumbling stone wall. Five generations of the family were buried in a circle, feet pointing inward.

"When the Hubbards arise at the Last Trump, they'll be facing one another," Alice Hubbard said. "Opening their eyes upon the elect of God, they'll see nothing but Hubbards. No boring outsiders. *That's* called the Hubbard heaven."

"What about Indian Joe?"

"Here he is."

Paul found the granite boulder, marked with the words the second Aaron had chiseled into it.

"Very advanced about Mahican Indians, the Hubbards were," Alice said. "It must have been guilt; they never got over the shame of stealing their land from the poor savages. They name everything for them. Is your father that way, too?"

"Our boat is named *Mahican.*"

"Of course it is. Imagine! Indian Joe's ghost, sailing around in the Baltic."

Alice thought that her husband's family, so close-knit and so proud of its history, was comical.

"What you really must understand, in order to understand the Hubbards, is the Hubbard brides," she said. "They're all here."

Moving from one tilted headstone to the other, Alice read off their ages. "You see?" she said. "All the Hubbard women die young, right down to the last generation. They were buried every one before they were forty—here's your grandmother, snuffed out at thirty-four, and Elliott's mother, dead at twenty-five. What a tragic history, what a mystery, or so I thought until Elliott shanghaied me into this summer in the country among his pals. Now I understand: all these women died of boredom."

As she spoke, the pure silence of the country morning was shattered. One of Elliott Hubbard's houseguests, an Italian tenor, had come onto the lawn of the Harbor to sing his morning scales. Alice and Paul could see him, far below them, his portly body wrapped in a white bathrobe, as he projected his voice against the stony mountainside. The Harbor, a sprawling white clapboard structure with innumerable ells and wings, stood on the banks of a brook in a mowing between two mountains. The brook was cold and as gray as a trout's back; the mowing, planted in timothy and redtop, was silvery green; the mountains were blue. Before the tenor began to sing, it had been possible to hear the sound of the brook. Now, as he sang the first few bars of "Una furtiva lagrima," a whitetail deer that had been grazing among a herd of Jersey cows lifted its head. Its horns were in velvet.

Elliott Hubbard was a collector of houseguests. Everyone was interesting to him, and he invited everyone who interested him to stay at his country house. In the room next to Paul's, a playwright composed dialogue, reading his lines aloud far into the night and crumpling up sheet after sheet of paper as he failed to achieve the effect he wanted. In the barn, a retired professional lightweight named Battling Jim Cerruti gave Paul boxing lessons. At the end of the summer, he made his report to Elliott: "The kid's fast and he's not afraid of getting hurt; he won't back off. He's going to get his bell rung a lot as he goes through life."

Alice said, "Elliott is like the college boy who sent his mother a telegram from New Haven: *Bringing 16 for Easter.* She had beds made up for sixteen guests. Her son got off the train on Good Friday accompanied by the entire Yale Class of 1916. Is your father like that, Paul?"

"He brings a lot of people home."

"What sort of people?"

"All sorts. Painters, writers, actors . . ."

"No actresses?"

"No."

"Elliott doesn't bring them home, either. Who else? Any bank robbers? Elliott brings clients home; we had a man who dressed up to rob banks. He'd be a monk, then an admiral, then a nun. Mostly it was ecclesiastical. He said he liked the costuming; he wasn't in it for the money. Elliott thought he was fascinating. He got him off with only a year in jail. You'll probably be just like them when you grow up. It's the Hubbard enthusiasm."

In the evening, when Elliott's guests came down to dinner, the conversation ran on until well after midnight. Usually Alice was the only female present. Whatever she may have said in the graveyard, she never seemed to be bored, but she did like to go to bed with her husband at a reasonable hour. When she wanted to end the jovial male conversation she would cry, *"Bones!"* and Elliott's Yale friends would get up and leave the room, as members of Skull and Bones, the university's secret society, were obliged to do on hearing that word spoken aloud. The others, respecting a mysterious ritual they did not understand, would follow.

— 6 —

"This is not the time to educate a boy in Germany," Paulus said.

Lori agreed, but she could not send Paul as far away as America again. When he returned to Europe at the end of the summer, he went to school in Switzerland. The school, a former monastery standing among vineyards on a knoll above Lake Geneva, was the coldest place in which Paul had ever been. From October to April, the sun disappeared, a bitter wind scoured the playing fields, and the lake was hidden behind a perpetual cloud bank. The school was as much like a prison as it was possible to make it. In the vaulted dining room, the boys ate thin soup, root vegetables, pasta, and salt fish, never meat, while in a loud voice a prefect read elevating passages from French literature. There were two huge paintings in this room, portraits of Saint Joan and St. Cyr, darkened by candle smoke, and these were the only pools of color in the whole gray place.

There was no mercy. In lightless classrooms, the students memorized facts and learned how to speak the French language; even the French boys were obliged to start over, to eliminate bad habits of speech and ugly accents. War with Germany was approaching. The younger masters, most of whom were officers in the French reserves, seemed eager for it to begin. They assured the boys that France would win because she was the stronger of the two powers. Paul, half American and half German, the worst possible combination of blood from the French point of view, maddened his masters by never forgetting anything while French boys stumbled over their lessons. It was clear to him from the first day that the only useful thing he could take away from this place was its language. After the first few weeks, he made few errors in French, but when he did mispronounce a word or commit a grammatical error, the masters struck him on the backs of his fists with the baton, a thin hardwood wand, raising red welts on chapped skin. During these beatings, the doubled hands had to be held, rigid and immobile, over the desk; it was a sign of defective character to move them. Paul did not move his hands.

Paul was called *Boche-Boche.* Soon after his arrival, four older boys with overgrown adolescent noses came into his room (a cell, really: iron bed, chair, desk, dresser, chamber pot, striped curtain over the window, writhing china Christ on a varnished pine cross) and found him wearing his sailing sweater as he studied. This was a violation of good form. The sweater was fastened at the shoulder with a row of bone buttons. While three of the boys held Paul down, the fourth, Philippe by name, cut off the buttons with a penknife and attempted to force Paul to swallow them. Paul clenched his teeth and, though Philippe broke off the corner of an incisor, refused to eat the buttons. Fighting all four of the boys at one time was beyond Paul's capability, so he let them walk away.

His revenge came soon enough. Sport at this school meant soccer, played every afternoon from two to five-thirty. After the soccer master watched him practice, Paul was put into a team with older boys. One of his opponents was Philippe. Dribbling toward the goal, Paul ran into Philippe at full speed and broke his nose. The next day he ran into him again and knocked him to the wet turf. Philippe leaped up and threw a wild punch at Paul. Paul ducked. Philippe swung his fist again. As Battling Jim Cerruti had taught him, Paul blocked it and hit Philippe with four straight lefts on his swollen nose and a right cross that broke a front tooth. Philippe put his hands over his bleeding face and howled in pain. After that, Paul was left in peace.

— 7 —

Paul returned to Rügen in the summer of 1939, the year of his fifteenth birthday. There were E-boats in the harbor and sometimes, looking down from the cliffs in the early morning, he could see German submarines, like great black fishes that had been thought to be extinct, cruising again on the surface of the Baltic. Otherwise, the island seemed unchanged. Life at Berwick was just as it had always been: the conversation, the long walks, the reading, the swims from the shingle beach.

The Christophers sailed much less, but sometimes Hubbard and Lori went out alone at night. Paul, a light sleeper, would wake at dawn and hear their footsteps on the gravel as they hurried toward *Mahican*'s mooring in order to get aboard before the tide began to run. They never asked him to come along as crew. He never asked them why.

One night, soon after his return, he heard the sound of boots on the gravel beneath his window. He looked out, but there was no moon and he could see no one. The sound of footsteps continued, pacing back and forth on the gravel. Paul looked at his watch. It was three-thirty, nearly dawn, and he smiled, imagining Paulus striding back and forth in the darkness, waiting for Paul to wake at sunrise. Sometimes the old man did that; on chilly mornings he would put on a long sheepskin jerkin that he had worn in the Russian campaign, wearing this garment over his old-fashioned ankle-length nightgown.

Paul dressed and went outside. He used the kitchen door and walked around the house on the soft grass, hoping to surprise Paulus.

It was a windless night; there were no stars. Paul walked in the blackness toward the sound of the footsteps. Suddenly, he smelled cigarette smoke. Paulus did not smoke; no one in the family smoked.

"Who is that?" Paul asked.

The footsteps ceased, but Paul could still hear the man's feet shifting in the gravel. The man switched on a powerful flashlight and shone it in Paul's face. Shielding his eyes, Paul could make out a leather coat and riding boots. The man did not speak. The flashlight went off. A lighted cigarette spun through the darkness and landed on the gravel in a shower of sparks. Brisk footsteps moved away, over the gravel.

Paul ran after the man. He confronted him. "Who is that?" he asked again. There was no answer. The man turned on his flashlight again and shone it into Paul's face. Paul jumped to one side, out of the light, and as the man searched for him with the beam of the electric torch, he saw that it was Stutzer, the Gestapo dandy, who had been standing in the darkness, watching Berwick.

Stutzer finally located Paul with the flashlight beam. Still he did not speak, but stood silently in the black, starless night, running the light up and down Paul's figure for several moments more before switching it off and then marching away over the gravel.

When Paul told this story at breakfast, Lori smiled.

"Ah," she said, "the Dandy. We should have warned you. He lurks about a lot. You never know when you might run into him."

"Lurks? Why?"

Lori shrugged. "I think he thinks we're smugglers. He's always searching the boat. We hardly ever sail anymore, it's such a bother to have him come aboard and turn everything inside out."

"Can't you do something about that?"

"Maybe someone can give him another crack on the head."

Hilde von Buecheler cut a piece of cheese and gave it to Paul. "Don't joke, Lori," she said. "Don't teach Paul to joke about these things."

Paulus was silent; he had been silent all summer.

Paul and Lori, on a morning in August, set off for a walk in the forest. It was an invigorating day, with the smell of fall already in the air. A stiff wind blew in from the Baltic and the sky and the sea were the same luminous shade of gray, the sign of a storm.

It was gray inside the forest, too. They were approaching the Borg, where they always paused to eat their lunch, when Lori sniffed loudly. "Cigarette smoke," she said. "It can't be the Dandy at this time of day. He's a night creature."

Lori scowled; intruders were common in the tourist season and she was cordial to them, but tobacco smoke annoyed her. She quickened her step, as if determined to drive this intruder, and the fumes of his cigarette, out of the wood.

The cigarette smoker, legs crossed, lounged indolently on one of the temple stones, reading a book; he might have been sitting in his own living room, so much at home did he seem in this forest. He drew deeply on a long cigarette; the smoke hung motionless for a moment in the heavy air, then found a current of wind and vanished. The man caught sight of Lori and Paul; He smiled, stood, and watched them approach, cigarette poised in his left hand. It was a Russian cigarette, a cardboard tube.

The intruder was Otto Rothchild. He stripped off his right glove and held out his hand.

"Baronesse; young Paul. What a surprise. I was just reading some poetry. Really these trees should be Russian birches, but your beeches are rather nice. One *can* get used to these drab colors; they go with the German light."

Lori glanced down at Rothchild's book, a limp volume of Pushkin, bound in leather. "Ah, yes, Hubbard's Russian," she said.

Just as she had predicted, Lori had never learned to like Otto Rothchild; she never called him anything but "Hubbard's Russian."

"I thought you had left Germany," Lori said.

"I was in Spain for the war."

"Naturally you were."

It exasperated Lori that Otto Rothchild always did the fashionable thing at the fashionable moment. When Bolsheviks were in style, he had collected Bolsheviks. Now he had Nazi friends: not louts who were real believers, but acceptable people who were willing to trade a little decency for an appointment or a uniform or the opportunity to know influential people and make money. Hubbard was intrigued by Rothchild's lack of scruples. He enjoyed his gossip: the Russian was the best talker Hubbard had ever known: informed, witty, and malicious. Lori never stayed at the table to listen to him.

Rothchild brought adventurers by to meet Hubbard, young men and women. They were invariably beautiful. To a dinner party for Zaentz, just before Zaentz escaped, Rothchild had brought a young lieutenant of army intelligence.

"His name is Bülow," Rothchild had said. "He's not one of the real Bülows, but he's perfect for his new career. He speaks Russian—I taught him myself, he has a lovely accent, like an intelligent serf who's played with his owner's son—and he's willing to betray absolutely anyone. Except, of course, the nobility, so *you* are immune, Baronesse."

Perhaps in retaliation for being called Hubbard's Russian, Rothchild called Lori Baronesse, the title used by the unmarried daughter of a baron, as if marriage to an American changed nothing for a member of her class.

"Otto is a rat," Lori said to Hubbard. "The rat population always exactly equals the human population. For every human being, living out in the open, there is one rat, hiding between the walls, existing on the garbage of his human host. Otto is your rat, Hubbard. In the days of the valuta it was your dollars. Now it's your respectability. He gets fat, gnawing away under your table."

"Nonsense. Otto knows everyone in Berlin."

"Thanks to good old lovable Hubbard. If he rides around in your pocket, peeping out and sniffing and wiggling his whiskers, then people stop noticing how disgusting he is. You've made him into a pet rat."

"Probably he's a spy," Paulus said. "Russians are famous for it."

Whatever he was, Otto Rothchild prospered. Reading Pushkin in the beech forest by the Borg, he seemed not to have a care in the world.

"It's marvelously peaceful here," he said. He sniffed, gazing fixedly at Paul. "What's in the package?" he asked.

Paul carried their lunch, wrapped in brown paper and tied with string. "Bread and cheese," he said.

"I thought I smelled sausage. One gets very little sausage in Spain. It's spoiled fish, mostly, and gummy rice."

"There is sausage," Lori said. "If you're hungry, by all means have it."

Rothchild untied the package. He ate greedily, poking one piece of

[57]

cheese or sausage into his mouth with another and chewing very thoroughly. He wiped the sausage fat from his fingers and lips with bread, and ate that too. Then he stretched out on his stomach beside the lake and drank like an animal at a water hole. Lori watched every move. Rothchild caught her glance.

"Skills from an earlier existence," he said. "Paul, would it be a great deal of trouble to bring your father here?"

Lori was glad of a chance to escape. "I'll fetch him," she said. "You remain with our guest, Paul."

Lori tramped away toward Berwick. Paul offered Rothchild the apple he carried in his pocket. Rothchild bit into the apple, removing large circles of white flesh. He chewed noisily and, when he was finished, dropped the core onto the floor of the forest. Paul had never seen such a hungry grown-up. Now that they were alone, Rothchild made no effort to talk to Paul; he was not the sort of man to spend the coins of charm on adolescent boys. He sat down on the stone and went back to reading Pushkin.

It was some time before Hubbard arrived. When he came into the glade, Rothchild made a sweeping gesture of welcome, as if he owned the forest, inviting him to sit down on one of the broken temple stones.

"Have you heard the radio?" Rothchild asked.

Hubbard shook his head.

"Yesterday Germany and Soviet Russia signed a treaty of friendship and military alliance."

"Nazis and Communists in an alliance?" Hubbard said. "The lunatic Right and the demented Left in bed together? How can they do that?"

"They can do whatever they like," Rothchild said.

He was never long without a gesture. To punctuate the sentence he had just spoken, he ground the core of the apple into the powdery dirt of the forest floor with the heel of his suede shoe.

"I caused the Bolsheviks some inconvenience in Spain," Rothchild said. "Now that they are Germany's allies, things are going to be inconvenient for me, Hubbard."

"Inconvenient for you, Otto? In what way?"

"In the way things were inconvenient for Zaentz," Rothchild said. "In the way they were inconvenient for Blau, Schwarz, Eisner, Gerstein, and all your other . . . passengers. Shall I go on? It's a long list. Everyone knows what you and Lori have been doing with your sailboat."

"Oh? What do they know, Otto?"

"That the Christophers are angels of mercy. Even the Gestapo knows. In other circumstances I'd advise you to stop your humanitarian work."

"But not before we smuggle you out of Germany?"

"Exactly. Unless you only help Jews." Rothchild drew on his Russian cigarette. "I do have a Jewish name—false, but Jewish," he said.

"And if we don't?"

"What does that mean, Hubbard—'And if we don't?' If you don't, you don't, and that's the end of it. Did you think I'd denounce you? Do you really imagine that I'm a danger to you?"

"Why not? You know half the Nazi Party."

"Lucky for me that I do. Horst Bülow told me that my name was on a list handed to the Germans after the pact was signed in Moscow."

As he spoke, Rothchild tied and untied a knot in the string that had held Lori's lunch package together. Hubbard took the string and paper out of his hand and stuffed it into the pocket of his jacket.

"What happens," Hubbard asked, "to those whose names are on the list?"

"They vanish, handed over to the Bolsheviks. They think they can find their way to many others through me."

"Can they? Are you a Bolshevik?"

"Of course not. Are you? But how many do we know between us? Nobody ever stands up under questioning, Hubbard. You only hold out long enough to lull your conscience for betraying your friends. They wouldn't kill me, you know; or you, or Lori. Or your child. It would be the camps. Slave labor."

"All right," Hubbard said.

"Friendship," Rothchild said, "is the exile's only capital."

— 9 —

It was Paul who led Rothchild down the cliff at midnight and swam with him to *Mahican*. They sailed without lights, setting a westward course for Falster. Aboard the boat, with Paul at the helm, nobody spoke except Lori.

"Where do you plan to go?" she asked Rothchild. "What will you do?"

"To Paris. I'll do what I've always done."

"Make friends and use them, you mean."

Rothchild smiled at her: his charming smile, perfect teeth and liquid eyes.

At this moment, the jib broke loose and whipped wildly around the mast. *Mahican* had been sailing close-hauled before the wind, her rail awash in a four-foot sea. Hubbard hurried forward and began to struggle with the sail.

Lori leaped out of the cockpit to help him. Hubbard's big feet slipped on the scrubbed oak planking as he tried to gather the sail into his long arms. He had captured most of it, but when he slipped he lost his grip on the stiff wet canvas and the wind took it, unfurling it like a flag. Hubbard grinned at Lori. She lunged for the sail and went overboard. Hubbard reached for her and missed and then the sail came back and wrapped itself around his head.

Paul dove into the sea after his mother. Though it had been pitch-black aboard *Mahican,* there seemed to be a little light below the surface. Paul struggled to swim downward. His chest hurt already. He hadn't got much air in his lungs before he went into the sea. He had seen the place where Lori went under, and his mind had been entirely concentrated on following her into this seam in the heaving water. Ten feet below his outstretched hands, he could see his mother. He couldn't reach her; she didn't seem to be swimming, but sank with terrifying swiftness, as if she were holding on to a weight.

Paul pressed his arms against his sides and kicked. The water wasn't deep here, no more than twenty feet, and there were rocks, bearded with weed, on the bottom. Lori settled between two rocks, one arm uplifted, her hair floating away from her face. Paul seized her hair, put his feet on the rock, and pushed off as hard as he could, kicking for the surface. He wanted desperately to take a breath; he did not know how much longer he could keep from opening his mouth. He clenched his teeth and let the water take him up, but he did not move. He kicked, but still his body did not rise. He seemed to have no buoyancy at all.

It did not seem to matter. It occurred to him that his mother might be dead; perhaps she had struck her head when she went overboard. Perhaps it would be best to remain here, to give up the struggle. He knew that he must fill his lungs with water in a matter of seconds; he could not control the instinct to breathe for very much longer. It was very calm down here out of the wind. Paul and Lori were part of the sea, a particle of the deep, moving with it.

Then he saw why they could not float upward toward the surface: Lori was wearing Paulus's old sheepskin jerkin and the weight of it, soaked with seawater, was drowning them. Paul wrenched his mother's arms and pulled her out of the sheepskin. Lori began to rise toward the surface. Clutching her hand, Paul kicked against the water, grinding his teeth together to keep from opening his mouth.

Their heads broke the surface and Paul saw the hull of *Mahican* less than a hundred feet away, mainsail shuddering as her boom swung and she came about. Paul filled his lungs with air and looked into his mother's face. Her hair was plastered tight against her skull. Her huge gray eyes were the color of the sea. Treading water, she kissed her son. Hubbard, shouting with joy, splashed into the sea beside them, carrying a line.

When they put Otto Rothchild ashore on Falster at dawn, Lori stayed below, so as not to have to say good-bye to him.

— 10 —

As *Mahican*'s sail entered the harbor at Rügen next day, the Gestapo launch put out from the quay to meet her and Stutzer the Dandy came aboard.

Once on deck, the Dandy did not look at the Christophers' faces; he held out his hand for the boat's papers and examined them. With a stiff forefinger, encased in its snug kid glove, he turned each page of Hubbard's passport, each page of Lori's, each page of Paul's. He never lifted his eyes from the documents.

"You are married to this American?" he said to Lori at last. When she didn't answer, he raised his triangular face an inch and his eyes peered out at her from beneath the shiny beak of his cap.

"Yes," Lori replied.

"Your husband and child have American passports; yours is German. Why?"

"They are Americans. I am a German."

"You don't hold an American passport as well as a German passport?"

"No."

"You consider, nevertheless, that your son is an American, not a German?"

"My son will make his own decision on that matter when he comes of age."

Belowdecks, a heavy object fell with a crash. Two other policemen, the Dandy's assistants, were searching the cabin. The Dandy, unruffled by the noise, went through the passports again.

"Paul Christopher," he said, "born in Rügen, fourteenth June 1924. Why do you travel so much to Switzerland, Christopher?"

Paul said, "I go to school there."

"What school?"

Paul named it.

"A French school?"

"Yes."

The Dandy closed the passports. He then examined Hubbard, Lori, and Paul, moving his eyes from their hats to their shoes as if he were still reading the stamped pages of their passports. His eyes flicked upward and caught the expression on Lori's face; it was very like the expression he had seen on her face three years before, in the café. The Dandy's pink lips pressed together.

"What is the purpose of this examination of our boat and ourselves?" Hubbard asked.

"You are enthusiastic sailors."

"We come to Rügen every summer for the sailing."

"For the sailing. You leave in the dark always."

Hubbard looked at the sky, flooded with the thin light of midday. "We try to catch the tides," he said.

"How many persons were aboard this vessel when you sailed?"

"My wife, my son, myself."

"Not more? You've been at sea for twenty-nine hours. Where did you go?"

"To Falster."

"In Denmark. Your passports and the boat's papers show no entry stamps, no exit stamps."

"We didn't go through formalities at Falster. We went ashore in the dinghy, had a picnic on the beach."

The Dandy opened the wicker picnic hamper. He examined the knives and forks and plates strapped to the lid of the basket. He unbuckled the straps and examined each utensil and dish.

"Four dirty forks, four knives, four spoons," he said. "Also four dirty plates. If there are only three of you, why are there unwashed forks and plates for four persons?"

Lori gazed steadily into his eyes. "We invited a guest for dinner in Falster."

The Dandy pointed a finger at his assistant, who got out a notebook and pencil. When he was ready to write, pencil poised above the blank page, the Dandy asked his next question.

"Name of the guest?"

"We never asked. Informality is one of the joys of sailing."

The assistant wrote rapidly. When the Dandy held up a finger, he stopped.

"This man whom you invited to dinner was a Dane?"

"Probably. We didn't ask. We spoke English together."

"And you left him in Falster, on the beach?"

"Yes."

The Dandy handed Hubbard the passports, slapping them into his palm. "Do not travel abroad again without reporting first to the police, and without passing through formalities at your destination," he said. "Failure to do so is a serious breach of German law."

Hubbard put a warning hand on Lori's rigid back. The Dandy made a gesture and his men scrambled into the launch, holding it against the fenders while he climbed down the ladder. Holding on to the ladder with his kid gloves, he stared, expressionless, at Lori's breasts. Triumph, a pinprick of expression, came and went in his pale eyes. He knew all the Christophers' secrets, he seemed to be saying, even the look of Lori's flesh under her clothes; and he wanted them to know that he knew everything. At last, the Dandy smiled.

— 11 —

In the library at Berwick, Paulus listened to Lori's account of the Gestapo search of *Mahican*.

"The time has come to give up these night sails," he said.

"Suppose the Dandy had caught us with *Rothchild* hidden below," Lori said. "What a joke—to be tried for treason or whatever they try you for because you smuggled something like Rothchild out of Germany."

"Next time you will be caught. They know what you're doing. If you go on, Lori, you'll only lead the Gestapo to the people you want to save. They'll disappear one night."

"They're going to disappear in any case."

"You'll disappear with them. Paul is an accomplice. You'd better realize that no one has immunity from these people."

"No immunity from the Dandy?"

"No," Paulus said, holding Lori's eyes. "No immunity. You're behaving very stupidly. Like your father."

"Like my father?" Lori cried. "Stupid? Explain, Paulus."

"He too laughed at the wrong people, at the wrong moment. Because the people who killed him were not soldiers, he thought they weren't dangerous. Because this man you call the Dandy isn't the sort you're used to seeing in a uniform, you think *he's* not dangerous. He'll kill you for the same reason the mob killed your father, because you look as you do and because your voice sounds as it does. If you don't realize that, then you are very stupid indeed. You're unfit for politics, Lori. Everyone in this family has always been unfit for politics."

Lori turned away and walked to the window.

"Politics? I don't care what they believe in," she said. "It's the stupidity I hate. It *must* be opposed, Paulus. My son won't grow up in a country of the stupid, hearing people say that Jews smear themselves with goose grease and sew themselves up in their underwear for the winter. I won't have it."

They left Rügen that night and, after two hours of packing in Berlin, boarded the Paris express with two bags apiece. Hubbard rolled Zaentz's drawing of Lori into a tube and carried it in his hand. It was important not to look overburdened, like refugees.

After that, everything happened very quickly. At the frontier, an officer of the Gestapo entered their compartment. Like the Dandy, he was absorbed in the stamps in the Christophers' passports. He read out their names.

"Two American citizens, one German citizen, father, mother, and son," he said.

"That is correct."

"You will come with me."

As they followed, the man from the Gestapo strode over the station platform, the mills of the Saarland filled the evening sky with flame and smoke. The night air smelled like scorched wool.

"They have lower standards of dress down here," Lori said, nodding at the wrinkles in the back of the Gestapo man's ill-fitting jacket.

There was only one chair in the policeman's office. He sat in it and studied the passports for several moments.

"You're going into France. Why?" he asked at last.

"For a holiday."

"What sort of holiday? You will walk, swim, what?"

"Some of everything, no doubt."

Hubbard did the talking. He held Lori's arm firmly, to keep her quiet.

"Also sailing?"

The Gestapo man's head snapped back as he spoke these words, as if he expected to detect a look of guilt on Hubbard's face. Hubbard gave him his genial smile.

An assistant came in, carrying the tube containing Zaentz's drawing of Lori. The Gestapo man opened it.

"That is personal property," Lori said.

"Yes?"

With great sarcasm, the Gestapo man tapped the end of the tube on the desk and removed the drawing. He unrolled it and held it at arm's length.

"Why are you attempting to smuggle this out of Germany?" he asked.

"One does not smuggle a work of art," Lori said.

"A work of *art?*"

His contemptuous eyes ran up and down Lori's body, comparing her to the pregnant smiling girl in the drawing.

He opened the two American passports and stamped them; then he wrote at length on the stamped pages, signed with a flourish, and placed another, smaller stamp beneath his signature. He handed the two American passports to Hubbard.

"Kindly read the entries I have made."

Hubbard found the pages and read what the Gestapo man had written there.

"This says that my son and I are expelled from Germany. For what reason?"

"It is not necessary to state the reason."

Lori stirred. Hubbard could feel the anger in her. Paulus was right —she was stupid about danger. There was great danger here. He tightened his grip on her arm.

[65]

"When may we reenter Germany?"

The Gestapo man did not respond; his business with Hubbard was over. He must have rung a concealed bell. Four uniformed men, ordinary frontier police, had already come into the room. It was a hot night; the odor of sweat-stained wool was very strong.

"You will leave now," the Gestapo man said. "These men will escort you to the train."

Lori held out her hand. "My passport, please."

The Gestapo man did not look at Lori. Her passport lay on the desk, between his hands.

"This woman will remain in Germany," he said. "You have one minute to make your good-byes."

"What do you mean, *remain in Germany?*" Hubbard said.

"You're wasting your one minute," the Gestapo man said.

"Go, Hubbard," Lori said.

"I demand to speak to the American consul," Hubbard said.

"The American authorities will be informed of your expulsion. Now you must leave Germany."

"Without my wife?"

"Your wife is a German citizen. She may not leave Germany at this time."

"Go," Lori said.

"No," Hubbard said in English. "Paul, kiss your mother. Get on the train. As soon as you cross the frontier, send telegrams to the American consuls in Saarbrücken and Berlin, to Paulus, and to Elliott. Here."

Hubbard handed Paul his wallet, full of Reichsmarks worth four to the dollar. In Germany, the currency was normal again.

Lori kissed Paul. "Remember everything," she said. "Go."

Paul hesitated. In English his mother said, "Don't say good-bye. Don't obey them in anything."

"Now," Hubbard said to the Gestapo man, "I demand to see your superior officer."

The Gestapo man's hands were flat on the desk. He lifted his right index finger, the smallest possible gesture. One of the policemen hit Hubbard on the right kidney with his baton. Another looped a chain around Hubbard's thumb and twisted. A third seized him by the arm and twisted it to his shoulder blades. The last policeman stood, legs spread, baton held across his thighs, and nodded to Paul.

Lori's eyes were on him. She spoke English again. "Control your face," she said. "They mustn't make you feel anything."

The policemen walked Hubbard, doubled over in pain, and Paul, who stood upright, out of the room.

Paul turned, to look for a last time at Lori. Nothing showed on her face, not even love for him and Hubbard. She shook her head, forbidding him again to say good-bye, forbidding him to let these thugs see that they had touched his emotions.

"Mutti," he said, unable to help himself.

"No good-byes," Lori said. But at the last second she, too, weakened, and spoke his name.

The fourth policeman struck Paul on the elbow with his baton. When he neither moved nor flinched, he hit him on the other elbow, and because he was blinded by pain, Paul did not see his mother again.

In later years, when he tried to remember every detail of this moment, he was always surprised that everything had been so ordinary. Apart from the blows, there was practically nothing to remember except that his mother, knowing that she would never see him again, knowing that she was almost surely going to her death, had not been afraid. She had never been afraid.

— 12 —

On Friday, September 1, 1939, the day that Paul and Hubbard Christopher left Germany, the Wehrmacht invaded Poland. Two days later, France declared war on Germany. Communications between the two countries ceased.

They went to Strasbourg, because there was an American consulate there. There were troops everywhere, dark-jawed, unkempt, unsmiling. Unlike the pink-faced German soldiery, who never seemed happier than when they were in ranks, the French did not sing as they marched. Nothing Paul had heard at school about French military glory, or at Berwick on the same subject, had prepared him for these files of sallow, resentful men tramping through the streets of Strasbourg toward the Rhine.

Fourteen days passed before a message arrived from Paulus. In all that time, Hubbard did not speak a word except during his daily visits to the post office and the consulate. At last the consul handed Hubbard Paulus's telegram, transmitted from the American embassy in Berlin: *No word from Lori since your departure. Am making inquiries through army channels, unfruitfully so far. Imprisonment possible. Under no circumstances enter Germany yourself. Remaining in France will intensify suspicion. Strongly advise return to the United States in neutral ship. All messages hereafter will be sent in care of your cousin.*

A regiment of infantry marched past the consulate as Hubbard read Paulus's message, and the sound of thudding feet came through the open window.

"This whole episode may not last very long," the consul said. "France *is* stronger than Germany. Remember the Maginot Line. They have the Jerries outnumbered five to one on the western front, and of course Britain is in it too." He smiled at Hubbard. "The Polish Army is supposed to be very brave," he said.

But the French, with more than one hundred divisions facing only twenty-three German divisions in the west, did not attack. Warsaw fell on September 28.

The next day, Paulus sent another message through the American consul: *No word. No trace. Your presence in an enemy country is a danger to your wife and child. Go to America at once.*

— 13 —

On the voyage across the Atlantic, Hubbard stopped speaking even to Paul. Paul sat in silence with him in the cabin and walked silently by his side as he circled the deck, making as many as a hundred circuits in the early morning before the other passengers were up. He had the eerie thought that, huge as Hubbard was, some even larger being, insane with anger, was struggling to burst through his skin in a shower of blood.

Paul was absolutely certain that his mother was dead, perfectly sure that she had been tortured before she died. He remembered the look in the Dandy's eyes as he stared at her breasts as he climbed down *Mahican's* ladder. The Gestapo man at the frontier, looking at Zaentz's drawing, had had the same look. All his life, Paul had heard about his mother's beauty; he knew what beauty meant to men like the Dandy. For the first time in his life, he hid his feelings from Hubbard. He realized that he was, in some way that he could not control, obeying his mother's orders not to let others see his emotions. He dreamed about Lori constantly. In his dreams she drowned, she fell from great heights, she sailed like a kite among clouds. Each time she died, he tried to say good-bye, and each time, she laid a finger on his lips. He woke up sobbing. Hubbard, who never slept, heard him, but he never spoke to him across the dark cabin.

In New York, Elliott Hubbard met them on the pier.

"What word from Paulus?" Hubbard asked, his first spoken words in more than a week.

"Nothing," Elliott said. "I would have cabled the ship if he had sent any word at all. Wouldn't Lori have gone straight to Paulus?"

"Yes," Hubbard said.

Elliott took them to the house on Ninety-third Street that he had bought on his marriage. Alice had given birth to a son called Horace. "No surprises," she said, dismissing the experience. "He's all Hubbard. How did *you* escape, Paul? Your mother must have amazing genes." This was her only reference to Lori.

Alice chattered incessantly, describing the strange friends Elliott had brought to the Harbor that summer. "This was our summer for bizarre Englishmen," she said. "They were all rabidly anti-German. Good thing *you* weren't there, Paul, as you're half German; they would have run you through." Hubbard listened to her, unsmiling, unspeaking.

In the library after dinner, Elliott poured brandy from a decanter and handed a glass to Hubbard. Hubbard took the glass, then put it down, untouched.

"Hubbard," Elliott said, "what are you going to do?"

Hubbard responded in a strong voice, as if the answer to Elliott's question was so obvious that it hadn't needed asking.

"I'm going to find my wife," Hubbard said.

"Where do you think she is?"

"In prison."

"You think it's possible to find her?"

"I don't know."

"And if you find her, do you think it's possible to get her out of a country at war—especially if that country is Germany?"

"It'll be very difficult."

Hubbard was speaking in a toneless voice. There was no more expression on his face than in his voice.

Elliott picked up Hubbard's brandy glass and gave it to him again. "Drink that," he said. Obediently, Hubbard did so. Elliott took the glass out of his hand. "Now," Elliott said, "how do you plan to get into Germany?"

"Why do you want to know?"

"Why do you think? So that I can help you."

"Sail, walk, parachute," Hubbard said. "Once I get inside the country I'll be all right. Nobody can tell from my speech that I'm not a German."

"You'll have no papers. You're six feet four inches tall. Do you think the Germans won't know you're there?"

Hubbard did not listen. "I must get Paul into a school, then I'll go back," he said.

Hubbard's speech was brisk now. He had made a decision; he had made a plan.

"Hubbard," Elliott said, "there's a man I want you to meet. I'll ask him to meet you at the club tomorrow." .

"What man?"

"An Englishman," Elliott said. "One of the Englishmen who spent the summer at the Harbor—Alice mentioned them."

"What kind of an Englishman?"

Elliott smiled. "A baronet," he said. "He's an ingenious sort of fellow."

Sir Richard Shaw-Condon, Bart., wore a dove-gray billycock bowler hat like Winston Churchill's, and he left it on his head while he sipped Scotch whisky in the library at the Yale Club. Sir Richard had remarkable facial hair: thick flaxen eyebrows and a matching Hitlerian mustache. In these strange American precincts, he was utterly at ease. His legs were crossed at the ankles, and his feet, encased in glossy oxfords, rested on the table. He seemed to want to look like a very young minister of the Crown, lounging on the front bench at question time in Parliament, dealing jauntily with attacks from the opposition. In the peculiar English way of breaking the ice with a stranger, he asked Hubbard a series of rude personal questions.

"Whatever made you live in Germany for all those years?"

"I had a German wife," Hubbard said.

"A beauty, I hear. German women can be extraordinary—that perfect skin. But *sixteen years*, my dear fellow. Didn't you ever long for civilization, tucked away in Berlin, munching on sausages and listening to drinking songs?"

Hubbard did not answer; he knew that this waggish interrogation must run its course.

"You write books," Sir Richard said. "Your cousin lent me one.

Difficult for an Englishman to understand all those American attitudes, of course, but I thought the writing was first-rate. Is that what you lived on, your royalties?"

"In part," Hubbard said.

"What was the other part? Have a bit of income of your own?"

Hubbard, still silent, ordered another whisky for Sir Richard. The waiter looked the Englishman up and down; a lot of eccentrics belonged to this club, but nobody had ever before worn a hat indoors here or put his feet on the tabletop.

"What really engages my curiosity, *our* curiosity," Sir Richard said, "is why you and your wife smuggled all those Jews and Bolshies out to Denmark. Was it politics, Christopher?"

"No."

"You're not a Bolshevik yourself?"

"No."

"*What* are you, then, may one ask?"

"Those people were our friends."

"*All* of them?"

"Nearly all."

Sir Richard took off his billycock bowler and spun it on his index finger. For a long moment, he was absorbed in this trick.

"Look here, Christopher," he said at last, placing his feet on the floor and his hat neatly upon his knees, as if this were some signal that the mood of the meeting had changed, "the fact of the matter is, we're most awfully sympathetic about your wife. D'you reckon we might put our heads together and think of something?"

"Think of something?"

"Something to help—to find her, to bring her back. Elliott told you nothing about our work?"

"No."

"You look remarkably like him, you know. Are you like him in other ways?"

Sir Richard had a high-pitched boyish laugh and now that he had abandoned his junior minister pose, he crackled like a schoolboy with mischief and curious intelligence. Hubbard had never seen a grown man with such a lively face. Sir Richard waited alertly for Hubbard's next question. Knowing the right question to ask was a test of breeding; Hubbard had the impression that he would be admitted to some sort of club if he asked it. He hadn't run into this situation since his first years

[71]

at college: you were supposed to ask a man from Boston if he knew another man, and then ask if old so-and-so still rode that black gelding called Domino—all of which told your listener that you knew the names of the horses belonging to people who rode with the Myopia Hunt, and it was therefore all right to go on with the conversation.

"In point of fact," Sir Richard said, when no question came, "we're not supposed to talk absolutely frankly to Americans inside the borders of the United States. It's your Neutrality Act. However, I'd like to talk frankly to you."

"Talk frankly about what?"

"About choosing sides. Your country is neutral, but in times like these, there can be no neutral men."

"Really? Why should I choose sides?"

"You must answer that question. You *are* faced with a grave personal dilemma. Perhaps we can help you to resolve it."

"Look," Hubbard said, "why don't you tell me whatever it is you're not supposed to say frankly to Americans?"

Hubbard's bluntness startled Sir Richard. The charm vanished from his face, like a smooth blank lid closing over a sparkling eye.

"Very well," Sir Richard said. "I hear you want to go into Germany."

"Yes."

"We might be prepared to help you."

"How?"

"I'll come to that. Are you willing to discuss the matter?"

"Why should I? You *are* asking me to become a British spy, aren't you?"

"Would it be so painful to spy against the people who have arrested your wife?"

"No. But how would that help my wife?"

"It wouldn't be all spying, you know. It's possible that you could find your wife."

"And rescue her?"

"You've rescued others from the Gestapo—all those Jews and Bolshies. Eisner, Blau, Gerstein, Zaentz. I realize that is by no means the complete list. You're greatly admired for what you've done, you and your wife. I'm offering you the chance to get her out. Surely you want to do for her what you've done for your . . . friends."

Hubbard lifted his glass to his mouth but could not drink; the liquor burned his lips.

"How would I enter Germany?" he asked.

"By train from Switzerland, like any other neutral."

"You must know that I was expelled from Germany."

"Yes. But we can get around that."

"Get around the German police? In time of war? How?"

"You must tell me if you're interested," Sir Richard said.

"I'm willing to hear what you have to say."

"It's a rather obvious idea. For the purposes of your visit, you would become your cousin Elliott. Travel on his passport."

"It would never work."

"Why not? You already answer to the name Hubbard. All you'd need to do is dye your hair and remember not to speak German quite so fluently. The other things you need to know we can teach you—knives, guns, poison, invisible ink. It's most enjoyable."

"What about Elliott?"

"Elliott arranged our meeting."

Hubbard heard his heart beating in his ears. Of course it was possible. It was so brilliantly simple. Why hadn't he thought of it?

"Really," Sir Richard said, "I think you'll find the whole thing is rather good fun. Leaving out your worry over your wife, of course."

"I accept," Hubbard said.

Sir Richard tilted his billycock bowler over his flaxen eyebrows and gave Hubbard a merry, conspiratorial smile.

Three

— 1 —

On the day before Christmas 1943, Paul Christopher took his second cousin Horace Hubbard sledding on the mountainside above the Harbor. After the long climb, the two boys paused for a moment and looked out over the valley. It was a bright day, so cold that the sunlight, reflecting from the snow and ice, seemed to be tinged with blue. The low mountains, thick with hemlocks, were a deeper blue. They could hear the wind in the trees, a constant low whistle, and dervishes of light dry snow spun across the open spaces.

Paul swung Horace onto his back, and the child wrapped his arms around Paul's neck and his legs around his waist. Paul threw the two of them, belly down, onto the sled. Horace grunted at the impact but held on. The Flexible Flyer gathered speed, its steel runners whispering over the snow; the pitch of the land was so steep that it seemed to Paul and Horace that they were flying into the bare limbs of the hardwoods and the feathery blue-green boughs of the conifers. The sled came out of the woods into a pasture strewn with boulders and ledges. The ground grew even steeper. Paul steered to the left in order to avoid a ten-foot drop off a hidden granite ledge, and the sled passed within inches of the high wall of loose stones that surrounded the cemetery. Now they could see the Harbor, a few hundred yards below, and smell the woodsmoke rising from its chimneys.

Two people, a woman and a tall man, had come out of the house to watch the end of the sled ride. They were directly in the path of the Flexible Flyer. The sled was traveling at fifteen or twenty miles an hour. The west wind had drifted snow to the sills of the second-story windows. Paul steered for the drift. When the runners bit into the softer snow, the sled slowed and then flipped over. Horace's small body flew through the air and plunged into the drift.

By the time Paul got to his feet, Horace had been rescued; Alice, his mother, was still floundering through the snow, holding her skirt high, but the man with her, whom Paul had mistaken for Elliott Hubbard, had hauled the child out of the drift and was brushing snow off his face. Horace was laughing: this was the way he liked the sled ride to end. His rescuer swung Horace above his head, and kissed him.

"Horace, you've got your father's looks, poor fellow," Hubbard Christopher said.

He handed Horace to Alice and turned to his own son, opening his arms.

"Hello, Paul," he said.

Paul hugged his father and kissed him. It was the first time he had seen him in nearly four years.

Half an hour later, Hubbard and Paul were alone in one of the small sitting rooms at the front of the house. They stood side by side, holding out their hands to a fire of apple logs.

"There's no trace of her at all, Paul," Hubbard said. "None. There are no papers, no record of an arrest or a trial. Officially, she doesn't exist."

"Does that mean that she's dead?"

"It means that she's alive."

"If she's alive, where is she?"

"Hiding, possibly."

"Do you really believe that?"

Hubbard, after a long pause, shook his head. "No," he said. "I think she's in a camp. I think the Germans have some reason for . . . erasing her existence."

"Then she'll die."

"No," he said, eyes glittering. "Your mother will not die. Remember what she was like. She won't yield. She will live to the end."

Hubbard had lost the air of hiding a joyous laugh that had made him so charming. He had become a fierce, unsmiling man. He sat down in a Shaker chair that creaked under his weight. He was as erect as Paulus. His eyes rested on Paul, who wore the uniform of a Marine Corps second lieutenant.

"Are you going to the Pacific?"

"Yes, right after this leave."

Hubbard, in an old gesture from Paul's childhood, laced his fingers through his son's. "We won't have much time together, then," he said.

Alice had left a tray of cocoa on the table. Hubbard poured two cups and handed one to Paul. They stood side by side, backs to the spitting apple logs, and sipped the cocoa. Through the windows with their small panes of wavy glass they could see the snow blowing; the wind moaned in the eaves and howled in the stone chimneys of the old house.

A car horn sounded and a green Packard convertible coupe, the top down despite the cold, turned in from the road and was climbing toward the Harbor. Every few yards the driver pressed the horn button and the klaxon sounded its peculiar hoarse *ah-OO-ga!*

Alice came into the room, carrying Horace, and held him up to the window so he could watch the car as it approached.

"It's brother Waddy," Alice said. "He thinks Horace likes to hear him blow the horn."

Horace grinned in delight as the horn sounded again. "I *do* like it," he said.

"I've given birth to the Hubbard cretin," Alice said. "Can it be a recessive gene? Will Horace grow up like his Uncle Waddy?" She peered out the window. "My God," she said, "he's brought a friend."

Stamping snow from his feet in the hall, Waddy introduced his friend.

"This is Wolkowicz," he said, "my secret weapon. Snow is nothing to Wolkowicz. As a child he walked from Kiev to Shanghai with a little pack on his back—five thousand miles over the Urals, across freezing Siberia, through the burning Gobi. It's a proletarian epic. Wolkowicz ate raw pony meat in Mongolia."

Barnabas Wolkowicz was a squat, muscular man with a big chin and high Slavic cheekbones. His nose had been broken and rebroken. He looked as though he had played the line in football, blocking for

[76]

men like Waddy. He wore the insignia of an army warrant officer. Beside willowy, blond Waddy Jessup he looked like a Neanderthal man. He put down Waddy's suitcase and nodded to Alice, unsure of what to do next.

Alice lifted Wolkowicz's large hairy hand and shook it. "Did you really walk all the way across Asia?"

Wolkowicz nodded. "I don't remember much about it. My father was with me," he said. "We didn't walk the whole way. There were trains."

"All the same," said Alice, "it sounds like a lot of effort. But what luck for Waddy. He's always wanted to meet a real Russian. He's the family Red."

— 2 —

That evening, Christmas Eve, Alice insisted that all the men wear uniform to dinner. "It gives the party exactly the hectic wartime flush I want," she said. "Who knows when there'll be another Hubbard Christmas at the Harbor?"

Alice was speaking to Wolkowicz. Waddy Jessup joined them. His eyes were bright, his speech a little slurred. "Why shouldn't there be any more Christmas parties?" he asked. Waddy had a weak head for liquor and he had already drunk three glasses of Scotch.

"You're all marching off to war," Alice said. "Elliott has been learning to parachute. I've never seen him so happy. You're *all* happy. It's this Outfit you all belong to. What is it?"

"You mustn't ask."

"Why not? Why doesn't it have a number, like everybody else's outfit? How can Army, Navy, and Marines be all mixed together? Why is a forty-year-old sailor like Elliott jumping out of airplanes?"

Waddy Jessup put a finger to his lips. "It's oh, so secret," he said.

Alice gave him a look of bitter annoyance. "God, men are clumsy," she said. "It's a good thing you only have secrets in time of war. Women live by secrets all the time; we *have* to in order to inhabit the same planet with men. You can't be trusted with the facts."

Waddy was not listening. His eyes were fixed on Paul, and he wore a look of amused calculation, like a rake noticing for the first time that a friend's daughter has grown breasts.

"Handsome young man, Hubbard's boy," he said. "What are his interests? Give me an icebreaker."

"An icebreaker? You've known him for years."

"I want to know him better. What are his interests?"

"Girls; he always seems to have one. He reads German poetry for relaxation."

"German poetry! Just my thing."

Waddy gave Alice a bright smile and crossed the room to Paul. He put a hand at the small of Paul's back. " 'Werd ich zum Augenblicke sagen,' " he said, " ' "Verweile doch! Du bist so schön!" ' "

"Hello, Waddy," Paul said.

"They say you spoke German even as a very small child," Waddy said. "What did I just say?"

"Were you speaking German?"

"Of course I was speaking German. I was quoting Johann Wolfgang von Goethe, the immortal bore. I can't remember what it means."

Paul translated: " 'If I say to the moment, "Stay now! You are so beautiful!" ' "

"That's it! The immortal Goethe." He beckoned to Wolkowicz, who left Alice and joined them. "Here's the immortal Wolkowicz," he said. "What're you drinking there, a boilermaker?"

"No, sir, a Rob Roy."

"A Rob Roy? Is it your first? Do you like it?"

"It's very good, sir."

"Drop the 'sir,' Barnabas. Call me 'you.' It's Christmas. WOJG Wolkowicz hails from Youngstown, Ohio," Waddy said to Paul. He pronounced *WOJG*, the abbreviation for Wolkowicz's rank, warrant officer junior grade, as if it were a word: *wojjig*.

"They drink boilermakers in Youngstown, Ohio," Waddy continued. "I knew a fellow at Yale who grew up in Youngstown, Ohio. His family owned a steel mill that made sheets and tubes. After a hard day of putting sheets and tubes into the blast furnace and taking them out when they were done, everybody would go down to the tavern and have a boilermaker. My pal didn't say anything about Rob Roys."

Waddy handed Wolkowicz his glass. "Why don't you have another Rob Roy? Bring me a boilermaker," he said. "Paul, what do you have there?" He drank from Paul's glass. "Plain soda water!" he said. "You must have crystalline piss, like mineral water. You can write your name invisibly in new-fallen snow—in Mary Lou's handwriting, of course."

Waddy kept Paul's glass, sipping from it, until Wolkowicz returned

[78]

with a fresh drink for him—not a boilermaker, but three fingers of
Scotch whisky, neat. Waddy tossed off the Scotch and gave Paul back
his soda water.

"What I think you ought to do, Paul," he said, "is *verweile doch*. It's
not too late to get out of the Marines. They'll just get you killed, you
know. That's what Marine second lieutenants are for—to show the
troops how to die."

Waddy put an arm around Paul's shoulders and his other arm
around Wolkowicz's shoulders and drew them close. A few drops of
whisky dribbled out of his glass and stained the shoulder of Wolkowicz's uniform.

"*Force Jessup*," Waddy whispered. "I want you for Force Jessup. Isn't
Elliott your godfather? He can fix us up."

"Force Jessup, Waddy? What's that?"

"Crack outfit, soon to go into action—expert killers, linguists, very
advanced in woodcraft. Wolkowicz will do the shooting, you'll do the
German poetry, and I'll do the leading. Stealth and cunning behind the
Jap lines, that's our game. *Much* better than hitting the beach with a
bunch of pimply Marines on some godforsaken atoll."

Alice joined the group and took Waddy by the arm. "Supper is
ready," she said. "I want you to sit with me, Waddy." She led her
brother away.

Wolkowicz, holding Waddy's dirty glass in his hand, watched him
go. His eyes were as colorless as rain.

After dinner, in another room, Wolkowicz examined an old spinet. It
was a lovely instrument: rosewood case, ivory keys the color of candle
flame.

"Someone always plays the spinet on Christmas," Alice said. "It's
more than two hundred years old. The first Hubbards brought it up
from Connecticut on an oxcart. Have you ever heard a spinet?"

"Yes, I have," Wolkowicz replied.

"Really? Most people haven't. There are quills inside that pluck the
strings."

Wolkowicz touched a key and a note sounded.

"Time for the gifts, but you must play for us later," Alice said.

Elliott handed out the packages. Paul got the last gift under the tree,
a long tube wrapped in white paper.

"You may want to open that when you're alone," Hubbard said.

"I'll do it now."

Paul left the room, taking his present with him, and walked through the house. Some of the rooms were heated by stoves and fireplaces; others were not. The house was made of pine and hemlock, wide boards whipsawed from huge virgin trees, and it murmured and squeaked as it moved in the winter wind; it had a scent like no other house: old lumber that had captured two hundred years of weather, wax, sachet, and woodsmoke.

The bedroom Paul used had been Hubbard's room, and the walls were hung with photographs of Hubbard's dead mother and father. Paul had added pictures of Hubbard and Lori and Paulus and Hilde. There was a large drawing of Berwick and a shelf of Hubbard's books, bound in blue goatskin. Alone in this room, Paul unwrapped the tube, removed the picture it contained, and spread it out on the bed. It was Zaentz's drawing of Lori in her pregnancy, a smiling girl, carrying him within her body. Lori had been younger than he was now when this drawing was made.

The latch lifted. Paul heard the door open and turned around. Hubbard had joined him. Paul held out the drawing and Hubbard took one edge of it while Paul held the other.

"How did you get it back?" he asked.

"It's not the original," Hubbard said. "Zaentz did this from memory. He lives in New York now."

"From memory? It's exactly the same."

"Yes. Just as I remember the two of you."

They went downstairs together through the cold house. The strains of the spinet, quavering like an old voice, grew louder as they opened door after latched door and drew closer to the old parlor. They paused and listened to the music. The player finished the piece and in the silence Hubbard and Paul once again heard the wind, also like an aged voice.

"I've always felt, when I find myself alone in this house," Hubbard said, "that they're all here, the Hubbards and the Mahicans, all of them."

"Only the Hubbards?"

"Only the dead. Not your mother, Paul." Hubbard paused. It was very cold in this room, which had no stove or fireplace, and his breath was visible. "She *is* alive," Hubbard said.

On the other side of the door, the player struck the keys of the spinet again. Paul lifted the latch. The room beyond was dim, lit by one small lamp and a few candles.

Barney Wolkowicz, drab army blouse wrinkled across his broad laborer's back, his thick hairy fingers spanning the keyboard, was playing a Bach fugue. The notes were so lovely, and so perfectly struck, that it seemed to Paul that they ought to be visible in the flickering warm atmosphere of the room.

Hubbard stood stock-still, his eyes fixed on Wolkowicz. When the last note had been played, he put his arm around Paul's shoulders.

"You see?" he whispered, as if it could just as well have been Lori who smiled at them from the spinet, instead of Wolkowicz; and indeed it was just as likely that Paul's mother should have come back to them, as young and lovely as she was in Zaentz's drawing, as that this ugly man should have such music in him.

BOOK II

Wolkowicz

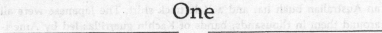

One

One

— 1 —

Captain Wadsworth Jessup was obsessed by elephants. He lay on a hilltop in Burma above the Shweli River, gazing through binoculars at an outpost of the 56th Division of the Imperial Japanese Army. Half a mile away, in a clearing in the dense rain forest, the Japanese were building a fortified position for a light tank at the junction of two trails. Three elephants worked steadily, piling huge logs around a pit gouged out of the bright brown earth.

"There, my dear Barnabas," said Waddy Jessup, "are Force Jessup's elephants."

Barney Wolkowicz crouched on the spongy floor of the jungle next to Waddy. Twenty Kachin tribesmen, the men of Force Jessup, as Waddy called this band of guerrilla fighters operating behind the Japanese lines, were deployed in the undergrowth. Some of the Kachins, slim cheery men hardly larger than American grammar school boys, were armed with muzzle-loading fowling pieces; Waddy had heard that these weapons were highly prized by the Kachins because it was easy to make ammunition for them, and he had brought along a half-dozen when he and Wolkowicz had parachuted into Burma a month earlier.

Waddy himself was armed with a Thompson submachine gun and a samurai sword he had bought from one of the Kachins. He wore an Australian bush hat and a Yale track shirt. The Japanese were all around them in thousands; bands of Kachin guerrillas led by American and British officers harassed the Japanese; Communist bandits struck at the enemy from camps just across the border in the Yunnan Province of China. Waddy was feverishly excited by the atmosphere of danger and murder. Since landing in Burma he had talked in a British accent, calling Wolkowicz "my dear Barnabas" and treating him like a manservant.

The rain forest was a stinking green haze in which the human eye could see no more than twenty feet. Anything might lie in wait, silent and murderous, beyond the impenetrable curtain of vegetation six paces away. The Kachin tribesmen were brave and well trained. Under Waddy's command, however, they had seen little action. No longer did Waddy prowl the narrow trails that threaded through the rain forest. On his first patrol, he had marched around a bend in a trail and come under fire from a Japanese machine-gun position. Three of his Kachins had been killed. As a squad of bowlegged Japanese soldiers rushed down the trail, dropping every few paces to fire their rifles, Waddy had led his patrol into the forest, ordering Wolkowicz to cover the retreat with fire from a Browning automatic rifle.

Wolkowicz drove off the enemy. Then, his ammunition exhausted, he fell back into the trees, expecting to find the rest of Force Jessup waiting for him. But the others, Waddy and his Kachins, had vanished. Wolkowicz was alone. He had rations for one day and water for half a day. He carried a compass, but no map. Only Waddy, the commander, carried maps; this minimized the possibility of their falling into enemy hands and revealing the secret location of Force Jessup's base.

Nevertheless, Wolkowicz found his way home. When he arrived at the base, starving and dehydrated, three days later, he found Waddy Jessup seated on a chair in front of his hut, drinking tea.

"Back at last?" Waddy said to his exhausted second-in-command. "Never mind. Have some tea. Sit down. I've been ruminating, my dear Barnabas. There's a lesson in our last action. One really can't beat the Jap by letting *him* kill *you*. The Jap sets up his machine gun, shakes out his riflemen, and waits for the impetuous white man to blunder into his hail of lead. No, no, not for Force Jessup."

Thereafter, Waddy led his Kachins on several long patrols, moving foot by foot through the jungle, shunning the trails. It was hot, hard, fruitless work. Often the Kachins had to cut a passage through the bush with machetes.

The Kachin headman had an unpronounceable name. Waddy called him N.S., short for Noble Savage. N.S. did not understand Waddy's tactics. Each night, after the force made camp, the headman demanded to know when Waddy intended to attack the Japanese. "The Japs are on the trails," the headman said. "We must get back on the trails."

Waddy would listen, a pleasant smile on his lips, affectionate mockery in his eyes. But he would not go near the trails. Finally, the Kachins threatened to take their arms and join another band that saw more action. It was then that Waddy had revealed his plan to capture elephants.

"Elephants?" Wolkowicz had said. "What the fuck for?"

Waddy gave him a pitying glance. "Let me explain, my dear Barnabas," he said. "How does Force Jessup move? Through the jungle. What is the main impediment to moving through the jungle? Why, the jungle itself. If, however, we had elephants, we could flatten the jungle and move through it at will."

Waddy unrolled a map and weighted it down with his samurai sword. Japanese strongpoints along the jungle trails were marked on the sweat-stained paper in red pencil.

"Look here," Waddy said. "We know the Jap has a machine gun dug in here, aiming south. The Jap wants us to march north, around this bend in the trail, into the muzzle of his gun. Instead, we follow our elephants up the trail to this point, just before the bend. Then we nip into the jungle and, moving with amazing swiftness and stealth, cut across the bend and strike the enemy from behind. Then we melt back into the jungle. If the Jap follows, we lie up and wait and wipe him out."

Waddy straightened his back and peered into the expressionless faces of Wolkowicz and those of the Kachin headman. "Brilliant but simple," he said.

"Captain," Wolkowicz said, "do you know how to ride an elephant?"

"I've been riding all my life. But *I* won't be riding them. We'll liberate their bloody mahouts along with the elephants."

Now, on the hilltop above the Shweli River, Waddy wriggled backward into the jungle and handed his binoculars to the Kachin who carried them for him. He cut a map of the enemy camp into the dirt with the tip of his sword and briefed Force Jessup on his plan of attack. It was a model of simplicity and aggressiveness.

"I count twelve Japs on foot, three in the tank," Waddy said, carving out the positions. "The tank must be neutralized before they can get it into action. It's inside the log position the elephants built. We have to keep it there. Barnabas, you are our demolition expert, so you and this splendid-looking Buddhist will go in first, wiggling on your bellies, and plant charges in the treads and under the tank. When you hear a burst of Thompson fire, at precisely 2300 hours, blow it up. Then start shooting. I'll be coming in from the river with half the force while old N.S. charges down the trail from the rear with the rest of the troops, cutting off the Jap's retreat. Do not, repeat do *not*, shoot the elephants. Kill all fifteen Japs and cut off their dinguses."

"What about taking some prisoners?" Wolkowicz said.

"My dear Barnabas, it's elephants we're after, not apes. We *have* apes."

Waddy, rolling up his map, grinned at Wolkowicz. "Hit the line for dear old Kent State," he said. Wolkowicz was a graduate of Kent State College in Ohio; he had majored in music. These facts deeply amused Waddy Jessup. In the falling twilight, Wolkowicz could read the word *Yale* on the chest of Waddy's blue track jersey. He turned away and rummaged in a pack for explosive and detonators.

— 2 —

In seven hours of hacking and marching, Force Jessup covered the half-mile of jungle between the hilltop and the Japanese outpost. Wolkowicz and the Kachin, laden with explosive, wire, and weapons, began crawling toward the Japanese emplacement at 2130 hours. By 2215, they had dragged themselves about fifty yards, moving a fraction of an inch at a time, and were only ten yards or so from the logs.

The tank's turret was a darker silhouette against the black night. Even now, three hours after the sun had gone down, the temperature was at least 100 degrees Fahrenheit. Sweat seeped from Wolkowicz's crawling body. He had been soaking wet with perspiration ever since he struggled out of his parachute harness, two minutes after hitting the ground in Burma. This disgusting body that he inhabited in the jungle, slippery with its own fluids like an intestine turned inside out, did not seem to be his own. He was wracked with dysentery. He had had to stop several times during the crawl to relieve himself. Between bowel movements, he had a tendency to break wind. The noise worried him. He was afraid it would arouse the Japanese. An excruciating cramp began just behind the base of his penis and spread, growing stronger with every second it lasted and every inch it traveled up his entrails. He rolled over on his back and pressed his buttocks into the dirt, squeezing the cheeks together to muffle the explosive sound of escaping gas.

In thirty minutes, he covered the ten paces that had separated him from the rear end of the tank. He could see the metal glistening in the dark and smell the oil on the machine. He put up a hand and touched warm steel, then felt the treads of the tank. One of the Japanese was inside. Another was on guard in the turret. Where was the third? Wolkowicz farted powerfully, and the remaining member of the tank crew, standing six feet away yet utterly invisible, laughed. Wolkowicz thought, He'll smell me. But the sentry did not stir again.

Wolkowicz took off his pack and got out the TNT and the detonators. Doing this simple thing in absolute silence, doing it so slowly that he could not possibly betray his position by even the flicker of a movement, required the use of every cell in Wolkowicz's brain and the control of every nerve in his body. He wedged the TNT between the tread of the tank and the bogie wheel, and inserted a detonator.

Then, crawling again, he moved away from the tank, paying out wire as he went. He had lost track of the Kachin who had crept into the outpost with him. Then he heard a gasp, not loud, like air being let out of a bicycle tire. Wolkowicz froze. Someone was crawling along the ground toward him. Wolkowicz drew his .45 automatic from its shoulder holster and waited. When the crawling man was six inches away, Wolkowicz recognized him: it was his Kachin comrade. The Kachin, his grin white in the ink of the jungle night, thrust his knife, reeking with the blood of the Japanese sentry whose throat he had just cut, under Wolkowicz's nose.

At precisely 2300 hours, Waddy Jessup fired a burst of tracer ammunition from his tommy gun into the Japanese outpost. Wolkowicz twisted the handle on his detonator box, and while Waddy's weapon was still emptying lazily into the darkness, the charge under the Japanese tank went off. The explosion looked like three cans of paint, red and yellow and white, smashing one after the other against the black wall of the night. The ammunition inside the tank went off in a series of shattering explosions and the tank burst into flames. In the jittery light, Wolkowicz could see Kachins leaping about, firing their weapons. Japanese soldiers scooted like rodents through the firelight and were cut down by bullets. The elephants trumpeted, shrieks of outrage amid the hoarse coughs of the heavy American weapons and the titter of a Japanese light machine gun. Wolkowicz heard no human voices.

Abruptly, as if someone had turned off a loud radio, the firing stopped. In the firelight, the Kachins were working, teeth and knives flashing, on the stripped corpses of the Japanese. The elephants, still trumpeting, threw themselves against the chains wrapped around their front legs. Their mahouts danced around them, shouting what Wolkowicz supposed were reassurances. A chain broke and the end whipped a mahout across the kidneys, folding his body back on his spine like a strip of cardboard. The elephant dashed down the trail, away from the burning tank, dragging his clanking chain behind him.

Waddy Jessup stepped out of the darkness at the edge of the outpost, waving his samurai sword.

"Stop the elephant!" he cried in Kachin. "You three men, fetch me that elephant!"

The Kachins, busy with their mutilation of the dead, paid no attention to him. Waddy didn't really seem to expect them to. He walked over to a little group of them and watched them as they butchered the dead, his jaunty smile fixed to his lips. There had been no sign of Waddy up to this point, and Wolkowicz had wondered, fleetingly, if he might have been killed or wounded; now he suspected that Waddy had lain hidden in the darkness until the firefight was over: there was something false in the captain's nonchalance. Wolkowicz approached him.

"Ah, the mad bomber," Waddy said, looking Wolkowicz up and down. "Good show, Barnabas. Let's have a look at our elephants."

"I think we ought to clear out of here, Captain."

"Do you really, wojjig?" Waddy said. He turned on his heel and strode across the beaten dirt of the track toward the elephants.

One of the beasts lay on the ground, weakly lifting its trunk, then letting it fall. Blood oozed from a row of wounds in the elephant's side; the animal had been machine-gunned. The remaining elephant stood over the fallen animal, nudging its body gently with its face. The two trunks touched and intertwined. The unwounded elephant uttered a mournful trumpet note.

"Bad luck," Waddy said, gripping the shoulder of a weeping mahout. "Is this elephant going to die?"

Waddy spoke in Kachin, but the mahout, a black-skinned Dravidian Indian, did not understand this language. Waddy gazed for a long moment into the native's tear-stained face. Then he drew a .45 caliber pistol and shot the wounded elephant in the forehead.

The elephant, screaming in torment, leaped to its feet and charged. Waddy dove into the fringe of the forest. The elephant tore at the underbrush with its trunk and tusks. The mahout, sobbing and shouting, danced beside the elephant, dodging the great round feet that stamped the ground, groping for Waddy in order to crush the life out of him. Waddy rolled around on the ground, samurai sword in one hand, pistol in the other. A young Kachin darted in front of the elephant, planted his bare feet, and grinning happily, fired an entire twenty-round magazine from a Thompson submachine gun, every third bullet a tracer, into the elephant's brow. The animal fell, uttering no sound except for the shuddering thud that its great scruffy body made when it struck the ground.

Waddy leaped to his feet. "Jesus!" he said, rolling his eyes. He was trembling. The Kachin who had killed the elephant calmly reloaded his tommy gun. The unwounded elephant, trumpeting, was loping away down the path, its mahout on his head. The sight of this beast escaping infuriated Waddy.

"Stop that man!" he shouted.

Though he spoke no English, the Kachin understood his meaning. He lifted his weapon and knocked the mahout off the elephant with a five-round burst. Then he seized the surviving mahout and dragged him down the trail in pursuit of the fleeing elephant.

"Shit," Waddy said.

He might have said more, but the Kachin headman trotted out of the darkness and began to speak to him.

"Not *now*, N.S.," Waddy said, and moved away, so as to peer down the trail after the escaping elephant. A smile crossed his face. The elephant was coming back with the mahout and the Kachin on its back. The headman caught Wolkowicz's eye and pointed his bare arm at the flames of the burning tank. Half a dozen Japanese soldiers, brandishing their immensely long Arisaka rifles with their glittering sword-bayonets, were leaping over the log barrier and advancing into the camp. They were killed almost immediately by fire from the Kachins. Waddy, who had begun to trot down the trail in the opposite direction to meet the returning elephant, skidded to a stop, then turned around and ran at top speed toward the burning tank. Wolkowicz, assuming that Waddy was charging back to meet the enemy, felt anger erupt in himself: he hated this evidence of his commander's bravery.

Then Wolkowicz looked farther down the trail. Beyond Waddy's sprinting figure in its Yale track shirt, beyond the clumsy galloping bulk of the elephant, a whole platoon of Japanese infantry, led by an officer who waved a bright samurai sword, were trotting down the trail, firing as they advanced. The outpost was being counterattacked from two directions. Waddy, shouting at the top of his lungs for his troops to follow him, started to run into the forest. A machine gun winked among the trees. The Japanese had outflanked them through the jungle as well.

More enemy soldiers were entering the outpost from the direction of the burning tank. Kachins, falling back as they fired, ran into a hail of bullets from two other directions, and were cut down one after the other.

Wolkowicz fell to his knees and began firing his BAR at the Japanese officer. The man fell, his sword spinning out of his hand. As the Japanese officer died, gouts of blood flying from his spinning body, Wolkowicz saw a map of Burma in his mind—the Shweli River flowing out of China to the north between two green mountain ranges, and all the vast impenetrable wilderness that lay to the south and west between him and the sea, between him and India, where he would be safe. Wolkowicz believed that his life was over. The Kachin leader was kneeling too, his back pressed against Wolkowicz's, firing in the opposite direction. Wolkowicz felt a tremor in the body of the other man, and then felt—he always remembered this—a brief cold puff of wind against his sweating back, as if a door had been opened a crack on a wintry day and then slammed shut, as the headman fell away, a bullet through his brain.

Wolkowicz looked around him. The elephant, trunk swinging idly, stood a few yards away with the mahout on its head. The animal was quiet. Bullets chewed the dirt at its feet and clipped leaves from the trees above its uplifted trunk, but they did not touch the elephant; the elephant, so calm when it should have been fleeing in panic, seemed to know that it was safe.

The fact that any creature so huge, standing in the middle of such a storm of fire, should not only be alive but be untouched seemed to Wolkowicz a religious miracle. He did not believe in God, he had been raised to laugh at the idea of God, and even now, at the point of death, it did not occur to him to speak God's name, much less to pray to Him. But it was obvious to Wolkowicz that the elephant was in touch with a higher power; the elephant itself had the power to protect Wolkowicz and save him. If he could touch the elephant, no harm could possibly come to him.

Wolkowicz, gripping his BAR, staggered through the singing bullets toward the elephant. The animal turned its massive head and gave him a look of deep enchantment; the mahout, his black face glistening beneath a white turban, seemed to nod in calm benediction from his seat on the elephant's skull. Wolkowicz reached out to touch the elephant. As he did so, a Kachin standing beside him was shot through the skull.

"Wolkowicz! Wait!"

Waddy Jessup, trembling violently, lay on the trail, his body pressed into the dirt. One trouser leg had ridden up, and Wolkowicz saw that the muscles on Waddy's calf were bunched and knotted, so great was his effort to drive himself into the ground and escape from death.

Wolkowicz slung his BAR, picked up Waddy's Thompson submachine gun and a pack of ammunition, and seized Waddy by the ankle. Dragging the leader of Force Jessup after him, Wolkowicz walked the last three steps to the elephant, and pressed his forehead against its bristly hide, which was dusty and cracked like sunbaked mud. The sound of firing seemed to fade to a whisper.

The elephant started to walk. It plunged into the jungle, flattening the tough springy growth as it went, just as Waddy Jessup, who scuttled along behind with empty eyes, clutching his samurai sword, had predicted it would do.

— 3 —

The elephant, carrying Waddy and Wolkowicz on its neck along with the terrified mahout, walked steadily forward into the rain forest for about five hours. Just at sunup, as it reached the crest of a hill, it trumpeted, dropped to its knees, and rolled over onto its side. The three men leaped free, flinging their weapons away. The mahout, tears streaming down his cheeks, darted to the elephant's head and began speaking to it in a soothing chirpy voice.

Waddy searched frantically through the underbrush, muttering.

Wolkowicz found the Thompson and the pack of ammunition, but he could not locate the BAR. As the firepower of this gun represented their one slim hope of withstanding a Japanese attack, Wolkowicz assumed that Waddy was as anxious to find it as he was. But Waddy was not looking for the lost BAR. He was looking for his samurai sword.

"Wolkowicz!" Waddy said, his voice cracking. "My sword is missing. Find it."

Wolkowicz pointed at the ground, next to the elephant. The curved handle of the samurai sword protruded from the elephant's hip. The animal was lying on the sheathed sword. Waddy fell to his knees and tugged at the handle. The crescent blade slid out of the scabbard, winking in the filtered early sun that slanted through the branches and vines of the forest.

Waddy's eyes were so unfocused that Wolkowicz thought he must have struck his head when he jumped off the elephant. Waddy's bush hat was still on his head, secured by a chin strap. This outlandish headgear made his face look pinched; his narrow shoulders, freckled by the sun, seemed frail and childish beneath the blue shoulder straps of his Yale jersey.

"Do you know why this sword is curved?" Waddy asked.

Wolkowicz shook his head.

"The steel is contorted by its own strength," Waddy said, speaking in an easy conversational tone. "The steel is heated in a charcoal forge, then hammered into a strip twice the desired length of the blade. Then it is heated and folded and hammered out again, then heated and folded and hammered and heated and folded and hammered. Each time this is done, the number of layers of steel in the blade is *squared,* not merely doubled, so that the curved blade of a samurai sword consists of tens of thousands of layers of tempered steel. The ideal sword will cut through the torsos of two enemies with a single stroke. To a Japanese of the samurai class, a sword such as this is a metaphysical object, a gift from the gods, embodying the fighting spirit of his race. You can understand why, yes?"

Smiling his genial smile, Waddy drew back the sword, holding the handle in both hands as if he meant to cut Wolkowicz in half, then threw it, spinning and flashing, into the forest.

"They'd kill me," Waddy explained, "if they captured me with that sword in my possession."

Wolkowicz looked carefully into Waddy's cheery face and empty eyes, and decided to change the subject.

"I think the BAR is underneath the elephant, too," he said. "We've got to get him up."

The elephant was lying flat on its side. All its little signs of life—the sinuous movements of the trunk, the twitching of the tail, the flapping of the ears—had ceased; the elephant might have been dead. Wolkowicz floundered through the undergrowth to the elephant's head. The animal's round greenish eye, the size of a mango, looked out of its face but did not seem to notice Wolkowicz or Waddy, who was following along behind.

Wolkowicz could hear the mahout's voice but he could not see him. Waddy, smiling dreamily, stood on tiptoe and peered over the motionless head of the elephant. Two skinny black legs, webbed with leathery scars, protruded from the elephant's head but the rest of the mahout could not be seen. Waddy giggled and leaped gracefully over the elephant's outstretched trunk. Wolkowicz, burdened by the Thompson and the ammunition pack, struggled after him.

The mahout lay on the ground with his head inside the elephant's ear; the ear itself covered his shoulders like a gray cape. His muffled voice droned on; the elephant stared with his mango eye at the canopy high above.

Waddy kicked the mahout on the leg. The man lifted the elephant's ear.

"What's the matter with the elephant?" Waddy asked in Kachin.

The mahout shook his head. "No Kachin," he said in English. These were the first words he had spoken through the long hours they had spent together.

"English, then," said Waddy. "Why is the elephant lying down?"

"He is disgusted."

"What are you doing inside his ear?"

"I am explaining."

"Then tell him we must go on."

"He will not do that, master."

"Let me talk to him."

"He will not listen to you."

"He doesn't seem to be listening to you, either. What language do you speak to him—Hindi? Tamil?"

The mahout grinned, embarrassed. "No, master."

"What, then?"

"I am speaking elephant. He only understands elephant. But he is not paying attention just now. He is disgusted."

The mahout, with a smile that asked Waddy's pardon, lifted the great rubbery leaf of the elephant's ear and thrust his head beneath it. His voice resumed its muffled cajoling.

Naturally, the elephant had left a highly visible trail through the forest. As soon as it was light, the Japanese followed it. Just as the mahout began to talk to the elephant again, a Japanese scout pulled the pin from a grenade and heaved it. Wolkowicz, who had excellent eyesight, caught the glint of sun on metal, looked up, and saw the grenade turning lazily in the air, end over end like a punted football.

"Grenade!" he shouted, diving over the elephant's head.

The grenade exploded with a flat noise and a puff of dirty smoke. The elephant snorted and heaved its forequarters upward. Wolkowicz, lying flat against the elephant's ribs with his face pressed to the ground, saw the butt of the BAR. He seized it and pulled it free before the elephant fell back to its former position, flat against the earth.

Wolkowicz stood up and, using the elephant's supine body as a breastwork, fired a burst at a flash of movement he saw in the brush fifty yards away. Waddy stood upright, gazing in the direction of the attacking Japanese with a smile of amusement on his lips.

Another grenade exploded between the mahout's legs. The mahout, now legless, twitched and lay where he was, with his head inside the elephant's ear.

Blood welled up from a wound in Waddy's left arm. He looked at it, still smiling, then turned his head away. A jet of yellow vomit squirted out of his mouth, then another. Wolkowicz clambered over the elephant, firing into the undergrowth with the BAR.

"Captain," he shouted, "take cover."

Waddy vomited again. The half-digested C rations from his stomach smelled exactly like the jungle itself: foul and slimy and in a state midway between ripeness and shit. Wolkowicz picked Waddy up, surprised by the lightness of his tall bony body, and threw him over the elephant.

The Japanese withdrew. Wolkowicz knew that they would soon be back in greater force. He sprinkled sulfa powder on Waddy's wound, a superficial cut an inch long, and bandaged it.

In addition to his U.S.-issue .45, Waddy carried a captured Baby Nambu pistol concealed inside the crown of his Australian hat. This was a tiny Japanese weapon, little more powerful than an air gun, that was sometimes given to officers by their families as a going-away gift. While

Wolkowicz stripped down and cleaned the BAR, Waddy examined the miniature Japanese pistol.

"I suppose I'd better get rid of this, too," he said.

Wolkowicz reassembled the BAR, deftly fitting the parts together.

"Waddy," he said, "I don't think it's going to make a fucking bit of difference to the Japs if you've got one of their guns. They're going to kill you. They're going to kill both of us."

"*Kill me?*" Waddy said. His pale hair, soaked with sweat, stood up in peaks. It gave him a look of even greater bewilderment. He clenched his lower lip between his straight, even teeth, and uttered a shrill whimper, like the outcry of a child in a temper. Then he drew back his fist and punched the elephant.

Wolkowicz heaved himself to his feet, rested the barrel of the BAR across the elephant's ribs, and looked out over the approaches to their hilltop. The mahout lay where he had died, the shredded flesh of his legs already crawling with vermin. The elephant, still in its reverie, continued to lie flat on its side, unmoving as a rock.

Waddy began to sing Yale songs. He had a surprisingly deep voice, almost a bass, that burbled on the low notes. Wolkowicz's trained ear detected that Waddy's singing became progressively more sharp as he rendered "Bright College Years," "Aura Lee," "Bingo, Bingo, Bingo," and other airs that Wolkowicz up to then had only heard about, but never actually heard.

"Were you happy in college, Barnabas?" Waddy asked after a silence.

"I don't know, Waddy," Wolkowicz said, his eyes searching the jungle. "Were you?"

"Yes, I was—tremendously happy. 'It was a shady gentle time and we were all in leaf.' Hubbard Christopher wrote that line about Yale. You remember Hubbard from the Christmas party."

Waddy, leaning against the elephant, his legs crossed at the ankles, his Australian hat once again firmly in place, smiled sweetly at Wolkowicz.

"I can accept death, having had so much in life," he said. "But it must be awfully hard for you."

"I'm not looking forward to it," Wolkowicz said.

"Is there anything I can do to make it more bearable?"

"*Do?* Like what?"

"I don't know. But whatever it was, I would do it, Barnabas. Have you thought about what we're dying for?"

Wolkowicz was outraged to think that Waddy actually expected him to listen to a patriotic lecture moments before he was going to be shot or bayoneted, moments before the eyes were going to be gouged out of his dead body, before his genitals were going to be sliced off. Wolkowicz visualized his mutilated body, hidden by the vegetation, rotting as it was eaten by insects, bursting as it was cooked by the sun and became part of the general stench of the jungle.

"I'm not going to wave the flag," Waddy said, suddenly sensitive to Wolkowicz's mood. "But let me ask you a simple question that contains the meaning of this whole experience. Is your father a worker, Barnabas? Does he work in the steel mills in Youngstown?"

"A worker? My father? Yes, sure he is."

"Then we're dying for him."

"We're dying for my father?"

"For the workers, yes," Waddy said. "This is the fight against fascism, right here, on this spot of earth. And we're fighting it, you and I together."

Waddy's voice trembled with tender sentimentality. In his last hour he seemed to have taken a genuine liking to Wolkowicz—or, rather, to Wolkowicz as a symbol of the proletariat.

"I'm proud to tell you," Waddy said, "that I am a member of the Communist Party."

Waddy, shoulders thrown back, chin raised, posed like a figure holding a flowing red banner on a Soviet poster. He wrung Wolkowicz's hand. Wolkowicz, permitting Waddy to fondle him, gazed with disgust on this silly, vain, stupid rich man's son who was responsible for the death of Wolkowicz, son and grandson of a worker. He shook his head and pulled his hand away.

Waddy was not through speaking. "There's something you can do for me, if you will, Barnabas," he said.

"What's that, Waddy?"

"Before they kill us, when it seems inevitable that they will kill us —*wait!* Do you think they'd kill a wounded man, an officer? Wouldn't they want information?"

"They know why we're here, Waddy. They might torture us for the fun of it, but what can we tell them?"

"We?" Waddy said. "Just a minute, wojjig. I didn't know you were an expert on the Japanese mind. Or did they have great courses in Japanese culture at Kent State College? You're certainly not an officer."

Waddy's mood had changed. No longer mellow, he was attacking what he imagined were Wolkowicz's soft spots—his Ohio origins, his immigrant family, his ridiculous college. What could Wolkowicz possibly know? Waddy said none of this aloud; he could convey it in the way he shaded the pronunciation of the word *Japanese,* making his tone even plummier than it usually was.

"Well, look, what does it matter?" Waddy said, changing his tone again and speaking to Wolkowicz as an equal. "What I want you to do, just before the final moment, is to shout the word *Bones."*

"Bones? What for?"

"I can't tell you why. It has to do with a secret Yale thing called Skull and Bones; I shouldn't have told you that much, even. No outsider is supposed to know."

"What happens after I yell *Bones?"*

"I go. You see, if anyone says the word *Bones,* I am required by the rules of this Yale thing I belong to, to leave the room at once. You see? It's what I want; it's a way to die—a game to play on the Jap."

"A game?" Wolkowicz said.

"You'll do it?"

Wolkowicz nodded.

"Good," Waddy said. He sat down again; he seemed content. Wolkowicz thought that he might begin to sing once more.

Wolkowicz searched in the ammunition pack; only one magazine, twenty rounds of .30 caliber ammunition, remained for the BAR, which fired six rounds per second. There was plenty of ammunition for the Thompson, Waddy's weapon. Waddy had not taken part in the firefight; instead, he had sat on the ground with his back against the elephant, toying with his Baby Nambu pistol. The submachine gun was propped against the elephant.

"Tell me something, Barnabas," Waddy said. "Does death hurt?"

Wolkowicz, leaving the BAR balanced atop the elephant, checked the action of the Thompson. His lack of response did not disturb Waddy, who went on with the conversation.

"My wound didn't hurt at all," Waddy said. "Was that because my mind was elsewhere, or do bullets just not hurt?"

"I don't know, Waddy." Wolkowicz's eyes were not on Waddy; he was searching the approaches to the hill. The Japanese were trying to encircle the position, trying to get behind them. They would succeed. They never gave up. Wolkowicz knew that the Japanese were not drugged or mad or gripped by a religious ecstasy. They fought as they did, caring nothing about dying, because it seemed obvious to them that dying was the natural consequence of charging a machine-gun position. Their bravery was an alien form of intelligence, dazzling but incomprehensible.

Wolkowicz heard a weak gunshot, a Japanese sound, very close at hand. Whirling, ready to fire with the Thompson, he saw Waddy with the Baby Nambu in his right hand. Waddy was looking at his left hand, upraised at arm's length with the fingers spread. A dribble of blood ran over his wrist from the tiny hole made by the bullet he had fired into his own hand with the little Japanese pistol.

"Jesus!" Waddy said, his lower lip trembling. "It *does* hurt."

At that moment, there was a tremendous explosion in the tree above their heads, a bloom of red flame and yellow smoke. Shrapnel rained down on them. The Japanese had brought up a mortar. Three more shells burst in the branches, then the rounds began to walk up the hill toward their position as the Japanese mortar crew shortened the range. Wolkowicz had been wounded in half a dozen places by the ricocheting shrapnel. Nausea flooded his body. Waddy, pressed against the elephant with his wounded hand clutched in his armpit and his other forearm thrown across his eyes, had no visible new injuries.

A mortar shell exploded within six feet of the elephant, opening a long oozing slash in its hide. At last the elephant sprang to its feet, trumpeting. It looked around, still remarkably calm, and ran its snuffling trunk over the corpse of the mahout. Wolkowicz dragged his weapons out of the way and threw himself to the ground as more mortar rounds exploded, scattering dirt.

Waddy ran to the elephant's head and seized its trunk. He uttered an excellent imitation of the deep-throated command, half threat and half song, that the mahout had used to mount the elephant. The elephant obediently curved its trunk. Waddy put a foot on it. The elephant lifted him onto his head. Waddy had taken possession at last of the Thompson submachine gun and he held it aloft in a gesture of romantic defiance.

Wolkowicz lifted his bleeding face out of the dirt. The elephant towered above him like an idol carved from stone. Waddy sat easily just behind the ears, and Wolkowicz realized—a dreamlike thought—that Waddy Jessup really had been riding all his life. He imagined him as a child, mounted on a Thoroughbred as it moved from a walk to a trot, wearing a polo helmet on his head, learning how to post.

"Say it!" Waddy called.

"Bones!" Wolkowicz shouted.

Waddy Jessup kicked the elephant. Moving at great speed, it crashed into a bamboo thicket, striding away from the exploding mortar rounds, away from the valiant murderous Japanese, abandoning Wolkowicz, who knew that Wadsworth Jessup was going to live and he was going to die.

The mortar barrage ceased. Wolkowicz heard the exuberant shouts of the enemy as the attack resumed. He put the scorched muzzle of the BAR into his mouth and felt a horrifying pain, filled with flame and noise, inside his skull.

— 4 —

The Japanese interrogator could not understand Wolkowicz's name.

"Say your name!" he shouted.

"Wolkowicz."

The interrogator drove a fist, surprisingly hard and sharp-knuckled, into Wolkowicz's naked stomach.

"Say your name!"

Wolkowicz had never for a moment been blessed with the illusion that he was dead. He had known, touching the muzzle of the BAR with his swollen tongue, that he had not pulled the trigger. He realized, at the moment in which he felt the pain of the blow, that a Japanese soldier had crept up behind him and smashed a rifle butt against the back of his head. He had known in that instant, before he lost consciousness, that what was now happening to him was surely going to happen to him: if the Japanese had not wanted to question him, they would have bayoneted him or shot him.

His captors had cleaned his wounds and given him rice and water. Now, even as they beat him and shouted at him, Wolkowicz could not suppress his admiration for them. They seemed to think well of him, too, in their way; the interrogator had told him, grunting out the English words in a matter-of-fact tone of voice, that he had killed twenty-eight Japanese soldiers and wounded fifteen others with his BAR. The Japanese giggled; laughing at death seemed to be their way of displaying emotion.

The interrogator, after two days of blows and questioning, had got Wolkowicz's name, rank, and serial number written down in English and Japanese on a sheet of crumbling rice paper. Now he proceeded to more important questions.

"Where is your base?"

Wolkowicz did not answer. He was thrown to the floor and kicked repeatedly in the stomach and kidneys. The pain was so great that Wolkowicz once again began to believe that the body that was being tortured was not really his own. This was a body he would leave behind in Burma; his own original flesh was somewhere else. He would not answer the questions.

"Why do you not speak?" the interrogator demanded, face contorted like a theatrical mask, after Wolkowicz had regained consciousness.

Wolkowicz could not speak. He did not know why. He knew no secrets that would be of the slightest use to the Japanese. Yet his mind refused to send his larynx, tongue, and lips the necessary signals. Wolkowicz did not leave his body, as people are supposed to do when on the threshold of death. He flew back into himself, into his family. He tried to remember the long journey across Asia. In some village where he had been caught digging turnips out of the earth, his father had been whipped. Wolkowicz saw the bloody stripes on his dead-white back. Later, he had lost his shoes and left bloody footprints in the snow. In spite of all this blood, Wolkowicz's father had gone on loving Russia. He had bribed Wolkowicz in his childhood to speak Russian—a penny for a new word, a nickel for a sentence, a quarter for a memorized stanza of poetry.

Now, as the blows of the Japanese interrogators rained down on him, Wolkowicz began to speak to them in Russian: noble resonant words, majestic sentences. Ah, the language was as beautiful as music!

The interrogators seized Wolkowicz's jaw and thrust a piece of wood between his teeth. He gagged. One of the interrogators drew a bayonet; it was much longer than an American bayonet, it might have been twenty inches long. The Japanese set his feet and squinted his eyes in concentration. Then, uttering a bloodcurdling samurai war cry, he placed the point of the bayonet against the root of Wolkowicz's left incisor and drove it up under the gum. With a quick, expert turn of the wrist, using the block of wood as a fulcrum, he pried the tooth out of Wolkowicz's jaw.

Wolkowicz screamed, gagging on the blood that spurted into his throat. The tooth had seemed to be attached to the roof of his skull and he believed, during the long-drawn-out agony as it was pulled, that it was bringing a jagged bit of skull with it, dragging this sharpened fragment of bone down through his brain. The Japanese asked him no questions. Before he could forget how it had felt, his tormentor pried out another tooth.

With each twist of the bayonet, the torturer uttered his horrible shout. Then Wolkowicz screamed. Time after time, their voices merged in this shrill diphthong of cruelty and agony.

Wolkowicz never knew how long they worked on him with the bayonet or what he had told them. To keep his sanity, he counted the teeth as they came out. He had a few seconds of consciousness between each extraction in which to remember the number that had already been pried out of his jaw, and to add another. He had begun with thirty-four teeth—yellowish crooked teeth, not straight flashing ones like Waddy Jessup's. When his interrogators were finished, he had twelve teeth left, six molars on each side. When he lost consciousness, he was convinced that his eyes had been pulled out too, because the world was black.

— 5 —

But when Wolkowicz awoke, his mouth tasting of salt and his skull still throbbing with pain, he realized that he had not been blinded. The reflection of flames danced on the wall of the room where he lay. He knew exactly where he was: in his cage, a bottomless box, covered by a grating that let the sun beat on him. He was chained to a post driven into the ground.

When, however, he lifted his arm and shook it, there was no rattle. His captors had forgotten to chain him. That was odd. Wolkowicz saw that the door of the cage was open. He got to his hands and knees and crawled out, thinking that he might find some water to drink; he knew he could not escape in his condition. The Japanese must know this too, if they had not bothered to lock him up.

A disorderly crowd of soldiers milled around in the encampment. Several huge fires had been lit. The soldiers were shouting and laughing. Their babble had a different sound from the noise usually made by Japanese troops. Wolkowicz wondered if the war was over, if the enemy had won and were celebrating their victory. He could think of no other explanation for this raffish atmosphere.

Wolkowicz got to his feet and staggered toward the nearest fire. A row of stakes had been driven into the ground. He drew closer and focused his eyes on one of the stakes. The severed head of a Japanese soldier stared back at him. Each of the other stakes, perhaps twenty of them, had a head driven onto its sharpened point. One of the soldiers ran up and grasped a head by the ears, twisted it, wrenched it off the post, and offered it to Wolkowicz. Wolkowicz, opening his mouth in a black ruined grin, accepted the gift.

The soldier, laughing, hooked arms with Wolkowicz and led him to a fire. Several other soldiers crouched around the fire, toasting gobs of meat on the end of long sticks. They were wild-looking youngsters, round-faced and dark-skinned, with black bristly hair that looked as if it had been trimmed with a bayonet. Only a few wore uniforms, shoddy soiled clothes that did not fit.

Realizing that he was holding a human head by the hair, Wolkowicz gave it back to the soldier. The soldier took it and made a face that said, "You really don't want it?" and punched Wolkowicz in a friendly way on the chest. Wolkowicz shook his head. The soldier threw the head into the fire. It lay with its ear pillowed on a burning brand, gazing resentfully out of the flames at Wolkowicz.

A hand fell on his shoulder. Wolkowicz paid no attention. He was hypnotized by the face in the fire. Wolkowicz looked closely at the soldiers who were cooking their dinner like boy scouts around a campfire and realized that they were Chinese.

The hand turned him around, firmly. "Well, mate," said a voice speaking English, "up and about, are you?"

Wolkowicz found himself looking into the bearded face of an Englishman. The man wore khaki shorts, knee socks, and a green turban. Wolkowicz himself was stark naked; the hair on his chest was filled with his own clotted blood.

"Come along," the Englishman said. "I'll give you a cup of tea. Unless you fancy a bit of broiled liver."

Wolkowicz looked again at the jovial Chinese soldiers. They were chewing happily on the charred livers of the Japanese they had just slaughtered.

Wolkowicz remained with his rescuers for six months. This was in many respects the happiest time in his life. The guerrilla band led by the Englishman was a mixture of Chinese and Kachin fighters. These courageous, merry young men were in action almost constantly, falling on Japanese patrols on forest trails, blowing up Japanese bridges and ammunition dumps. The Chinese invariably decapitated the Japanese dead and opened them up for their livers. The Englishman did not know why.

"They seem to thrive on human flesh," he said, "and it must have a hell of a psychological effect on the Nips. It'll be interesting to see if they eat Trotskyites when they get back to killing them after the war. Burmese are much more appetizing than Japs."

"Trotskyites?"

"Yes, the Burmese can hardly wait to have at each other again. You see, these chaps are White Flag—Stalinists. There are other bands of them, also fighting the Japanese during this temporary truce, composed of Red Flag chappies—Trotskyites."

"What about the Chinese?"

"Stalinists too. They're just lending a hand."

"There's a Communist civil war going on in this godforsaken place?"

"Oh, yes. Jolly important to the world struggle for social justice, this bit of bush."

The White Flag camp was located in a village that lay at the head of a high valley framed by crags. Here Wolkowicz and the Englishman lived, in the ruins of a bell-shaped pagoda with a huge pipal tree in the dooryard. Between cannibal feasts, the guerrillas went to English classes conducted by the Englishman and gathered flowers for him; he was cataloging the flora of the region. On the roof of the pagoda, hundreds of tiny wind-bells tinkled in the night. The bamboo, which grew to a height of sixty feet, burst into flower while Wolkowicz was in the village, smearing color over the steep mountainsides.

"The bamboo only blooms every forty years or so," said the Englishman, "so no one in this camp is likely to see this again."

"How do you know all this stuff?" Wolkowicz asked.

"I'm a student of Asiatic trivia. Fascinated by flora and fauna."

A Burmese doctor treated Wolkowicz's ruined mouth with sulfa and surgery. The camp abounded with pretty young Burmese women, and one of them moved into Wolkowicz's bed. The Englishman, who spoke fluent Chinese in several dialects as well as Kachin, did not report Wolkowicz's rescue to his headquarters for a long time.

"I enjoy the company, it's rather nice to jaw in our native tongue," he said. "Sooner or later, of course, we'll have to reveal your presence to headquarters. We'll say you had amnesia and babbled in Russian for ages before crying, 'I remember! I'm a Yank!' Meantime, since you're such a handy sort of chap with guns, you can lead the odd sortie, if you don't mind."

Wolkowicz, using a Sten gun instead of a BAR, killed many more Japanese. Twice he saw wild elephants in the forest. Once a tiger came into a Japanese outpost after a fight, ignoring the fires and the noisy victory celebration, and fed on a headless body, like a dog lying under the table at a drunken banquet. Wolkowicz's wounds healed. There were no mirrors in the camp in which he might have seen his sunken mouth.

"It is wonderful, that," the Burmese girl giggled, stroking his quivering penis with hands dipped in sandalwood oil.

Finally, an Anglo-American army penetrated to the Shweli River, and Wolkowicz, dressed in British shorts and a turban that had been wound by his Burmese girl, walked into an encampment of Merrill's Marauders and identified himself as a member of the Outfit.

"What the fuck is the Outfit?" asked the major in charge.

— 6 —

In Ceylon, Wadsworth Jessup, impeccably turned out in a khaki uniform that still smelled of the hot iron, smiled at Wolkowicz. He had come into his room at six in the morning to wake him. Wolkowicz sat up in bed; the sheets were as thick as sailcloth. Waddy had lifted the mosquito netting and stuck his head inside. He was wearing Air Force sunglasses. Brilliant sunshine fell through the windows onto a polished teak floor; through the window Wolkowicz could see a man in knickerbockers swinging a golf club. He heard the head of the club hit the ball.

"Barnabas," said Waddy Jessup. "It *is* you. Thank God."

Beaming with good fellowship, Waddy took off his aviator's sunglasses for a moment so that he could look directly into Wolkowicz's eyes.

"Thank God for what?" Wolkowicz asked.

"For your deliverance."

Waddy had abandoned his British accent and spoke again in his normal prep school drawl. He wore a major's gold oak leaves on his collar and a row of ribbons, surmounted by his paratrooper badge, over his shirt pocket. Among his decorations was the ribbon of the Distinguished Service Cross, the second-highest medal for bravery awarded by the United States Army.

"I mean, my God, Barney," Waddy continued, "when that elephant stampeded away with me, leaving you to the mercy of the Jap, I really thought I'd seen the last of you."

Wolkowicz looked Waddy up and down. "I'll bet you did, you little cocksucker," he said.

Waddy tilted his head in puzzlement, as if Wolkowicz had cracked a joke that he didn't quite understand. There was a knock at the door. A Ceylonese servant, all in white, scuttled in, balancing a huge silver tray on his head.

"Ah, breakfast," Waddy said. "Sit ye down, Barney, sit ye down. They do a much better breakfast here than what we used to get in Burma."

They were in a hotel in Nuwara Eliya, the highest and most beautiful place in Ceylon. Before the war, the British had used it as a hill station, a place to go in the hot season. Now it was headquarters for the Outfit, and for British special operations, in the China-Burma-India Theater.

The servant plucked silver domes off plates of food and poured steaming coffee into china cups. He stood back, one bare foot on top of the other, in case he was needed.

"That's all right," Waddy said. "You can go away now."

The servant left. Wolkowicz, wearing nothing but his wrinkled khaki drawers, got out of bed and sat down at the table. Waddy was energetically spreading marmalade onto a piece of toast.

"Cream? Sugar?" Waddy asked. "Is this room all right?"

Wolkowicz, arriving in the dark the night before, after a flight from the battlefield, had not appreciated the splendor of the Grand Hotel. He looked out the window again. He could see crimson rhododendron bushes, hundreds of them, all in bloom. A silvery lake lay in the middle distance, the reflection of cypresses and pines shimmering on its placid surface. Wolkowicz drank an entire cup of coffee in three swallows. Waddy poured him another cup, then watched in satisfaction as Wolkowicz demolished the rest of the breakfast, porridge and eggs and sausage and bacon and a grilled tomato. As Wolkowicz mopped up the yolk with bread, Waddy urged more of everything on him: he hadn't touched his own food.

While Wolkowicz ate, Waddy told him the story of his own miraculous escape from Burma, eyes dancing as if no one on earth besides the two of them could understand what a delicious joke their firefight with the Japanese had been. The bolting elephant had carried Waddy straight to the nearest trail, and there he had encountered what was left of Force Jessup. The Kachins had whisked him back to their base, fighting their way through Japanese positions. Waddy had been delirious as a result of his wounds and unable to fight himself. He had just managed to get the radio working in order to call headquarters and report Wolkowicz's death and his own disabling wounds. The Kachins had cleared a runway in the jungle, a DC-3 had made a daring landing, and Waddy had been flown out to Ceylon.

Wolkowicz eyed Waddy's ribbons.

"Is that what you got the D.S.C. for?" he asked.

"I myself think it's excessive," Waddy said. "But they insisted. They've made me acting C.O., too, so the world's your oyster in Nuwara Eliya, my dear Barnabas. Golly, it's good to see you back from the dead!" He filled their coffee cups again. "Now, tell me your story."

Waddy sat back expectantly and lit a British cigarette with a Dunhill lighter. Wolkowicz remained silent. Waddy peered across the table at him. "Is it true you hitched up with the Brits?" he asked. "There're rumors that you had amnesia and still killed half the Jap Army."

Wolkowicz had been staring fixedly at Waddy the whole time he ate the two complete breakfasts, his greenish eyes dull with contempt, but he had not uttered a sound except for the peculiar sucking noises that resulted from the techniques he had invented in order to eat without teeth: he soaked his toast in coffee, mashed his sausage with his fork, swallowed his fried eggs as if they were oysters. Finally, wiping his greasy lips with an egg-stained napkin, he spoke. "I'm not going to tell you a fucking thing," he said.

"You're not?"

Waddy held the cigarette in the center of his mouth, puffing rapidly as he continued to give Wolkowicz a look filled with cheery comradeship. His voice trembled slightly and he kept his hands out of sight beneath the table; Wolkowicz supposed that they were trembling, too.

"Look," Waddy said in a bluff tone of voice, his cigarette bobbing up and down as he spoke, "you know *I* don't care what you've been up to. But you've been missing for six months, Barnabas. Headquarters wonders where you've been. They want to hang a medal on you. You and I have to put something on paper, send in a report."

Wolkowicz stood up, hairy and broad, and opened his toothless mouth in a black grin. "Waddy," he said, "just get the fuck out of here. I'm going to turn in a report, all right. But it won't be to you."

Boyish animation, Waddy's habitual expression, drained out of his face. He blushed under his tan, and then he looked deep into Wolkowicz's eyes, like a schoolboy trying to conceal his sullen resentment of punishment from a headmaster who had seen through his lies.

"Out," Wolkowicz repeated.

Waddy put on his sunglasses. Wolkowicz reached across the table, removed the cigarette from Waddy's lips, seized him by the hair, and ground out the burning end on the lens. Sparks fell on Waddy's perfectly laundered shirt, burning little holes in it.

— 7 —

At midnight, carrying a sheaf of papers in his hand, Wolkowicz stalked through the long corridors of the vast old Victorian hotel to Waddy Jessup's room. The door was unlocked. Wolkowicz opened it and stepped inside.

Waddy, dressed in a fitted silk dressing gown, stood by the window with a glass in his hand. He was all alone. A half-empty bottle of Glenlivet Scotch stood on a baize table. The Baby Nambu pistol lay on the green cloth beside the bottle. Waddy did not greet Wolkowicz, but turned and walked back to the table and poured him a drink. Waddy's hand was still unsteady. He spilled whisky on the tabletop, creating a spreading dark stain in the felt. The whisky was colorless in the glass. Waddy drank it off.

"I've brought you a couple of things to read," Wolkowicz said. "Are you up to it?"

"Of course."

Waddy put down his empty glass with a thump and accepted a handwritten document from Wolkowicz. It was a detailed description, ten pages long, of the action in the jungle. Slumped in a chair, turning the pages, Waddy struggled to understand what he was reading. The style was dry and factual. Wolkowicz's handwriting was strange: line after line of perfect Palmer Method penmanship.

Waddy paused to pour himself another drink. His hands quivered. Scotch splashed over the rim of the glass. Wolkowicz reached across the table and gently removed the tumbler from Waddy's fingers. When he had finished reading, Waddy picked up his glass again and drained it. His hand was quite steady now.

"Is that what you think happened?" Waddy said. His look of friendliness had given way to an expression of sullen resentment.

"There was a witness."

"A witness?"

Wolkowicz handed Waddy the other paper. It was written in a flowing British hand, as handsome in its way as Wolkowicz's. Within the sentences, words were joined together like a parade of elephants by a sweeping stroke of the pen that tied the last letter of one word to the first letter of the next. Each letter was perfectly formed: the ys were particularly fine. Waddy, though he realized that he was reading his death warrant, giggled. It was uncanny that any two grown men should write in this inhumanly perfect way. And it appeared that they had met in the Burmese jungle. What were the odds on *that!*

Waddy, intending to laugh aloud at this absurdity, instead uttered a sob. The paper he held in his hands was a narrative account of Wolkowicz's workmanlike bravery, and of Waddy's shameful cowardice, during the attack by the Japanese. It was signed by some British captain: Wolkowicz's "witness." Neither of these champion penmen had an ounce of pity for Waddy; neither had room in their dry sentences to mention the simple truth that Waddy had been driven mad by the Japanese, by the jungle, by the war, by the strain of living through what he had thought was the hour of his own death. His insanity was temporary. It was understandable. There was no guilt involved. It had happened to others; Waddy wasn't the only one.

"This Brit is willing to say that he watched the whole thing from hiding?" Waddy said in an unsteady voice.

"Why not? It's the truth."

"Why didn't he attack, then? Why didn't he come to our aid?"

"You can ask him that at your court-martial, Waddy."

Waddy fell silent. His breathing was very loud, almost a snore, as a result of the alcohol he had drunk. He worked his tongue as if it were coated with some ill-tasting substance. He was unable to talk. His eyes, red-rimmed and watery, stared with a faraway expression at the Baby Nambu.

"Just leave me alone with that," Waddy said dolefully, nodding at the pistol. "Is that what you want?"

Wolkowicz picked up the ridiculous little weapon, removed the clip, and ejected the round from the chamber. He then slid it into his trousers pocket. Waddy, spilling Scotch down the front of his iridescent blue robe, struggled to speak. At last, sound issued from his mouth.

". . . Sorry," he said.

Tears slid down Waddy's smooth-shaven cheeks. Wolkowicz picked him up, surprised again by how little his angular body weighed, and threw him onto his bed.

At eleven the following morning, Wolkowicz found Waddy on the practice green, putting, his narrow body hunched over the club, his face frozen in concentration.

There was no sign, in the bright early sunlight, that Wadsworth Jessup had ever had a drink. Attired in faultless starched khakis, decorations glowing on his breast, he flashed his eager smile and clapped Wolkowicz on the shoulder.

"Great news, Barnabas," Waddy said. "We've won in Burma."

He beamed at his subordinate, a confident man certain of admiration. He was behaving as if he had never read the reports Wolkowicz had given him the night before.

"I don't know what's next for types like us," Waddy said. "Anyway, everybody who's been in Burma will be coming out." He grinned again. "I have more good news. To begin with, I've confirmed your battlefield commission as a second lieutenant and recommended that you be promoted to first lieutenant."

"What battlefield commission?"

"The one I gave you under fire in Burma."

Waddy reached into his shirt pocket and produced a pair of gold second lieutenant's bars. He pressed them into Wolkowicz's hand.

"That's not all," Waddy said, "I've put you in for the D.S.C. If your Brit will back up what I say, you ought to get it. Even without his corroboration you'll get the Silver Star."

Wolkowicz stared steadily into Waddy's eyes. In the look that Waddy returned, there was no trace of embarrassment or shame or fear.

"The great thing, as our gallant British allies would say, is to avoid a bad show," Waddy said. "Barnabas, what's past is past. Neither one of us can go back to that day in the jungle and change what happened. I don't remember events quite the way you do; maybe I was affected by my wounds. But after all, Barney, only you and I were there and"— Waddy was grinning again—"only the elephant will never forget."

"Meaning?"

Waddy went on smiling, less buoyantly. "Meaning that you have me in your power," he said. "What else do you want?"

"It's as simple as that?"

"When it comes down to it, Barnabas, things are always simple. What else do you want? Just tell me."

"Europe."

Waddy frowned, a mere flash of expression, before he understood that Wolkowicz was not making a joke. "Europe?"

"By the time I get new teeth and take leave in the States," Wolkowicz said, "the war in Europe will be over. I want to go to Germany for a while, just to see what it's like."

"Why Germany, for heaven's sake? The Air Force has blown it to smithereens."

"I want to stay in the Outfit and go to Germany as a civilian. Can you arrange it?"

"What is the quid pro quo?"

"Only the elephant will remember."

"And your Burmese Brit, of course."

"You'll never hear from him."

Waddy studied Wolkowicz's contemptuous eyes, his sunken mouth, his blunt peasant hands. "I'll see what can be done," he said. "Hubbard Christopher—you remember, the Christmas party again—has been appointed to run the Outfit's postwar operation in Berlin. He's in Washington now. I'll give you a letter of introduction."

"That's all that's necessary?"

"Well, yes," Waddy said. "We're cousins by marriage. Anyway, Hubbard'll want you. You're a Russian-speaking Deadeye Dick with the heart of a lion. I only wish I could keep you on my team."

Two

— 1 —

When Hubbard Christopher returned to Berlin was chief of U.S. intelligence in the summer of 1945, the city, once so beautiful and green, had vanished. In its place was a vast smoking plain covered by heaps of rubble. From 1940 to 1945 the RAF and the U.S. Air Force dropped 76,652 tons of bombs on the city, and in the last ten days of April 1945, during the final battle for the city, the Red Army directed more than 40,000 tons of artillery shells on Berlin. In 1945 there were 1,153,040 fewer persons living in Berlin than there had been in 1939. Not all of those missing had been killed, but in the last year of the war the death rate was 55.5 persons per thousand, for a total of approximately 200,000 dead in that year alone. By way of comparison, total American dead in all theaters of operation in all of World War II amounted to 292,100.

Many of Berlin's dead still lay buried under the smashed masonry. An army of women in black dresses, gathering up the smashed city stone by stone, uncovered the corpses as they worked and laid them out on the rubble—old people, women, children. A few walls, ripped out of dead buildings like flesh torn from a carcass by the teeth of a predator, still stood, and here and there a blinded stone face, the fragment of one of the ornamental cornices, could be seen. The Tiergarten had been cut down for firewood. Berlin, which had been a great metropolis only five years before, now looked like a lost city that had been dug out of the earth centuries after its fall by some colossal archaeological expedition. Hubbard wrote:

> *What beast slouched here in our sleep,*
>   *crunching the brittle bones of our illusions*
> *in its jaws? Only our old affectionate*
>   *pet: he grew hungry in the dark house.*

These were the first lines Hubbard had put on paper since 1939. He had never really broken the silence he had fallen into after the Gestapo took Lori from him. It was necessary for him to speak to people in the course of his work, he had to get food and answer the telephone, but he never talked for pleasure again.

In carrying Lori away, danger had done everything to him it was possible to do; he cared nothing about it after that. By the end of the war he was a legendary operative. As a novelist, he had a trained imagination; as the man who loved Lori, he had the ruthless will to do whatever was necessary to find her and to stay alive long enough to be reunited with her. Not many men possessed such a combination of talent and motive. Following his recruitment by British intelligence, Hubbard Christopher had spent a year in Germany, pretending to be his cousin Elliott. The work the British asked him to do—recruiting Germans, the most obedient people in Europe, to betray their country—seemed to Hubbard so absurd as to be insane.

Sir Richard Shaw-Condon had been surprised that Hubbard had missed the point. "The point is, we *must* have networks," Sir Richard had said. "Naturally you'll have a high percentage of duds. That doesn't matter. Once you've turned a chap into a spy and made him realize that he's a traitor who will be killed by his own tribe, the silly bastard is yours for life. You must know masses of Hun idealists—Social Democrats, crypto-Communists, cabaret politicians, that lot. Sign *them* up."

"I'd be sending them to their deaths."

"Bad luck. We *must* have networks."

Hubbard understood that Sir Richard and his masters were not really interested in results. They were interested only in the style of the thing; spending the war in secret work was just another of the things fashionable people did to make themselves envied. The world of espionage was a region of the mad, in which men who could not write or paint or sculpt created distorted works out of the flesh of living persons and said—*believed*—that the result was art. It was like watching the inmates of an asylum daub an army of stick figures onto an enormous canvas, using buckets of blood for paint.

Hubbard did his secret work with painful care. All of his agents lived to the end of the war, and one of them became the most valuable spy the Western Allies had inside the German Army. His name was Friedrich Zechmann. When Hubbard first met him, at one of Otto Rothchild's dinners in 1935, he had been a young major on the general staff. Zechmann, who had the sly blank face of a cabaret comedian, had poked fun at the Nazis, who were then still a novelty, by pretending to admire everything they did.

"The concentration camps in Thuringia!" he would say, fingering the stem of a wineglass. "The Communists and the Social Democrats are benefiting greatly from the program of healthful outdoor exercise at Buchenwald. Pallid intellectuals are now as ruddy as their politics; sunken chests have been replaced by manly bosoms."

"Disgusting," Lori had said.

"Exactly. A Communist ought to *look* like a Communist, not like an example of healthy German manhood. It may be necessary to kill all the Communists in order to avoid confusion. The party admits its mistakes and corrects them."

A few months after his return to Berlin in 1940, Hubbard, disguised as Elliott, had been strolling in the Tiergarten when Zechmann greeted him.

"Christopher!"

"Good afternoon, Colonel. But you've mistaken me for my cousin. My name is Elliott Hubbard."

Hubbard now spoke German with a broad American accent. As he could not prevent himself from speaking the language grammatically, he spoke slowly, to give the impression that he was groping painfully for the right place in the sentence to put a verb he could not quite remember. Zechmann quizzically examined Hubbard's dyed hair and eyebrows.

"I beg your pardon, Mr. Hubbard. The resemblance is startling. Even the name is reminiscent. What brings you to Germany?"

"My cousin's wife is missing. I'm trying to find her."

"Have the authorities been able to help?"

"She doesn't exist in their files."

The British had not, of course, been able to give Hubbard any direct help in locating Lori. They had never intended to help him—of what use was a female prisoner of the Gestapo to them? Hubbard had always understood that there would be no help.

Zechmann slapped the palm of his open hand with his folded gloves. "That's very distressing," he said. "I knew her father. I served in the last war with her uncle."

Zechmann stood for a moment on the gravel path, eyes averted from the soldiers who strolled by, hugging their girls. He was deep in thought. Hubbard knew that Zechmann was not fooled by his alias. At last Zechmann made a decision.

"I'm on my way home," he said. "Follow me." He strode off in his burnished boots.

In his apartment, a tiny unheated place in the Englische strasse, a five-minute walk from the edge of the Tiergarten, Zechmann poured Hubbard a glass of beer.

Hubbard, still in his role as Elliott, described what had happened to Lori and Hubbard at the frontier. Zechmann, never questioning Hubbard's disguise, listened to the end. He asked no questions; there was no need.

"I'll do what I can to help you," Zechmann said brusquely. "But do not permit yourself to hope. In the end, we may only know how much she suffered."

Zechmann had been on Paulus's staff during the Russian campaign in the First World War. Because of this experience, and because Paulus had insisted that he learn Russian, he was now in charge of the section of military intelligence that dealt with the East. He met every month with his counterparts in the SS. He brought Hubbard dozens of photographs taken in the camps, with the blurred faces of women who might be Lori encircled with black crayon. Hubbard never saw a face he knew to be Lori's.

Soon Zechmann saw through Hubbard's second disguise and realized that he was a British agent. He began to give him other information, always delivered verbally, always perfectly accurate. He never explained why he was doing this.

Zechmann and Hubbard met, during the spring and summer of 1940, at Paulus's apartment in Berlin, during the coffee hour. After the

United States entered the war, they met in northern Italy, Hubbard crossing over from Switzerland on a Swiss passport. In 1944, Zechmann told Hubbard that Paulus, recalled to active service as a Russian expert, had been killed in the Urals. Until the end, Zechmann brought Hubbard the photographs of women in the camps, though Zechmann had never believed that Lori was among them. By prearrangement, Zechmann and Hubbard met in a meadow in Bavaria a week before the Russians entered Berlin. Zechmann had surrendered, to Hubbard personally, with all his files and all his officers and agents. His section of German intelligence was reconstituted intact as the Zechmann Bureau, an arm of the Outfit.

— 2 —

Barney Wolkowicz had no high regard for the Zechmann Bureau. In Berlin, in 1946, he explained why to his silent chief, Hubbard Christopher.

"Every time we try to run an agent who doesn't come from the Zechmann Bureau," Wolkowicz said, "he gets flyswatted. You *have* noticed the pattern?"

Two of Wolkowicz's agents had been killed in a week, both of them smashed against one of Berlin's sawtooth rubble walls by a speeding car. This method of assassination was called flyswatting because the victim was crushed against the masonry, leaving a mark (blood and flesh and the tattered black cloth that all the defeated Germans seemed to wear) which resembled the remains of a fly that had been smashed on a windowpane.

"It's the fucking Russians," Wolkowicz said. "They've penetrated the Zechmann Bureau."

Hubbard looked calmly across the desk at Wolkowicz. This suspicion, voiced by any other man, would have been regarded as the first sign of a nervous breakdown. The Zechmann Bureau *was* American espionage in Berlin. But Wolkowicz was the best man Hubbard had. All the others, more than twenty intelligent, brave young men, did not together produce the results that Wolkowicz produced by himself.

This astonished his colleagues. When he arrived from Burma, still suffering from the effects of malaria and dengue fever, wearing his new false teeth, speaking no German, not much had been expected from him.

It was thought that Waddy Jessup, who had sent him to Hubbard, was doing this crude, foulmouthed man a kindness—letting him see Berlin before he was sent back to Ohio, or wherever it was he had come from. Sniffing this atmosphere, Wolkowicz insisted on working alone; he radiated class hostility. Soon this created difficulties.

"I know he killed a battalion of Japs and got the Silver Star, and everybody knows how talented he is," an exasperated colleague said to Hubbard, "but he's a pain in the ass. He thinks everybody in the Outfit except him went to Yale and had their brains fried. He calls Yale the fool factory. I didn't go there, but Jesus!"

Hubbard grinned. "If you'd been marooned in Burma with Waddy Jessup you might be anti-Yale, too," he said.

Hubbard had liked Wolkowicz the first time he ever saw him, at the Christmas party at the Harbor. The rudeness, the obscene speech, the coarse table manners meant nothing. In everything that counted, Wolkowicz was a gentleman: truthful, loyal, brave, kind, generous. To women he was chivalrous, and perhaps because his ugliness made them feel more beautiful than they were, they often succumbed to him.

Also, it was evident to Hubbard from the day Wolkowicz arrived in Berlin that he was the finest natural spy he had ever encountered. There was no easy explanation for this talent. Perhaps the first reason for his excellence was his truculent refusal to believe in anybody's innocence. Wolkowicz treated all men, and especially all women, as enemy agents at all times; they could be used, paid, praised. They could even be loved. But they could never be trusted. What might seem paranoia in another man was shrewd intuition in Wolkowicz.

"You penetrated Zechmann's operation in 1940, right?" Wolkowicz said to Hubbard, pursuing his latest suspicion.

This was, of course, a secret. It did not surprise Hubbard that Wolkowicz knew it, or suspected it. Wolkowicz seemed to absorb other people's secrets through the pores of his skin. Wolkowicz did not pause.

"Now the *Russians* have penetrated Zechmann," he said. "If you could do it, they can do it; anyone can do it. You can't expect a man like Zechmann to admit this. I say we should penetrate him too, for his own good—find the infection, clean it out, and never say a word about it to Zechmann."

"If your theory is correct, the Russians will know what we're up to."

"Good. It'll teach them a little respect."

Wolkowicz, in the strident voice he never lowered, outlined his plan for finding the traitors in the Zechmann Bureau. He disliked putting things on paper: the Army clerks who did the Outfit's typing could be assumed to be sleeping with girls who were in the pay of the opposition. Wolkowicz's plan, like all his plans, was beautifully clear and brutally simple. He relied entirely on low cunning—the old, old tricks that had worked for thousands of years. His approach to human nature was so primitive that more sophisticated men could scarcely understand it.

"It's more complicated than that," they would say.

"Like shit it is," Wolkowicz would reply. He was invariably right.

Wolkowicz proposed baiting the trap for Zechmann with a female. Hubbard had no trouble understanding what Wolkowicz had in mind for Friedrich Zechmann. "Why do you think this girl, Ilse Bauer, is the key?" he asked.

"Because Zechmann's queer for virgins."

Another secret. Wolkowicz handed a large glossy photograph across the desk. Ilse Bauer, Wolkowicz's agent, was a girl of twenty with spun blond hair, flawless skin, and slightly slanted eyes set above high cheekbones. Even in a photograph, she glowed with virginal innocence.

Wolkowicz reclaimed the photograph. When he opened his coat to put it safely in an inside pocket, Hubbard saw the butt of a Walther P-38 automatic thrust into the waistband of his trousers. Wolkowicz was never without this weapon; his attachment to it was an office joke.

"Why does it have to be the Russians?" Hubbard asked.

"If it's not the Russians," Wolkowicz said, "it's got to be Zechmann."

"You think he's killing your agents to keep down the competition?"

"Why not?" Wolkowicz said. "I'm taking bread out of his mouth."

Of course this was a possibility, though a more civilized man might not have realized it and certainly would not have mentioned it.

"All right," Hubbard said. "Go ahead, slowly."

Wolkowicz nodded firmly and smiled with his perfect white false teeth.

Every Thursday at five o'clock, Hubbard called on Hilde von Buecheler. This had always been Hilde's time to have people in for coffee. She lived now in two rooms in the basement of the house she and Paulus had inhabited in the Charlottenburger chaussee. It was a' cave, really, beneath the heap of rubble that was all that remained of the house in which the Christophers' old apartment had been located. The Russians had confiscated Berwick as their headquarters on Rügen.

Hubbard brought Hilde a pound of Maxwell House coffee and enough canned food to last her for a week. Because she would not accept money from him, he left a carton of Camels on the hall table for her each week. On the black market, the cigarettes were worth 2,500 marks, $625 at the prewar rate of exchange. (A common whore cost five marks or five cigarettes, a girl of good family twenty-five or more.) "It's just like it was when you came after the last war," Hilde said. "American cigarettes are the new valuta."

Somehow Hilde had preserved her photographs, and cabinet portraits of Paulus and their sons in uniform, and of Lori before her marriage, and of her great-nephew Paul Christopher were displayed on the table. She had grown thin. She had developed a tendency to chatter.

"Is Zechmann coming?" Hilde asked.

Zechmann came every Thursday, too. As in 1940, this was a convenient way for Hubbard to see him.

Zechmann, when he came, brought chocolate for Hilde, carrying it in his briefcase. While he drank his coffee, he and Hilde repeated ten-year-old army gossip. Free at last to tell anything she knew, Hilde provided details of old romances that sent the icy Zechmann into gales of laughter.

At six o'clock, as Wolkowicz had arranged, Ilse Bauer knocked at the door. Hilde opened it. Snow was falling and the ruins beyond Ilse in the lightless city were dusted white.

"Frau Colonel Baroness von Buecheler?" Ilse asked in a firm, middle-class voice.

"Yes." Hilde saw that snowflakes were falling through the shaft of yellow light from the open door and that the shoulders of the girl's thin coat were covered with snow. "Please come in," she said.

Ilse came into the candlelight, her face glowing from the cold, snowflakes shining on the yellow wing of hair that escaped from her kerchief. She smelled of roses, the scent of them came in with her like an aura. Hilde hadn't smelled such a perfume since her own girlhood. Her eyes, still animated from the gossip, shone with pleasure on seeing Ilse's fresh beauty. Not many German girls looked like this, so pure and untouched, in 1946.

It was an uncomfortable moment for Hubbard. Zechmann was, as Wolkowicz had predicted, entranced by Ilse's looks. But Hubbard doubted that any cover story Wolkowicz had provided to Ilse would fool Zechmann. What plausible reason could this girl, a total stranger, give for rapping on Hilde's door?

"My name is Ilse Bauer," Ilse said. "I don't know if I'm doing you a kindness, Baroness, but I promised I would come."

"Promised? Promised whom?"

Ilse Bauer reached down and took Hilde's hand, a startling liberty.

"Your niece, Lori, long ago," she said. "I have a message from her."

Hilde smiled giddily, extended her free hand on the end of her rigid arm to Hubbard, and fell to the floor in a dead faint.

After Hilde revived, Ilse sat beside her on the sofa, holding her hand in both of hers and urging her to take a sip of coffee.

"No," Hilde said. "The message."

Ilse stroked her hand. "This happened a long time ago, a few days after the war started," she said. "I lived then in Weimar, a bit outside of the town."

"This was in 1939? You must have been very young."

"Thirteen, Baronin. I was riding on a road. A big Mercedes, one of those dark official cars, came up behind me, going too fast, and struck my horse. I was thrown and knocked unconscious. The horse was a Lippizaner gelding, but gray, not white as the ideal type is supposed to be. All the same, this Lippizaner was my pride and joy. I heard a shot and came to. A man from the Mercedes held a pistol in his hand; he had shot my horse. I became hysterical. There were three men in long leather coats. They couldn't deal with me. Finally one of them said, 'She needs a woman.' There was a woman in the car. She seemed to be a prisoner. She had—forgive me—the marks of a beating on her face. She wore— forgive me—manacles on her wrists. All the same, they treated her with respect, as if she was somebody. They let her out of the car. She comforted me, bathed my head, and got me to get into the car so they could take me to the hospital. She hugged me, like a mother, whispering in my ear. I was still hysterical. She herself seemed to be very, very tired, but she said a wonderful thing to me. Stroking my cheek, she said, 'Now he can run as much as he likes.' Then she whispered to me, the name of Colonel Baron von Buecheler, Charlottenburger chaussee, Berlin. And she said, 'Tell him Buchenwald. My name is Lori. Tell my uncle I am alive.' "

Dark eyes shining in her powdered face, handkerchief balled in her fist, Hilde listened.

"That was seven years ago," she said. "Why do you come only now?"

"I couldn't come sooner. My mother is Swiss. She took me to Switzerland the next week. She wouldn't let me write to you; she was afraid."

"What did this woman you believe to be my niece look like?" Hilde said.

Ilse crossed the room and touched Lori's photograph. "Exactly like her picture," she said.

Zechmann had been listening from his chair in the corner, outside the glow of the candles. His voice came out of the shadows.

"What was the name of your horse?" he asked.

Ilse gave him a smile in which her sadness over the Lippizaner still lingered. "Hugo," she said.

Hubbard said nothing at all.

— 4 —

Wolkowicz apologized to Hubbard for the cover story he had given to Ilse.

"I know it was a pretty bad thing to do, using your wife's death—"

"Disappearance."

"Disappearance. It must have been a hell of a shock. I couldn't warn you. But I knew Zechmann would be watching your reaction. He had to see real feelings on your face. He knows you too well to take a chance on your faking it. I'm sorry."

Hubbard nodded. After years of secret life, no outrage seemed unpardonable to him. This was simply the way things were done. You learned not to be emotional about it. After a time, the ordinary feelings of ordinary people became unbelievable, they made you uncomfortable, like amateur theatricals badly done. Hubbard did not bother to acknowledge Wolkowicz's apology. He wanted to know more about Ilse.

"Did Ilse actually live near Weimar in 1939?" he asked.

"Yes. Also, she spent the war in Switzerland, in Geneva. That's why she looks so healthy—she hasn't been living on potato soup like all the other girls. Zechmann will find that everything about her checks out, even the horse, except that it wasn't shot by the Gestapo. But even Zechmann can't run down a detail like that."

"I want to talk to her."

"Okay," Wolkowicz said.

He was puzzled by Hubbard's interest. It wasn't until much later that he realized Hubbard believed Ilse had actually seen Lori on that road outside Weimar. Even knowing that what Ilse had told Hilde was a carefully rehearsed lie, invented by Wolkowicz, Hubbard chose to believe in the Mercedes, in the girl on horseback, in the gray Lippizaner, in the kind prisoner with Lori's face.

Now he can run as much as he likes.

Hubbard could hear Lori's voice speaking these words, so typical of her.

"But you told him it was a lie, a cover story," Ilse said to Wolkowicz, later. "Is he crazy?"

"On this one subject, you'd have to say yes. Maybe he thinks he can keep his wife from being dead by insisting that she's alive."

"How can he believe such a thing?"

"I guess he loved her."

Hubbard cultivated a friendship with Ilse, chatting with her about her girlhood, about the future she might have. Hubbard did not understand why such a girl, who even in a destroyed capital could have had anything she wanted, was willing to do the work Wolkowicz gave her to do. One night, when Wolkowicz had brought her to Hubbard's quarters for dinner, Hubbard put this question to Ilse. She turned her face away.

"I'd rather not explain," she said.

"I think you ought to tell him," Wolkowicz said.

This was unusual. Wolkowicz seldom intervened in a conversation between Ilse and his chief. Ilse gave Wolkowicz a desolated look and went into the bathroom. She had drunk a lot of whisky that night and she staggered slightly. She wore white knee socks. It was shocking to see her drunk, she was so luminous with youth and physical innocence.

Hubbard did not pursue the subject after Ilse left them, though it was obvious that Wolkowicz knew the answer to his question. Wolkowicz had never known such a quiet man. Hubbard's reserve was frustrating: you never knew whether he believed what you said to him, or if he even heard you.

"You got onto kind of a painful subject for old Ilse," Wolkowicz said. "I should have explained it all to you before this. Her father was an officer in the Waffen SS, on the Russian front. About three months before the war ended, he got in touch and said he wanted to see his wife and daughter. They left Switzerland and came to Berlin to wait for him —bombs and shells falling day and night, the Russians getting closer every day. It's hard to imagine anyone being that stupid. He never showed up. Ilse's mother was killed by a Russian shell. The kid was left all alone, with no relatives and very little money. The Russians got to Berlin before Ilse could get out."

Wolkowicz paused, embarrassed. Hubbard realized that Wolkowicz was angry at Ilse's dead mother for leaving her daughter in a burning city that was about to be pillaged by an enemy army. Wolkowicz made himself another Rob Roy. He had an astonishing capacity for liquor, frequently drinking a whole bottle of whisky, mixed with sweet vermouth, in the course of an evening. He never showed the slightest effect.

"Ilse seems attached to you," Hubbard said.

He did not think that Wolkowicz would go on without encouragement, and it was evident that he hadn't come to the end of the story. Hubbard was sure that Ilse was listening through the door.

"Yeah. Well, there's a reason for that," Wolkowicz said. "Let me tell you how I met her. Right after I got here, I was driving by some woods and I saw this fucking Mongolian coming out of the bushes, grinning and buttoning up his fly. Russian soldiers were trotting into the trees, stumbling over their hard-ons. It was obvious they were having one of their gang rapes. So I parked the car and went into the woods myself. Another Mongolian was just rolling off this German girl. She was lying on the ground *on her face.* They had pulled her dress up over her head. Two of these Mongolians had hold of her legs, pulling them apart, and two more were sitting on her head. I know the Russians do this all the time. I know I should have left quietly. But instead I kicked the guy who was humping her on his bare ass and pulled out my gun."

"How many of them were there?"

"A dozen or so. Maybe twenty had already passed through the line."

"They left her alone when you arrived?"

[124]

"Well, I speak Russian. I explained things to them. I may have fired a couple of shots. I took Ilse to a doctor and then took her home."

"The doctor said she was all right?"

"Physically, yes. It wasn't as bad as I thought when I saw them coming at her from the rear. That's just the way they do it. They think they're horses.

"She's okay now. But when you add what happened to her to the fact that her father was probably killed by the Red Army, you can understand why she isn't crazy about the Russians."

Ilse came back into the room. She had been crying. A look came and went in Wolkowicz's face. Rapid though its passage had been, Hubbard saw it for what it was: love.

— 5 —

Friedrich Zechmann had taken Ilse home from Hilde's. On the way, driving down a ravine between snowy heaps of rubble, the headlights picked up two figures in the shadows. An American soldier, his cap on the back of his head, leaned against a ruined wall, gripping the head of a woman who knelt in front of him. The woman was trying to break away. After a little struggle, the soldier let her go and slumped against the wall, depleted. The woman scrambled to her feet and turned her haggard face toward the car.

"Dear God," Zechmann said. "Margarete."

The woman spat and retched and, as the headlights continued to shine in her eyes, covered her face.

"Who?" Ilse asked.

"The widow of a brother officer," Zechmann said, driving on.

In the days that followed, Zechmann sent his driver to Ilse's apartment with invitations to concerts, to the theater, to dinner. She accepted one invitation in three. Zechmann offered her food, clothes, coffee, cigarettes; she would accept nothing. Far from going to bed with Zechmann, Ilse would not even kiss him. Her virtue, in a city of rubble in which countesses would fellate American corporals in return for a handful of cigarettes, inflamed Zechmann.

"Are you a virgin?" he asked Ilse in his mocking way.

"Of course," she replied.

Zechmann went absolutely still. The look of mocking flirtation he had been wearing disappeared from his face and was replaced by an expression of longing. He looked for an instant as if he might weep with joy. He drew air in through his nostrils and when he spoke there was a tremor in his voice.

"If that's true, it's a great triumph in these times," Zechmann said. "How have you stayed alive in Berlin?"

"People will always pay to see a curiosity," Ilse said.

"This idea that I am a virgin seems to have panicked him sexually," she told Wolkowicz. "Really, it's quite pornographic."

Zechmann did not lose his head altogether. As Wolkowicz had expected, he investigated the possibility that Ilse was an opposition agent. Zechmann assigned a team to watch her, to search her room. The team found correspondence from the Union Bank of Switzerland in Geneva. The letters from the bank explained how Ilse had managed to preserve her virginity: she had been living on withdrawals from a small account; the money was almost exhausted. Zechmann knew that his moment would come. Very soon, when her Swiss money ran out, Ilse would become a black-market commodity like most of the other women in Berlin.

Six weeks after Zechmann had met Ilse, she withdrew the last hundred francs from her Geneva account. Zechmann gave her ten days in which to spend the money, and then he asked her to marry him.

"No," Ilse said.

"Why not? Am I really so repulsive?"

"Not at all, Friedrich. But I want to marry for love, not for self-preservation."

"God in heaven, Ilse, don't you realize that ideas like that are buried under this rubble forever? Do you think that Berlin is a city of romance?"

"Not buried forever," Ilse said. "Not for me."

They were sitting in Zechmann's car, a nondescript gray Opel. All around them the smashed stones of Berlin were heaped into hillocks. A few walls still stood, fragments of masonry punctuated by rows of empty windows. It was raining. Under the air raids, Berlin had burned for five years and the last flames had been extinguished only a year before. The fiery smell of the blackened stones, washed up by the rain, filled their nostrils. It was a nauseating odor, like the stench of a burnt carcass.

Ilse still smelled of roses. Breathing her fragrance, Zechmann imagined a garden filled with delicate pink blossoms, petals velvety to the touch. He seized Ilse and kissed her.

"No," she said, twisting her face away.

Zechmann paid no attention to her protests. Holding her down, squeezing both her biceps with paralyzing strength, throwing a leg across her thrashing ankles, he covered her face with kisses. They were tender kisses, chaste as the kisses of a schoolboy. He wore a long leather coat; it squeaked as he wrestled with Ilse, and she could smell the leather. She stopped struggling and let him kiss her. He went on with it, eyes tightly shut, trembling, as if he were tasting her heart. He stroked her hair, touched her cheeks, traced the line of her jaw with a fingertip. Ilse expected him to fondle her breasts, to force a hand between her legs, but he used only his mouth, and his mouth never left her face. Finally Zechmann released her and stared through the windshield at the black glistening dunes of brick and stone.

"This has gone out of control," he said.

Ilse sat quietly, her hands folded in her lap. At dinner, Zechmann had noticed that her knuckles were a bit chapped; the sight of her reddened flesh had sent a pang through his heart.

"This is not what I had hoped for, that's certain," Ilse said. There was a note of despair in her voice.

"What had you hoped for?"

"I'm all out of money. I'd hoped that you'd help me to find work."

"Work? What sort of work do you want to do?"

"Whatever will get the bastards who did this to Germany," Ilse said, staring with hate-filled eyes at the rubble.

"That will take a long time."

"I don't mind. Let me work with you."

"I have no work for virgins."

Ilse's face glowed with its angelic smile. She put her hands, small and warm, on either side of Zechmann's face. He moved his head impatiently. Looking into his eyes, she shook her head. "Be still," she said. She began to kiss his face in the way in which he had kissed hers. He submitted.

"Why did you do that?" he asked when she was done.

Ilse paused. "I felt your love just now," she said. "Thank you. Good-bye."

She opened the car door.

"Wait," Zechmann said.

Ilse strode toward the path in the rubble that led to her room.

Zechmann, heels ringing on the cobbles, hurried after her, calling her name, but she closed the door in his face.

Wolkowicz was waiting for her when she went inside. While they talked in the dark, Ilse stroked the coarse springy hair that grew on his broad chest. She told him what Zechmann had done in the car.

"Maybe he's a eunuch," Wolkowicz said.

"No," Ilse said. "He's a romantic. All cynics are romantics."

"Save the epigrams for Zechmann."

The next week, Ilse went to work for the Zechmann Bureau as an interpreter. In addition to her fluent French, she spoke fair English and even a little Russian.

— 6 —

While Ilse overpowered Zechmann, Wolkowicz recruited an agent from East Berlin, a former captain of the Abwehr who had a minor sidewalk job in the Soviet security apparatus. The agent had no great value, but Wolkowicz developed him with scrupulous care. He had met him at a performance of *Die Meistersinger*.

"Thank God for tobacco," Wolkowicz said to Hubbard afterward. "At the intermission I went outside for a smoke, and in the shadows I spotted these two hungry eyes. 'Cigarette?' I said. '*Jawohl!*' he said."

Wolkowicz spoke all foreign languages with a Russian accent; even his English was tinted by his father's way of speaking the language; he jammed gross English words into the Russian alphabet like a foot into an elegant slipper that was too small for it. Horst Bülow, on hearing Wolkowicz's accent in German, changed to Russian. He spoke it well, but with the upper-class intonation that the Soviets hated.

Wolkowicz invited Bülow to join him for supper after the opera. Bülow devoured his steak and fried potatoes and drank Steinhaeger and beer like a man who had just been released from prison. He wore a threadbare suit cut from his Wehrmacht uniform, the cloth dyed black, with bilious green lights in it. Bülow liked to talk; he liked to play the man of culture to an unlettered American.

"Even in the ruins we Germans have great music played by great musicians," he said. "Perhaps you should get some ruins in America so that you can have music, too."

Wolkowicz invited Bülow to a Mozart recital the following week. After that concert he gave him a ticket for *The Magic Flute* the following week; Bülow, sitting next to Wolkowicz with a whole carton of cigarettes on his lap, laughed like a giddy girl at the antics of Papageno.

"I am a student of conspiracy," said Bülow over dinner, discussing the Masonic rituals in the libretto. "To be successful over the long term, a cabal must have a religious basis—Mithraism, the Jesuit Order, Freemasonry."

"Communism?"

"Of course. There is great religiosity in all political movements, especially revolutionary political movements."

"That was true of the Nazis too, would you say?"

Bülow looked about him with quick birdlike turns of the head. It was a small restaurant that Wolkowicz had taken him to, another cave in the ruins, with only five or six tables. The owner had recognized Bülow when he came in, Bülow had seen it in his eyes; the man had worked before the war at the Jockey Club, one of Bülow's favorite places. It was gone now, of course.

"Excuse me, please," Bülow said. "I will talk about anything but the Nazis."

"All right. What's it like, working for the Russians?"

"Maddening. They are not a nation of watchmakers, the Russians. They do everything with a sledgehammer."

Without preamble, in a loud voice, Wolkowicz asked Bülow to bring him a document in Russian. Bülow's eyes flickered over the room again, looking for signs that Wolkowicz's grating voice had been overheard.

"I can't possibly do that," Bülow said in a startled whisper.

"I don't mean a *secret* document," Wolkowicz bellowed. "It can be anything—rip a notice off the bulletin board."

"Why would you want such a thing?"

Wolkowicz put a forkful of food into his mouth and talked as he chewed. "Humor me," he said. He wanted it for the simplest of reasons: if Bülow would steal even the smallest thing from his masters, on Wolkowicz's orders, and accept money for it, then Wolkowicz would be his new master. It was the first step. Bülow knew it was the fatal step. He drank his Steinhaeger and his eyes watered.

After the next concert, Bülow gave him a paper typewritten in Russian. It was an exhortation to the workers of liberated Germany to fulfill their work norms for the last quarter of 1946. Wolkowicz chuckled as he read it.

"Great stuff," he said. "Let me pay you for your trouble."

Bülow waved away the fifty-mark note, two weeks' salary for him. "No, no—take it," Wolkowicz said.

Bülow put the money in his pocket and excused himself. He was urinating into the foul toilet, in the open air behind the restaurant, when Wolkowicz came up behind him.

"While you're doing that," Wolkowicz said, "sign this."

Reaching around Bülow, he handed him a slip of paper and a pen. The paper was a receipt for fifty marks. Bülow hesitated, then signed the paper.

"Write *For Information* above your signature," Wolkowicz said.

Bülow, his flaccid penis hanging out of his unbuttoned fly, felt embarrassed and vulnerable. It seemed more important to cover his flesh than to resist Wolkowicz's outrageous command. He signed.

"Now," said Wolkowicz, "one more thing. Just ink your thumb on this stamp pad and put your thumbprint on the receipt."

Again Bülow did as he was told, then scrubbed his inky thumb against his trousers.

Wolkowicz patted him on the shoulder. "Here's a ticket for the Haydn concert on the twelfth," he said. "Bring the telephone directory for your section with you."

"The telephone directory! That's very dangerous. They regard telephone directories as state secrets. It's impossible, what you ask."

"Nothing is impossible, Horst," Wolkowicz said. "I want you to remember that."

— 7 —

Wolkowicz had identified two men inside the Zechmann Bureau who were possible Soviet agents. Ilse had no trouble making friends with either of them. Her beauty would have been enough by itself to attract them. But, as Wolkowicz told Hubbard, she had something more.

"When you add to her looks the fact that Zechmann is crazy about her," Wolkowicz said to Hubbard, "you've got a great aphrodisiac working for you. Everyone wants to be pals with the boss's girl friend."

Ilse made no secret of her friendship with Hubbard. She even made a gentle joke of Wolkowicz, saying that he had begun to court her. Explaining that they were presents from Wolkowicz, Ilse brought nylon stockings, candy bars, round tins of American coffee into the office and distributed them to the other girls.

"This American leaves treasure on my doorstep while I'm out," Ilse explained. "He's such a clumsy bear! He wants me to go to a Haydn concert with him. He plays the piano—Chopin, everything, to entertain me when I visit Christopher. I think I'll go."

"Go? With an Ami?" one girl said. "With *that* Ami?"

"He's really rather sweet."

"Beauty and beast."

Horst Bülow came to the concert, too. Wolkowicz pretended to have got the dates mixed up. He introduced his agent to Ilse, using a false name for her but identifying Bülow, who twitched in fear at the sound of it, by his true name. Bülow left the concert hall midway through the last selection. On his empty seat, after the lights came up, Wolkowicz found a thin mimeographed telephone directory, wrapped in a sheet of grease-stained paper.

Next day, at morning coffee, Ilse shared a chocolate bar with the first of the two possible Soviet agents inside the Zechmann Bureau. Giggling, Ilse described Horst Bülow and the package he had left on his theater seat.

"Evidently Wolkowicz meets this amazing spy at the concert every other Thursday," Ilse said, making a gay joke.

This information planted, Wolkowicz waited to see if Bülow would be flyswatted. Two concerts went by. Bülow arrived in safety and left in peace. Each time, trembling, he signed a receipt for the trifling sums that Wolkowicz paid him in return for the useless routine material that he had copied from the files.

"There's not even any surveillance on him," Wolkowicz told Hubbard. "The first guy must be clean. It's time for Ilse to tell the other guy."

"How are you going to prevent these people from killing your agent?" Hubbard asked.

"Prevent them? I don't want to prevent them. He's not an agent; he's bait. If I can shove him out of the way of the death car, I will. But the whole idea is that they will kill him. Then *we'll* know who to kill."

Ilse confided her knowledge about Horst Bülow to the second suspect in the Zechmann Bureau. The results were the same. No attempt was made on Bülow's life.

"That doesn't mean that the Zechmann Bureau isn't penetrated," Wolkowicz said. "I know fucking well it is, Hubbard. All it means is that we've got the wrong suspects."

Hubbard was not so sure. As the operation had unfolded, Hubbard had grown more skeptical of it. There had never been a shred of evidence that anyone in the Zechmann Bureau had betrayed Wolkowicz's murdered agents. Their deaths might even have been bona fide traffic accidents, unlikely as that seemed. In espionage there wasn't usually any evidence of anything. Those who committed crimes in this world were not criminals, they were government servants. In the real world, a murderer will leave clues because his mind is clouded by passion or fear, because he lacks the money to obtain suitable weapons, because there is no place to hide. Usually he is alone—nobody has taught him the proper way to murder a man, nobody has gone over his plan for the crime, pointing out flaws, suggesting a better technique; he feels remorse, guilt, shame, self-disgust: he is an outcast; imprisonment is a relief. The man who kills at the orders of an intelligence service has none of these practical or psychological problems: in committing a murder that in other circumstances would be regarded as the work of a psychopath, he has done his country a service and his country pays him, gets rid of the murder weapon, and folds him in its maternal embrace.

That was why Wolkowicz had no hard evidence that two of his agents had been flyswatted by the Soviets. He had to rely on intuition, suspicion, patterns of events that were slightly askew. That was sufficient. Often enough in Berlin in 1946, suspicion was reality. Faceless men *were* trying to kill you. It was prudent to look into every petty detail, to spend the enormous amounts in time and money that it took to live like a paranoiac who had the inexhaustible means to check out all of his delusions.

It was especially wise to suspect the people you had the greatest reason to trust. Hubbard had compelling reasons to trust Friedrich Zechmann. Therefore he had to force himself to be suspicious of him.

Because of his own friendship with Zechmann, Hubbard had let Wolkowicz run this operation without interference; he had not even asked to know Horst Bülow's true name. To Hubbard, Bülow was Bowstring, an alias buried in the text of a report in Wolkowicz's safe. Had he heard the true name, he would, of course, have recognized it. Hubbard had not forgotten that Bülow was the Abwehr officer who had warned Otto Rothchild in 1939 to get out of Germany; and Rothchild had got out, aboard *Mahican*.

"I think you ought to drop this operation," Hubbard said to Wolkowicz.

"Drop it? Why?"

"Because it's leading nowhere. Because it's reckless. There's too much to lose. We haven't just penetrated the Zechmann Bureau, we've humiliated Zechmann. I thought he'd try to seduce Ilse; in fact, I assumed he'd succeed, he's always been such a sexual buccaneer."

Hubbard's words, delivered in his steady voice, were a blow to Wolkowicz; he was sure his plan would work. But instead of protesting, he made a joke.

"A sexual buccaneer?" Wolkowicz said. "Jesus, Hubbard, now *that* was a touchdown for Yale. I wish I could talk like that. But I don't get the part about how we humiliated Zechmann. How did we do that?"

"He fell in love with Ilse."

"That wasn't part of the plan."

"Exactly. His emotions are involved. If he finds out that she's been using him, that she—or rather, you—have been running him like some little sex-starved clerk, all hell will break loose."

"He's not going to find out."

"Then you'd better stop sleeping with Ilse."

Wolkowicz had remarkably steady eyes. Now, for the first time in the years that Hubbard had known him, his gaze wavered for a moment. He hadn't realized that Hubbard knew this secret.

"Zechmann is capable of killing you both," Hubbard said. "That is the lesser danger. He's also capable of taking the Zechmann Bureau, intact, over to the other side."

Wolkowicz raised his hand, like a hardworking boy in a classroom. "You think he hasn't already done that?" he asked. "Hubbard, think about it. It would be the greatest penetration in history. We think Zechmann's working for us. We think he's so great we don't even bother to do any work on our own. Zechmann becomes U.S. espionage in Berlin. *But all the time he's working for the other side.*"

Hubbard closed his eyes for a moment. Wolkowicz saw, in that instant, how tired this man was, how old he was becoming, how little interest he had in this work. All that kept Hubbard Christopher upright was his mad belief that his wife, who had been arrested by the Gestapo more than six years before, was somehow still alive, though ten million other prisoners had been murdered during those years by the Nazis. Briefly, Wolkowicz felt sadness for his chief. Then he felt very uncomfortable. Hubbard had opened his eyes, and there was an expression on his face—not anger, not contempt, not surprise—that Wolkowicz could not read.

"If that sounded crazy I'm sorry," Wolkowicz said. "You always told me I had freedom of speech."

Hubbard's face cleared; he smiled. "You do," he said. "Zechmann may be a Soviet agent. Anyone may be a Soviet agent. Even you."

Hubbard smiled deep in his eyes. It was a joke. Wolkowicz knew that; Hubbard found his suspiciousness amusing. It made him uncomfortable just the same. He plunged on, keeping to the subject.

"Then you think I may be onto something?"

"It's not an untenable theory," Hubbard said. "I think you're onto a Soviet operation, all right. I think the Soviets *did* flyswat your agents. But not for the reasons you stated. I think they *want* us to think that the Zechmann Bureau is penetrated. I think they hope that we'll even suspect that Zechmann is their agent and that we'll stop trusting him, that we'll get rid of him. They want us to think the Zechmann Bureau is a Soviet operation."

"Why?" Wolkowicz asked. But he already knew why. He already knew that Hubbard had seen the true pattern of the Soviet operation against the Zechmann Bureau.

"Because Zechmann is hurting them," Hubbard said. "They couldn't get control of the Zechmann Bureau, so they want to neutralize it. Think about it. All the raw material for a delusion of treachery is present: Zechmann betrayed his own country during the war by working with me, so why wouldn't he betray me? We don't even have the reassurance that Zechmann and his men are Nazis and therefore hostile to communism: Friedrich Zechmann would never have a Nazi in his section, only Wehrmacht staff officers who weren't interested in politics. If Zechmann looks so innocent, he *must* be guilty. Therefore we'll kill off our own best asset. It's very elegant."

"You think the Russians are that smart?"

Hubbard looked at Wolkowicz for a long moment. He liked this ugly, brilliant, brave man so much.

"Yes, I do," he said. "The operation against the Zechmann Bureau is terminated."

"Today?"

"This moment."

"You don't want Ilse to tell Zechmann himself about Bowstring, as long as we've gone to all this trouble?"

"No."

"I think that's a mistake."

Hubbard, after his burst of speech, had retreated into his silence again. He picked up his reading glasses and opened a file. He was already thinking about something else: all the interest had drained out of his face.

Wolkowicz rose to his feet and silently left the room. He was overwhelmed by admiration. Of course Hubbard was right—but what a leap of instinct, what effortless powers of the mind had landed him on the answer. Not one man in ten thousand would have been able to see what the Russians were really up to—or, seeing it, have had the courage to risk everything by betting on his own instincts. If Hubbard was wrong, he had just wrecked the American intelligence service in Germany for at least a generation. But Wolkowicz, who had a mind to match Hubbard's, knew that he was not wrong.

It was amazing how well Hubbard did his job without really being interested in it. He did it with 10 percent of his intelligence. What did he do with the other nine-tenths: write books? dream about his wife? Wolkowicz used every atom of his own ability in everything that he did, every day. He shook his head and laughed, then turned on his heel and went back into Hubbard's office.

"Sir?"

"Yes, Barney?"

Hubbard wore a look of mild puzzlement: Wolkowicz had never before called him "sir."

"If we're through with Ilse, I think I'll marry her," Wolkowicz said. "Will you be best man?"

"Of course," Hubbard replied, pushing back his chair and rising to his enormous height to congratulate his protégé. "Of course."

Wolkowicz beamed in pleasure.

— 8 —

A month after he returned from the honeymoon in Paris, Wolkowicz burst into Hubbard's office, still wearing a rain-soaked hat and the British trench coat Ilse had made him buy in the Faubourg Saint-Honoré. He was clutching a large stack of eight-by-ten photographs. He clicked his false teeth and gave a mocking smile, a mannerism of his when he was ill at ease.

"Got a minute?" he asked.

"Draw up a pew."

Hubbard stood up and held out his hand for Wolkowicz's raincoat. Struggling out of the garment, Wolkowicz passed the photographs from one hand to another as if they were too valuable, or too sensitive, to leave unguarded even for an instant. When he sat down again, he held the photographs on his lap.

"Even though we've closed down the Zechmann op," Wolkowicz said, "I kept running Bowstring. The stuff he brings in is mostly garbage, but then it turns out that he has access to captured SS and Gestapo documents—mostly files on dead Germans who were suspected of being politically unsympathetic."

Wolkowicz had given Horst Bülow a miniature camera and instructed him to photograph the files and deliver the film to him.

"It scared the guy shitless to do this, photographing one file at a time, working his way through the alphabet, but he's doing it," Wolkowicz said. "To me, it was just a way to break him in. Last week he got up to the Cs. I gave the film to the lab, but even if you kick their asses it takes them days to develop anything, so I just ten minutes ago picked this up."

Wolkowicz leaned forward and put the stack of photographs on the edge of Hubbard's desk. Hubbard had been sitting with his big shoes on the desk. Now, without moving his feet, he leaned across the desk and picked up the photos; they were still a little sticky from the developing bath and he had to peel each successive print away from the one below it. The first sheet was the standard cover page with its secret stamp and file number. Hubbard peeled it away.

The second page read: *CHRISTOPHER, Hannelore, born Buecheler.*

Above the name was a police photograph of Lori. The quality of the print was not good, but it appeared that Lori had been wearing a striped prison uniform when the picture was made. Her eyes, wide and clear, staring straight into the camera, pierced the fuzzy surface of this blurred photograph.

"Would you like me to leave for a while?" Wolkowicz asked.

"No," Hubbard said in a calm voice. "Stay."

He put his feet on the floor and hunched over the file, concentrating deeply. Each page was filled from top to bottom with neat typewritten sentences. Hubbard read each page twice. Finally he lifted his face.

"Did you read this?" he asked in his even tone.

"Just the first couple of pages. When I saw what it was I brought it right in to you."

"It's not complete. Part of the file is missing—everything after 1939. This only goes up to her arrest."

"He must have run out of film. We'll get the rest of it in the next batch."

"When?"

"Next Thursday. We have a meeting every other Thursday."

"It has to be sooner than that. Contact him and tell him to bring the rest tomorrow."

Nothing about Hubbard had changed, now that he had found what he had been searching for. There was no tremor in his voice, no difference in the way he looked across the desk at Wolkowicz.

"There is no secure way to contact this agent," Wolkowicz said.

"You don't have a dead drop, a chalk mark on a wall, any kind of signal for him?

"No. He's such a zero I never thought it would be necessary to see him in a hurry. I just tell him each time where and when to show up for the next meeting."

"There must be a way."

"It will scare the shit out of him. He's a bundle of nerves. It would have to be a brush contact, on the street."

"Can you do that yourself?"

"If you want me to. I'd have to catch him on the way to or from work. I've never gone into his neighborhood. It could blow the whole thing if I'm seen."

"Haven't you been seen with him at all those concerts?"

"We don't usually sit together. I'll do it, Hubbard, but if things go wrong, we'll never see the rest of the file. The Russians will grab him. I know how you feel, but it's only a week until the next routine contact. It's better to wait."

Hubbard cleared his throat. "I'd rather not wait," he said.

The two men sat in silence for long moments.

"There's another way," Wolkowicz said. "Ilse."

"He knows Ilse?"

"He met her once, remember. She could find some way to talk to him—get on the same streetcar and tell him what we want."

Wolkowicz looked at his watch.

"If I call her at the office," he said, "she can probably catch him on his way home from work. But that means talking on the phone."

Ilse still worked at the Zechmann Bureau. Hubbard pushed his telephone across the desk. Wolkowicz put his hand on the instrument and gave Hubbard a look in which sympathy was mixed with anxiety.

"Are you sure you want me to do this?" he said. "It's Zechmann's phone at the other end."

Hubbard nodded. Wolkowicz cleared his throat, twice. What he was about to do was such a breach of secrecy that he had to force his muscles to disobey the warning signals sent out by his brain in order to make the various parts of his body pick up the receiver, dial the number of the Zechmann Bureau, and tell Ilse, in a tangled web of hint and innuendo that even Hubbard could not follow, to accost Horst Bülow and tell him to come to an emergency meeting. He called Bülow the Music Man. By some miracle of quick wits, Ilse understood who he meant and what he wanted.

— 9 —

Horst Bülow chose the meeting place, a streetcar stop on a broad avenue running through the Wilmersdorf Wood, a point nearly as far from the Soviet Zone as it was possible to get. He set the time at 4:30 A.M., the hour of first light in Berlin in mid-August.

Hubbard and Wolkowicz, riding in the backseat of Hubbard's car, drove past the rendezvous point at 4:20. There was no sign of the agent. The street was deserted except for an old woman in black who came out of the forest carrying a bristling load of dead twigs slung over her back in a shawl. Hubbard's driver, a U.S. Army sergeant in civilian clothes, yawned.

"Keep awake, Mitchell," Wolkowicz said to the sergeant. "Drop me here and turn into the woods. I'll make the meeting, cross the street, and walk down this way. You watch my every move. If I lift my right arm, even if I only lift it three inches, put the car in gear and pick me up. Got it?"

The sergeant, yawning again, nodded. He smelled of schnapps. Wolkowicz got out of the car. Hubbard got out the other door.

"Are you coming too?" Wolkowicz said.

"I want to talk to him."

Hubbard got out of the car. He carried an envelope in his hand. Wolkowicz automatically registered this detail.

Wolkowicz hesitated, then set off, walking with his oddly endearing gait, feet slamming into the ground, elbows wagging. Hubbard sauntered along behind. A yellow streetcar, squealing and hissing sparks, stopped a couple of hundred meters up the street and a man got off. It was Bülow. He carried the inevitable briefcase in one hand and a rolled newspaper in the other. The old woman with the load of sticks climbed laboriously onto the platform after Bülow got off; he made no move to help her.

"That's him," Wolkowicz said.

The agent was on the opposite side of the street, too far away for his face to be visible, but it was obvious how nervous he was; he darted glances up and down the street and finally shrank into the fringe of the woods.

After the streetcar had passed and Wolkowicz had seen that there was no one aboard as it traveled away from the center of the city, the two Americans stepped off the curb and started to cross the road. Hubbard saw the sun flash on glass, but paid no attention. His eyes were on the agent, who was making a signal to indicate that it was safe to approach.

At that moment, Hubbard recognized Horst Bülow. He was older and thinner, but he was the same man he had known before the war. Out of the corner of his eye, Hubbard saw the sun flash on glass again and then he heard the shriek of tires. The car struck him.

"Jesus!" Wolkowicz said. He began to run, turning his wide face over his shoulder as if to warn Hubbard.

Hubbard saw the envelope fly out of his own hand, spinning. Then it froze in midair, stopped by some mysterious force. Hubbard felt his own body for the last time as it was lifted into the air. The impact ruptured his aorta, and in the fraction of a second of life that remained to him, he believed that he was flying. He descended into a beech forest. There was no pain. Freed from the lifelong weight of his long bones, he flew even more swiftly into the chalky light of the German morning.

Wolkowicz, who had leaped out of the way of the Mercedes, watched it turn around, leaning on its springs, and head back toward him. He pulled out his P-38 and, standing with one foot on either side of Hubbard's fallen body, methodically put all eight rounds through the windshield of the approaching car, into the face of the driver. The car crashed into a tree and began to burn. Wolkowicz, cursing in a steady roar, pulled the dead driver out of the flaming automobile.

Horst Bülow fled through the trees. The sergeant, who had leaped out of the car, fired five shots from a .45 automatic at his darting figure, missing all five times.

Wolkowicz carried Hubbard's body to his car and loaded it in the back, tenderly arranging the long twisted limbs on the seat.

"Aw, shit," he sobbed, tears flowing down his face. "Aw *shit!*"

Refusing all help from the sergeant, Wolkowicz heaved the leaking corpse of the German into the trunk and drove with both dead men to American headquarters, weeping and cursing and fumbling with loose cartridges as he attempted to reload his pistol.

Three

Wolkowicz delivered Hubbard Christopher's ashes to the Harbor on a
day in late September. Among the hemlocks the leaves of the swamp
maples had already turned scarlet, and higher up the mountain some of
the birches showed bright amber foliage. As the family stood in the
graveyard above the house, inside the circle of headstones, there was no
sound at all apart from the low moan of the wind through the woods,
and that seemed to make the hush deeper. Wolkowicz had never ex-
perienced such silence, not even in the Burmese jungle with its constant
hum of birds and insects. There were no prayers; Alice Hubbard had
wanted to have the Order for the Burial of the Dead read by an Episcopal minister, but Paul and Elliott would not agree. Neither had ever
heard Hubbard mention God.

Hubbard's friend Sebastian Laux, a small pale banker who looked
like a porcelain figurine among the gigantic Hubbard men and the
plump Hubbard aunts, read some of Hubbard's verses. A flight of crows
passed overhead, cawing raucously. Turning his back to the wind, Paul

opened the urn and let his father's ashes go, a puff of gray. As they drifted away toward the blue hills their parched scent was briefly noticeable. This only lasted a moment. There were no tears; no one comforted Paul. They all walked down the hill together through the pasture and then ate lunch in the sunny dining room, laughing and telling anecdotes about Hubbard's childhood. They did not seem to acknowledge that he was dead.

"The Hubbards are not natural mourners," Alice explained. "Death, to them, is Hubbard heaven. When their hearts stop, they go to an eternal family reunion in the sky. Even on earth, they never get bored with each other."

She was speaking to David Patchen, Paul's roommate at Harvard. Patchen had been surprised by the merriment. He was a gaunt young man, as tall as the Hubbards, with a vivid scar on the left side of his face. The whole left half of his body had been damaged in the war: he had an artificial eye, his eyelid was paralyzed so that he never blinked on that side of his face, his arm was withered, his leg was lame.

As the family rose from lunch, Alice took Patchen by the hand and led him into the library. She gave him a glass of port wine and lit a fire in the fireplace.

"Do you mind being alone?" she said. "We won't be missed, and now and again I do like talking to a non-Hubbard." They discussed Post-Impressionist painting; this had been Alice's passion at Vassar. "Elliott has custody of the Hubbard Cézannes," Alice said. "Some old uncle bought them from the artist for pocket money. I'm plotting to get half of them in a divorce settlement." With the living side of his face, Patchen smiled at the joke, but it was no joke. Alice had learned, the month before, that Elliott was sleeping with another woman. She chattered on. Patchen had never heard so many witticisms. From the next room came the plangent sound of the spinet. Wolkowicz was playing Bach again.

In his room, Paul sat by the window, reading the book of his father's poems:

> *Our son was born, you know, at the instant*
> *you took flight on the summer wind of*
> *your imagination, carrying that chalk island*
> *above the sun-drenched cloud tops,*
> *lifting my bones out of the muffling earth*
> *and putting eyes and tongue into my skull*

so that I might know the splendor of your gift
(a child with your heart and face and voice).

The music that had been floating through the house ceased and Paul heard someone in the hall outside his door. Wolkowicz knocked and entered, carrying an old scratched Gladstone bag that had belonged to Hubbard.

"Your father's things," he said, setting the suitcase down.

Wolkowicz was ill at ease, looking around the room at the pictures. His eyes examined Zaentz's drawing of Lori; when he saw that Paul was watching him, he looked away.

"My mother," Paul said. He smiled. "And me."

"You look a lot like her."

Paul nodded. He had heard this all his life.

"Was she quiet, too?"

"Quiet? No, not at all."

"Then you've got your father's personality."

Paul made no answer to that, but he gestured toward a chair. Wolkowicz hesitated, then sat down.

"Your friend is in pretty bad shape," Wolkowicz said.

Paul peered at him, puzzled. He had expected him to say something about Hubbard and it took him a moment to understand. Wolkowicz touched the left side of his face, tracing the line of Patchen's scar with a blunt forefinger.

"Oh, you mean Patchen," Paul said.

No one else at the Harbor had mentioned Patchen's wounds; Paul himself ignored them. But Wolkowicz had already memorized the shape of Patchen's scars.

"What happened to him?" Wolkowicz asked.

"Grenade. I don't know the details."

Wolkowicz nodded briskly. The moment Paul stopped speaking, he seemed to lose interest in this subject and be ready to go on to another. This was one of the marks of Hubbard's behavior; it seemed odd to Paul to see Wolkowicz, a stranger, using one of his father's mannerisms.

"About your father," Wolkowicz said. He had to clear his throat twice to get the sentence out. "Do you want to hear what happened?"

Paul nodded. Wolkowicz described Hubbard's death—just the way in which the car ran him down. Wolkowicz left out the meeting with Horst Bülow, the gunshots, the dead German. All that was secret; even Hubbard's son had no right to know such details.

Holding Wolkowicz's eyes, Paul listened intently to Wolkowicz's words. Wolkowicz saw that he didn't look exactly like his mother after all: he had his father's intelligence, so intense and silent that it seemed to be a danger signal.

Paul said, "You're telling me my father's death was a traffic accident?"

"He was hit by a car."

"At four-thirty in the morning, in the middle of the Wilmersdorf Wood?"

Paul, still staring into Wolkowicz's eyes, would not break off his glance. This scrutiny made Wolkowicz uncomfortable; he made no effort to conceal this. He held up his hand, as if to ward off more questions.

"That's all I have to tell you," he said. "I'm sorry."

Wolkowicz got to his feet. "I have to be going," he said. "There's a train to New York at four o'clock."

"Are you going back to Berlin?"

"No, I'm through in Berlin." Wolkowicz did not offer to explain further.

"Wait," Paul said. He heaved his father's heavy bag onto the bed and opened it. It contained no clothes, just Hubbard's reading glasses and wallet and his steel watch and wedding ring, and a thick package. Hoping that the package contained a manuscript, his father's last work, Paul ripped it open. There was no manuscript inside. The package was full of blurry photographs of concentration camp prisoners.

In each picture, a ring was drawn around the unrecognizable head of a woman. All the women were fair and small. Paul spread the photographs out on the bed. He gave Wolkowicz a puzzled look. Wolkowicz looked uncomfortable again, and once more he had to clear his throat before he could speak.

"He kept hoping he'd find your mother," Wolkowicz said. "He studied pictures from the camps and sometimes he'd find a woman who might be her. The same physical type, about the same size and age. People changed a lot in the camps. Still, he thought he might recognize her."

"But he never did?"

"No."

"He never found any trace of her at all—no file that mentioned her, no witness?"

"Your father never talked to you about this?"

"No, not about this part of it. He believed that my mother was alive. Did he find any trace, anything at all?"

"No," Wolkowicz said. "A lot of pictures, but no proof."

Wolkowicz said nothing about the file Hubbard had seen on the last day of his life. For all practical purposes, there was no file; it couldn't be completed. Horst Bülow, living in terror in East Berlin, would never obtain the missing pages, if missing pages had survived.

Paul studied him with Hubbard's calm, intelligent gaze.

"It wasn't a reasonable thing, Paul," Wolkowicz said, "to think there might be hope. It was sad, being with your father when he wouldn't give up hope. I'm sorry."

Wolkowicz gripped Paul's hand, a painful pressure. "I'm not telling you anything you don't already know," he said, "but your father was a great man. I'll never owe any man more than I owe him. If I can ever do anything for you, and I mean anything, just tell me. Elliott will know how to find me."

There were tears in Wolkowicz's eyes, the only tears that anyone had shed for Hubbard that day.

— 2 —

Before he returned to college, Paul went to New York. He found Zaentz in Greenwich Village and gave him the photographs Hubbard had collected. Opening the package, Zaentz recoiled.

"What are these, for God's sake?"

Paul explained.

"Why bring them to me?"

"You knew my mother's face better than anyone."

"I?"

"You drew her from memory after fifteen years. If anyone can recognize her face, if it's in those photographs, you can."

Zaentz spent the afternoon by the high window of his studio, an aging man with gleaming white hair, looking at the photographs again and again. Finally he stacked them together neatly and took off his steel-rimmed spectacles, unhooking the wire bows from his ears. He spoke to Paul in a low voice, in English.

"No," Zaentz said. "These women are not your mother. Your father is dead, Paul. You should let this obsession about your mother die too."

A week after Hubbard's funeral, Sebastian Laux came to Boston to see Paul. Paul thought that Sebastian wanted to discuss his father's will with him. He had been the family's banker and now, as trustee under the will, he had custody of Hubbard's estate.

In his suite at the Ritz-Carlton Hotel, Sebastian looked out the window onto the English Gardens.

"This is only the second time I've been to this city," he said. "It's just as I remembered it—a nice little park, lots of brick, and absolutely no sign of life. You must be very glad this is your last semester at . . . college." Sebastian, a Yale man, did not like to speak the word Harvard.

A waiter brought hot water and Sebastian made green tea, stirring it energetically with a bamboo whisk. As a young man, before the war, Sebastian had spent a year in Japan and ever since he had carried Japanese tea and Japanese tea bowls with him wherever he traveled. According to Elliott, Sebastian had brewed green tea for them behind the German lines in France, where they had been together, fighting with the Maquis.

He watched Paul drink the bitter tea. "Maybe you'd prefer something else?" he said.

"No, this is fine," Paul said.

Holding his bowl in both his tiny hands, Sebastian sipped his tea, inhaling a big gulp of air to cool each mouthful of liquid. During Paul's boyhood visits to the Harbor, Sebastian had explained that this vulgar noise was considered good manners in Japan. Paul had not seen him since those days, though Sebastian's bank, D. & D. Laux & Co., had paid his tuition bills and sent him his allowance when he was at school.

Sebastian had already told Paul that his father had left his entire estate to Lori. Paul would inherit if he petitioned the courts to declare his mother dead. This Paul had refused to do.

Sebastian finished his tea. "I suppose you still want to leave things as they are with your father's will," he said.

"Yes."

"The cash value of the estate, as of today, is $78,587.56," Sebastian said. "That may be a smaller sum than you imagined. Your father and mother gave a lot of money away before the war, almost their entire capital."

"They gave it away? How much?"

"Just over a quarter of a million dollars. I was always sending drafts to people with odd names in Copenhagen. I suppose they were the ones you and your parents smuggled out of Germany on that sailboat."

Paul, hiding a smile, looked into his tea bowl. He seemed pleased at the thought of Hubbard and Lori squandering his inheritance. This didn't surprise Sebastian. He had been handling the family's financial affairs for a quarter of a century and he didn't think it was possible to explain the way money worked to anyone who had a drop of Hubbard blood in his veins. Both Elliott Hubbard and Hubbard Christopher had always taken pleasure in giving money away—Elliott to his legion of girls and friends, Hubbard to terrified refugees. The cousins were not spendthrifts. They just seemed to find money slightly comical, like sex —one of the things in life it was impossible to understand and useless to resist.

"It isn't a bad idea to leave the money where it is," Sebastian said. "You ought to be able to earn your own living, and in time the balance will grow."

"Is there enough for my Aunt Hilde to live on?"

Paul's question was the first real sign of interest he had shown in this subject.

"Your father was quite specific about Aunt Hilde," Sebastian said. "We've been making quarterly transfers to Berlin from the interest. Their banks are operating again; things are getting back to normal with the Germans."

Paul nodded and looked around the room. He seemed ready to change the subject. So was Sebastian: he had not come to Boston to talk about money to Paul Christopher. Yet he didn't quite know how to start the conversation he wanted to have with him.

Gathering his thoughts, Sebastian went to the window and looked down again on the English Gardens. In the deepening twilight, crowds of people were streaming through the gates of the park. Sebastian had keen eyesight, and even from this distance he noticed that there was something odd about the Bostonians. With a small thrill of satisfaction, he realized what it was—they looked alike; most of them had Irish faces.

"Did you know, Paul," Sebastian asked, "exactly what it was your father was doing in Berlin?"

"What he did, Sebastian? Of course."

"He told you? I don't mean his writing."

"He was a spy. He didn't tell me. He didn't need to. It was obvious."

Sebastian lifted his eyebrows, then chuckled. "I suppose it was. Nevertheless, your father was extremely good at the work. When he died, he was chief of American intelligence in Berlin." Sebastian paused. "I used the word *died,*" he said. "But you do realize that he was murdered?"

Hearing this, Paul did not move or speak; he simply continued to listen, waiting for Sebastian to go on. Sebastian searched Paul's face for some sign of surprise, for some flash of anger or hatred. Like Wolkowicz before him, he saw only the calm, sad intelligence he had witnessed so often in Hubbard's face. Finally, Paul asked a question.

"Why are you the one to tell me this, Sebastian?"

"Elliott couldn't bring himself to do it. I'm . . . *trusted* by the men your father worked with. I knew them in the war."

"Do they know who did it?"

"In a general way," Sebastian said. "It was the opposition."

"The Russians? Why would they do it?"

"One never knows the answer to that question, not the exact answer. I gather they had a lot of respect for him; he was too good at his work. They feared him."

"Was it really as simple as that? As stupid as that?"

Sebastian thought the question over carefully. "Yes," he replied. "Very probably."

— 4 —

The next day, Sebastian and Paul went down to Washington together. The Outfit was giving Hubbard a posthumous medal; that was why Sebastian had been sent to tell him that his father had been murdered. Hubbard's colleagues wanted Paul to accept his father's decoration. On the train, Sebastian gave Paul a slip of paper to sign. It was a promise never to reveal what Sebastian had told him; it asked him to promise, too, never to reveal that he had attended the ceremony.

"It may seem strange to you, to decorate a man in secret, after he's dead, but those are the rules," Sebastian said.

Paul signed the secrecy agreement.

In Washington, Sebastian led him down a dim corridor past rows of tall polished doors. Sebastian opened one of them and they walked across an empty anteroom into a paneled conference room. Prints of square-rigged sailing ships decorated the walls. A little group of men stood by the window, talking. Among them was Elliott Hubbard, who hurried across the room to greet Paul. Behind him, at the edge of the group, stood Wolkowicz. At his side was a remarkably pretty blond girl. She smiled brilliantly at Paul, as if he were an old friend for whom she had been waiting.

Elliott led Paul to the window and introduced them to the other men. Wolkowicz waited, hanging back, until this was over. Then, in his clumsy way, he stepped forward and shook hands.

"My wife, Ilse," Wolkowicz said.

Ilse shook hands and repeated her smile. She wore white gloves. Paul was astonished that Wolkowicz should have married a girl who looked like this. Ilse read the surprise on his face but made not the slightest acknowledgment.

"I knew your father very well, so I know what you have lost," she said in German, squeezing his hand. "You have my sympathy."

Elliott touched Paul's arm. "I think they want to begin," he said. He and Paul joined the others. Except for Wolkowicz, who wore a brown gabardine suit, all the men were dressed alike, in well-pressed dark suits with vests and striped ties. Their shirts were very fresh, as if they had changed them specially for the ceremony.

The ceremony was brief. Wolkowicz and Paul Christopher stood shoulder to shoulder, facing the Director, while an aide read a citation. It was a description of Wolkowicz's actions on the morning of Hubbard Christopher's death. In this way, standing at attention in a room full of strangers, Paul learned the full, bloody circumstances of his father's death.

The Director hung a medal around Wolkowicz's neck and gave him a sympathetic look, as if he, rather than Paul, were the bereaved son. "It wasn't your fault we lost him, lad," he said.

The aide read Hubbard's citation and the Director gave Paul his father's medal in its open case.

Champagne was served. It was nine o'clock in the morning.

"From now on I think we'll have these things a little later in the day," the Director said. "This is the first time we've done it, so whoever is responsible for the champagne must be interested in establishing a tradition. Do you think your father would have minded the festive atmosphere?"

[149]

"No. He liked champagne."

"I admired Hubbard," the Director said. "Everyone did. No one will ever know the great things he did. I suppose he would have preferred it that way, but to me it's sad. He did so much for his country and nobody will know it."

"Perhaps nobody wants to know," Ilse said. The waiter passed by and she held out her glass for more champagne.

"Who do you mean?" the Director said, smiling. Ilse was so pretty, so fragrant in her spotless linen suit and her white gloves. She smelled of her rose perfume.

"Those outside. They prefer to think that men like Hubbard, men like my husband, do not exist—that they are not necessary. Protect me and say nothing! That is what they want."

The Director was taken aback. "Do you really think so?" he said politely.

"Our German poet Schiller wrote, 'Against stupidity the gods themselves struggle in vain,'" Ilse said. She repeated the words in German, looking directly into Paul's face. Wolkowicz, his medal dangling from his neck, stood with them, unsmiling.

"Ah, yes," the Director said. "Schiller."

The aide approached, holding the box for Wolkowicz's medal in his hands.

"Time to give that back," he said. Wolkowicz took off his decoration and handed it over. The aide held out his hand for Hubbard's medal. Paul gave it to him; the aide snapped the leather boxes shut.

"I'm afraid this is the last you'll ever see of these," he said. "We lock them in the Director's safe. "It would be quite a coup to the opposition to know who we're decorating. You'll know the medal's there; that's supposed to be enough."

— 5 —

In the spring, the Director, finding himself in Boston, invited Paul and David Patchen to supper at Locke-Ober's restaurant. While Patchen was out of the room, he asked Paul to join the Outfit.

"Even if you weren't your father's son and Elliott's nephew, we'd want you," the Director said. "You understand the Germans and the

French, you speak their languages. That's pure gold to us. Besides, I've been reading your poems."

During the war, and afterward at Harvard, Paul had written enough poems to be collected into a book, and his father's publisher had printed them. He thought that the mild publicity his book received—a few brief reviews in newspapers and magazines—might disturb the Outfit.

"No, no, it's wonderful cover," said the Director.

"Cover?"

"Yes. You're a genuine poet, a hell of an advantage. You can live anywhere, see anybody. You don't have to explain yourself. You have a reason to live in the real world. Damn few spies do."

Christopher had been concerned about Patchen's future. He decided to put in a word for him. The Director listened with twinkling eyes.

"David Patchen is already with us," he said. "Fine boy. He was with us in the war. We dropped him into a hornet's nest on Okinawa, you know—that's where he got his wounds, going in ahead of the invasion. He radioed the information in spite of his wounds. David is remembered. He'll always have a home with the Outfit."

Paul accepted the Director's offer. In later years he would try to remember his feelings at this moment, when he stepped out of the real world and into the secret world. Had he thought about his father? Had he remembered the hidden Jews aboard *Mahican*, the Dandy, the Gestapo men who had beaten his father and arrested his mother? Had he been motivated by love of America, by the idea of freedom? He didn't know. What he remembered was a great feeling of relief: the Director had offered him privacy, a world in which honors were locked in a safe, a world in which everything could be known and nothing revealed, a world in which there could be no inexplicable disappearances.

— 6 —

Because he could speak French, the Outfit sent Christopher to Indochina, where the French were fighting a war against Communist guerrillas. Wolkowicz seemed to know of this assignment even before Christopher did. On the day his orders were issued, Wolkowicz invited him to lunch.

Christopher was surprised to hear Wolkowicz's voice on the telephone. In the six months he had been working for the Outfit, he had seen nothing of Wolkowicz. There was nothing unusual in that: the Outfit had no central headquarters; its staff was scattered around Washington in temporary buildings, in odd corners of other departments of the government, in private office buildings and safe houses. There was no telephone directory. Wolkowicz knew Christopher's number in the way that he seemed to know everything else, by that superdeveloped instinct for learning secrets that Hubbard had noted in him.

"Do you like oysters?" Wolkowicz asked on the phone. "Good. Meet me at twelve in the aquarium."

Wolkowicz was watching the tropical fish when Christopher arrived. He opened a grease-stained paper sack and handed Christopher his lunch—a hamburger bun with a deep-fried Chesapeake oyster the size of a flattened tennis ball inside it.

"I put ketchup on it," Wolkowicz said. "I hope that's okay." He bit into his own sandwich. "Best oyster sandwich in town," he said. "I get them from this takeout place down by the river."

The aquarium was crowded during the lunch hour with other government workers. Wolkowicz, wolfing his sandwich as he went, led Christopher outside. They walked in silence across Constitution Avenue to the mall. Wolkowicz sat down on a park bench.

"I think we'll be all right here," he said. "I wanted to talk to you about what you're going to run into in Hanoi."

"Have you been there?"

"Not to Hanoi, but I spent part of the war with the guy who's going to be your case officer out there. Waddy Jessup."

"You spent the war with Waddy?"

"We were together in Burma. He's a touchhole cousin of yours, I hear."

Wolkowicz curled his upper lip and tapped his false teeth with the nail of his index finger. "Burma," he said. "Jesus." He seemed to be speaking to himself. Then his eyes came back into focus and he spoke to Christopher.

"Look," he said, "I've got a strange feeling about you, like you're my responsibility. It's because of your father, but not all because of him. You seemed like a good guy the first time I met you, at that Christmas party. Then at your father's funeral I felt like a shit. What happened in Berlin shouldn't have happened. Not to him."

"I agree, but nobody thinks it was your fault."

"Fuck what anybody thinks. I was there."

Wolkowicz shook his head, a bearish movement. His muscles seemed to work involuntarily, like an animal's: one moment he was at rest, utterly motionless, and the next he was moving at full speed.

"What you want to do when you get to Hanoi," Wolkowicz said, "is watch it with Waddy Jessup. He's dangerous."

"Dangerous?"

"Dangerous." Wolkowicz dug a finger into Christopher's thigh to emphasize the word. "Waddy used to wear a Yale track shirt out in the jungle. They fried his brains at Yale. They do that to everybody—the Outfit is full of the cocksuckers, they hire each other—but Waddy is something special. He's not only a fool, he's yellow, and if you don't watch him he'll get you killed."

Christopher could think of no reply. Wolkowicz peered into his face.

"I take a short lunch hour," Wolkowicz said. "You're leaving. It would have been better to lead up to what I'm telling you instead of just hitting you with it, but we haven't got the time. If I'd known what was going on I would have found a way to keep you out of Indochina as long as Waddy is there. I *didn't* know. So I'm telling you now: watch out for Waddy. And for Christ's sake, don't go out on any ops with him, especially not in the jungle."

"I'll remember what you've said," Christopher said.

He got to his feet. Wolkowicz, still seated on the bench, looked up at him. While he spoke about Waddy Jessup, his broad face had been twisted in disgust. Now his expression changed and once again he looked sad—close to tears, even, as he had looked at the Harbor when speaking of Hubbard.

"I hope so," Wolkowicz said. "Waddy's done enough damage." He cleared his throat and spat, another automatic response, like a dog biting at a wound on its own body. "So have I," he said.

A month before Christopher's arrival in Hanoi, Waddy Jessup smuggled fifty copies of his book of poems into Vietnam by diplomatic pouch. Waddy's agents then distributed these volumes surreptitiously on the shelves of bookstores, returning every other day for two weeks to see if they had been sold. Fifteen of them were sold. Waddy bribed a local journalist to write a favorable review of Christopher's book.

Waddy was convinced that his book-smuggling operation had eased Christopher's passage into the heart of the local avant-garde when, only days after reaching Indochina, Christopher met a fellow poet, a Tonkinese who had studied at the Sorbonne, who introduced him to the local café intelligentsia, a mixed group of European and Vietnamese Communists and fellow travelers. The fact that the Tonkinese poet was a female who fell in love with Christopher did not seem important to Waddy.

"She read your poems," Waddy said to Christopher; "that was the key—your aura as an *artiste*. I fixed you up with the aura. All you have to do now is glow."

Waddy and Christopher met once a week, in the cool of the early morning, to play tennis on a court owned by a French colon. The tennis gave them a reason to see each other; even to the Tonkinese girl, it seemed natural that a man with Christopher's athletic body might want to play a bourgeois game once a week. Between sets, Waddy outlined Christopher's mission in Indochina.

"The job of an intelligence service," Waddy said, "is to stay in with the outs. Just now the Vietminh are the outs, but not for long. The French are going to lose this colony, thank God, and when they do the United States must have friends among the new people. That's where you come in."

"Why do you say *thank God*, Waddy?"

"Because Vietnam belongs to the Vietnamese, because colonialism has had its day, because the white man must lay down his burden. You and I are going to help the white man do that."

"The French are our allies."

"Of course they are. That's why you don't have to waste time making friends with them. Your job is to make friends with their enemies; love their enemies, Paul—that's your credo."

"The French won't love me for that."

'Well, I ask you: who *do* the French love? Do you want to be the first American they've ever admired? The worst they can do is throw you out of Indochina, but before they do, the Vietminh will love you. You're already sleeping with one of them. By the time the French have you out, the country will be teeming with little brown friends of yours."

Christopher's Tonkinese girl taught him Vietnamese. He learned languages easily and within a few months he was able to converse with fair fluency. Her poems were too angry to be published in an occupied country, but they were distributed by an underground press: Waddy provided money for the purchase of a printing press, and this was set up in a house in the native quarter. Christopher's girl worked as a printer and she would come home late at night with the smell of ink on her golden skin. So long as the sun was out or a lamp was lit, she talked politics, but in bed she never spoke; she would fall asleep lying on top of Christopher and in the night he would lift her feathery body with its fragile bones and place it on the mat beside him. She was called Lê, a common Vietnamese name that means "tears."

Christopher had a commission from an American magazine that had printed some of his poems to write about Indochina. The American press was filled with stories written from the French point of view: American correspondents in Indochina drank in French clubs, ate in French restaurants, went to briefings by the French military. They went out with French troops and watched as the rebels—fragile, fleet young people in black pajamas—were hunted and shot like deer as they sped through the trees or went to the river at dusk.

Christopher, who on Waddy's instructions had not met a single French person in Hanoi, proposed to write about the other side. By now the Vietminh trusted him. One night, guided by a friend of Lê's, he got onto a boat in the Red River, and a few hours later was put ashore. There he was met by a Vietminh patrol. In their company, he walked a hundred miles through the jungle to an underground encampment, a whole town hidden beneath the earth. As his guide led him through miles of tunnels, running beneath the forest, Christopher asked what had happened to the dirt; not a single shovelful could be seen aboveground. "It was carried away in cloths, a shovelful in each cloth, and put somewhere else," the guide said. Christopher realized that Waddy Jessup was right: the French had lost this colony. There was no possibility of defeating an enemy who would carry away a thousand tons of dirt in handkerchiefs.

Christopher spent a month with the Vietminh, lying hidden during the day, moving and attacking by night. While Christopher accompanied them, the Vietminh were ruthless and destructive, but they fought with scrupulous honor, never harming a civilian. Their targets were exclusively French: patrols of French soldiers, outlying French plantations. They fought the French in the way the Japanese had fought Christopher and the U.S. Marines in the Pacific jungles: with animal stealth and fearless skill.

Then one morning the patrol walked into a quiet village. There was no sign of life. While the guerrillas waited, weapons at the ready in case this should be a French ambush, their leader went into the headman's hut. Christopher heard voices inside and the sudden piercing cry of a child. Before the Vietminh could stop him, he ducked into another hut. A woman crouched on the dirt floor, clutching two children, a boy of five or six and a girl of three. Both children had chopsticks driven into their ears. Evidently this had been done to them during the night, because the blood on their cheeks was still wet: the girl was unconscious and Christopher touched her face with his forefinger. The mother spoke to him in broken French; she did not seem to be afraid of him, but when two Vietminh soldiers came into the hut, she gasped and stopped speaking. The Vietminh herded everyone outside. Every child in the village had chopsticks driven into its ears.

At the edge of the village, lying in an uncovered grave, were the bodies of a dozen men and women; their right hands and their heads had been cut off. Among them was a Catholic priest, a Frenchman who had had a bald head and a peevish sharp face; even in death he seemed sure of his opinions. He reminded Christopher of one of the masters at his school in Switzerland. The guerrilla leader found Christopher at the edge of the open pit. Lifting his voice above the sound of the droning flies, the Vietminh officer said, "This is what the French do to our people." Then he saw the priest's body in its cassock and the priest's severed head, and he called for a working party of villagers to fill the grave.

Christopher wandered away. He asked no questions of the villagers, but he listened to what they were saying to one another. A Vietminh educational squad had done all this as a lesson to the village. It was a Catholic village; they had heard that the priest had come to live there because he believed that his presence, as a Frenchman and as a priest, could protect the villagers.

It was important to the Vietminh to prove him wrong. First the educational squad had cut off the right hands of every Catholic in the village (because those hands had been used to make the sign of the cross), then they had beheaded them, then they had held a lesson in revolutionary doctrine, then they had sung patriotic songs. And then they had driven the chopsticks into the children's ears.

"What's the point of writing about the *chopsticks?*" Waddy Jessup asked, back in Hanoi. "It's an isolated incident, not at all typical of the Vietminh. It could have been a French trick, they could have sent out some of the thugs posing as Vietminh."

"The French beheaded a French priest? Do you really believe that, Waddy?"

Waddy toweled his sweaty hair; they had just finished their tennis. "You're new to this work, Paul," he said. "Trust me. If what you've written appears in print, you'll throw away everything you've worked for here. You'll lose that delicious Tonkinese girl, you'll lose all your friends."

Christopher sent off his story as he had written it. Waddy needn't have worried: the editors of the magazine removed the description of the chopsticks. When he returned to New York, Christopher asked why.

"Didn't you think it was just a little racist?" asked the editor who had handled the story. "I mean, really, Paul—fiendish Asians pounding things into the ears of babies. It's like eight-millimeter pornography run backward. The stuff about the patrol and the city of tunnels was great, though."

By that time, Waddy Jessup had already been back in America for nearly a year. Christopher had received news of his departure from Hanoi from David Patchen. One morning, when he arrived for his regular tennis game with Waddy, David Patchen awaited him. He had come out from Washington to introduce him to his new case officer.

"Waddy was called home pretty suddenly," Patchen said. "You were upcountry, he said—*upcountry* was Waddy's word—so he couldn't say good-bye."

"Will he be back?"

"No," Patchen said. He was wearing his summer clothes, a wrinkled seersucker suit and a black knitted tie. The new man, dressed in tennis whites, volleyed off the board fence of the court. Patchen shot him a look, to be certain he wasn't within earshot.

"It was the polygraph," Patchen said.

As a security measure, the Outfit had given all its officers lie detector tests. Strapped to the machine—"fluttered," in the argot—they were asked if they were enemy agents, if they had stolen money, if they were homosexuals.

"You can guess which questions gave Waddy trouble," Patchen said. "They've given him a job in the Foreign Service. Nothing sensitive. I believe he's in the protocol office. He's good with wives."

— 8 —

When, after the defeat of the French at Dien Bien Phu, Christopher returned to the United States, he stayed with Elliott Hubbard at his house in New York. The house looked as if it had been burglarized. Half the paintings were missing, leaving patches of lighter paper along the walls. The pictures had gone with Alice when she divorced Elliott.

Elliott's new wife, a dreamy woman about Christopher's age, was a painter. Three or four of her muddy abstractions hung in the places where the Cézanne, the Seurat, the Cassatt, the Hicks had formerly been displayed.

The new wife's name was Emily. She had turned the attic into a studio, and Christopher followed Elliott up the stairs to be introduced to her. She wore a smock smeared with paint; the brush she gripped in her teeth had left a streak of vermilion on her cheek. A big window had been built into the roof to admit the light and through it there was a view of Central Park. Emily seemed to be painting a landscape of the park, for she peered intently through the window as she worked.

"Oh," she said, greeting Christopher. "I've dreaded meeting you. You've had such a sad life, and I can't understand your poems. This is Julian."

She led Christopher by the hand to a playpen where a child slept in a litter of educational toys made of unpainted blocks of wood.

"He looks like Elliott," Christopher said, gazing at the sleeping baby.

"Yes. Elliott's family has very strong genes. You're the first relative I've met who doesn't look exactly like them."

Emily did not seem to expect him to answer. Even as she spoke, her attention slipped out of Christopher's grasp like a trout and she turned without another word and strode across the room toward the huge unfinished painting that stood on her easel. The picture looked to Christopher like a gutter puddle on a gloomy day. Frowning in concentration, Emily added more red to what seemed to be a rainbow of motor oil in the lower left-hand corner. She was a serious painter, but not a very talented one.

Alice Hubbard agreed with this judgment. On Saturday morning, Christopher went to Alice's new apartment, on the other side of Central Park, to fetch Horace, who spent weekends in his father's house. Alice had obtained the missing Post-Impressionists as part of her property settlement, and these hung on her walls, illuminated by spotlights.

"You're staying with Elliott?" Alice said. "How do you like the Hubbard abstractionist?"

"Emily? I've just met her. She's very good-looking."

"And so talented. I hear her paintings are hanging where these outmoded things used to be. We all get what we deserve. May one ask where you've been all this time?"

"Indochina."

"Indochina? Did you run into Waddy out there?"

"Yes."

"He never mentioned it. Don't tell me you're a spy now, too?"

Alice laid a hand on Christopher's arm, apologizing for her remark. Divorce had changed her: the old headlong Alice would never have made such a humble gesture.

"No matter," she said. "Maybe you can talk to Waddy about old times and cheer him up. He's terribly depressed."

"I don't know if I'll see him."

"Of course you'll see him. He's staying with me, poor fellow. Join us for lunch. It'll do Waddy a world of good. Me, too."

Christopher took a breath, then smiled. Waddy Jessup was the last person in New York with whom he wanted to have lunch.

"All right," he said.

Alice saw what was passing through his mind. "Trapped," she said. "Too bad. But it can't be worse than eating raw fish with that trollop who's doing the new paintings for Elliott. At least Waddy doesn't smell of turpentine."

They could hear Horace running down the hall, calling Christopher's name, and Waddy's laughter, a wild tenor trill that ended in a fit of coughing, in the background.

After he had completed his greetings to Horace, now sixteen years old and taller than his mother, Christopher said hello to Waddy. His handshake, once so firm, was weak. He seemed to have a tremor, and this was transmitted through his limp hand. His eyes were rimmed in red. He needed a haircut. His clothes were rumpled. He had gin on his breath.

Alice shooed them into the dining room. The table was already laid for four. Waddy poured the wine, a yellowish Mosel. While Alice and Christopher ate their asparagus, each taking two or three sips of wine, Waddy finished off the bottle and went into the kitchen to open another.

"What's wrong with Waddy?" Christopher asked.

"He's being investigated."

"Investigated?"

"By Congress. They think he's a Communist."

"He *is* a Communist."

Waddy returned with a tall green bottle. With trembling hand, he poured more wine—droplets for Alice and Christopher, a brimming glassful for himself. He stared resentfully at Christopher.

"I was listening in the kitchen," he said. "Why do you say I'm a Communist, Paul?" These were very nearly the first words he had spoken.

"You've always said you were."

"Have I? I don't recall that at all. It's that lout of a Wolkowicz who's spreading these lies about me."

"Oh, Waddy, come off it," Alice said. "It's just us. You've always been a raving Red."

"A progressive, maybe. A man with progressive friends, people with a little human feeling . . ."

"Then why did you call yourself a Communist? You drove Father to distraction with it. You came home from Yale spouting Marx."

"That was meant to be a joke. *You* know that, Alice."

Alice, taking away the plates, paused at Waddy's shoulder. He handed her his untouched asparagus.

"Is that going to be your defense?" Alice said. "That you were just kidding? For fifteen years?"

"It happens to be the truth."

"Really? You had me fooled."

Alice went into the kitchen. Waddy poured himself more wine. The

[160]

sweetish burnt aroma of a cooking omelet drifted into the dining room along with the noise of a pan being shaken on the stove. Waddy gazed out the window, saying nothing.

When Alice returned with a copper skillet in her hand, Waddy began talking again. Christopher wondered if he thought he should have a witness or if he simply needed the reassurance of his sister's presence.

"You've been abroad, Paul," Waddy said, "so you don't know what's been going on in this country. The Republicans have taken over Congress and they're after the intellectuals. It's a putsch."

Alice held the omelet pan over Waddy's plate.

"Are you going to have eggs?"

Waddy nodded. "A *putsch*," he repeated.

Alice put a small portion of omelet onto his plate. "Eat it up, Waddy," she said. "Your liver is going to kill you before the Republicans do."

Waddy put a fragment of omelet into his mouth but did not swallow it. Horace, shoveling his own eggs into his mouth, watched in fascination. Waddy seemed to have forgotten how to eat.

"Chew, Waddy," Alice said. "Swallow. I don't understand why you want to deny that you're a Red. Fight for the cause, that's what you always said."

Waddy gave her a furtive glance. "Not in front of Paul," he said.

"Not in front of Paul? Do you think *he's* an agent of the Republicans?"

"I'm not sure what Paul is. Paul has strange friends. Wolkowicz and Hubbard were close. What a joke! I *sent* that ape to Hubbard, and now look where he is."

"Oh, for heaven's sake," Alice said. "What can you say that Paul doesn't already know? He's been listening to you rave for years. So has everybody else. It's not against the law to be a Communist. It's stupid, but it's not against the law. Stop being such a rabbit, Waddy. Go before that congressional committee and say, 'You're damn right I'm a Communist. Proud of it!' I mean, really—what can they *do?*"

"They can send me to prison."

Alice laughed. Waddy winced.

"It wouldn't be a *long* sentence, Waddy," Alice said. "Besides, think what a hero you'd be to all your revolutionary pals when you got out. 'They couldn't break old Waddy!' That's what they'd say."

Christopher had been watching the play of amusement and mischief over Alice's face. She had popped a morsel of bread into her mouth as she finished speaking, and was chewing rapidly.

"Besides," she said, "prison might be very satisfying in certain ways. I hear the jailbirds go in for free love. That was always one of your revolutionary principles."

Alice broke off more bread. Her eyes were on Waddy. She stopped chewing, her jaw to one side, her mouth slightly ajar. A look of alarm spread over her face.

"Waddy," Alice said, her voice muffled by the food in her mouth.

Waddy seemed to be having a seizure. His eyes were wide open, his lips were pulled back from his teeth. His body shuddered, every jointed part quivering, as if some living thing were rushing through the passages of his belly and throat and would soon leap out of his mouth onto the table. He uttered a huge dry sob, then another, and with his eyes fixed on Christopher he went into hysterics.

"He's having another crying jag," Alice said. "Shake him, Paul." She swallowed her bread and leaped to her feet.

Christopher pulled Waddy out of his chair and spoke his name, but Waddy continued to sob in a hoarse, heartbroken voice. Christopher shook him. It had no effect.

"Harder," Alice said.

Christopher, who was younger and much larger than Waddy, shook him as hard as he dared. Waddy's head rolled, his arms flapped, he continued to stare into nothingness. Christopher slapped him. The sobbing broke, then started again. Christopher slapped him again. Waddy stopped making noise.

Alice put an arm around Waddy's waist and led him into a bedroom. In a moment she came back.

"I think he'd better have a talk with Elliott, don't you?" she said. "Nobody else can reassure him. Waddy's such a spineless fool. Forget I said that, Horace, but for God's sake, *you* be a man, will you?"

Four

While Wadsworth Jessup was having hysterics in New York, Barney
Wolkowicz, in Washington, was supervising the search of an apartment
belonging to a government secretary named Jocelyn Frick. It was a fussy
spinster's flat, furnished with antiques that were too beautiful for the
tiny rooms. There were stuffed animals on the bed. Wolkowicz watched
while a federal agent, not a member of the Outfit, took apart a Teddy
bear, searched the stuffing, and then, glasses perched on his nose, sewed
it together again, using the original thread.

Jocelyn Frick was a Soviet agent. Wolkowicz, tracking another
suspect, had found a faint sign that this might be true; he had followed
it up, and now, six months later, a team of agents trained in surreptitious
entry, the euphemism used to describe the burglary of the homes of
suspected spies and traitors, had taken her apartment to pieces and put
it back together again.

Jocelyn Frick was the youngest daughter of a justice of the Supreme
Court of Virginia. His photograph, a Bachrach portrait of a white-

maned man in judicial robes, stood beside her bed; her father had autographed the picture: *To my darling "Cinders," from her vy. affect. Daddy, R. Beaulieu Frick.* Her father had called her Cinders, short for Cinderella, because she had been a helpful child who had waited long to blossom into prettiness. Even then, her sisters considered her plump; men thought she was voluptuous. Like her beautiful sisters, she had gone to Sweet Briar and been presented to society at the Spring Cotillion, but she had not married. Instead, she had fallen in love with a gloomy Armenian named Mordecai Bashian. This was entirely unexpected. Three boys from good Tidewater families had proposed marriage to Jocelyn, but after graduating from college in the middle of the Great Depression, she had wanted to be a bachelor girl for a year or so. Her father, who had influence with the New Deal, had got Jocelyn a job in the Bureau of Labor Standards.

All this, and a good deal more, Wolkowicz knew. His full-field investigation of Jocelyn had turned up many facts. The microphones he had planted in her apartment gave him a glimpse of the inside of Jocelyn's mind and heart, because she had the habit of talking to herself —or, rather, to an imaginary friend. When she was all alone in her apartment, especially if she had had a secret drink or two, Jocelyn would pour out her heart to the empty air, exactly as if she were confiding in an old and trusted friend. Wolkowicz's listening devices heard everything she said.

The Armenian Jocelyn loved, Mordecai Bashian, was her supervisor at the Bureau of Labor Standards. Jocelyn's jolly manner and her pretty clothes, when she reported for duty, did not impress Bashian. He seemed to take an immediate dislike to her, a new experience for Jocelyn, who had been teased and petted by males all her life. At twenty-one, she was flirtatious, but she was sexually innocent, unless you count, as Jocelyn did not, an occasional game of mousy-mousy. Mordecai Bashian seemed to be offended by her femininity. He loaded her with dull paperwork, document after document written in stuffy bureaucratic language she could hardly understand, and he made her stay in the office deep into the night, typing, so that whatever silly report he had demanded would be on his desk when he came in in the morning. Tears fell onto the spongy mimeograph paper as Jocelyn typed away in her little island of electric light with the dark hushed city all around her.

After months of this torture (her boss never seemed to read her work, certainly he never commented on it) Mordecai Bashian came into

Jocelyn's office one evening, took her camel's-hair polo coat off its hanger, and threw it onto her desk, sending documents flying. "Come on, let's go to dinner," he said. Surprised into agreeing, Jocelyn got into a cab with him and went to an Italian restaurant in a cellar, way down on Maine Avenue, by the Potomac.

Jocelyn had never thought of Mordecai Bashian as being good-looking; he was swarthy and long-nosed and he slouched. He never smiled. He spoke in a hard monotone; there were no masculine ripples in his voice—no humor, no undertone of teasing. But in the smoky light of the Italian restaurant Bashian looked quite different. The waiters knew him. He laughed and joked with them and ordered veal par-migiana and a bottle of Chianti. Somebody was playing a concertina in the next room. Jocelyn had never eaten real Italian food before. The wine bottle in its basket, the crusty veal with its rubbery slab of strange white cheese covered with tomato sauce (Bashian even knew the name of the cheese), the waxy smell from all the candles guttering in the necks of bottles, the lilting notes of the concertina—the atmosphere hypno-tized Jocelyn. Also, she drank a lot of sour red wine; Bashian kept filling her glass from the enormous bottle. All the while, he talked to her steadily, staring at her. His dark brown eyes were like the eyes of a Negro except that Bashian's eyes were unkind.

Mordecai Bashian talked about Negroes. He seemed to know an entirely different type of darky from the ones Jocelyn had grown up with in Virginia. Her stories about her mammy and the pickaninny playmates of her childhood infuriated Bashian. "Pickaninnies?" he said. "Pickaninnies! Those pickaninnies are going to smear the blood of people like you all over the pages of history." Bashian grinned sardonically, the first sign of humor she had ever detected on his face, when Jocelyn recoiled at these words. "Afraid?" he said. "You'd *better* be afraid." But Jocelyn was not afraid of Negroes; she was shocked that Bashian could even imagine that the fine colored people she had known all her life could be capable of such horrors. She told him how much she loved her family's Negroes and how much those Negroes loved her family. "Don't you smirk at me, Mordecai Bashian," Jocelyn cried as another nasty smile twisted his lips. "I don't know what a smart-mouth Jew from New York City thinks he knows about my mammy!"

At that, Bashian rose from his chair, the brownish skin of his face turning red. "So you're a dirty little anti-Semite too," he said. "It so happens I'm an Armenian. I don't suppose you know what that is, do you?" He stamped out of the restaurant. Jocelyn, who had never known that a man could be insulted by anything a girl said to him, tried to run after Mordecai Bashian to apologize, but the waiters stopped her and made her pay the bill, which amounted to almost four dollars.

When Jocelyn did get outside, there was no sign of Mordecai Bashian. The street was empty. A fog had come in, hiding all but the masts of the boats that lay at anchor in the river. It was spooky: all was silence except the hulls of the boats squeaking as they rolled in the tide or the current or whatever made them move. Jocelyn drew on her gloves (she never felt fully dressed without gloves). There were no taxis in sight. Jocelyn had never been in a situation in which there was no one there to take care of her. Her bosom filled up with tears, as it always did when her feelings had been hurt really badly. She sniffled. Then, deciding to make the best of things, she walked bravely into the wall of fog.

Jocelyn didn't know exactly where she was. She didn't really know Washington very well; she was always getting turned around. This old street was paved with stones and her heel went into a crack and she turned her ankle. She remembered the wounding, nasty words Mordecai Bashian had spoken to her. She began to cry in earnest. The fog was thickening by the minute; she could barely make out the shapes of buildings only a few feet away. Presently Jocelyn arrived at the Fourteenth Street bridge. She thought she knew where she was and hurried on. Then, with a leap of the heart, she heard a man cough, a frightening noise distorted by the fog. Jocelyn quickened her step. Out of the corner of her eye, she saw a shape moving in the mist. She was sure it was the coughing man. He was following her. She could hear his cough.

There wasn't a soul in sight. Jocelyn could see streetlights on the bridge, gauzy in the fog, but she heard no sound at all—not a car, not a voice. Jocelyn's stomach knotted. She had a stitch in her side. She couldn't get the sound of the man's footsteps out of her ears. It was March, a chilly night. The bare skin on Jocelyn's thighs between the tops of her stockings and the bottom of her girdle suddenly felt cold. It seemed wrong to run, but nevertheless she broke into a trot. Her heavy breasts jounced in her brassiere, her ankles kept turning in the high-heeled shoes. The silk of her undergarments whispered against the lining of her dress, a feminine noise that always before had given her pleasure but now sounded like the sibilant voice of her rapist, calling to her out of the fog.

Suddenly a strong, angry male hand seized her arm, dragging her to a halt. Jocelyn opened her mouth to scream but no sound came out.

"Slow down, for Christ's sake," Mordecai Bashian said. "Oh, Mordecai, thank God it's you!" Jocelyn cried in gratitude.

Mordecai led her away from the river. They walked together in the fog along the Mall, all the way from the Washington Monument to the Lincoln Memorial, then across the bridge to the Jefferson Memorial. Jocelyn held on to Mordecai's arm with her gloved hand. He was much gentler now. He told her about his childhood in a tenement in New York, about his father who sent his sons to CCNY by selling things that nobody wanted—pots and pans, books of knowledge—from door to door. Mordecai described human suffering the like of which Jocelyn had never imagined. At home, when as a child Jocelyn did not eat her dinner, her mother would say, "The starving Armenians would be glad to have those carrots." Mordecai's family *were* the starving Armenians; his grandparents, his uncles and aunts, his cousins had been driven into the desert by the Turks. All had died. "America would do nothing. What does Christian civilization care about the murder of two million Armenians?" Mordecai said. "Was there outrage in your stately Virginia mansion because my grandmother was dropping in her tracks from lack of water, because my uncles were being flogged to death, because my cousins were being raped and bayoneted by the Turks?" Mordecai tapped his bony chest. "There is outrage in here, but what can a white girl like you know about that?" he said contemptuously.

It was a terrible thing to be a member of the downtrodden classes. Until just then, strolling along beside the Reflecting Pool with Mordecai Bashian, Jocelyn had never truly understood that. She had hurt Mordecai with her mean words about his being a smart-mouth New York Jew, even though he wasn't Jewish. And, as he explained, she had hurt him, too, by just being what she was: a pretty, well-to-do, joking girl with a state supreme court justice for a father. That was why Mordecai had been so unkind, because Jocelyn was unattainable. He kept on calling her a "white girl," as if, in some sardonic sense that she could never understand, he was colored.

Mordecai led her into the rotunda of the Jefferson Memorial. Fog draped the brooding statue of Thomas Jefferson like a toga. It was awfully picturesque and romantic. Mordecai's face was really a kind and sensitive face. A lock of black hair had fallen over his forehead. Jocelyn reached up and pushed it back. She gave him a sweet smile, and then on a generous impulse she kissed him, a warm soft pressure right on his lips, to show that she forgave him and knew that he forgave her.

Mordecai kissed her back, very sweetly, and pulled her to him. Chastely, Jocelyn let herself be kissed, as she had learned, arms hanging loose at sides, eyes shut, lips soft but firmly together. When Mordecai stopped, she opened her eyes and smiled. He put his arm around her and they walked outside. Mordecai led her down toward the Tidal Basin. She assumed that that was the way home.

They were inside a grove of trees. The fog was so thick that they had to grope their way among the trunks with their hands outstretched before them. It was like being in the dark in a haunted house. Jocelyn shivered and giggled. Mordecai pulled her to him again and kissed her. What harm can this do? she thought. She knew how to handle amorous boys. Mordecai smelled different from the other men she'd kissed, more pungent; she wondered if it was because he was an Armenian. Again she shivered a little. Mordecai took her lower lip between his lips and gave it delicious little kisses, a new way of doing things in Jocelyn's experience. She was aware of his body. He stepped back, untied the belt of her coat, and put his arms around her inside the coat. His hands caressed her back. He touched her breasts. "No," Jocelyn said. But Mordecai didn't stop, the way the boys from Washington & Lee most always did. He licked her ear and kissed her neck. She supposed he was swelling up, though she couldn't tell through the armor of her girdle. "Come on," Mordecai said, drawing her under a big tree. "No," Jocelyn said, "I think we'd better go." Mordecai uttered a sigh of wounded despair, and Jocelyn realized that he thought once again that she was rejecting him because he was Armenian. She couldn't see his face; they were hidden from each other in the fog. Jocelyn sank to the ground with her back against the trunk of the tree.

Mordecai caressed her breasts. He unbuttoned her blouse and unfastened her bra. Jocelyn had permitted this to happen a time or two before; she was proud of her breasts. Mordecai touched them with his tongue. Jocelyn struggled, then relaxed and let him do it; it was dreamy and warm to be caressed as she gazed into the fog that hid them like a cloud of white tulle. Jocelyn felt wetness between her thighs. Now it really was time to go. But Mordecai wouldn't let her leave. He put his face very close to hers. The tenderness she had detected earlier was mixed now with a petulant, hard selfishness. She was moved by the way he looked; she was a little frightened, but moved. His hands were under her skirt. This was the first time she had ever permitted this. Mordecai unhooked her garters and caressed the insides of her thighs. He removed her pantaloons, and then, as she found herself raising her hips to make things easier, he peeled off her girdle. When Mordecai removed her petticoat and her skirt she didn't resist.

Naked, she lay on her outspread polo coat with her arms at her sides, accepting his hands and his fingers and his lips and tongue. He kissed her body all over. She felt something happening. He was kissing her mouse! She leaped in astonishment and tried to scoot away over the whistling silk lining of her coat, but Mordecai had hold of her buttocks and he followed her with his quick tongue.

Jocelyn stopped trying to escape. A great shuddering sensation seized her. She buried her hands in Mordecai's thick hair, loving the coarseness of it and imagining how dark it was, and then she wrapped her legs around his neck. She had a long, sweet orgasm like a whisper that ran from her toes to her crown, and felt that her bones, her skin, her hair, and the blue veins inside her body were all one thing. As she lay on her polo coat, dazed by pleasure, Mordecai lifted his head. She kissed him in gratitude on the cheek. He thrust his tongue into her mouth. She expected to retch, but when she tasted herself on the tongue of a man she clutched Mordecai's head again and began to use her own tongue. She felt something. She knew what it was, yet she was amazed by it: she had always imagined that it would be like a bone, cold and sharp, but it was a lovely, smooth, limber muscle that slid into her, reaching and reaching. She wept. "Move your ass!" Mordecai said. He showed her the rhythm, pulling her toward him with hands locked on either buttock. She whirled like a person going under ether into a blackness, her whole being swelling inside her glowing skin.

After that, Jocelyn naturally considered that she was Mordecai's wife. But when she spoke of marriage, his face grew black with disgust. "Get this," he said. "I'll *never* marry you. But I will make an honest woman of you. I'll teach you how to think."

Mordecai was the smartest person Jocelyn had ever known. He insisted that she believe every single thing that he believed. In a way, Mordecai reminded Jocelyn of her mother: like her mother, he had no doubts about anything. He *knew* what to wear, what to say, what to believe, what to despise, and he could not bear to be in the room (could not bear to be in the same world, if truth were told) with any outsider who didn't have the right clothes, words, beliefs, and taboos.

Jocelyn didn't find it hard to please him, though it was time-consuming. Being his mistress was like rehearsing a part: she had to know her lines by heart. If she said something wrong, Mordecai would make her say it over again until she had it exactly right. He made her read *Das Kapital* and *Ten Days That Shook the World* and *The New Masses*. They went only to Soviet films, which always seemed to be overexposed and speeded up, so that Jocelyn formed the impression (she knew this wasn't so) that Russia was a country bathed in blinding sunlight, inhabited by bearded wild-eyed men who scurried around like mice, waving rifles over their heads. Mordecai and his friends talked incessantly about these few books and periodicals and films. There was nothing worth knowing in American literature, nothing worth looking at in American art: there couldn't be, because the United States was still a bourgeois capitalist society. It was a terrible sin to read the books that Jocelyn's father had always called "the dear, old books." It was a shocking breach of manners to mention one's family in the presence of Mordecai's friends: Jocelyn embarrassed him more than once with her empty-headed chatter about her parents and her sisters and her funny cousins before she learned to be more serious.

Mordecai made Jocelyn feel guilty about everything. "If you want to come into my life," he had said, "you can't bring any bourgeois baggage with you." She sacrificed her magazines, her Bette Davis movies (except for *Watch on the Rhine*, a wonderful treat on her twenty-eighth birthday), the Episcopal Church with its sweet boy sopranos singing "Hear My Prayer," and jokes. It made her sad to think of what she'd lost, but she knew that she could not live without Mordecai. She came to be bored by his talk, but her passion for his body grew so strong that she thought sometimes that she was going crazy. She wondered if any woman had ever done the things she did and lusted to do again. She didn't think it was possible.

Jocelyn's affair with Mordecai, which lasted for nearly twenty years, was a deep secret. In the office he treated her as he always had: with such cruel unfairness that the other girls came to love her and hate him. She was not permitted to mention Mordecai to her parents, not even his name. Mordecai would not come to her apartment, and she never knew where he lived or even if he had a telephone. They made love in borrowed rooms or in the car or in the lonesome Virginia woods beyond Mount Vernon. Sometimes Mordecai would call her at midnight and tell her where to meet him. She'd drive through the deserted streets to the rendezvous and he would pull her into an alley and stand her up against the wall and have her.

She knew that she was in the grip of a sexual obsession. If it was a sickness, then there was no cure for it, because the sickness *was* the cure.

After a few years, Mordecai started to send Jocelyn on errands. She delivered messages for him to people whose names he never revealed to her: he called them "Addressees." Sometimes she carried an envelope to an Addressee, sometimes she had to repeat a phrase that Mordecai had made her memorize; sometimes she picked things up from one Addressee and delivered them to another. Mostly she called on Addressees—scruffy people with contemptuous eyes and hateful masks for faces, like all of Mordecai's friends—in Washington. But sometimes she went to New York or Baltimore or even to Boston. She knew better than to ask questions: she just made her deliveries. Mordecai began to talk about the need for her to have a reason to call on the Addressees. Jocelyn said she didn't know why she needed a reason when no one even knew she was doing it, and she had no friends to tell. Mordecai was so angry that he refused to give her any relief for a whole month. They would meet and get undressed, but he would not touch her. He would masturbate while she watched, writhing in frustration. Once she tried to do the same, thinking that perhaps that was what he wanted.

"I don't want *that,*" Mordecai said. "If you love me, you have to do exactly what I say, with whomever I say."

The next time Jocelyn delivered a package to an Addressee, she slept with him, as Mordecai had instructed her.

When she staggered out of his room into the street she found Mordecai waiting for her. He made her describe every act she had performed with the Addressee, exactly as he required her to repeat the ideas that he approved of. Afterward, he was very tender to her in the back of her car. "You must have a reason to call on the Addressees," Mordecai said, bestowing one of his rare smiles on her. "Being a whore explains everything." After that, she committed some sexual act with many of the Addressees. Mordecai invariably rewarded her after a delivery of this kind by being passionate and virile.

At the end of a wonderful hour in a hotel room—it was the eighth anniversary of their night by the Tidal Basin—Jocelyn asked, her voice quavering, if she could please stop being a whore. She hated it; she wanted only one man, Mordecai. He pushed her away. "The others are the only thing that make it possible for me to fuck you," he said.

[171]

Wolkowicz arrested Jocelyn on a Thursday in the spring, in a Peoples Drug Store. Sometimes, on her lunch hour, Jocelyn made a delivery to a man she never spoke to. This always happened on a Thursday, the day that *Newsweek* came out. Jocelyn would go to the drugstore and look at the magazines. Her job was to leave an envelope inside the third *Newsweek* from the top. The man would buy that particular copy and walk out with it while Jocelyn looked through other magazines, making sure the wrong person didn't get the loaded *Newsweek.* As a reward, she always bought herself a copy of *McCall's* to read in the ladies' room.

One day, as the man was paying for his *Newsweek,* two young men in dark suits and straw hats took him by the arms and seized the magazine. They found the envelope inside.

"I am an official of a foreign embassy," the man said in a loud voice. "I have diplomatic immunity. I demand that you return my property."

He attempted to free his arms; the young men resisted. There was a wild struggle and all three men fell to the floor, punching and cursing. Their straw hats fell off and rolled down the aisle toward Jocelyn. She was terrified. A strong male hand seized her arm. *McCall's* fell from Jocelyn's hand and fluttered to the dirty floor.

A burly man with cold, cold eyes was showing her some sort of identification in a leather case. Through the thin sleeve of her blouse she could feel the sweat on his hand.

"I want you to come with me, Miss Frick," he said in a conversational tone. "Don't look at what's happening up front. Just walk out of the store like you always do. I'll be right behind you."

He unbuttoned his coat. She saw the butt of a gun protruding from his waistband.

It had been Jocelyn's great fear, when she was taken into custody, that the whole story of her becoming a whore would get into the newspapers. Sitting on a straight chair in the bare room Wolkowicz took her to, she had wide-awake dreams, a whole series of them, in which her father read the unspeakable truth in the Richmond *News Leader* and then did the only thing he could do: Jocelyn flinched when she heard the gunshot in the library, cried out when she saw the judge's flowing white hair stained with blood.

Wolkowicz seemed to understand her burden. For the first few hours, she would tell him nothing. He didn't bully her at all; for a man who looked like a brute, he was remarkably kind, even courtly. Finally Wolkowicz gave her a long look, filled with sympathy, then opened an envelope he had brought with him. It was a holey government messenger envelope, closed by a cord that wound around two little cardboard buttons.

"Jocelyn," Wolkowicz said, "I want you to look at some pictures."

Then, one by one, he laid out glossy photographs of Jocelyn engaging in sexual acts with the Addressees. She stared in fascination at the shiny enlargements. Men with slack faces and rumpled hair penetrated her, kneaded her breasts, and did worse. The pictures were bleached and jumpy, like Soviet films. She hardly recognized her own face, twisted as it was into a shame-filled mask with wild eyes. Jocelyn had never realized how ugly copulation looked.

Wolkowicz let her cry for a long time. Then he pulled one of her hands away from her face and placed a clean handkerchief in it. Jocelyn dried her eyes and blew her nose. The first sight she saw, when she was finally able to look at a human face, was the homely features of Wolkowicz, and there wasn't a trace of blame or disgust or cruelty there. While she cried, he had put the photographs away.

"Jocelyn," he said, "I want you to look at one more picture."

She covered her eyes again. Gently, he pulled her hands away from her face and held them. On the table, all by itself, lay a photograph of Mordecai Bashian. It was a group portrait. There was a woman in the picture too, and three children. All had dark, sullen faces like Mordecai's. Jocelyn tugged at her hands and Wolkowicz let them go. She picked up the photograph and a spear pierced her heart.

"Then he was married every minute of the time I've known him," Jocelyn said, dabbing her eyes with the handkerchief.

"That's about the size of it," Wolkowicz said sympathetically.

"*Aaaaaaaaaaaaaaaaaaah!*" Jocelyn cried.

Wolkowicz let her go on until she was all cried out and racked by dry sobs, like a child whose heart has been broken. Then he took one of her hands in his and apologized.

"I'm sorry," he said. "We didn't take those pictures. I'm sorry you had to see them. Mordecai Bashian had them taken; we found them hidden in his house. When you wouldn't talk to me, Cinders, I thought it might be because you were afraid everyone would find out what's in the pictures—afraid that we'd use this evidence against you, to hurt you and your family. Was I right about that?"

Jocelyn nodded. Hearing him call her Cinders perked her up some-how. She'd never dared to reveal this old pet name to Mordecai. Sud-denly she was bright-eyed and deeply calm. Wolkowicz squeezed her hand reassuringly.

"That doesn't have to happen," he said. "I promise you. The pic-tures can be destroyed. No judge would ever see them, no other human being would ever see them. Nothing would happen to you. You've suffered enough. None of this was your fault. Do you believe me?"

"Yes."

Wolkowicz smiled at her until she smiled back. Then he touched her cheek, gave it a little pat.

"Mordecai meant the world to you," Wolkowicz said, "but I think you know what he's done. He betrayed you, Cinders. He betrayed his country, too. He's put the United States in terrible danger. Will you help our country?"

Jocelyn nodded. Wolkowicz patted her cheek again.

"Good girl," he said.

In after years, remembering that little tap upon the cheek, Jocelyn wondered what Wolkowicz's name might have been. Though they spent days together, going over photographs and documents and re-hearsing her testimony before the Committee, he never once told her what to call him. It seemed rude to ask: she should have been able to read his name on his badge when he showed it to her in the drugstore. It was her fault that she didn't remember.

— 3 —

In her testimony before the House Committee, Jocelyn forgot no names, as she had forgotten Wolkowicz's. Among her Addressees were officials of the Defense Department, the Treasury, the Immigration and Natural-ization Service, and one officer of the Foreign Service. Like Mordecai Bashian, they were all medium-level civil servants who had no great power or influence. But, as the fiery young counsel of the Committee, a man named Dennis Foley, kept on saying, they were inside the gov-ernment like maggots.

The officer of the Foreign Service named by Jocelyn Frick was Wadsworth Jessup. Waddy was accused of being a Soviet agent. He denied it. But Dennis Foley insisted that Waddy had worked in subtle ways to bring about the defeat of the French in Indochina and the establishment of a Communist regime there. Haggard and trembling, his voice breaking as he tried to answer Foley's barrage of accusations, Waddy was not a believable witness.

Midway through the testimony, as Waddy drew closer and closer to the edge of hysteria, Waddy's lawyer asked for a conference with Foley and the committee chairman. Elliott Hubbard had been engaged by the Outfit to represent its interests in the case. After all, Waddy was a former Outfitter and it was obvious that he was ready to confess to crimes he had never committed, just to put an end to his ordeal.

"If you'll plead him guilty," Foley told the lawyer, "we'll recommend a minor charge—perjury, say—to the Department of Justice. His D.S.C. will get him a token sentence."

"Plead him guilty?" Waddy's lawyer said. "He's not guilty and you know it. You have nothing to go on but innuendo and supposition."

"Is that so?"

Foley pressed a buzzer and Wolkowicz came through the door.

"This is the man who broke the case," Foley said. "I think you know each other."

Elliott was astonished. No hint that Wolkowicz was involved in the Addressees Spy Ring, as the press called Mordecai Bashian's network of shabby failures, had reached his ears. Elliott asked to speak to Wolkowicz in private.

"How are you mixed up in this?" Elliott asked when he and Wolkowicz were alone. "This is not Outfit business, catching spies for Foley's wienie roast."

"It's Outfit business if there's a threat to the security of the Outfit," Wolkowicz said. "The Director thought there was a threat. Waddy was mixed up with this Mordecai Bashian, who was seeing the case officer from the Polish Embassy we picked up in the drugstore."

"Waddy, mixed up? How?"

"Mordecai let him frig Jocelyn Frick."

"*Waddy?* For Christ's sake, Barney—Waddy's a homosexual."

"So she gave him a blow job. Maybe he closed his eyes and thought about boy scouts."

"Barney, be honest. Do you really think Waddy's a Soviet agent?"

Wolkowicz, in a heavy silence, shrugged. "I think he used to be your brother-in-law, Elliott," he said. "I think you were at the Fool Factory together."

Elliott tapped the table. "Barney, this whole hearing is a farce and you know it," he said. "There's absolutely no proof that any of these people, except Bashian, ever lifted a finger to commit espionage for the Soviet Union or Poland or anyone else."

Wolkowicz yawned. "Of course there's no proof," he said. "The international Communist conspiracy is a *conspiracy*. They don't scatter clues around. The fact that there are no clues, or almost none, is a very convincing detail in the eyes of Dennis Foley."

"You served with Waddy in Burma. He's an ex-Outfitter."

Wolkowicz held Elliott's eyes. "You want the world to know that?" he asked. "Do you think I'm not trying to protect the Outfit? Do you think it was easy to talk Foley into offering Waddy a deal?"

"You did that?"

"Yes, but not for Waddy. I did it for the Outfit. I don't want it said in public that we've been penetrated by the fucking Communists any more than you do, Elliott."

Elliott managed to get the charge reduced to contempt of Congress. Waddy Jessup was sentenced to one year in the federal prison at Danbury, Connecticut. There, most of the Addressees were fellow prisoners. Mordecai Bashian sought out Waddy during the exercise period, and as they walked round and round in circles inside the prison fence, droned on and on about Waddy's affair with Jocelyn Frick.

Waddy said, "Mordecai, I don't know Jocelyn Frick from a load of cucumbers."

"Of course you'd say that, you're a trained agent, under discipline," Bashian replied. "But how did you get to her, exactly? How did you persuade her to be unfaithful to me?"

Waddy did not understand how this boring Armenian had ever got into the Party.

Five

— 1 —

For killing Hubbard Christopher's murderer in Berlin, Barney Wolkowicz had been given the Outfit's highest decoration. Now he was being awarded the same medal again for his work in breaking up the Addressees Spy Ring.

The ceremony took place at eleven in the morning in the Director's office. Paul Christopher was surprised to find himself among the dozen men who had been invited to attend.

"Wolkowicz asked for you," David Patchen explained. "He seems to have a kind of family feeling for you."

At the decoration ceremony, Patchen was in charge of the box containing Wolkowicz's medal. The Outfit had discovered his gift for administration early, and made him a member of the Director's personal staff.

"Are you getting a medal, too?" Wolkowicz asked derisively, delivering a soft punch to Patchen's sunken chest.

Patchen had handled the inside work—the paper, the money, the bureaucratic niceties—for Wolkowicz's operation against Mordecai Bashian and his network.

Wolkowicz, dressed in a gabardine jacket that seemed to be the upper half of an old suit, plaid trousers, and scuffed shoes, stood by himself. The other men in the room, dressed alike in their dark three-piece suits from Brooks Brothers, striped ties, and glossy shoes, chatted easily with one another. Wolkowicz's wary eyes moved from one impeccable figure to another, a tiny smile tugging at his lips. He saw Christopher watching him and lifted his thick eyebrows in greeting.

Patchen opened one of the leather boxes and offered it to Wolkowicz.

"Are you making the award?" Wolkowicz asked.

"No. This is your other medal," Patchen said.

"What's it supposed to be for?"

"You're supposed to wear all your medals when you get another one."

Wolkowicz lifted the medal out of its velvet nest and hung it around his neck. Patchen opened the other boxes, revealing a Silver Star and a Purple Heart, the decorations Wolkowicz had won in Burma.

"Come on, kid," Wolkowicz said. "I know you're efficient, but I'm not going to wear those things."

Patchen shrugged. The Director came in, escorting the Vice President of the United States. The Vice President hung the second medal around Wolkowicz's muscular neck. Wolkowicz, a flute of champagne going flat in his hand, listened in silence while the Vice President entertained the Director with tales of his experiences during the war in the Pacific as intelligence officer of a navy shore installation.

Wolkowicz stripped off the decorations, ducking his bullet head. He wadded ribbons and medallions into a ball and dropped them into Patchen's hand. He beckoned to Christopher.

"I've got to have lunch with these clowns," he said, with a gesture of the head to indicate the Vice President and the Director. "But I want to talk to you. Come to the house for dinner tonight."

"I don't think I can," Christopher said. "I have a dinner date."

"Bring her with you."

"It's Patchen."

Wolkowicz hesitated. "Bring him, then," he said. "But I may send him home early."

Ilse had made *Bowle*, a punch consisting of Rhine wine and fruit, with a bottle of German champagne added at the last moment to give the mixture effervescence. It was very sweet and the strawberries that floated on the surface of the cup bumped against Christopher's teeth as he drank.

"To the son of our beloved friend," Ilse said in German.

Wolkowicz paused, looked downward, and closed his eyes for a moment. It was a mannerism Christopher already knew well; Wolkowicz used it to conceal the embarrassment that any display of sentiment seemed to cause him. Then he poured his *Bowle*, strawberries and all, into his wide mouth, swallowing the wine and chewing the fruit.

Patchen sipped the mixture politely but refused a second glass. At dinner, Wolkowicz eased his P-38 in its soft holster out of his waistband and laid it on the table beside his plate. In order to please Christopher, Ilse had gone to great trouble to serve Berlin specialties. Christopher, who did not particularly like German cooking—Lori had believed in lighter fare—complimented Ilse on each dish.

Throughout the meal, she chattered in German to Christopher. Wolkowicz, eating with great speed, finished each course long before the others and waited for the next to be served, occasionally running a fingertip over the blue metal of the pistol beside his plate, saying nothing.

Ilse, turning to Patchen, changed into English. "Isn't it wonderful, getting two medals?" she said.

Patchen inclined his head. "Very unusual."

"Well, Barney is an unusual fellow."

"That's absolutely true."

Wolkowicz roused. Placing an elbow on either side of his plate, shoulders hunched, jaw propped on his fists, he stared at Patchen.

"Patchen thinks I blew the whole operation," he said. "That's what he told the Director."

The smile left Ilse's face. Patchen, who had been cutting up a strip of veal with his good hand, put down his knife.

"Go over it again for us, Patchen," Wolkowicz said. "I missed part of your critique at the morning meeting."

The Outfit permitted absolute freedom of speech: the most junior man could question the methods of the highest-ranking one without fear of reprisal. Patchen had chosen to question Wolkowicz's methods in the presence of the Director at the morning meeting of division chiefs and other senior officers.

Patchen had asked why Mordecai Bashian and the other members of his cell had been arrested. Why, instead, hadn't they been watched, followed, manipulated until they led Wolkowicz to bigger fish? Why hadn't they been blackmailed, doubled, used against the enemy? Patchen asked why the Outfit was even interested in a domestic spy ring —that was the FBI's function, not the Outfit's.

"Patchen thinks I put on a circus," Wolkowicz said to Ilse, in German. "That's what he told the Director: 'Intelligence services are supposed to win secret victories, not put on circuses for politicians.' "

Ilse drew in her breath and glared at Patchen. Thick silence descended over the Wolkowiczes' dinner table. Patchen, who did not understand German, caught the word *Zirkus* and guessed at the meaning of Wolkowicz's speech to Ilse.

"It was nothing personal," he said.

"No shit?" Wolkowicz said. "I thought maybe you belonged to Skull and Bones with Waddy Jessup."

Patchen smiled his saturnine smile.

"How old are you, kid?" Wolkowicz asked.

"Thirty."

"And you're already asshole buddies with the Director. You must have a lot of natural ability."

Wolkowicz lifted his backside and broke wind. That seemed to end the conversation as far as he was concerned. He threw his napkin on the table, picked up his P-38, and went into the sitting room.

Ilse served cake and coffee. Wolkowicz played Chopin on the grand piano. The mood lightened. Ilse's face was flushed with wine, and as she listened to the crystalline notes of a polonaise, she moved her head in rhythm to the music. She took Christopher's hand and held it until Wolkowicz finished playing. When Wolkowicz turned around, his eyes fell on their clasped hands and a flicker of jealousy crossed his face. Ilse smiled at them all, though her eyes changed when they fell on Patchen.

"You can't imagine, Paul, what it was like to hear this strange American play for the first time," Ilse said to Christopher. "It was at your father's apartment in Berlin—such beauty created by those hairy hands. I thought he was a gangster, but he turned out to be Franz Liszt. No wonder I fell in love."

Wolkowicz smiled, the first time Christopher had ever seen him do so. Ilse crossed the room and kissed her husband tenderly. The face Wolkowicz lifted to her lips was full of trust and affection.

"I'll say good night," Ilse said. "Come often, Paul." She kissed Wolkowicz again and smoothed his hair. "I have such a funny feeling about Paul," she said to her husband, "as if I'd known him in another life. When he came in tonight, it was like a dream of the time before the war." She hugged Wolkowicz's hunched figure and smiled brilliantly at Paul.

"Paul looks the way German boys looked, long ago, before they lost everything," she said.

To Patchen she said nothing at all, but merely shook hands, nodding as if to indicate that she had forgotten how to say good night in his language.

"I'll get your coat," Wolkowicz said to Patchen. "I want to talk to Christopher."

When Patchen had left, Wolkowicz poured two glasses of schnapps and handed one to Christopher.

"Prosit," he said. "I hope you like this stuff, because you're coming to Vienna with me."

"Vienna? I didn't know you'd been assigned to Vienna."

"Nobody knows it except the Director and me, and now you. I want you to be my number two."

Wolkowicz's face glowed with pleasure. He put a heavy damp hand on Christopher's shoulder and squeezed. "It's going to be a *great* operation," he said.

"What kind of an operation, exactly?"

"The real thing. We're going to break some Russian balls. I'll tell you all about it in Vienna."

Christopher watched Wolkowicz drain his schnapps, then pour himself another.

"Why did you ask for me?"

"You speak German," Wolkowicz said. "In spite of Waddy, you did good things in Indochina—a little spooky, the way you walk right in on the customers, but I like that. You're your father's son. It's mostly that, Paul—I miss the hell out of your father."

Patchen had bought a house near Georgetown University, and the next afternoon, a Saturday in May, he invited Paul Christopher to watch the Georgetown baseball team play Harvard. After the game, at the end of the afternoon, the two friends walked across the campus. Patchen's Doberman pinscher trotted ahead of them along a patch of beaten red soil. Patchen walked briskly, dragging his ruined leg. Before being wounded, he had been an athlete. He still craved exercise. He liked long walks.

"Wolkowicz," Patchen said, "has the right spirit. Audacity, audacity forever."

"Do *you* know what the operation in Vienna is all about?"

"It's something the Director cooked up with the Brits. He says it's the biggest coup the cousins have had since the war. It must be big if they want to cooperate. They only run us in when they need money. It's all very odd."

Patchen paused, a gaunt twisted figure, and watched his dog race through the deserted campus.

"Very odd," he said again.

The Doberman ran from one tree to another, leaping and whining at squirrels who scurried along the branches, scolding. The peculiar molten light of the Washington springtime shone on the mellow brick like oil on skin.

"It should be fascinating, explaining Wolkowicz to the old Etonians," Patchen said. "I hope you'll tell me what it was like when you get back."

Six

— 1 —

That summer in Vienna, Paul Christopher, like his father before him, conceived a great affection for Barney Wolkowicz. Though there was a difference of only five years in their ages, Wolkowicz treated Christopher with gruff tenderness, as if he were a much younger brother. Hubbard's death was a strong bond between them. Neither man ever mentioned it, but both knew that no son could have done more than Wolkowicz had done at the scene of the murder. Christopher felt that Wolkowicz was in some sense his real brother.

On his arrival in Vienna, Christopher was met at the airport by Wolkowicz's driver, an Austrian in a leather coat. The man approached Christopher as he waited with his bags, as he had been instructed, at the bus stop outside the terminal. They uttered the prearranged greetings, some nonsensical exchange in German about a hotel. It was well after midnight. The Austrian picked up Christopher's bags and led him to a dark green Mercedes. He drove to a restaurant in the Vienna Woods and parked in the lot next to a second, identical Mercedes.

Wolkowicz emerged from the other car and looked around, then got into the front seat with Christopher. With a flick of the hand, he told the Austrian to get out of the car.

"Drive," he said.

As Christopher would learn, Wolkowicz liked his men to perform small services for him: he never drove if a subordinate could take the wheel, never fetched himself a drink if a man of lesser rank could be sent to the bar. With Wolkowicz giving directions and watching the street behind them for surveillance, they drove to a bombed neighborhood just outside the Ring.

"Make a hard right, *now,*" Wolkowicz said.

Christopher turned into a passage in the rubble. The nose of the car dipped and he found himself driving down a curving stone ramp.

"This used to be an underground garage," Wolkowicz said. "Now it's an underground garage again. We run it. It's surprising how much of a big city is underground—most of the important stuff."

They were in a large room, brilliantly lighted with arc lamps. Mechanics worked on several cars.

"The garage is good cover," Wolkowicz said. "You can drive into a garage anytime without arousing suspicion. But we have a hell of a time getting enough cars to fix; it's always the simplest details that take up the most time."

Another man in a leather coat and a Tyrolean hat awaited them here.

"Hi," he said in a chipper American accent. "Want to go below?" He unlocked the door of a van and slid it open. Wolkowicz jumped in. Christopher followed him. The van, a boxy vehicle like an American bread truck, was parked with its rear door flush against the wall. Wolkowicz slid the door upward with a clatter and shone a flashlight against the steel plates of a door set into the stone wall of the garage. The door swung open. A second American, this one dressed in denim coveralls, stood inside, at the head of a steep flight of stairs. He wore a military-issue .45 Colt automatic in a shoulder holster and carried a submachine gun slung across his chest. The submachine gun was fitted with a thick silencer that was nearly as long as the weapon itself.

Wolkowicz plunged down the stairs, his feet rattling the iron treads. As he got to the darkness at the bottom he handed Christopher a flashlight and led the way through a long tunnel; beyond its walls, which were encrusted with dead lichens, Christopher heard the rush of running water and detected the sweetish odor of decomposed excrement.

"You're in an old sewer," Wolkowicz said. "Everybody had forgotten about it until we came along."

They were in a labyrinth, with smaller passages leading off the main tunnel and smaller ones yet branching off the secondary tunnels. Wolkowicz moved briskly, sure of the way. He fell to his knees and crawled into a low tunnel. A long narrow carpet of the kind usually laid in hallways had been put down on the floor. At the end, Wolkowicz pulled an army field telephone out of its box and turned the crank. He spoke a phrase Christopher could not understand into the mouthpiece, then replaced the phone.

"We're there," Wolkowicz said, sitting with his back pressed against the wall.

"What language was that you just spoke on the phone?"

"Kachin." Wolkowicz grinned. "Let the fucking Russians figure *that* out," he said. "You'll have to learn the daily passwords in Kachin. It's not hard."

A door opened. The colors in the rug, which was at least thirty feet long, glowed in the sudden bath of stark electric light.

Wolkowicz crawled through the door into a long room that had been created out of a section of tunnel. The walls were padded with soundproofing material. The word *Silence!* was painted on every wall in letters two feet high. Half a dozen men sat at a long table, each tending a bank of tape recorders.

Wolkowicz ignored them. He led Christopher through another door. It opened into a guardroom where three men waited alertly, submachine guns at the ready. Christopher saw a detonator box wired and ready, inside the cover of an ornate birdcage. Wolkowicz followed his glance.

"The birdcage is the Brits' idea of a safety device," Wolkowicz said. "They don't want to fall on the handle when drunk and blow everybody up. Right?" The guards smiled at the tired joke.

"Beyond this point, everything is wired. We can blow it if we have to," Wolkowicz said. "The code word is *Birdcage*. The charges are a mixture of TNT and phosphorus; when they go off, this sewer becomes one big burn bag."

In the next room, Wolkowicz slapped the metal case of a chattering machine that looked like a very complicated teletype. It was one of five identical devices that were spewing out streamers of white paper. Wolkowicz tore one off and handed it to Christopher. It was covered with Russian text.

"This is the operation," Wolkowicz said. "This room is directly underneath the Imperial Hotel, which is Russian headquarters. These funny-looking typewriters are replicas of their decoding machines. We're intercepting and decoding and reading every fucking word they send and receive. Come on. We'll see if the genius is here."

Wolkowicz swung open another steel door and strode into a smaller room. The floor was covered with Persian carpets, laid edge to edge, and more carpets had been hung like paintings on the whitewashed walls. A dark-haired girl sat behind an antique desk, working on a streamer from the decoding machine. She was rolling the paper into a tube; a pyramid of similar tubes, fastened by rubber bands, stood in a basket on the floor. She, too, was equipped with a silenced submachine gun; it lay on a fragment of carpet, to protect the desk from scratching.

"Hello, Rosie," Wolkowicz said. "Where is he?"

"Not far," the girl said in a British voice. She had frank eyes, large and violet—the only violet eyes Christopher had ever seen. "You must be the new Yank," she said to Christopher.

"Paul Christopher."

"Rosalind Wilmot."

"Rosie works for the head Brit," Wolkowicz said. "In actual fact, this is her show. She's the queen of the underground."

"I do make tea," Rosalind said. "Very tricky at this depth. Would you like a cup?"

"No, thank you."

"Very negative about tea, the Americans. Here's Robin."

A man came into the room with a stack of fluttering streamers across his arm. He laid them on Rosalind Wilmot's desk. He did not give Wolkowicz and Christopher so much as a glance.

"We *must* have more Russian speakers," the man said. His accent was the British equivalent of Wolkowicz's: street English, with the shadow of a foreign intonation. There the resemblance ended. Where Wolkowicz was squat and muscular, Robin Darby was tall and thin; instead of a squashed Slavic face, he had a large hooked nose and a domed forehead. His eyes were bold and expressive rather than slanted and guarded. He wore a full beard, a mixture of gray and ginger hairs, an unusual adornment in the well-barbered years just after the war.

"Do *you* speak Russian?" he asked Christopher.

"No."

"Neither does Rosalind. How are we supposed to read all this bloody stuff?"

"Christopher reads Russian," Wolkowicz said. "He just doesn't speak it."

"Ah, *Christopher*. I knew your late father. Welcome to Plato's cave. My name is Darby."

"How do you do?"

"Bloody badly. Too much of a good thing, all these ribbons of paper. You can't visualize how boring—*boring!*—these cretinous Soviets are. Sit down. I'll put you in the picture."

A year before, in Berlin, Robin Darby, an officer of the British intelligence service, had completed the theft of a Soviet coding machine.

"I say *completed*," Darby said, sipping tea from a mug, "because it took three perishing years to steal the thing. My man inside Soviet headquarters smuggled it out a part at a time. He was the repairman, you see. Every time a machine needed maintenance, which was often —the Russians aren't terribly mechanical, you know—he'd winkle out some cog or gear in his toolbox. Eventually we had enough of the vital parts to deduce the rest of the machine. Then we built one of our own, hooked it up to a landline running out of the Soviet Embassy in a European capital that shall be nameless, and lo! it worked. We went into mass production."

"How did you recruit the repairman?"

"*Recruit* him?" Darby said. "We could hardly keep him out by barring the doors. He was a German Communist who'd vanished into Russia before the war. He just popped up in Berlin after the fighting was over, looked us up, and said, 'Look here, old chaps, how would you like a decoding machine?' Well, of course we smelled a rat, but we led him on in our super-clever way, and what do you know? The bloody thing worked. The whole scenario was so implausible that London and Washington had no choice but to believe it. That's so often the way, though, isn't it?"

"If he was a Communist, trusted by the Russians to repair these machines," Christopher said, "why did he do it? *How* did he do it?"

Robin Darby shrugged his sharp shoulders. "Who knows?" he said. "I suppose he was disillusioned with Soviet life. Agents are very strange, you know. We did pay him a hundred thousand pounds."

"Is he now spending it somewhere?"

"No, poor chap," Darby said. "He died of rabies just after he delivered the last bit of clockwork, though I don't know where he found a dog to bite him in Berlin; I thought the Germans had made them all into stew. It's a fearsome death, rabies—the spine bends, the jaws

[187]

clench, the mouth foams. It was enough to make one think that God is a Red."

Robin Darby stretched, yawned, and departed. Rosalind lingered for a moment.

"As you've just arrived, would you like to meet for dinner?" she said to Christopher. "I know Vienna intimately. There's a marvelous place where the waiters are ex-SS troopers, dressed in cowboy suits."

Christopher agreed to meet her at seven. Wolkowicz waited until the door closed behind her before speaking.

"Now you know who the world's greatest spy is," he said. "Darby is such a Britshit. *'Our* agent, *our* operation!' The decoding machine was bought and paid for with Outfit money and this whole operation is Outfit planning. Darby was a messenger."

"You don't like Darby?"

"I can't stand the la-de-da son of a bitch."

— 2 —

Both Christopher and Rosalind Wilmot thought it strange that Wolkowicz and Darby were not compatible. They had a great deal in common. Darby was the anglicization of some long Lithuanian name: his parents, like Wolkowicz's, were refugees from eastern Europe. Both had grown up in working-class neighborhoods, the sons of self-educated factory workers. Both had gone to universities on scholarships. To carry coincidence to unlikely extremes, both had parachuted into Burma during the war and fought with the Kachins behind the Japanese lines.

"Good job they landed in different parts of the jungle," Rosalind said. "They're too much alike. Both despise the old-school-tie crowd— it's an obsession with Robin, and with Wolkowicz, too. Then they look at each other, poor devils, and see what the truly awful alternative is —*each other.*"

"Is that it?" Christopher asked.

"Not entirely. There's Frau Wolkowicz. Ilse rather fancies old Robin, you know. Not so much as she fancies delicious you, Christopher, but she does fancy him, rather."

This conversation took place in the fall, as Christopher and Rosalind sat in his car outside her apartment building. They had come from a dinner party at the Wolkowiczes'. Throughout the evening, Robin

Darby had carried on a comic flirtation with Ilse, quoting love lyrics in German and inviting her to run away to Paris. Ilse had countered Darby with a joke of her own, pretending to a passion for Christopher; she had stroked his hand, gazed at him and sighed, and finally even sat on his lap. Ilse had drunk a lot of wine.

"Sometimes, when Ilse's a bit tiddly," Rosalind said, "I get the impression she even fancies *me.*"

"All that's a joke," Christopher said.

"Old Wolkowicz doesn't see the joke, you know," said Rosalind. "Tonight he kept on glowering and fingering his heater."

"Fingering his what?"

"His heater. Isn't that what you Americans call a firearm?" Rosalind put a hand on Christopher's arm. "Really, I think Ilse is unsafe for you," she said. "But do you think there can ever be love between the two of us?"

Christopher smiled at her. She stroked his face.

"I don't know," he said. "You have nice eyes, but you say 'Ameddican' and 'heatuh.' You don't seem to be able to talk like a regular person."

"Actually there's no hope of love for you and me, Christopher. There's someone else in my life. It's hopeless, but there it is."

"Not a married man, Rosalind?"

"Worse than that—incest." In the feeble roof light, Rosalind's great limpid eyes shone with mirth. "But look here," she continued, "we *could* be friends—wouldn't that be all right?"

"Yes. It would be torture, but it would be all right."

"Not torture. Bliss. We could be sexual friends."

"Sexual friends?"

"You don't believe in sexual friendship?"

"Oh, yes. But I didn't know that women believed in it, too."

"Oh, dear—you're not telling me you're queer?"

Christopher laughed. "No."

"Well, then. Shall we try it?"

They went upstairs together.

Months later, Rosalind turned to Christopher in bed and seized his ears in her two hands. It was a large double bed in her overheated bourgeois flat at the top of an apartment house; from the windows they could see the roofs of the royal palace. Christopher's pistol in its shoulder holster hung from one bedpost, Rosalind's from the other. She kneeled astride Christopher, her black hair swinging, and laughed.

"Pistols on the bedposts," she said. "Really, it's like some perverse Teutonic brothel. We owe so much to Wolkowicz and Darby."

"Can we change the subject?"

"You don't want to gossip about our masters? Such an honorable Ameddican. I thought it was all right to backbite if one was in bed."

Christopher looked at his watch and stirred. Rosalind pinned his shoulders to the mattress.

"Do let me gossip," she said. "Robin can be terribly funny. Do you know what he calls you and Wolkowicz? 'Tall-blond-and-handsome and Short-brutish-and-ugly.' "

Christopher picked Rosalind up—she was a small girl—and set her on the other side of the bed. He went to the window and looked out. Fat snowflakes drifted out of a gray sky, turning the rooftops white. Rosalind called to him; he didn't answer. She crossed the room and climbed naked onto the windowsill.

"Snow," she said. "If we start now in that great beast of a car of yours, we can be in St. Anton by morning. Wouldn't it be lovely to get out of this filthy city and up into the lovely clean mountains? *Skiing*, Christopher."

Rosalind always called her sexual partner by his last name, a reminder of the terms of their contract. Love was never mentioned between them; as Rosalind had specified, they had remained friends.

"I'm the duty officer this weekend," Christopher said.

"In the absence of Robin and Short-brutish-and-ugly, you're in charge. Call in somebody else."

Wolkowicz was away, meeting the Director in London. Darby had left Vienna, too. Christopher hesitated.

"*Sun*, Christopher," Rosalind said. "We'd see the sun. Remember the sun? Driving up the Vorarlberg, we'd break through the clouds into dazzling sunlight. The virgin snow would be gleaming on the mountainsides, we'd breathe the Alpine air."

"All right. Pack."

They drove all night, and as Rosalind had foreseen, they arrived in St. Anton, in brilliant sunshine, at midmorning. They skied until late afternoon and then came down to the hotel for hot chocolate. They sat on the terrace, basking in the sun; Rosalind had got a light tan and her eyes were more beautiful than ever. Suddenly they brimmed with laughter.

"Ah," she said.

Rosalind was gazing over Christopher's shoulder at a couple in ski clothes who stood on the path leading to the hotel. They were kissing passionately; the woman's fingers clawed at the man's back. They separated and walked on, still kissing, toward the hotel. Desire had made them unsteady and they staggered slightly as they groped their way along the snowy path, eyes shut. The woman took off her cap and shook her blond hair loose. She looked directly into Christopher's face. It was Ilse. Robin Darby's hand clasped her breast through the wool of her sweater.

Rosalind covered her mouth and laughed.

— 3 —

If Wolkowicz, with his sensitivity to the moods of others, suspected his wife's adultery, he did not betray his suspicions to Darby or to Ilse by so much as a gesture, and he never mentioned them to Christopher. But he often left the Sewer during his shift on duty, leaving Christopher in charge. The schedule was ideal from the point of view of the lovers: when Darby was off duty, Wolkowicz was on duty, fifty feet underground, sealed in a secret installation. This gave Ilse and Darby a sense of freedom: they lunched together in restaurants, went to tea dances in hotels, strolled through the Prater.

Nevertheless, Wolkowicz, using all his professional skills, watched them, collecting evidence. One day he came to work an hour early, bringing Christopher with him. He carried a large yellow envelope, the flap secured with tape. He closed the steel door behind him and threw the envelope onto Darby's desk.

Darby lifted his amused eyes. "What's this?" he asked.

"Open it up."

Darby slit the seal and emptied the contents, a stack of glossy photographs bound with a rubber band, onto the polished surface of the desk. Darby removed the rubber band and began to look at the pictures. A look of mild interest spread over his face. Rosalind, standing beside him, flushed and bit her lip.

"Christopher," she said, "shall we go check the machines?"

Wolkowicz stood in front of the door. "Stay put," he said, "both of you."

Darby, still amused, looked from Rosalind to Wolkowicz to Christopher. He separated the photographs into two stacks and put the larger stack back into the yellow envelope. Then he held up the top photo from the smaller stack: it was a clear, perfectly exposed candid portrait of Darby and Ilse, naked together in an overstuffed chair.

"I'll have copies of each of this lot," Darby said. "I don't think the outdoor shots are up to much, do you? Too many clothes."

Wolkowicz took the photographs out of Darby's hand. Darby offered no resistance.

"What we have here, in this sewer," Wolkowicz said, "is a very good operation. Nothing should spoil it. So what I want is peace and brotherhood down here. But at four o'clock this afternoon, I want you to meet me, Darby, out in the woods. Christopher will bring you to the place. I'll take Rosalind with me now."

Darby wasn't smiling, but no hint of guilt or embarrassment crossed his face. "Is Ros to be a hostage?" he asked.

"Just show up," Wolkowicz said.

On the way to his rendezvous with Wolkowicz, while Christopher drove, Robin Darby chattered. "You're remarkably like your father," he said. "Not in looks, really—it's the manner. You seem to have the same sort of super-absorbent mind. Rather scary, actually; your father was otherworldly. Ros loaned me the book of your poems. The poetic voice is *quite* similar. Is all that deliberate? Do you consciously emulate him?"

"We're almost there," Christopher said.

The Mercedes was rolling along a narrow road in the woods. The windshield was steamy. Christopher rolled down the window and the sound of the tires crunching on the snow came inside. The shuttered façade of a *Heurigestube,* closed for the winter, came into view. Wolkowicz waited in the parking lot, a squat figure in a duffel coat.

"An encounter in the woods over a lady's virtue," Darby said. "How very Ruritanian."

Darby alighted. He wore a green Loden cape. Wolkowicz said nothing, but his eyes never left Darby's smiling face. Wolkowicz took off his coat and hung it on the hood ornament of his Mercedes. He gave his P-38 to Christopher, and then drew a snub-nosed .38 caliber revolver from an ankle holster.

"Is it to be pistols, then?" Darby asked.

Wolkowicz gave the second pistol to Christopher. Then, without so much as drawing in his breath, he launched himself across the five or six feet of space that separated him from Darby and smashed his fist into the other man's bearded face. Darby's thin body flew backwards, cape fluttering as he fell.

Christopher had never seen anyone move so fast and so violently as Wolkowicz. Before Christopher heard the sound of Wolkowicz's fist smashing the cartilage in Darby's nose, the two men were on the ground, flailing each other. Neither used his voice; the only sound was the fall of fists, the impact of feet, and gasps of pain and effort. Both men were trained fighters. Wolkowicz used no judo, only his fists and feet; perhaps he was too angry. Darby, who knew that he had no chance against Wolkowicz in a fistfight, did use his training. He kicked Wolkowicz in the groin and pounded his stomach and kidneys with cleaverlike blows with the edge of his hands. The struggle might have lasted three or four minutes, a long time. Neither man won. It just ended.

Wolkowicz and Darby lay together for a moment in the trampled snow, which was pink with their blood. Then Wolkowicz, sobbing for breath as the result of a blow to the sternum, got to his feet and struggled to the car. He put his hands on the fender and fought to breathe. Darby, still lying in the tangle of his ruined cape—Wolkowicz had used it to sling him against a tree—gazed at his adversary. All the sparkling expression had been beaten out of Darby's eyes. Blood poured from his broken nose into his beard; he reached into his mouth and brought out a broken tooth.

Wolkowicz picked up his P-38. Darby's eyes did not change expression. Christopher moved quickly to place his body between the two enemies. But Wolkowicz had no plan to shoot Darby. Chest heaving, he tucked his holstered pistol into the waistband of his trousers and put a hand on Christopher's shoulder, moving him to one side. He spat a globule of reddened saliva into the snow and pointed a finger at Darby. The finger was broken.

"I just want you to know," Wolkowicz said, coughing, "that this was only round one. Nothing's over yet. Got it, Limey?"

Darby held Wolkowicz's enraged glance for a long moment. Then he scooped up a double handful of snow and pressed it against his ruined face.

Christopher was awakened the following night by a pounding on his door, hammer blows that echoed through the apartment. Rosalind was with him; she stood behind Christopher in the darkened room with a pistol in her hand while he opened the door.

Ilse Wolkowicz stood on the landing, holding the valise with which she had been battering the door panels.

"Paul, Paul," she said. "You have to let me in. Barney is drinking, he's gone crazy, he went out. He's going to do something terrible."

Christopher turned on the light. Rosalind's nude figure, white skin and black hair, leaped into view; she was still pointing her Walther, which she held in the approved two-handed grip, at the open door. Ilse looked her up and down.

"Dear God," she said with a shrill laugh, "what a picture." With her eyes still on Rosalind, she seized Christopher's arm, pinching the flesh between her nails, pulling his ear toward her mouth. He leaned over.

"The Russians," Ilse hissed.

Rosalind, frowning at Ilse, shielded her pubis with the pistol, a perverse gesture of modesty. Abruptly, she turned and left the room.

"It's true," Ilse said to Christopher, whispering rapidly. "He's going to tell them about me."

"Tell the Russians about you? Tell them what?"

"About my father. He wasn't in the Waffen SS, he was in the other SS. He was in charge of a camp in Poland. It's so terrible to be a German. Our home was in the Soviet Zone; I come under their jurisdiction. They'll kill me for what my father did."

Images flooded into Christopher's mind: the faces of the women in the camps, dozens of them, who had looked like Lori, each with a black circle drawn around her head. Ilse's fingernails dug into the flesh of his arm. He pried her fingers loose and pushed her hand away.

"I can't help you," he said.

"For God's sake, Paul—I was only a child! I was in Switzerland, going to school. I knew nothing. Do you think my parents *told* me what my father was doing in the camps?"

Christopher was wearing a dressing gown. Ilse slid her hand under the lapel, onto his bare skin. He stepped away from her.

Ilse stared at him in disbelief. "Your father wouldn't have let this happen to me," she said.

Christopher didn't answer her. He went to the telephone and dialed a number. She rushed after him and snatched at the telephone.

"Not Darby," Ilse said. "Don't call him." She was still talking in her urgent whisper. She hung up the phone. "I don't want help from either of the bastards," she said.

She seized the lapels of Christopher's dressing gown again. He stepped back.

"Then you'd better stay here with Rosalind," he said. "I'll try to find Barney. He won't go to the Russians."

"You don't know Barney," Ilse said. "You don't know what was between us."

Rosalind came back, fully clothed, her coat over her arm. Her face was cold and composed.

"Rosalind will stay with you," Christopher said to Ilse.

"Like hell I will," Rosalind said. "I heard every word." She walked out the door.

Christopher found Wolkowicz in the Sewer, sitting in the inner office at Darby's desk, reading a streamer from one of the decoding machines. He appeared to be perfectly sober, but then he always did.

"Ilse is at my place," Christopher said.

"Is she?"

Wolkowicz did not raise his eyes from his reading. Presently he got up and left the room. For the rest of the night he avoided Christopher. Christopher stayed in the Sewer until Darby and Rosalind came in at dawn. He took Wolkowicz home with him. Wolkowicz knew where the car was going as it passed through the streets leading to Christopher's apartment house; he sat with the brim of his hat pulled down over his eyes, battered hands in his coat pockets, saying nothing.

In Christopher's apartment, they found a note from Ilse; she had gone home to pack; she had decided to go to the States. Christopher called Wolkowicz's number; there was no answer. He went to Wolkowicz's apartment; the porter had not seen her come in.

Wolkowicz's Austrian driver arrived with a message. In a destroyed street between Christopher's apartment and her own place, Ilse had been kidnapped from her taxi. A truck had backed into the taxi and when the driver leaped out to remonstrate, two men had wrenched open the back doors and pulled Ilse into another car.

"She resisted, she was screaming for help," the taxi driver told Christopher. "She was holding on to my taxi like this, very strong, I thought she was going to pull the door off the hinges, and when she wouldn't let go, one of the Russians punched her in the stomach. Then she was limp, yes? So they just stuffed her into their car."

"They were Russians?"

"Certainly they were Russians. In overcoats made by chimpanzees. You know."

"Oh, you bloody man," Robin Darby said. "You bloody, bloody man."

"This is a security matter," Wolkowicz said. "Whatever Ilse may have told Christopher, I did not contact the Russians. I didn't know about her father."

Teams flew in from Washington and London to investigate. Wolkowicz submitted to a lie detector test and passed.

"It's a fucking mess," Wolkowicz said. "She knows all about the Sewer, all about the decoder."

"If Barney didn't tell the Russians," Rosalind said, "who did?"

Darby ran his fingertips over his bandaged face. "I think Barney knows," he said.

They were all together in the Sewer, discussing the problem. Only Darby was angry. Wolkowicz seemed to feel no sense of loss, no remorse: Ilse might as well have been any other German—a defeated enemy, an agent, lost in an operation that went wrong.

"Ilse told them—who do you *think* told them?" Wolkowicz said. "She belongs to the opposition. She belongs to the fucking Russians. She always has."

Rosalind didn't believe this. "Why would she go back to them? Why would they stage this silly kidnapping? She was far more valuable to them in place, where she was."

"Because I caught her with Darby. Catch them in one lie and all the other lies run out of the hole like mice. She lost her head."

As Wolkowicz described the consequences of his wife's adultery, impatient with Rosalind's stupidity, they listened to the rustling rodent noise of the decoding machines.

"Maybe you're wrong," Christopher said.

"I'm not wrong now," Wolkowicz said. "I was wrong before. I trusted her. I made an exception."

"Bad luck," Darby said. He had regained some of his good humor.

"I take it we agree that something must be done? Shall I deal with that?"

Wolkowicz nodded; Christopher and Rosalind watched their chiefs in silence as they agreed, without exchanging a word, to kill the woman who had made them hate each other.

But Ilse had vanished. Darby's hunters could not find her. In the Sewer, the decoding machines continued to spew out their ribbons of secrets; new teams of experts were brought in from Washington and London to see if there was any change in the character of the Soviet transmissions. Had Ilse alerted the Russians? Were they now mixing disinformation into the flow of coded transmissions? The experts said that there had been no change; the same information, reams of it, was still coming over the wires faster than it could be translated.

"You know," Rosalind said to Christopher, "I wonder. It's all very odd, the way things just go on as if nothing has happened. Do you think Ilse was *not* a Soviet agent? Did the Russians simply ship her off to the labor camps without questioning her at all, without ever dreaming that she knows what she knows?"

"Why would she keep quiet?"

"Why did she keep quiet about her father?"

"But the Russians know what Barney is."

"They knew what her father was, too. For someone who smells like a rose, old Ilse has a marvelous combination of men in her life, hasn't she?" said Rosalind, and went to sleep.

— 6 —

But Wolkowicz was sure that Ilse would betray them. He expected the Russians to attack the Sewer. He sent teams deeper into the warren of abandoned tunnels to plant listening devices and explosive charges.

"If the fuckers come," he said, "I want to hear them."

Wolkowicz was right, as usual. Just before dawn, on a night in spring three months after Ilse's disappearance, one of the listeners pushed the alarm system. Red lights flashed up and down the Sewer. Wolkowicz ran to the listening post.

"What do you hear?" he asked the listener.

"Footsteps, running. A lot of men."

Wolkowicz pulled the headset off the listener's head and clapped it to his own ears. Even as he heard the scuffle of boots running toward them through the sewers beyond the wall, he gave the order to evacuate. Rosalind rolled up two of Darby's Persian carpets and stood waiting with them clasped in her arms. The silenced submachine pistol was slung over her back.

"Christopher, come on," she said. "Bring that Qum—the silk one on the wall."

Wolkowicz shoved her roughly through the door. "Get out of here with your fucking rugs," he said. "Call Darby. Go."

Rosalind unslung her weapon and handed it to Christopher. The Sewer emptied. Only Christopher and Wolkowicz remained. Wolkowicz drew his P-38 and took the birdcage off the detonator box. He jerked his head toward the exit. "Time to go," he said.

"I'll stay," Christopher said.

"Like hell you will—"

Wolkowicz did not have time to finish. The wall of the inner office blew in with a tremendous noise. The blast lifted the nearest steel door, which had been fifty feet from the explosion, off its hinges; it sailed toward Christopher and Wolkowicz, lazily, like a bit of foil in a gust of city wind. Wolkowicz did not move; he seemed to be hypnotized. Christopher threw him to the floor. The door rang against the stone wall, then fell onto Wolkowicz, pinning his lower body to the floor.

Wolkowicz's face was contorted with pain. He was bleeding from his nose and ears. "Birdcage!" he said in a loud voice. "I can't move. *Blow* the fucking thing."

Wolkowicz jerked his head again, toward the detonator box. The handle had not been twisted. Christopher realized that the attackers had blown out a wall in order to get inside the Sewer.

A Russian soldier emerged from the haze of dust. He fired a burst from a Kalashnikov submachine gun into the room. Christopher saw the flame and heard the rapid reports. He killed the Russian with the silenced machine pistol Rosalind had given him. Two more Russians rushed into the room, firing. The rounds from their weapons passed over the heads of the two Americans who lay prone in the dust. Christopher shot both of the Russians.

Christopher pulled the steel door off Wolkowicz's legs, seized him by the shoulders, and dragged him through the rest of the Sewer, into the low tunnel. Wolkowicz's bulky body slid easily over the carpet, cloth whistling against cloth.

[198]

"Birdcage! Birdcage!" Wolkowicz shouted. "God damn it, Paul, *blow* it."

Christopher, stooping low, ran back into the debris and got the detonator box. Paying out wire from the spool, he scuttled backward into the tunnel and sprawled beside Wolkowicz. It was dead quiet. Christopher could see through the open doors the length of three rooms.

Christopher saw figures running among the decoders, firing as they came. Rounds slammed into the stones and sang as they ricocheted around the arched walls. Christopher twisted the handle on the detonator box. The decoding machines exploded one after another like a string of firecrackers. Then the main charges went off and the running men vanished in a flash of blinding white light, as if the film had broken in a movie house.

— 7 —

In Washington, as winter ended, Christopher walked with David Patchen across the Georgetown campus. A cold rain pattered on the umbrella they were sharing. Patchen, who felt the chill more than other men, was bundled up in a duffel coat, a long school scarf wound around his neck, a knitted cap pulled down over his ears.

"I remember saying I thought working with Wolkowicz would be interesting," Patchen said, "but I had no idea *how* interesting. What is your dominant impression of your year abroad?"

"It was a fiasco."

"Don't say that to anyone else. The Sewer—capital *S*, in Headquarters usage—is regarded as the greatest coup in the history of espionage."

"It is? But if Ilse *was* a Soviet agent, then the Russians knew about the whole thing from the start."

Patchen's Doberman saw a stranger approaching and stopped frisking, his whole attention focused on this possible threat to his master. Patchen, too, stopped talking until the outsider, a student who gave them a cheery hello, passed by.

"That argument has been discredited," Patchen said. "The official view is that Ilse was not a Soviet agent until she started sleeping with Darby. The Soviets found out about her adultery and blackmailed her."

"That's an ingenious theory."

"It's Wolkowicz's theory. There's a will to believe the wronged husband. If you accept the other explanation—*your* cynical explanation, Paul—then you have to accept that the Outfit, not to mention the Brits, not to mention the invincible Wolkowicz, were all hoodwinked, used, and humiliated by the Soviets. And that simply cannot be."

"Do they think that way at Headquarters? It's crazy."

"Not in their eyes. They believe they're *avoiding* paranoia by refusing to suspect the enemy of being smarter than they are. That's the real madness, to choose madness as a way of remaining sane. Do you follow me?"

"I don't think so."

"Think about it. Then again, maybe you shouldn't think about it. Maybe you've been thinking too much. You seem awfully sad, for a hero."

Christopher had been decorated that day, along with Wolkowicz, in one of the secret ceremonies in the Director's office. As Patchen spoke, they were passing under a lamppost. By its weak light, Patchen searched Christopher's face.

"They think you should go outside, under deep cover," Patchen said.

"What deep cover?"

"Your book of poems again. Maybe you could write for that magazine."

"What would I do under this impenetrable deep cover?"

"You'd be a singleton. You'd work alone. You could go anywhere, do anything, become a legend in your own time. *If* you can escape from Wolkowicz. He doesn't want to give you up."

Christopher had lost none of his affection for Wolkowicz, but he could not work with him again. He knew too much about him.

"Who would I be working for, under deep cover?" he asked.

"You'd report to me," Patchen replied. "But as I said, you'd be working alone."

"All right," Christopher said.

"Good." Patchen coughed, then petted his Doberman when it bounded back to him in sympathy. "I think working alone will suit your temperament better," he said.

Seven

— 1 —

Years afterward, in an expensive Washington restaurant, Rosalind Wilmot put the last forkful of food into her mouth, chewed, and swallowed.
She drank some wine and touched her lips with a napkin.

"I think it's marvelous, the way one can now just ask for a bottle
of wine in America and have actual Algerian Beaujolais brought to one's
table," she said. "The last time I was in Washington my brother took
me to a little place that had been recommended by someone in your
State Department. 'Wine list?' Clive said. 'I'll ask the bartender,' said the
waitress. She came back with two great mugs of something Americans
call Muscatel. We drank it down. Clive thought that it tasted like
Algerian mead. He called for more. 'This is absolutely delicious!' he said.
'Do you make it right here in America from the fermented honey of
American bees?' The waitress said, 'I'll ask the bartender.'"

Rosalind smiled across the table at Christopher.

"You don't look so very much older," she said. "But then, you
haven't been working with Wolkowicz, have you?"

"No."

"Lucky chap. For me, there's been no escape from Robin. You know, of course, that he's in Washington?"

Darby was now the head of British intelligence in the United States.

"I'd heard that," Christopher said.

"What else had you heard about Robin?" Rosalind asked.

"Nothing much."

Rosalind gave Christopher a measured look. "That hardly seems possible," she said. "Robin is the talk of the town. He drinks like a fish and makes the most awful scenes."

"Darby drinks and makes scenes?"

"You find that odd, do you? Robin is taking this posting badly. His duties consist of going to lunch with someone from the Outfit a couple of times a week. He's expected also to be charming at parties. He's not very charming, I'm afraid."

"I thought there was more to his job than that."

"Ordinarily there is. But Robin's been shut off by the Americans. They refuse to put him in the picture. On important things, they deal direct with London through your chief of station there. Robin thinks there's a plot against him."

"If he's behaving as you say, maybe they just think he's a drunk."

"If drunks were mistrusted by either side there'd be jolly little Anglo-American collaboration," Rosalind said. "No, he thinks it's Wolkowicz."

"Really?"

"Really. Wolkowicz is a vengeful bastard, isn't he? And now he's such a figure of mystery and power."

It was true that Wolkowicz had come up in the world. Dennis Foley, Wolkowicz's old friend from the congressional investigations committee, had become the President's assistant for intelligence matters. Foley had borrowed Wolkowicz from the Outfit for special duties. No one knew the exact nature of these duties.

"Is Barney a figure of mystery and power?" Christopher asked.

Rosalind's violet eyes glittered with mistrust. "You know he is. Aren't you part of his team?"

"Hardly. I've been abroad."

"But now you're back. One would suppose that you'd join up with your old chief again."

"Would one?" Christopher said.

Christopher called for the check. When it came, Rosalind paid it with a new fifty-dollar bill.

They went outside and got into Rosalind's car, an inconspicuous gray Chevrolet. The paint gleamed with wax and the upholstery had been vigorously brushed: it could only be a vehicle from the motor pool of the British Embassy. Rosalind was giving Christopher every possible signal—the blurted questions about his reasons for being in Washington, the crisp new fifty out of the petty cash drawer, the car—that she was on duty and he was her target.

Now, as she drove him through the darkened streets of Georgetown, she began to talk again in the same rude tone she had used in the restaurant. It occurred to Christopher that, in two hours of conversation, Rosalind had made only one joke, the story about the Muscatel.

"Robin has suggested that I should resume my friendship with you; he thinks I can get you to whisper secrets in bed," she said. "That should tell you that he's not quite the man you knew in Vienna."

"You mean he wouldn't have suggested such a thing in Vienna?"

Rosalind gave a little grunt, as if the car had hit a hole in the pavement.

"No," she said. "That was true lust. Besides, Robin wasn't quite so desperate in those days. His current case of nerves must have something to do with that business with Ilse. One wouldn't think that a bit of warmed-over sex could mean all that much, but Americans do brood so about such things. It must be because you never seem to *know* the people you marry, they're strangers you meet at the office. And of course Ilse was a bloody romantic German, which adds to the lunacy. Remember how Wolkowicz looked, pounding Robin's face to a bloody pulp in the snow in the Vienna Woods. Quite mad."

Rosalind, when she spoke of Americans to Christopher, implied that they were foreigners to him, too. In a way, they were. She stopped the car in front of Christopher's hotel. "I'm quite desperate myself," she said. "I've asked to be posted away from here. They're going to let me join my brother in Baghdad."

"Do you get along well with your brother?"

"Madly. It was Robin who suggested it, before he knew you were coming back to assist Wolkowicz."

"Why do you have this fixation about my assisting Wolkowicz, Rosalind? In what way am I going to assist him, do you think?"

"In this vendetta Robin believes is going on against him."

"Robin is having alcoholic delusions."

Rosalind sat with both hands on the wheel, staring straight ahead. However her manner had changed, she looked the same. It was raining and her white face, framed by its dark hair, was reflected in the windshield. She turned her luminous eyes on Christopher.

"Delusions, are they?" she said. "Robin will be happy to know that. I'll tell him. It will give me something to report. It ought to comfort him."

She took Christopher's face between her hands and kissed him on the lips. It was a sisterly kiss, dry and cool.

"On the other hand, Robin always said of you that you never told unnecessary lies," she said. "When he remembers that, he may not be so comforted."

Both she and Christopher knew that they had been lying to each other all evening. It was part of the work. In Vienna it had been a joke, their professional secrets had been no more important to them as they lay in bed than secrets about old lovers were to an ordinary couple who decided to have an affair.

Rosalind drove away, weaving a bit as she maneuvered the clumsy American car. She had gone to a lot of trouble to warn Christopher that this business with Darby was no joke. He wondered what her reasons could be.

— 2 —

Next day, Wolkowicz and Christopher met by the elephant cage in the zoo. Wolkowicz had made elaborate meeting arrangements, as if they were running an operation in a city behind the Iron Curtain. Christopher had been instructed to approach on foot, through the park, in order to be able to spot surveillance. There were other signs of excessive tradecraft, not typical of Wolkowicz: a figure eight had been drawn in chalk on the sidewalk at a designated place to signify that the meeting was on, and there were to be elaborate signals between Wolkowicz and Christopher before they approached each other. Christopher had been warned not to discuss the meeting with anyone, not even Patchen.

When Wolkowicz saw Christopher, he took a sack of peanuts out of his pocket and began to feed the elephants; Christopher slapped the folded newspaper he was carrying against his thigh. These were the all-clear signals.

The formalities over, Wolkowicz seized Christopher by both biceps and gave him a shake. His rubicund face with its button nose and its fat cheeks glowed with pleasure.

"You seem happy," Christopher said.

"I must be glad to see you. I didn't think Patchen would be smart enough to let me have you."

"He knows about this?"

"Sure he knows. That's the whole idea."

Wolkowicz fed more peanuts to the elephants, who thrust their trunks through the bars of their enclosure; it was obvious that the animals knew Wolkowicz; he must come here often. Christopher grinned. Wolkowicz frowned.

"What's so funny?" he asked.

"The elephants like you."

"I like elephants," Wolkowicz said. "Do you know what I'm doing?"

"No."

"I'm running a counterintelligence op."

"Who are you running this op for, Barney?"

"I report to a guy in the White House named Foley. It's the god-damndest setup. I'm not supposed to tell the Outfit a fucking thing, and so far I haven't. Patchen is having a fit. That's why I asked for you. I figured Patchen would try to penetrate this operation. I *wanted* it to be penetrated. The Outfit has to know what's going on. I'm under orders from above not to tell the Outfit what I'm doing. How do we handle a situation like that? We use you, the one man who will not screw either me or the Outfit."

"You *want* me to report to Patchen?"

"Somebody has to."

Wolkowicz placed his last peanut in the pink nostril of the nearest elephant and crumpled the empty bag.

"What about your orders from the White House?" Christopher asked.

"Fuck the White House," Wolkowicz said. "Let me give you the scenario."

Wolkowicz told Christopher who their target was, and why. When he was finished, he looked into Christopher's cold, guarded face.

"You don't believe it, do you?" Wolkowicz said.

"It's a surprise."

Wolkowicz's perfect false teeth appeared, briefly. Over the years, he had grown steadily more corpulent. His flesh had taken on a kind of gloss, like a sausage casing. Now, sprawled on the bench with his legs spread and his hands thrust into his pants pockets, he stared belligerently into Christopher's eyes.

"I know what you're thinking," he said. "You think I'm out for revenge."

"That's what Rosalind Wilmot thinks."

"Is that so? Did you enjoy your dinner with her last night?"

"Not especially."

"I heard you made an early night of it. Darby knows we're on him, right?"

"According to Rosalind, he knows you have him under surveillance. I don't think he knows what you suspect him of."

"He knows, all right," Wolkowicz said. "I wouldn't go to all this trouble over what's-her-name, my ex-wife." His dentures gleamed again, white in his pink face. "Not that I mind a little bonus."

— 3 —

Later, walking the Doberman, Patchen philosophized. It was early in September and the night was mild, but Patchen wore his scarf and his cap.

"I sometimes think there is some sort of psychic link between Wolkowicz and me," Patchen said. "I can't stand the man and he can't stand me, but we seem to be overcome by the same suspicions at the same time."

"You suspect Darby, too?"

"Oh, yes. I would have gone after him myself if the White House hadn't preempted the investigation."

"You must be glad they did. It saves the Outfit the necessity of embarrassing the British service."

"That, or it saves the British service from being as embarrassed as it ought to be. Us, too."

"What do you mean by that?"

Patchen hurried along, dragging his leg. It had rained that day and in the washed air his breath smelled faintly of the Bordeaux he had drunk with dinner.

"The first thing I did when I got this new job, which theoretically gives me access to everything," Patchen said, "was to look into the history of operations against the Soviets."

A month or two earlier, Patchen had been made chief of operations; he ran the entire espionage service.

"It's a strange history. In nearly twenty years of trying, the Outfit, on its own, has never initiated a single successful operation within Russia or against a Russian target outside of the Soviet Union. Does that surprise you?"

"What about the Sewer?"

"What about it, indeed? Perhaps this merry little jape you and Wolkowicz are putting on will answer that question. But there are so many other questions. You can't imagine how many."

"You think Darby can answer these questions?"

Patchen cleared his throat. "I think," he said, "that nearly everyone will be satisfied with his answers. 'My God,' they'll say when Wolkowicz is done, 'now we know the worst!' "

It was time to turn back. Patchen called his dog.

"But will they know the worst?" he said. "I wonder."

— 4 —

Christopher had not imagined that he would see Rosalind again, but within a week he was invited to a British party, and she was among the guests. It was a buffet dinner. Christopher arrived late and after he had filled his plate the hostess led him to the last empty place, a chair that formed part of a circle in front of the fireplace.

"Do you know all these dreadful foreigners?" she asked. "My niece Charlotte Grestain and Robin Darby, Rosalind Wilmot and—"

"My dear Paul," Darby said in a slurred voice, "what a magnificent surprise." He gave Christopher an elaborate wink. The hostess gave Darby a worried look.

"You do know one another," the hostess said. "Marvelous. I'll leave you to it, then."

"Tell me the rest of your name, Paul," Charlotte Grestain said, patting the chair beside her. She was a lean girl, no more than eighteen, with the face of a huntress and a fresh English complexion. She sipped what seemed to be a glass of milk.

"Christopher."

"Really? I think it's very matey the way you Americans have Christian names for surnames. Do you like milk?"

"Not especially."

"I drink nothing else when in America. It's your national drink. I wonder if I can have another?"

She gestured to a waiter. He took her glass. "Milk and whisky, Lady Charlotte?"

"Yes, please. The whisky improves it enormously."

Robin Darby plucked a drink off the waiter's tray as he passed. He ran his eyes over the long legs of Charlotte Grestain.

"Whisky and milk is my idea of bridging the Atlantic," Charlotte said, "mixing the best of the Old World with the best of the New."

Darby drained his glass. "You're a silly little brat, Charlotte," he said.

"Famous for it," Charlotte replied.

Darby kneaded his empty whisky glass and looked around in naked desperation for another drink, gesticulating to waiters. They passed by, their trays out of reach.

"They've been told not to come near me, that much is plain," Darby said.

He uttered a sepulchral laugh. If Wolkowicz had grown meatier in the years since the fight in the snow over Ilse, Darby, who had always been thin, had become emaciated. His elongated body appeared to have been dropped into its chair like a doll, limbs askew, eyes glassy.

Darby breathed noisily through his nose. His beard was wet with dribbled whisky. When the waiter returned with Charlotte's whisky and milk, Darby helped himself to another drink.

Darby took no part in the small talk that ran around the circle of chairs except to laugh loudly, in a humorless voice, at the witticisms. He employed a different laugh for every member of the party, greeting Charlotte's sallies with a snort, Rosalind's with a phlegmy giggle. Only Christopher was spared this treatment; instead of laughing at his remarks, Darby fixed him with a demented wild-eyed stare, hand clapped over his mouth.

They were joined by two other latecomers, a U.S. senator called Oliver Brooks and his wife. Senator Brooks was in his sixties, but he looked much younger; he had the smooth face of a man of thirty and a magnificent head of coal-black hair. It was suspected that he had undergone hair transplants. His wife was an extremely pretty girl of twenty-two who had been a beauty queen, a final runner-up in the Miss U.S.A. contest, before she married the senator.

Mrs. Brooks sat down, her shapely knees primly together, and gave everyone in the circle a bright smile. Darby straightened his sprawled body and smiled back just as brilliantly. So long as Darby smiled, Mrs. Brooks continued to smile. She was a responsive girl, eager to be polite. For long moments the beauty queen and the Englishman faced each other, teeth bared. When she gave signs of relaxing her smile, Darby intensified his; she would then smile more brightly. At last she realized that Darby was mocking her. Her smile faded.

"God," Darby said, "that was lovely. Put up a card in Soho Square and you could get ten pounds for it—Miss Sourire, Charm School, one flight up. What do you think, chaps?"

Senator Brooks, who had been talking to Charlotte Grestain, saw nothing amiss. He glanced at his young wife, to see if she perceived the humor in this obscure English joke, but she was poking listlessly at the food on her plate and he couldn't catch her eye.

The senator began to tell political anecdotes. Darby, eyes goggling with exaggerated attention, greeted the end of each story with a basso buffo explosion of guffaws that caused heads to turn all the way across the room.

Senator Brooks was entranced by his wife's beauty. His face, when he looked at her, wore an expression of helpless adoration. He filled her glass, took away her plate. He asked her if she would like strawberries.

"Do you think they're real strawberries?" she asked in her soft southern accent. "I can't bear those hothouse berries that taste like wadded-up pages torn out of the telephone book."

"I'll find out if they're fresh," Senator Brooks said.

While he was gone, his wife sat quietly, turning a sapphire ring on her finger, her eyes fixed on the floor. As soon as her husband was out of eyeshot, her face lost its smiling charm. No one was watching her except Darby. Under his intense stare, her lips parted and she started to smile again. Senator Brooks returned with a dish of strawberries and a glass of champagne and she gained control of herself and gave him her brilliant smile.

The strawberries were heaped with whipped cream. She lifted some on her finger and licked it off. She had a quick, pink tongue. She giggled, dipped her finger in the whipped cream again, and thrust it into her mouth.

Darby laughed. It was a raucous, mocking laugh, different from all the others he had been using. Rosalind, who up to now had taken no interest in Darby's game, leaned forward and spoke to him. Darby lifted his forearm and shook it, as if he were flinging off an unwanted hand.

"I say, Senator," Darby said loudly. "Your wife is awfully good at that."

Senator Brooks turned his smooth face toward Darby and gave him a cordial politician's smile. "Good at what?" he asked.

"Getting her teeth out of the way."

Brooks lost his smile. His wife took her finger out of her mouth.

"I mean to say it's awfully good for the hair, or so I've heard," Darby said.

"Good for the hair?"

"Yes, the hair. You have a magnificent thatch of it, if I may say so, no sign of gray, unusual in a man of your years. Earlier, as I was admiring Mrs. Brooks's teeth, I wondered how that could possibly be, but now of course it's quite obvious."

Brooks had begun to smile again. This was going to be another strange transatlantic joke. Mrs. Brooks, holding her dish of strawberries in her smooth lap, sat quite still.

"The secret of eternal youth, at least so far as the hair is concerned, was told to me years ago in London, by the wife of an aging but vigorous poet. She got a bit tiddly at a party, did the poet's wife. Most of the people there were younger than her husband, but some of them already had gray hair. She looked round at the company and said, 'There seems to be a lot of gray hair here for such a young crowd.' I agreed. 'I give my husband three blow jobs a week and he doesn't have a gray hair in his head,' she said."

The party had gone silent. Darby raised his voice and addressed the rigid guests.

"I had no idea that sort of cure was possible in America, your women have such bloody great strong teeth," he said. "But the senator here is living proof, isn't he?"

Senator Brooks, moving with great deliberation, lifted the dish of strawberries from his wife's hand and led her from the room.

Darby watched them go, then shook hands with the hostess. *"Lovely* party, my dear Vera," he said, and left.

"Dear God," Rosalind said. "He *is* over the edge."

"Over the edge my ass," Wolkowicz said. "It's all part of the act. He's getting ready to disappear."

Wolkowicz believed that Darby's public misbehavior was an act, part of an elaborate scheme to make it seem that he was a lunatic rather than a criminal. On the table before Wolkowicz were the fragments of evidence that had led him to the conclusion that Robin Darby was a Soviet agent. The photographs, the dry typed reports of movements and contacts, the critiques of operations that had seemed at the time to be such triumphs for British intelligence—all added up, for Wolkowicz, to the sum of Darby's guilt. Darby's drunken outburst at the party was just another digit to add to the column.

"We're going to have to move," Wolkowicz said, "or we'll lose the cocksucker."

Wolkowicz closed the file. "Let's get Horace in here," he said. Christopher was surprised that Wolkowicz was willing to let the discussion of Darby's behavior at the party drop with so little discussion; usually he worried every bit of evidence for hours, sniffing it and turning it in the cunning paws of his suspicion.

When Horace Hubbard came into the room, Wolkowicz ignored him. His reading glasses sliding down his pug nose, he continued to read in silence. Horace, tall and gangling, waited patiently. He had graduated from Yale the year before and immediately joined the Outfit. This was his first assignment; Wolkowicz had chosen him because he was so clean. Horace had not had time to form friendships, much less loyalties, inside the Outfit. Besides, Christopher was his hero.

"Get me some coffee," Wolkowicz said at last.

"Something came in from the truck," Horace said.

"Coffee," Wolkowicz said. He went back to his reading.

Horace poured coffee from a Silex that bubbled on a hot plate within reach of Wolkowicz's hand. Wolkowicz sipped coffee and made a face.

"Okay," Wolkowicz said. "Now, what about the truck?"

The truck was a van—or, rather, several vans and limousines that were changed every day to divert suspicion—from which electronics technicians monitored the listening devices that had been placed in Robin Darby's apartment, car, and office.

"The listeners picked up the Russian accent again," Horace said.

"The same voice, the same telephone code. The caller said, 'The washing is ready, when can we deliver?' Darby said, 'After five is the best time.' The caller said, 'To your office or your home?' Darby replied, 'Not the office, if you don't mind.' "

Wolkowicz took the slip of paper from which Horace had been reading this dialogue, and studied it in silence for long seconds.

"It's a meeting," he said. "But where?"

Horace scratched his lower lip. He looked something like his father, but he had his mother's gift for mockery; when he spoke to Wolkowicz, he *looked* like Wolkowicz, adopting his facial expressions and sometimes reproducing his voice, like a ventriloquist. Wolkowicz seemed not to notice.

"This may not thrill you," Horace said, speaking this phrase in Wolkowicz's raspy voice before switching over to his natural way of speaking. "But I think I may know where the meeting is going to take place."

"Why the hell wouldn't it thrill me?" Wolkowicz demanded.

"Yesterday I was coming out of the Mayflower at about three in the afternoon—"

"What were you doing in the Mayflower?"

"I'd had a long lunch with a friend. As I came out the back door onto Seventeenth Street, I saw Darby. He was going into the National Geographic Building, trotting up the steps. I decided to see what he was up to."

"You *followed* him?" Wolkowicz said. "What the fuck's the matter with you, kid?"

"I told you you wouldn't be thrilled," Horace said.

There was no surveillance on Darby: Wolkowicz assumed that he would spot it immediately, scare, and ruin any chance Wolkowicz had of catching him. Not until the moment of the kill did Wolkowicz want Darby to see the men who were hunting him.

Horace waited, his brows lifted in his alert, attentive way, to see if Wolkowicz was all through rebuking him. Wolkowicz gestured that he should go on.

"It took me a moment to find him when I got inside," Horace said. "They have a replica of the Sistine Chapel on display. Darby was inside the display, admiring the ceiling—it's made up of backlit color transparencies. Very nice. Darby walked out, went back to the entrance, then seemed to change his mind, looked at his watch, and walked very briskly to the Sistine Chapel again and went inside it again. Then he walked right on out the back door into the parking lot. He looked at his watch again as he opened the door to go out. He was timing the whole thing."

"He was casing the place for a meeting," Wolkowicz said.

"That's what I thought."

"Did he see you?"

"Maybe. But he doesn't know me."

"He'll know you next time," Wolkowicz said. "If he's using the same tradecraft he's always used, the meeting will be today. If he said five o'clock, he means four. Let's haul ass."

— 6 —

That afternoon at precisely four o'clock, Robin Darby, walking with the springy step that Christopher remembered from the Englishman's triumphant days in Vienna, strode into the National Geographic Building and proceeded briskly to the Sistine Chapel display. Inside the display, he bumped into a man who was looking with rapt attention at the ceiling. There was a brief, embarrassed scuffle. Then both men made their excuses and Darby went on his way. It looked like the most natural behavior in the world.

As Darby emerged from the display, he saw Horace Hubbard. Just for an instant, recognition flickered in his eyes. He changed direction abruptly, walked to the bank of elevators, and stepped aboard a waiting car. Before the dull bronze doors could close, a uniformed guard stepped onto the elevator and confronted Darby.

"May I help you, sir?"

"No," Darby said. "I don't require any help."

"Do you have an appointment with someone?"

"Of course I have an appointment."

"Who with, sir?"

Darby looked over the guard's shoulder and saw Paul Christopher standing in the foyer.

"Hello, my friend," Christopher said. "You're lost. Here I am."

"My dear fellow," Darby said, "I think I may be under arrest."

The guard, unsmiling, stepped aside and let Darby go. He watched him shake hands with Christopher, then watched Christopher guide him toward the exit. As they went through the door, Christopher reached under Darby's coattail and grasped his belt. The guard thought that was queer. But he saw a lot of queer things in his job.

Christopher ran Darby down the short flight of marble steps. Darby had never realized how strong this American was. He did not attempt to resist; there was no point in it. He saw at least five Outfit toughs stationed in the parking lot. There were as many more in M Street: one loitering by an abandoned brick school, another in the doorway of a variety store, another no more than ten feet away.

This nearest tough held a rolled newspaper in his hand. He lifted it and a taxi sped toward him. Darby's contact, the man he had bumped into inside the Sistine Chapel, was walking along the sidewalk. The taxi rolled past him and stopped.

The tall youth Darby had seen inside—the same boy he had seen the day before when he cased the place—was walking after Darby's contact with long, rapid strides. The door of a waiting taxi opened just before the contact reached it. He saw the men in the street for the first time and tried to run.

Horace Hubbard seized him by the scruff of the neck and the seat of the pants and rushed him toward the open door of the taxi. A man inside the taxi reached out, grasped the contact by the lapels, and pulled him inside. The tall youth jumped in after him and the taxi drove away with its back door flapping.

"Here comes our car," Christopher said. A black limousine with smoked windows drifted to the curb and the door opened. Darby folded his skinny body and got inside. Christopher got in after him. Wolkowicz was already in the limousine, seated on the jump seat so that he faced Darby when the latter sat down.

"Hello, Limey," Wolkowicz said.

Darby pulled up his right pants leg, revealing a small automatic pistol in a leg holster. To Christopher, this seemed a gesture of surrender. But Wolkowicz seized Darby by the hair and beard and slammed his face against the glass partition that separated the backseat from the front. Blood spurted from Darby's nose.

The Englishman gave Christopher a look of appeal and pointed at the gun; Christopher took it. Wolkowicz seized Darby's lower lip between his thumb and forefinger and twisted. Darby, helpless in the pain of the grip, lay still.

"Whatever the Russian gave you, I want," Wolkowicz said.

Darby reached into the inside pocket of his coat and handed Wolkowicz an envelope. Wolkowicz ripped it open. It contained a Canadian passport bearing Darby's photograph and a false name, a driver's license and credit cards in the same fictitious name, and twenty brand-new one-hundred-dollar bills.

"Fucking amateurs," Wolkowicz said.

Darby straightened up and sat quietly between the two Americans. His nose was still bleeding. Christopher handed him a handkerchief. Darby took it and smiled, but he did not attempt to stop the blood that was flowing over his beard. His whiskers were quite gray now, with little trace of the ginger color they had had years before in Vienna.

Darby closed his eyes and put his head back against the puffy upholstery. Though he had spent his life in observing small details, he seemed now to take no interest at all in the route that the purring Cadillac followed as it carried him out of the city.

— 7 —

At his trial, held in secret in London, Robin Darby freely admitted to having spied for the Soviet Union. The man he had met in the Sistine Chapel had been an officer of the KGB, his case officer. He gave full particulars on this man.

During the brief brush contact inside the Sistine Chapel, the Russian had given Darby the money and false documents that had been found on him. Had the arrest been delayed by so much as a day, Darby would have vanished from the United States and from the West.

"You planned to escape to the Soviet Union?" the prosecutor asked Darby.

"Yes."

"You anticipated that you would be arrested for espionage?"

"It was obvious that something was on. My flat was bugged. I was *not* being followed, which meant that they didn't want to flush me. I knew that Wolkowicz was engaged in a highly sensitive counterintelligence operation."

"How did you know that?"

"Rumor. The members of the Outfit are a confiding lot. I assumed that I was the target."

"Will you tell this court why you became a traitor?" the prosecutor asked.

"A traitor?" Darby, who usually spoke in a cockney accent that was so heavy that it seemed affected, reproduced the upper-class diction of the prosecutor. "A *traitor?* To the likes of you? You must be joking," he said, laughing outright.

Robin Darby was convicted of espionage and sentenced to life imprisonment. During his trial, he had been held in a special cell on an army base. On the night before he was to be moved to his permanent place of imprisonment, Wolkowicz and Christopher visited him.

The jailer led them to Darby's cell and slid open the peephole, inviting the Americans to look at the prisoner before they entered. In this place, Darby had been permitted some comforts. The interior was brightly lit, as the Sewer had been, and as in the Sewer, the floor was covered with a Persian carpet. Darby sat with his narrow back to the door, reading a large illustrated book.

When the door opened, he turned around. Christopher did not recognize him at once: he had shaved off his beard. The absence of hair made his large nose seem even larger, and his crooked yellow teeth, which had formerly been hidden behind a fringe of mustache, glinted in a lantern jaw.

"Amazing transformation, isn't it?" Darby said. "No beards allowed at the Scrubs, I'm told."

"What about rugs?" Wolkowicz asked.

"I'm afraid not. It's Spartan rules for traitors. I'm just packing up my books. I don't know what I'll be allowed."

A couple of dozen heavy volumes were strewn on the narrow bed. Christopher examined them. Printed in most of the half-dozen languages that Darby was able to read, they all dealt with the same subject.

"Botany?" Christopher said.

Darby stroked his denuded chin. "My vice," he said, "but then, this is the hour at which all secrets of the heart stand revealed. Would you like one as a keepsake?" He handed Christopher a leather-bound volume on the flowers of the Andes, in Spanish. "It's a first edition," he said. "Do have it." He turned, with the same affable smile, to Wolkowicz. "Barney?" he said. "Something in Russian?"

"No thanks," Wolkowicz said. "I just came to say good-bye."

"Decent of you. Congratulations, by the way. You've done it again."

"Just lucky," Wolkowicz said.

Darby interrupted him. "No need to apologize," he said. "All in a day's work."

"No shit?" Wolkowicz said.

"You mean it *isn't* all in a day's work? You can't be upset still over that business with your wife in Vienna?"

Wolkowicz expelled an harsh, exasperated breath. "Not anymore," he said. "That's over, finally."

Darby studied Wolkowicz's glowering face for a moment. He never lost his own smile. " 'That's over, finally,' " he repeated. "Ah! Now I remember. 'This isn't over yet,' that's what you said, Barney, that day in the snow. But now finally it is? That's what you've come to tell me?"

Wolkowicz held Darby's eyes, and now he smiled.

Darby laughed one of his artificial party laughs, a wild whinny. He caught Christopher's eyes and held them and when he spoke, he spoke to Christopher, as if Wolkowicz, who had just put him into prison for life, could not be expected to understand what he was about to say.

"What an ending," he said. "The revolution destroyed by a wronged husband. How can such a thing be believed?"

Wolkowicz seemed not to hear Darby's words. He drew a paperback book from his overcoat pocket.

"Okay?" he said to the jailer.

The jailer glanced at the book, then nodded. "I don't know if he'll be allowed to have it when he moves."

"He can read it tonight," Wolkowicz said. He handed the book to Darby, who examined the cover.

"The Manchurian Candidate," Darby read. "Is that a thriller? I've never actually read a thriller."

"I think you'll enjoy this one," Wolkowicz said.

"Very thoughtful." Darby tossed the pulp book with its garish orange cover onto the cot with his first editions.

"I must give *you* something," Darby said. Stooping in the confined space, he rolled up one of the carpets and handed it to Wolkowicz. "It's an Isfahan, rather a good one, really," he said.

Wolkowicz made no move to accept the rug. Darby picked up the other man's arm by the elbow and thrust the cylinder of carpet beneath it. "Do take it," he said; "think of me when you tread on it."

That night, Darby killed two of his jailers and escaped. Autopsies established that he had used a needle to inject a deadly poison into his victims; it was a poison, derived from the bean of the castor plant, that was used only by the Soviet secret service.

Darby left a message for Wolkowicz, written in ornamental Cyrillic script on the flyleaf of *The Manchurian Candidate*.

When translated, it read: *Ilse was quite innocent. But she did like to lie face down on the Isfahan while one smelled the roses. Think of me.*

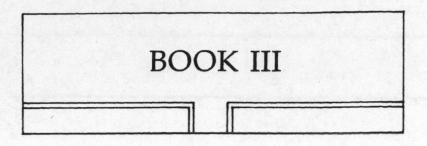

BOOK III

Christopher

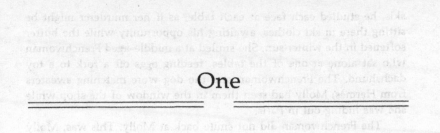

One

— 1 —

A week before the death of Molly Benson, she and Christopher went skiing in the early morning on the slopes above Zermatt. It was the day after New Year's, their last day in the mountains. By nine o'clock, when they came down to their hotel, the tables on the outdoor terrace were crowded for breakfast. A fierce white sun lit up the snowfields on the wall of the Matterhorn.

"Oh," Molly said, "but I've loved it here."

They had spent the holidays here after Christopher returned from America. Before that he had been in Vietnam. In Saigon, he had made enemies, and this had put both their lives in danger. Friends of Christopher's in Paris had hidden her while he was gone. *Hidden* her. Molly thought it was too farcical, it was like a film, being in love with a man who knew a dangerous secret, being in this glorious place with him, eating delicious food, drinking strange liqueurs, making love while the Alpine moon came in the window, being hunted by secret agents.

As Molly and Christopher came onto the hotel terrace with their skis, he studied each face at each table, as if her murderer might be sitting there in ski clothes, awaiting his opportunity while the butter softened in the winter sun. She smiled at a middle-aged Frenchwoman who sat alone at one of the tables, feeding eggs off a fork to a toy dachshund. The Frenchwoman and the dog wore matching sweaters from Hermès; Molly had seen them in the window of the shop while she was hiding out in Paris.

The Frenchwoman did not smile back at Molly. This was, Molly knew, a reproach for her lack of chic. She was dressed in a loose blue Guernsey sweater that was meant to be worn with rubber boots during long tramps over the English moors. She had bought her faded ski pants five years before during a school trip to Gstaad. Molly never looked at other women, never noticed what clothes they wore. She had no idea of fashion. Her transparent skin glowed, tanned after a week on the slopes. Her full lips needed no paint; she had green eyes with large brilliant whites and her thick hair had never been curled. When fashionable women looked at Molly, that was what they saw. Coldly, the Frenchwoman looked away, as if she hadn't seen Molly at all, as if she expected to see someone who was truly beautiful elsewhere in the crowd.

The waiter brought coffee and Molly poured from the silver pot for herself and for Christopher. She cut a brittle roll in half lengthwise, scattering flakes of crust on the tablecloth, and buttered it. She examined the little transparent packets of jam.

"Do you prefer grape jam or grape jam?" Molly asked. She spread jam on the bread and gave half to Christopher. Molly did many things for him that he preferred to do for himself. He opened the copy of the *Neue Zürcher Zeitung* that the waiter had brought with breakfast. He looked through the paper, sipping coffee, but left his bread untouched on the plate.

"Don't you like lovely bread and jam?" Molly asked, chewing.

With her shining hair falling down the back of her warm, sensible Guernsey sweater, she drank the last of her coffee and ate Christopher's share of the bread and jam.

Molly licked the jam from her fingers. Christopher had stopped examining faces; something in the newspaper interested him. Molly saw a chance to show that she had learned something about the spy's life.

"Do you know that man, the one in the trilby hat?" she asked.

Christopher looked over his newspaper at a squat, unshaven man who stood on the steps at the entrance to the terrace. The newcomer, coatless in the snow, was dressed in a safari suit. His short-sleeved jacket was open at the throat, revealing a mat of thick black chest hair. He wore a brand-new Tyrolean hat with a large feather stuck into a silver ornament. Molly's Frenchwoman stared at this newcomer in utter disbelief and gave her dachshund a reassuring kiss.

"Yes," Christopher said, "I know him."

Barney Wolkowicz doffed his Tyrolean hat to Christopher and Molly and started toward their table. As he crossed the lumber floor of the terrace the leather soles of his shoes slipped on the caked snow. He floundered and grasped the backs of chairs to keep his balance. Molly smiled at him and Wolkowicz grinned back with his false teeth.

Sitting down at their table, Wolkowicz took off his hat again and wiped the sweatband with Christopher's napkin. "How do you like my new hat?" he asked. "Fifty francs, Swiss. Pretty good, I thought, considering the size of the feather."

"I wish my chap had one just like it," Molly said. "I'm Molly Benson."

Wolkowicz didn't tell her his name. Molly asked no questions. She was still learning the manners of the profession. Though she and Christopher had been lovers—not just lovers, but in love every minute, absorbed in each other's bodies and minds—for two years, she had known for less than a month that Christopher was a spy. When he told her, she had laughed; it had been such a breathtaking surprise, as if he had invented some merry new way to make love. She believed him at once, it explained so much about him—his absences, the things he said in his sleep in foreign languages, his caution. She even believed, because he told her so, that men were trying to kill them. All the same, it seemed comical to her. Suppose they *were* killed, murdered by some seedy little man who was paid a thousand dollars for the job. Even death would be a joke.

As she watched Wolkowicz her eyes brimmed with merriment. From beneath the fuzzy brim of his trilby hat, he was examining the faces at the surrounding tables.

"Paul's already done that," Molly said.

"Done what?"

"Memorized all the faces. I should think you'd want some breakfast."

Christopher called the waiter and ordered coffee and rolls for Wolkowicz.

Christopher said, "You're a long way from home, Barney."

They had last seen each other in Saigon, a month before. Wolkowicz was the chief of station in Vietnam.

"Well, yeah," Wolkowicz said. "I'm on my way to the States and I thought I'd look you up and say hello."

"Isn't Zermatt a little out of your way?"

"Anything for an old friend. *Anything:* I've never liked Zermatt. There's no way to get off this frigging mountain except on that dinky train and every time you try to walk down the street you fall down in the snow. They ought to spread sand or ashes."

Wolkowicz shuddered violently.

"You don't have a coat?" Molly said, concerned. "I'll fetch Paul's for you. Unless you want to go inside."

"No. You've paid for the sunshine. Let's sit in it."

"Then I'll get the coat," Molly said.

Wolkowicz watched her walk into the hotel.

"She doesn't sound like an Australian," he said.

"She went to school in England."

"Where?" It was a silly detail, but Wolkowicz was still storing up details about Christopher as if he were a younger brother who needed to be protected from his own lack of experience. Wolkowicz resented any secret, however small, that Christopher kept from him.

"She went to Roedean," Christopher said. "Then Cambridge, Girton College."

"Isn't there a song about Roedean? Darby used to sing it: 'We are the girls from *Roe-dean.* . . .' "

"I remember. It's not one of Molly's songs."

The waiter brought Wolkowicz's tea and started to pour it. "Go away," Wolkowicz said, taking the pot out of his hand. He cut a piece of Gruyère, crushed it on his plate, and ate the yellow crumbs with a spoon. He was shivering again. His cup rattled in the saucer when he put it down.

Christopher said, "We can go inside."

"No, we'd better talk outside for now. Before your girl comes back I want to tell you why I came all this way to see you."

Christopher waited for Wolkowicz to continue. Wolkowicz watched the people at the next table gather up their jackets and hats and mittens. When they had left, he spoke again, in his normal grating voice.

"I'm all through in Saigon," he said.

"Why?"

"New assignment in Washington. I'm en route."

Christopher didn't ask what the assignment was; Wolkowicz wouldn't have told him.

"Your buddy Patchen was in Saigon a week or so ago," Wolkowicz said. "He said nobody is supposed to go near you. There are people in Washington who think you should be locked up in a mental institution. What did you tell them, for Christ's sake?"

"That the President was killed in revenge for the assassination of the President of Vietnam."

"Is *that* all? You *are* crazy."

"What if it happens to be the truth?"

Wolkowicz exhaled through his teeth. "The truth. The trouble with you is that you think that the truth and reality are the same thing. In this world, *lies* are the reality. People can't live without them."

Wolkowicz, shuddering with cold, lifted the cup to his lips with both hands and drank.

"I know you've resigned from the Outfit," he said. "I know you're not going to start babbling about your wacky theory to any outsiders, but your pal the Truong toc doesn't know that. You've covered his family with shit. He wants your ass."

Molly came out of the hotel, carrying Christopher's sheepskin coat. Wolkowicz spoke quickly, so as to get the words out before Molly came close enough to hear.

But Molly did overhear.

"What is a Truong toc?" she asked.

Wolkowicz grinned at her. She held the coat open for him and he got up and slid his arms into the sleeves. As he did so, his unbuttoned safari jacket parted and Christopher glimpsed the butt of his P-38.

"If it wants Paul's ass," Molly said, "I really must know what it is."

"In Vietnam, the Truong toc is head of the family—he represents all the dead members of the family, all the ones who are now living, and all the ones who are yet to be born."

"Represents them?"

"Kills people who insult the family honor," Wolkowicz said. "People like your boyfriend, here."

"Is it the Truong toc who's after us, then?" Molly said.

Wolkowicz sat down and huddled inside Christopher's sheepskin coat. He took Molly's hand.

"The warmth is back in my bones," he said. "You saved my life, sweetie pie. I'm never going to forget that."

"What about the Truong toc?"

Wolkowicz seemed to notice Molly's beauty for the first time.

"He's not going to forget about you, either," he said.

To the waiter, who had trailed along after Molly, gazing worshipfully at her body, Wolkowicz said in German, "Bring me some eggs and fried potatoes, quick."

— 2 —

From the window of their room, Molly and Christopher looked down on the terrace. Wolkowicz, as shapeless as a bear in Christopher's heavy coat, crouched over a plate of ham and eggs, a fork in his fist.

"What a thug!" Molly said. "Just what I imagined a spy would be like. You're a great disappointment to me in that regard, Paul. You wear such humdrum hats."

Down below, Wolkowicz tore the soft center out of a piece of bread and mopped his plate. "He's wonderful," Molly said. "Look! He has the table manners of a Russian prisoner of war."

It was taking Molly a long time to pack. Christopher folded her sweaters and put them, one after the other, into the bottom of her suitcase. She turned around and saw what he was doing. "No, that's wrong," she said. She spoke in a fluting headmistress's voice: " 'What is the cardinal rule of packing, girls? Boots, books, and bottles in the bottom of the box.' " She removed the sweaters and began to repack.

"He *is* a spy," she said. "Don't deny it. I saw his gun."

"Don't be fooled by his act," Christopher said. "He may talk like a gangster and fake his table manners, but he's an intelligent man."

"He *fakes* those table manners?"

"If you don't pack your box, we're going to miss the train."

"Each of your friends is more wonderful than the last," Molly said. "I had no idea Americans were so interesting."

They were not alone in the little cog train as it traveled down the mountainside. Three men in drab Swiss business suits, gray with dull orange stripes, sat at the far end of the car. Wolkowicz's eyes, glittering under his Tyrolean hat, never left them. Wolkowicz had drunk schnapps with his morning eggs, and his breath smelled of raw alcohol.

Molly held Christopher's hand, stroking the skin. Wolkowicz

watched with a mocking smile on his stubbled lips. Molly intercepted his look.

"It's the full moon," she said. "At this altitude, the lunar influence is very strong. It causes tides in the human body."

Wolkowicz paid no attention to her. The train stopped at one of the way stations and the Swiss businessmen alighted, leaving them alone.

"Excuse us for a minute," Wolkowicz said to Molly.

He marched Christopher to a seat at the end of the car. They sat facing each other. Wolkowicz leaned forward and pitched his voice so that it could just be heard above the rattle of the train.

"I'm going to peel off when we get to the valley and leave you and your girl on your own," Wolkowicz said, "but first I want you to have some information."

The train passed through a tunnel. Wolkowicz stopped speaking until it emerged into the light again. Molly was still sitting where they had left her, gazing out the window at the windblown snow.

"We've penetrated the Truong toc's establishment since the last time you were in Saigon," Wolkowicz said. "Horace got a girl inside who services the old man."

Horace Hubbard had become Wolkowicz's deputy in Saigon.

"Horace," Wolkowicz said, "gave his little girl a Minox, so she could take pictures of things."

Wolkowicz unbuttoned the breast pocket of his safari jacket and produced an envelope. He handed it to Christopher. The flap was sealed with Scotch tape. Christopher opened the envelope. Inside he found a picture of a Western woman, obviously a photograph of a photograph. It had been made in bad light by an amateur. It was grainy and blurred. But Christopher recognized it. The face in the picture was Molly's.

"Horace's agent said they put money on the table to pay for an assassination," Wolkowicz said. "And lying on the table, all mixed up with the blood money, was this picture."

Christopher lifted his eyes. Molly was still looking out the window of the train. After a moment, she felt Christopher's eyes on her and smiled. Wolkowicz turned in the wooden seat and followed Christopher's gaze. He winked at Molly, then looked at her for a long moment longer, a thoughtful expression on his face.

"They want to make you suffer," Wolkowicz said, looking at Christopher again. "I know you're not going to let them close to this girl. So what do you want to do, go back to Vietnam?"

"What else is there to do?"

"I thought so," Wolkowicz said. "Fucking Jack Armstrong. Can I talk you out of it?"

"No."

"Where are you going to store her while you're out there getting yourself killed?"

"In Paris, maybe."

"With Tom Webster?"

Christopher nodded.

"That should be all right," Wolkowicz said. "Have you got enough money?"

"Yes."

"Where did you get it?"

"Patchen gave me some back pay."

Wolkowicz snorted, as if Patchen's motives were laughably apparent. "It's nice to have friends," he said. "I'd take all the money I had with me. When you get to Saigon, Horace will do what he can to help you, even though nobody is supposed to help you; those are Patchen's orders. You've scared the Outfit shitless with your crazy ideas."

"Then why are you helping?"

"Fuck Patchen. Fuck the Outfit. What do they know? One thing you should know. The Truong toc has left Saigon."

"Where has he gone?"

"Up north somewhere. Check with Horace. You'll have to fly up there. Don't, for Christ's sake, trust *anybody* who isn't related to you. But here."

Wolkowicz pressed a slip of paper, about the size of a commemorative postage stamp, into Christopher's palm. A phone number and the name *Gus* were typed on the paper.

"If you need a pilot, Gus is all right," Wolkowicz said. "He's got a nice little airplane and he'll fly anywhere, anytime. Expensive, but he remembers who paid him."

Wolkowicz heard Molly's footsteps approaching and stopped talking. She had changed into a skirt. Wolkowicz admired her as she walked by, making no effort to hide his interest from Christopher. Since the loss of Ilse, he treated all women with contempt.

"Beautiful legs," he said of Molly. "Is she as intelligent as she sounds?"

Christopher nodded.

"Bad combination," Wolkowicz said.

Molly overheard and turned around. Wolkowicz looked into her face again, as if in deep study. He waggled his fingers at her and she continued on her way.

To Christopher, Wolkowicz said, "You know who she looks like, don't you? Your mother—her face is right out of that drawing you used to have."

"I still have it."

"Hold it up to your girl, then. You'll see the resemblance."

The train pulled into the station at Visp. Without another word or gesture, Wolkowicz got up and headed for the door. Molly came out of the lavatory and said something to him. Wolkowicz brushed by her, adjusting his Tyrolean hat, as if she were a stranger, speaking in a language he had never heard.

For a moment, Molly's face was lit by a chatoyant smile. Wolkowicz was right: she did look like the Lori in Zaentz's drawing.

— 3 —

Molly wanted to spend the night in Dijon. There was a hotel there that she liked. It had a one-star restaurant that served duck in orange, her favorite French dish.

"We had such a wonderful duck in Dijon last summer," Molly said. "Let's have it again, Paul. That's my idea of a proper hereafter, to go back in life while you're still young and re-create all the good bits, leaving out the nasty stuff like separations and lost jewelry and harsh words."

"We have to drive on to Paris," Christopher said. "The Websters are expecting us."

"I'm in no rush for Paris. It's such a cold, gray city, and Tom Webster keeps giving me those hangdog looks. You'd think he was your divorced wife and I was the other woman."

"If everything goes well on this trip, you'll never have to stay in Paris again."

"Of course I won't. Everything went so well the last time you went to Vietnam."

They were driving through three or four inches of fresh snow down the western slope of the Jura Mountains. Christopher's Lancia swerved and skidded. He pulled off the road, got the tire chains out of the trunk, and put them on.

When he crawled out from under the car, Molly had vanished. The tracks of her boots led down the mountain. Christopher locked the car and followed them. Dusk was beginning to fall and he hurried, fearing that he might not be able to see the tracks if it became much darker. In the valley below, a few dim yellow lamps were lit in the stone houses. The Angelus struck on a full-throated church bell. He could just make out the sharp profile of the church steeple. He had driven this way before, and he recognized the village though he could not remember its name.

Molly's footprints turned off the highway into a forest track. Christopher found her a few meters farther on. She had swept the snow from a rock, and she sat on it, huddled in Christopher's sheepskin coat, watching the sunset.

"Do you remember this place?" Molly asked.

Christopher nodded. The June before, they had stopped here and eaten a picnic. "We had that amazing sour pink wine called onion skin," Molly said.

She spread Christopher's coat on the rock. "Come," she said.

"You'll be cold."

"No, the air is warm. Look, it's beginning to snow again."

A moment later, as Christopher looked down into Molly's face, she began to weep. She made no sound; the tears glistened on her cheeks and she breathed a little more quickly, in rhythm with the movement of their bodies. She seemed to be dancing.

"You have such a sweet body," she said.

In the car, Molly grinned at Christopher. "Saved from freezing," she said, twisting the mirror toward her and combing her wet hair. "Before you," she said, "I'd never made love to someone I loved, really loved. Had you?"

"I thought I had."

"But had you?"

"No."

"I don't think I ever will again, do you?"

Christopher, staring into the snow whirling in the headlights of the car, shook his head.

"Good," said Molly. "Because I've been swotting up my sorcery. If you found another girl, even if I were dead, I'd climb into her body, my friend, so that in the middle of everything you'd say, 'Hello! What's this? Something familiar here. Hold on, it's Molly!' "

"What about the other girl?"

"I'd strike her frigid. No satisfaction in it for her at all."

"None?"

"That is rather hard on her, isn't it? I'd pretend to be asleep once a month—let her have you. What's the harm in your having a bit of a change so long as I don't know it?"

— 4 —

The Websters' apartment on the avenue Hoche had a row of high windows on a courtyard. In midafternoon, the weak winter light of Paris seeped into the salon.

"Blinding, the sun of Paris, isn't it?" said Sybille Webster. "At high noon, you can almost make out the features of the people on the other side of the room."

Sybille, a Virginia girl, considered Paris a hardship post. She held out her hands to the fitful blue flames of a coal fire.

"This fireplace is all that saves us from freezing," she said. "Poor Stephanie is covered in chilblains. I don't know how we're ever going to restore her circulation so that she can go to dances and get herself married like other girls. She has this awful splotchy chest as a result of living without central heating. And now she's decided to wear her hair in a tonsure. It took years to grow her hair down to her waist. It was glorious. One visit to the hairdresser by herself and I am given back a nun with jug-handle ears."

Stephanie, the Websters' daughter, paid no attention to her mother. Her small hand was buried in her shining monk's cap of black hair. Lying on the carpet with a book, she listened intently to the conversation between her father and Paul Christopher. Her father liked to believe that she could not understand the elliptical speech that members of the Outfit used when discussing their work. But Stephanie, who had learned Arabic as a small child in Amman, and who now spoke French in preference to English, had an ear for nuance.

Glasses glittered on her father's plain face, concealing his eyes. The soles of his shoes whispered over the carpet as he shifted his feet, a sure sign that he was nervous. Paul Christopher was his best friend; Stephanie had always called Christopher "Uncle Paul." Tom Webster was talking in a low voice about Molly, who sat at the other end of the long salon.

"She's welcome here, don't misunderstand me," Tom Webster was saying. "But this isn't the best place for her. They're watching my front door."

"You've seen them?"

"Photographed them." Webster handed Christopher a strip of photographs, close-ups of faces, taken with a telephoto lens. Webster put a forefinger on a genial, open Vietnamese face.

"Nguyên Kim," Webster said.

Christopher recognized Kim, the Truong toc's man in Europe.

"Nguyên Kim and his boys have killed a couple of Vietnamese here," Webster said. "The French told Kim he'd be dead if he killed anybody else. There are *rules*, they explained. But Kim doesn't know that there are rules."

Christopher leaned over and ruffled Stephanie's hair. "Stephanie," he said, "would you ask Molly if she has any aspirin?"

When Stephanie was out of earshot, Christopher turned his back on the room. "Is a safe house possible?" he asked.

"Technically, no. You're untouchable. Wolkowicz explained Patchen's orders to you. I can help you as a friend, and I will. Even Barney will do that, though I've never known him to risk his fat ass for anybody but Barney."

"That's a little harsh."

"You have your opinion of Barney. I have mine. But if Washington finds out we're even talking to you, we'll all be selling encyclopedias."

Stephanie slid back onto her spot on the carpet and reopened her book. "Molly's bringing your aspirin, Uncle Paul," she said.

Molly had put two aspirins into a tumbler of water. Christopher drank the mixture. Tom Webster offered Molly a drink.

"No, thank you," Molly said. "I must say you two seem to be hard at it. What's the subject? Can I join?"

"The subject was you, as a matter of fact. What to do with you."

"Going back to sunny Rome seems much the best idea to me."

"When Paul gets back from Saigon you can talk about that. Now, no."

" 'No'? You sound like the thought police. Am I under arrest, then?"

"I wish you were," Webster said. "You'd be well taken care of in a French jail."

Stephanie closed her book and slammed it against the carpet. "Jail! That's awful!" she said.

Sybille strode across the room and gently kicked her daughter's narrow hip.

"Out, Stephanie," Sybille said.

Stephanie uttered a theatrical sigh, rose to her feet, and went to the other end of the room. She lay down with her book by the fire.

"*All* the way out," Sybille said. "Bedroom. Door closed. Tom, she's a little spy. You should be more careful."

Sybille poured herself a vodka. "If it weren't for Stephanie, I wouldn't mind the bombs and bullets," she said. "We love having Molly here. But there *is* Stephanie."

Molly looked from face to face. "You're all absolutely serious, aren't you?" she said. "You think I need protection. I don't want to be locked up, in a French jail or any other bloody French thing. I want to go back to Rome."

"Listen to good advice," Sybille said. "Tom will take good care of you while Paul's away."

"I know of an apartment you can borrow," Webster said. "I can have it watched."

"And I'll be inside like Rapunzel?" Molly said.

"How can you do that without getting in trouble?" Christopher asked.

"It's a legitimate operation," Tom Webster said. "My job is to watch the Vietnamese in Paris."

"I'm not exactly Vietnamese," Molly said.

"No," said Webster, "but they'll be buzzing around you like bees around a honey tree."

"What poetry," said Molly.

— 5 —

Sybille helped Molly into her disguise: a curly black wig, sunglasses at three o'clock in the morning, a rabbit-skin coat, and baggy gold lamé harem trousers. The baggy pants were especially important, they had told her, because of her memorable legs; Sybille, giggling, had bought them for her in a tarty shop on the Champs-Elysées that catered to tourists from South America.

At ten minutes to three, the phone rang. Sybille did not answer. After a pause, it rang twice again. This time Sybille picked it up and spoke in her rushing Virginia voice to Tom, who was at the other end.

"It's all right," Sybille said to Molly. "Remember, now—walk up toward the Etoile to the rue Tilsitt. Tom will pick you up in a black Citroën. Make sure it's Tom before you get in."

Molly had been inspecting herself in a full-length mirror. Molly pointed to her changed self in the glass.

"Do you think Paul would betray me with this mysterious woman?"

Sybille kissed her. "I don't think you have a thing to worry about, cookie," she said.

Webster was waiting for her in the Citroën when she arrived at the rue Tilsitt. He flicked on the dome light so that she could see his face. Two caped policemen watched impassively.

"They'll think I'm a fifty-franc girl," Molly said.

"They know all the fifty-franc girls. They'll think your husband is in Brussels on business."

Webster put the car in gear. "We're going to take the long way around," he said, his eyes fixed on the rearview mirror.

During the long ride through the empty streets, Webster talked in code phrases on a hand-held radio. Molly opened the glove compartment, looking for a Kleenex, and saw a large blue pistol.

Webster closed the glove compartment. Molly sniffed. He gave her his clean handkerchief. "We're almost there," he said. "It's an unusual place, as safe houses go. It belongs to a sporting Brazilian."

"A sporting Brazilian?"

"You'll see."

Peering through her sunglasses, Molly read the street signs. They were in the 16th Arrondissement, near a Métro station called Muette. She had been here with Christopher, to go to a museum where they had a lot of Monets. After looking at blurry canvases from the artist's water-lily period, they had walked through a park among crowds of dressy French children who looked like midget graduates of the Ecole Normale.

Webster turned the Citroën into a cul-de-sac off the boulevard Beauséjour. This little street, hardly more than a courtyard, seemed to be deserted. Webster waited, the glove compartment open and his hand inside on the pistol. Then someone standing in a doorway lit a cigarette.

"Let's go," Webster said. "Take off your shoes. Quick."

They leaped out of the car. Webster drew Molly into an unlighted hallway and, pulling her by the hand, led her at a run in her stocking feet up the stairs. It was a long way up. Webster shone a penlight on the stairs at every landing and in these brief bursts of incandescence Molly saw that his face was wet with sweat. He panted loudly in the darkness.

At the top, the door of an apartment opened. Christopher stood in the doorway. Molly and Webster plunged by him and he closed the door. Molly looked around her. The sporting Brazilian had furnished his place with glass tables and cubical black chairs. Tiger skins were scattered over a fuzzy white carpet. The walls were mirrored from floor to ceiling and tinted blue and pink. Molly saw thousands of images of herself in her curly black wig, her rabbit coat, her gold lamé harem pants.

"I feel like King Zog's mistress," Molly said. "Is it *always* like this, Paul?"

"Always," Christopher said.

Because Christopher loved her so much, Molly had the power of drawing him out of his body and into her own. With a gesture, with a tiny change of expression, she did this now, and he saw the absurd apartment, the ludicrous situation through her eyes. He began to laugh. Molly joined him. Tears of merriment streamed from their eyes. Wearing her wig and her streetwalker's clothes, she embraced him and covered his face with kisses.

"Is it possible to be happier than this?" Molly asked, watching their image in the mirrors.

Tom Webster shook his head in disbelief. He sank onto a tiger skin, gasping for breath; his big toe protruded from a hole in his sock.

"I think I'll have a drink," he said.

Whisky and water in hand, Webster fixed Molly with a solemn look. "Listen to me," he said. "This is a safe house. You'll be safe here as long as you don't go outside. That's the cardinal rule, Molly. Stay in this apartment. If you do that, we can guarantee your safety. If you don't, nobody can protect you."

He gave her the little radio he had used in the car and showed her how it worked. He hung it around her neck by its strap, knocking her wig askew. Molly stripped off the wig and tossed it onto one of the glass tables. Her rabbit-skin coat already lay on the floor by the door.

"Wear the radio twenty-four hours a day," Webster said. "Take it to bed with you. There'll always be a man downstairs."

Webster led her to the window and pointed out the man standing in the doorway across the cul-de-sac.

"If you want us," he said, "just push the button to transmit and say *Australia*. That's your code word. If one of us is coming up, we'll call *you* and say *Sydney*. Nobody else gets through the door—not a woman, not a child, not a stray cat. Okay?"

"Right," Molly said. *"Australia. Sydney."*

She pressed a button and the radio emitted a squawk. She dropped it, startled.

Webster pointed at the radio, reminding her of all his warnings. "I'll see you tomorrow, after Paul is on his way," he said. "Paul, walk down with me."

In fact they took the elevator. Molly heard it whine down the shaft and heard the gates clashing far below in the night. She went to the window and looked out. Webster and Christopher were talking to the sentinel in the doorway. The man nodded as if to acknowledge an instruction, then dug in his pocket and searched through a handful of change. When he couldn't find what he needed, Christopher gave him what seemed to be a coin and he hurried away.

The face of a clock was reflected in the mirrored walls. Five minutes passed and the sentinel returned. Christopher looked up and saw Molly in the window. She waved. He made no sign in return. Molly's radio crackled.

"Sydney," a voice said.

"Where did the sentinel go?" Molly asked, when Christopher came back.

"To the Métro station to make a phone call."

"Was that a *jeton* you gave him?"

"Yes."

"You always have what they need, don't you?" Molly said. "What will they do without you?"

They embraced among the mirrors. The radio was caught between them. Molly unfastened the strap and let it fall with a thud onto the white carpet by her rabbit-skin coat.

"Time enough tomorrow for code words," she said.

Later, as he walked across the tarmac to board his plane for Saigon, Christopher thought of Molly: asleep as he had left her, and awake as she must soon be, filled with anger and sadness. She could not understand why he could never say good-bye to her. He had left her alone many times before in the same way, without a word.

"It's the only thing about you that I hate," she told him each time he returned. "It's such a simple thing to wake me up and kiss me before you go. Why can't you do it?"

Molly was right. It was a simple thing. But in the end, he never woke her.

Inside the plane, Nguyên Kim knelt in a first-class seat, gripping the fingers of a blond stewardess with one delicate brown hand while with the other he stroked the inside of her wrist. Kim's fingers moved sensuously from pulse to palm and back again, tracing veins and bones. The stewardess, a French girl with a meticulously painted face, stood with her legs apart, spike heels planted in the carpet, anger in her eyes that this colored man should dare to touch her.

Christopher sat down in the seat behind Kim's.

Kim spoke to the stewardess in the breezy American English he had learned at UCLA. The stewardess tugged, trying to free her hand, and when Kim did not loosen his grip, she flushed under her paint.

"I don't understand English," she said in French.

Kim switched to French. "I'll teach you," he said. "Tell me your name."

"Dominique, monsieur."

"English is a fantastic language, Dominique. You mustn't be against it just because it's spoken by Americans."

Kim had seen Christopher get aboard. He let go of the stewardess and she hurried away. Kim stood up and took off his jacket, folding it neatly and placing it in the overhead rack. He went on smiling even when he was alone; he had learned affability as well as English at UCLA. Kim was a member of the royal Nguyên family; his ancestors had been kings of Vietnam. Now he floated between the new order and the old, taking money and doing whatever was necessary to earn it. Because of his ancestry he believed that he had more right to live than others;

certainly more right than any pompous Frenchman or any hulking mongrel of an American.

"Hello, Paul," he said. "Did you notice the eyes on that stew? They're the eyes of a whore, very scornful. *Every man in the world wants to fuck me.* Bourgeois white women think that they understand everything because they understand lust. Why don't we sit together?"

The jet began to move onto the runway. Kim looked at his watch, a solid gold Patek Philippe with a gold band. He wore a heavy gold ring, set with large rubies, on each index finger.

The plane gathered speed and took off. Kim looked at his gold watch again, rings flashing.

"Right on time; good," Kim said. "I had to run to make this plane. It pisses me off when I do that and it takes off late."

The stewardess passed by and Kim caught her hand. "I'll bet you could find some champagne for my friend and me," he said. "Are we going to eat pretty soon?"

"There's a snack."

"Even the snacks are glorious in France. What food!"

"I'll have a Perrier," Christopher said.

When the stewardess brought the trays, Kim waved his food away and asked for more champagne. He had already drunk half a dozen glasses. His eyes were growing dull.

"This food is disgusting," he said to Christopher. "I'll tell you a strange thing. As soon as I get on a plane for Vietnam, I lose my appetite for everything that isn't Vietnamese. French food, French wine are so coarse, so crude. Frenchwomen are cows. Not like home—fragrant silky silent pussy. . . . Am I boring you?"

"I don't mind a little racism," Christopher said. "What's the Truong toc up to?"

"Brooding about you, mostly. I'm on your side, Paul. I *understand* Americans. I keep telling the old man there's nothing personal in your campaign to destroy him and his family and all he holds sacred."

"Does he believe that?"

"Of course not. 'Who is this mad American?' he asks. 'What does he want? What made him what he is?' "

"Will he talk to me?"

"What's the point? You've already told the U.S. government everything you know."

"Maybe they didn't believe me."

Kim laughed, a rare sound from a Vietnamese. "That *is* funny," he said. "I'll have to tell the Truong toc that one."

The jet was climbing through the clouds. As the lights of Paris vanished, the plane emerged into bright moonlight.

"You don't have the lovely Molly with you?" Kim asked. "But then you're not like the other Americans, are you? They make comrades of their women, taking them everywhere. No wonder they have so much trouble thinking clearly."

Kim moved to an empty row of seats, pulled out the armrest, and wrapped a blanket around himself. For the rest of the journey, he was silent. He did not look out the window. He ate no food, drank no alcohol. He sat with his legs folded beneath him, his back perfectly straight, staring ahead, like a monk in the act of meditation.

As the plane approached Saigon, Kim emerged from the lavatory and knelt on the seat in front of Christopher's, ringed hands folded on the backrest. He had transformed himself. Now he was dressed as a Vietnamese in a transparent white shirt, loose trousers, sandals. His black hair gleamed with oil. His face had lost its animation and was composed and solemn. He had stopped speaking English.

"I suppose you know the Truong toc is in Hue," Kim said.

"Do you have an address for him?"

"You really want to see him?"

"Yes."

"When you get to Hue, visit the royal palace at five in the evening. Carry a copy of *Le Monde*. Open it and read it by the royal tombs. Sometimes the old man posts lookouts there. They'll notice you."

In one final Western mannerism, Kim winked at Christopher. Then his face lost all expression as he waited for the wheels to touch the runway.

— 7 —

At the airport, Horace Hubbard waited near the entrance to the passenger terminal, a Vietnamese official at his side. Horace was very tall and the Vietnamese was very short; neither man seemed to be aware of the difference in stature. They chatted easily, smiling, and as Christopher approached, Horace lifted a negligent hand in greeting. He wore his embassy tropical costume: seersucker jacket, polka-dot bow tie, khaki trousers, loafers polished to a high shine. His handshake was strong and as he looked down into Christopher's eyes, his own blue eyes, set deep beneath bushy dark brows, twinkled benevolently.

"Horace," Christopher said. "I didn't expect to see you here."

"Barney's orders. Binh, this is my cousin."

The Vietnamese official held a stamp and stamp pad in his hands. He smiled and held out his hand. Christopher gave him his passport. The Vietnamese stamped it without looking at it and handed it back.

A Thai, a squat muscular man whose feet seemed to grip the earth as he walked, joined them. His powerful biceps filled the sleeves of his immaculate white jacket.

"Hello, Pong," Christopher said. "How are you?"

"Alive and well."

Pong was Wolkowicz's man: driver, cook, thug, bodyguard.

Horace walked Christopher to his car, an embassy Chevrolet guarded by a Vietnamese policeman. The engine was running; the air conditioner, set on maximum, blew lukewarm air into the baked interior. Pong trotted across the tarmac with Christopher's suitcase. He had taken it directly from the plane's baggage bay.

"I didn't know you provided these services," Christopher said to Horace.

"I have the loan of Pong until the new chief of station arrives. It's Barney's farewell gift to his faithful assistant."

"Why are you meeting me?" Christopher asked.

"Why not? It's not likely to destroy your cover. You don't have any cover left in this country."

"That sounds like a quote from Barney."

Horace shrugged. There was no need to explain Wolkowicz's pronouncements; they only startled because there was so much truth in them.

Horace started a Beethoven tape, the "Emperor Concerto," on a portable player. He pulled the curtains over the rear windows. Pong maneuvered the big shiny car through the jammed streets. A boy on a snarling Honda darted out of the shouting mass of pedestrians and bicyclists. Pong nearly hit him. He shouted angrily through the windshield at Pong and kicked the side of the Chevrolet, hard, with the sole of his glossy plastic shoe. Pong, expressionless, looked through the glass at the motorcyclist. The boy kicked the American car again. Pong reached beneath a newspaper on the seat beside him and produced the submachine gun that was hidden there. He stopped the car and, with the weapon in his hand, gazed calmly at the boy on the motorcycle. The boy sped away.

Horace put a canvas satchel into Christopher's lap. Christopher unzipped it. It contained the standard homemaker's kit for Outfit personnel in Vietnam: two grenades, a double-edged knife, a can of Mace, a loaded 9 mm Browning Hi-Power pistol with an extra thirteen-round magazine, and a Swedish Kulspruta submachine gun like the one Pong had pointed at the boy on the motorcycle. The designers of the submachine gun had done nothing to make it beautiful. It was all metal, brutal and clumsy with its long ammunition box and the thick cylinder of a silencer fitted to its muzzle.

Horace was embarrassed. "Barney asked me to offer this to you," he said. "Are you familiar with the Swedish K, also called the Carl Gustav? It shoots six hundred rounds of special secret Parabellum ammunition a minute. It's the most powerful machine pistol in the world, and we're the only ones in Vietnam who've got it."

Christopher smiled at Horace and closed the zipper on the canvas bag. "No thanks," he said. "I come in peace."

"Barney particularly wanted you to have this stuff."

"No."

The cousins had lunch together. Horace was staying in Wolkowicz's house until the new chief of station arrived.

"Maybe the new man will sleep here," Horace said. "Barney never would."

"No? I didn't know that."

"Barney keeps it quiet. He never sleeps where he lives. Someone might catch him asleep."

Christopher was amused. This was a new fact.

"Where does he sleep?"

"In secret places. He changes all the time. It started when his wife left him, he said. He'd slept with her all that time, and she could just as well have stabbed him in the heart as have committed adultery. Ever since, he's slept alone. He advises it for everybody."

"What secret places? Safe houses?"

Horace shrugged. "There didn't seem to be much point in asking. Barney has his eccentricities."

A python lay sleeping beneath a sofa. There was a lump in its smooth body. The snake was another of Wolkowicz's eccentricities.

"The python goes with the house," Horace said. "Barney fed it a

[241]

pig before he left; it's supposed to sleep until it has digested its meal. Snakes are not very responsive pets. I wonder how the new chief is going to feel when it wakes up and asks for the second little pig."

— 8 —

In the late afternoon, Horace took a nap. As soon as it was dark, Christopher went out. In a leather shoulder bag he carried a change of clothes and a toilet kit, enough for an overnight trip. He thought that Pong might follow him, but he did not.

As soon as he was sure that there was nobody behind him, Christopher called Gus, the pilot Wolkowicz had recommended, from a public phone.

In a ripe cockney accent, Gus gave Christopher instructions: "I do business on the roof of the Majestic Hotel. Show up at eleven-thirty. That's too late for the dinner crowd and too early for the serious drinkers, so there'll be nobody there but you and me and the spies. I'm always at the same table, northwest corner. Do you want to tell me your name?"

"Crawford."

"Crawford, right. Bring money. It's very dear, the Majestic is."

Walking toward the hotel through the nighttime crowd, Christopher heard a loud explosion in the distance. Neither he nor anyone else in Tu Do Street paid any attention to the sound; faraway explosions were not objects of curiosity in Saigon. He reached the Majestic Hotel and went upstairs. From the roof, he could see a large fire burning on the western edge of the city, beyond the weak glow emitted by the streetlights and the neon signs.

The headwaiter pointed out Gus at his table by the parapet.

Gus was a Chinese. Christopher was surprised: Gus's voice, coming over the phone, had evoked a picture of a stocky red-faced former sergeant-pilot of the RAF. Gus sipped beer from a bottle and watched the glow of the flames.

"What have you chaps got out there that would burn as bright as that?" he asked Christopher.

"I don't know."

"Lovely fire. You've got to hand it to the little sods. They know how to blow things up."

The waiter brought Christopher a Heineken beer. Gus clinked his bottle against Christopher's.

"So," he said. "You want to go for an airplane ride."

"What kind of a plane do you have?"

"Piper Apache."

"That has two engines?"

"Right. Where do you want to go?"

"North."

"Where precisely? I have to file a flight plan, consult my maps."

"Near Da Nang."

"Near Da Nang. That's a risky flight. It's always riskier to go near a place than to go bang to it, isn't it?"

Gus's eyes flickered between the flames on the horizon and Christopher's face. He looked away and said, "It'll cost you a thousand, American, before takeoff. If you change destinations, you'll owe more money."

"How much more?"

"Depends on the destination. The nearer Hanoi, the dearer. That's fair enough, ain't it?"

Gus drained his upturned Heineken bottle.

"I want to leave tonight," Christopher said.

"Right." Gus lifted a fresh bottle of beer. "As long as you don't mind the pilot having a bit of alcohol in his bloodstream."

"You're equipped for night flying?"

"You wouldn't believe the truth on that subject, mate. Time, gentlemen."

This stream of cockney jabber issuing from the flat wrinkled face of a Chinese, a painfully thin man who was no longer young, amused Christopher. Gus paid the check and overtipped the waiter.

He led Christopher at a fast walk down Tu Do Street. In the men's toilet of a cellar bar, Christopher handed over ten one-hundred-dollar bills. Gus counted the money as he urinated, placing his bottle of beer on the porcelain top of the urinal.

"We'll catch the floor show, then go," Gus said. "That way it'll look like we're just having a good time. Or don't you mind who sees us taking off under a von Richthofen moon?"

"That sounds fine," Christopher said.

There was no possibility of conversation outside the men's room. A band playing amplified instruments created a tremendous din. The bar was a hangout for American civilian pilots. Though there was a lot of cameraderie among the pilots, they ignored Gus, a fellow pilot, as he fought his way to the bar and ordered two more beers. They didn't treat him as a stranger—for that matter they didn't treat Christopher as a stranger—but neither did they treat him as a member of the club.

Christopher wondered whether it was Gus's race or his accent that made him an outcast; he hoped it had nothing to do with his skill as an aviator.

A drunken Texan in a stetson, waltzing to a rock tune, crushed a fragile brown girl to his chest. The girl's feet dangled two feet above the floor. The Texan swung her until her body was horizontal. Her shoes, red satin pumps, flew off her feet. "My shoes!" she cried. "My shoes!" The drums rolled for the floor show and the Texan dropped the girl. She scrambled on hands and knees for her shoes.

"Have you seen our Rosie?" Gus shouted. Christopher shook his head. "Ever been to the Green Latrine in Vientiane?" Christopher nodded. "Same sort of thing," Gus said. "Lovely."

The floor show began and ended with Rosie. She was taller than most Vietnamese girls. Several bright cloth roses were pinned to the curtain of black hair that fell to her knees. Otherwise she was naked. When she appeared onstage, the Americans gave her a raucous cheer. Christopher, seated at the bar, looked in the bar mirror at the men on the stools beside him. They were all drinking beer from the bottle. Each had an arm around a Vietnamese girl, and each wore a steel Rolex watch on his left wrist.

Rosie began to dance. As she swayed to a Hawaiian song, her hair parted like a hula skirt and cheers rose. There was a curious innocence about her frail body. The breasts were hardly more than swollen nipples. The faint shadow between her thighs might have been makeup.

The men began throwing packages of cigarettes onto the stage. Rosie caught a box of Winstons, extracted a cigarette, and danced to the edge of the stage to beg a light. She caught another package and lit another cigarette. The crowd cheered and peppered her with cigarette packages. Swaying and smiling, Rosie danced gracefully out of the way. Someone handed her a lighted cigarette. With a pretty gesture, she put it into her mouth. Now she was smoking two burning cigarettes and holding two others.

Her hair hung down her back, so that her doll's body was in full view. More lighted cigarettes were handed to her. She held four cigarettes in each hand and three in her mouth. Dancing all the while, whirling her magnificent hair, she transferred the burning cigarettes deftly from her fingers to her mouth, puffing rapidly to keep them all alight. There was something deeply perverse about the sight of this nude adolescent blowing clouds of smoke out of her nose and mouth. Excited hands reached over the edge of the stage, offering more lighted cigarettes. Rosie coquettishly refused them.

Finally Rosie accepted another cigarette. She had no place to put it; her hands and her mouth were full. She pouted and smiled and listened to the shouts of the men. She lifted one slender round leg and placed the foot on her other knee.

With a kittenish smile, she inserted a cigarette into her vagina. She moved the muscles in her stomach. The cigarette glowed. She inserted another cigarette, and another. The tips of the cigarettes glowed red as her stomach muscles contracted. Rosie did a full back bend, hands flat on the floor. The pilots, laughing and howling and slapping one another on the shoulders, watched as Rosie smoked six, then seven, then eight cigarettes at a time, the ends glowing between her splayed childish legs.

Gus touched Christopher's arm. "This is the right moment to slip away," he said. They moved through the crowd to the door.

"Rosie's a marvel, isn't she?" he said, when they were outside. "But I wouldn't touch her with a barge pole. Clap is bad enough, but cancer?"

— 9 —

Gus's small plane flew down the Mekong estuary, yawing and plunging as it crossed and recrossed water and land. "You cross seams in the air, flying over land and water this way," Gus said. The plane plummeted and Gus trimmed the nose. "See?" he said. It was a remarkably clear night. The river was bathed in moonlight, and from the plane Christopher saw the shadows of masts and rigging, trembling on the sluggish river water.

"It's the ocean route for us," Gus shouted. "Too much moon to fly over the jungle. Crawling with V.C. cockroaches with anti-aircraft guns, the jungle is."

Gus muttered into the radio, then twirled the dials on his radio navigation system. The plane had reached altitude. Unfolding a soiled aviation map, Gus pointed to the bulge of the Vietnamese coast.

"What we're going to do," he said, "is fly northeast until we're beyond the coast, then due north over salt water. It's farther, but there're no cockroaches in the South China Sea. Okay?"

To the west, like a fringed eyelid closed in sleep, lay the dark forested coast of Vietnam. The dappled water stretched to the horizon on all other sides. Christopher saw the phosphorescent wake of an American destroyer, on station off the mouth of the Mekong.

Gus took his hands off the controls. "George is flying the aircraft —automatic pilot," he said. "Are you going to stay awake?"

Christopher nodded. Gus pulled the beak of his baseball cap over his eyes. "Shake me up if you hear strange voices," he said, and went peacefully to sleep, chin on his chest, arms folded for warmth.

The monotonous noise of the engines rose and fell as the propellers bit into the thin air above the sea. The heater sent torrents of scorched air into the cabin. Christopher felt slightly ill, as he always did in airplanes. Gus slept for more than three hours. When he woke, he drank water from an army canteen and offered it to Christopher. Then, yawning, he crawled into the backseat and rummaged in a canvas duffel bag, placing a Kulspruta submachine gun, identical to the one Horace had offered to Christopher, on the seat while he searched in the depths of the bag. He found what he wanted and got back into the pilot's seat, leaving the weapon in full view.

"Breakfast?" He offered Christopher one of the two thick chocolate bars he had got out of the duffel bag. The chocolate bars had melted and solidified again, so that they were hard brown puddles in their foil wrappers.

Gus, chewing, checked his instruments. "Coming up on the moment of truth," he said. "We've flown right up the 109th meridian, and in a minute or two we'll have to make a left turn for Da Nang, if that's where we're going. But that's not where we're going, right?"

"We're going to Hue."

Gus stopped chewing his chocolate. His face twisted in disbelief. "Hue? All this mystery over bloody *Hue?* I thought at least we'd be landing in Laos to pick up a load of opium. Hue!"

"What's the charge for Hue?" Christopher asked.

"No bleeding charge for Hue. But I've got to have an extra two hundred to compensate for the disappointment. I had you figured for a real soldier of fortune."

Gus, working with his instruments, changed course. Hue, the royal capital of old Vietnam, lay about a hundred miles to the northwest of

Da Nang. He sorted through the charts, then threw them in the back-seat.

"No bloody chart for bloody Hue," Gus said. "I don't know if I can find the airport. You should've told me Hue. Have you ever landed in Hue?"

"No."

"It'll be the blind leading the blind, then. Neither have I."

Gus completed a long turn, leveled the wings, and put the controls back on automatic pilot. He folded his arms, pulled down his cap, and went back to sleep.

The moon, still large and bright, had moved to the western hori-zon. Christopher had not slept since he left Paris. He closed his eyes and dreamed of his childhood again. His mother gave him her brilliant slow smile; they were riding in the Tiergarten; she was looking down from a tall horse at Paul on his pony. She wore polished oxblood boots. She offered him chocolate. He could smell chocolate and boot polish in his dream. He realized that he was grown up and his mother had come back. Hubbard had been right: she had lived, nothing could make her die against her will. "Now it's all right to say good-bye," she said. "But remember, they cannot *order* us to say good-bye. What right do they have to look at our faces when we say good-bye?" She held up Zaentz's drawing of the Gestapo dandy; five policemen tore it out of her hands and beat it to shreds with their truncheons. Paul picked up the Gestapo dandy's severed hand and took Lori's passport from its grasping fingers. "Say good-bye *now*," Lori said; "I'm going straight to Paulus, don't worry." She galloped away. Paul could not utter the word. Molly was beside Lori on another horse. "Good-bye, good-bye," the women cried, galloping away with their sun-shot hair flying like pennons.

In a loud voice, Gus said, "Bloody hell!"

Over the nose of the plane, Christopher saw a coastline. The moon had set. The first bleached hues of the Asian sunrise touched the low-sailing clouds.

"Overbloodyslept," Gus said. "I thought you were going to stay awake."

"What's that coast?"

"Scenic Vietnam, of course, but where?" Gus said. "Look at the time. We flew through our destination."

Gus turned on the power for the radio. He switched bands and listened. The blurred chatter of pilots talking in English and Vietnamese, and in a language that wasn't Vietnamese, faded in and out behind the static. Gus switched off the automatic pilot and began a wide turn, slapping the nose trim control with his open hand to lose altitude. He craned his head, looking for landmarks.

"I'm going to be truthful with you," he said. "I don't know *where* the bloody hell we are. But I'm making a left turn here and that ought to bring us into Hue. I'm going to descend."

They flew a few feet above the treetops. "This is one way to find out if you're in cockroach country," Gus said. "Not recommended for the faint of heart. If we were, they'd be shooting at our arses."

He pointed forward. A complex of runways appeared a mile or two ahead.

"I think that's Hue," Gus said. "Anyway, we'll land and empty our bladders and tell 'em we got lost."

Gus spoke into the radio. The tower didn't answer. He overflew the field, still talking. There was no response to his radio call and no sign of life on the ground.

"Maybe the cockroaches have taken over in the night," Gus said. Into the microphone he said, "Wake up, you cockroaches." Still there was no response. "They're all asleep," he said. "No bloody radio, no bloody runway lights, no bloody anything."

Suddenly the runway lights came on. "Hurrah, the bloody janitor's turned on the lights," Gus said. "Hold on."

He made a tight turn, lined up with the runway lights, and made a fast, hard landing.

As the taxiing plane bumped along, propellers catching the colors of the sunrise, Gus grinned apologetically. He reached into his shirt pocket and returned Christopher's two extra hundred-dollar bills. "No charge for getting lost," he said.

It was a long taxi to the terminal buildings. Gus peered into the half-light. Christopher had no idea what the airport buildings at Hue looked like. These were the standard square concrete boxes, oozing with tropical lesions.

Men ran out of one of the buildings.

"Bloody hell," Gus said. He slammed on the brakes and revved the engines, racing across the tarmac.

Some of the men had leaped into a vehicle and raced across the field with headlights blazing. The plane shuddered as Gus increased speed. Beneath the peak of his cap his narrow face was grim; as he manipulated the controls, he ground his teeth.

Gus reached into the backseat with one hand and grabbed the submachine gun. He handed the weapon to Christopher. "If they try to get ahead of us in that truck, shoot the bastards," Gus shouted.

Christopher put his face against the Plexiglas window and looked back. He couldn't see the truck. The plane rose from the ground and fell again with a jar. Gus, his neck corded, pulled back on the control column, trying to get the plane to take off.

"Get up, you beast," Gus said.

The wheels hit the ground again. Then there was another, shuddering crash and the plane went over onto its nose. As it began to cartwheel, Christopher realized that the truck had rammed them from behind. Gus, hanging in his safety harness, frantically cut the engines and threw the switches to activate the fire extinguishers.

The machine landed right side up. "Out, out!" Gus cried. Christopher had dropped the submachine gun. Gus snatched it from the floor and kicked open the flimsy door of the plane.

Before Christopher could get his own door open, a rifle butt smashed through the Plexiglas; the edge of the plastic sheet opened a cut four inches long on Christopher's forehead. He felt nothing, but was blinded by the blood running into his eyes. He was pulled roughly out of the plane by at least two men and dragged away from the wreckage.

Christopher struggled free and wiped the blood out of his eyes. He could not see perfectly, but he could see well enough. Two young men wearing wrinkled mustard-colored uniforms threw Christopher to the ground; he got a mouthful of powdery dirt and coughed as he inhaled it into his lungs.

Gus was running for the tree line, a hundred yards from the edge of the runway. Three men in mustard uniforms were chasing him. Gus had covered about twenty yards. His pursuers shouted at him to stop. One of them fired a burst of automatic fire into the air. Gus lost his hat and Christopher thought he had been hit, but he kept running.

Gus whirled and fell to one knee. The muzzle of his submachine gun blinked very rapidly. Parabellum rounds ripped through the wrecked fuselage and kicked up dirt near Christopher. The men who had been holding Christopher's arms threw their bodies over his, as if to shield him from the bullets. He was still coughing uncontrollably, trying to expel the dust from his lungs.

Gasping, Christopher tried to raise his head. One of the men pushed his head down and lay on it. Christopher thought, I am going to choke to death in the middle of a firefight.

He squirmed until he could see. All three men pursuing Gus began to shoot. The noise of their weapons, firing on full automatic, sounded like a saw whirling through a log. The submachine gun flew out of Gus's hands.

Christopher thought afterward that he had seen parts of Gus's body torn away by the high-velocity bullets; perhaps it was the noise like a saw that made him think that. Then it was absolutely quiet except for the sound of men breathing very close at hand.

Still Christopher could not breathe. His arms were twisted behind him. These men, who were very young, did not smell like Vietnamese: their breath was clean, with no trace of the piercing fishy odor of Vietnamese food.

Christopher heard a sob. Thinking that one of his boyish captors had been wounded, he looked into the flat features of the soldier who was twisting his arm. Christopher realized that he was in China, and that the sobs were coming out of his own throat.

Two

1

In a secret trial, Christopher was convicted of espionage against the People's Republic of China. He was sentenced to "death with twenty years' suspension of execution and solitary forced labor with observation of the results."

"What exactly does that mean?" Patchen asked the Chinese intelligence officer who brought him the news. They faced each other across a table laden with food in the dining room of the Peninsula Hotel in Hong Kong. Neither Patchen nor the Chinese had much appetite, but both had wanted to meet in a public place.

"It means that he is under sentence of death but that the sentence will not be carried out for twenty years."

"That's a very cruel sentence."

"No, it is most clement," said the Chinese. "Many of the criminals who receive this humanitarian punishment are saved."

"How does that happen?"

"Through the observation of results. If the prisoner reforms, or if there are special circumstances, he may not after all be executed."

"Do you foresee such a result in this case?"

The Chinese let his eyes wander over the crowd of sleek Chinese capitalists and white tourists who were enjoying the Peninsula's famous buffet lunch. The serving tables groaned with more than two hundred different dishes, Chinese and Western. There was enough food in this room, for this one meal, to feed twenty imprisoned Christophers for twenty years.

Patchen repeated his question: "Do you foresee such a result in Christopher's case?"

The Chinese emerged from his reverie and looked into Patchen's impassive face. "It is for the prisoner to answer that question," he said, "the prisoner and his government. Christopher does not have a good attitude. He insists that he is not an American espionage agent."

"That happens to be the truth."

"Then why are you here, Mr. Patchen? We will make no progress if we are not honest with one another."

"I agree. That's why I'm telling you the facts. He had resigned before he landed on your territory. He was not on an official mission."

"Is that the position of your government?"

"It's the truth."

The Chinese frowned. "Then there is little hope," he said. "In order for the prisoner to be saved, he must admit his crime and understand it. That is the first condition. Equally important, the United States must admit officially that this man Christopher *was* an American spy; your government must apologize publicly to the People's Republic of China for having sent the terrorist Christopher into our country to commit his criminal acts."

Patchen and the Chinese looked at one another, two men with impassive faces, shabbily dressed by the flashy standards of the place they were in.

"How long are you prepared to wait for your apology from an American government?" Patchen asked.

"According to the terms of the sentence, twenty years. But that is a matter for your side to decide; it need not be twenty years."

"What, in the meantime, will happen to Christopher?"

"He will perform useful work."

"Will he be permitted to receive letters or parcels or visitors?"

"No."

"Will he mingle with other prisoners?"

"No."

"Then he has been condemned to twenty years of solitary confinement with the certainty of death at the end of it?"

"He is a dangerous counterrevolutionary. Perhaps he will yet show the right spirit. Perhaps a future American government will show the right spirit. We must hope that the right results will be observed."

Patchen did not nod or smile or make any gesture to signify that he understood. He tucked money under his plate to pay for the lunch. Then he and the Chinese stood up and walked out of the room, leaving their laden plates on the table.

— 2 —

On the anniversary of Christopher's capture, Tom Webster was the first to arrive at the club. Though he was not a member, the porters knew him, and when he came into the foyer out of the bitter January wind, they greeted him by name and asked the ritual question always put to strangers: "Would you like to use the facilities, Mr. Webster?"

Webster declined, and they showed him up the stairs to the private dining room that Patchen had engaged for the evening. It was a windowless, somber room, paneled in walnut. Four weak bulbs, screwed into a brass chandelier, gave off the only light. A silver candelabrum, charged with five unlighted candles, stood on the round table. Its mirror image, blurred and yellow, shone in the polished mahogany. Five places had been set with the club's worn silver.

As he waited for a drink, Tom Webster tried to imagine Christopher in his cell in China. He could not do it; instead, he pictured him as he would look on the day of his release twenty years hence—thinner, older, broken. Although it was only seven o'clock, Webster was already drunk. The death of Molly had broken his spirit; thinking of Christopher in prison, thinking of the dead girl, he could hardly live with his conscience. In his imagination, he shook hands with this ghost of the future and said, "I was the last one to see Molly alive; what happened in Paris was my fault." What would Christopher say?

An elderly waiter brought Webster a glass of Scotch whisky on a tray.

[253]

"Is that all right, sir?"

"Fine. Do you have a match? I want to light the candles."

"I can do that for you, sir."

"No. I'll do it."

When Horace Hubbard arrived, all five candles were burning. "Patchen is downstairs," he said, "waiting for Wolkowicz."

Webster nodded. "What is this all about?" he asked.

"Patchen didn't say exactly. It's about Christopher."

Patchen and Wolkowicz arrived, followed by the old waiter.

"Double Rob Roy," Wolkowicz said.

Patchen ordered a club soda, without ice, and drank it in silence. His graying hair was brushed flat on his long head. He wore spectacles with narrow black frames and small round lenses. These gave him a look of meekness. Even his enemies had always thought that he would become Director; now his chances were spoiled, some said, because he had tried to protect Christopher—and, worse, had believed his last terrible reports.

"I think we can sit down now," Horace said.

Another waiter came in carrying a tureen of soup. Wolkowicz caught him by the sleeve and ordered another Rob Roy. He was the last to sit down, and as the legs of his chair squealed across the floor he looked around the table with his hard eyes.

"Who's the fifth man?" he asked.

Patchen, filling the wineglasses, paused with the bottle in his hand. "The empty place is for Christopher."

Wolkowicz had been lifting his Rob Roy toward his lips. He paused, stared incredulously at Patchen, and then finished his gesture, drinking off half a cocktail.

Patchen lifted his own glass.

"Absent friends," he said.

Tom Webster and Horace Hubbard raised their wineglasses and drank.

Wolkowicz drained the dregs of his Rob Roy. "Boola boola," he said.

Patchen ate the least and was finished first. The level of wine in his glass had fallen about an inch. As the cheese was passed around, Wolkowicz filled Webster's wineglass to the rim and emptied the last of the Burgundy into his own.

"Okay," Wolkowicz said, "what's the news?"

"He's alive," Patchen said.

He told them what he had learned in Hong Kong.

"Where are they holding him?" Wolkowicz asked.

"We don't know."

"Was he wounded?"

"We don't know."

"What the fuck was he doing in China?"

"We don't know."

Webster struck the table with his fist, rattling the dishes. "What *do* we know?" he shouted. "What are we *doing* for him, God damn it?" His voice was slurred.

Patchen gave Webster a long, cool look. "What we are doing for Christopher, Tom, is having dinner together," Patchen said.

"I see," Webster said. "We're just old comrades keeping his memory alive. Is that it?"

"For the time being," Patchen replied, "that's it."

Webster drank more wine.

Wolkowicz had not taken his eyes off Patchen's face while Webster talked. Now he went on with his questions, as though the other man had not interrupted.

"Did you make any progress on identifying the plane and the pilot?"

"No. All our own pilots are clean. We polygraphed every one of them."

"Nobody is missing?"

"Nobody. Who would be crazy enough to fly into China? Anyone who did would certainly be in the next cell to Christopher."

"Then he must have been kidnapped," Wolkowicz said.

Horace Hubbard spoke. "That's possible. But by whom? It's a blank page. We have Christopher to thank for that. He covered his tracks in a routine professional manner. He didn't want us to know where he was going."

Patchen held up a hand. "Barney knows all this. We all know all this. We may never know more."

Webster rapped on the table again, a series of sharp knocks. "David," he said, "I don't like that. I don't like what you just said."

Patchen's expression remained the same. "I'm sorry. What would you like me to say?"

Webster had difficulty in forming words. "I'd like you to say that we're going to keep trying," he said, "that we're going to find out what happened, that we're going to get him out. I'd like somebody to say that

[255]

he was the best of us. Wasn't he? Wasn't he? Don't we have any obligation to him at all?"

There was no reply. Webster struck the table again. "God *damn* it, David!" he said.

Wolkowicz put his elbows on the table and leaned around Horace in order to speak straight into Webster's face. His voice was even rougher than usual.

"Let *me* answer Tom's question," he said. "The answer to your question, Tom, is no. No, we don't have any obligation to Christopher. When he went into China, was he on a mission for the Outfit? No. Had he torn the heart out of the Outfit by puking his crazy fucking theory all over everybody's shoes? Yes. Was he told to leave it alone? Yes. Could he leave it alone? Not Christopher. Paul Christopher got himself into a Chinese prison without any help from anybody. Do you think he expects the Outfit to get him out? No. Of course he doesn't. He may be crazy, but he's not stupid."

Webster seized the edge of the table. "Are you saying we're abandoning him?"

"Ask Patchen. I thought we'd go in and get him. That made sense to me—quick in and out. We've got all those fucking helicopters in Vietnam. Get him out before he talks. That was my suggestion. Patchen didn't buy it."

"Christopher won't talk."

Wolkowicz grinned, a long fixed grimace, giving them all time to remember what had happened to his teeth.

"Of course he won't," Wolkowicz said. "Nobody ever does."

Webster pushed back his chair, as if to walk out in disgust. It was not easy for Patchen to show sympathy, but he touched Webster—put his hand on the other man's hand.

"The fact is, Paul doesn't have very many friends," Patchen said. "The four of us are his friends. That's not much, Tom, but it's all he's got. Nobody else wants to think about him. He's an embarrassment. A few want him to rot in China."

"But we're not like them," Webster said. "We'll feel bad about him rotting in China."

"More than that. We'll get him back."

"How?"

"I don't know. Faces change in Washington. In China, too. The time will come, and when it does, we'll get him back."

Webster stood up. He steadied himself, gripping the back of his chair. He tried to say something, but drink had robbed him of the power of speech. He opened his mouth and shook his head, trying to force his voice and tongue to form words. The others looked up at him.

"Tom," Patchen said, "we all know you feel responsible because of what happened to Molly in Paris. But you're not responsible. Barney is right: Paul is responsible, and only Paul."

Webster shook the chair, banging its legs against the floor. Still he couldn't speak. Suddenly he began to cry. Fat round tears like a child's squeezed out of the corners of his eyes and slid over the broken drinker's veins in his cheeks.

"I don't think we can get him back and neither do any of you," he said. "Do you believe it, Barney? Horace?"

Wolkowicz said, "Patchen believes it. Maybe he knows something we don't know."

Patchen sat very still, saying nothing, watching Webster cry like a child.

"Christopher doesn't even know that Molly is dead," Webster said. "Who's going to tell him *that* when we get him back?"

"You can have that job if you want it," Patchen said. "In the meantime, I think the four of us should keep in touch. We're all Christopher has."

Wolkowicz looked around the table. "Lucky Christopher," he said.

Three

— 1 —

Seven years had passed since Paul Christopher had seen the dead man standing in a hospital room in Peking, and still he was not sure if the face he had glimpsed and the voice he had heard were real or if they were hallucinations.

As Christopher lay in the darkness in his cell, he reconstructed the incident in his mind, putting together fragments of memory like the smudged pieces of an old jigsaw puzzle. He did this every night, just before he went to sleep, and just after he wrote the single word of poetry that he permitted himself every day.

It took a long time, under the conditions of Christopher's imprisonment, to write a single word of poetry; he was allowed neither paper nor pencil, so he had to compose in his head. Before adding his daily word, it was necessary to recall the entire poem and visualize it as it would appear on a printed page. The poem was now 3,569 words long. It was his calendar.

He had actually been in prison 3,753 days—ten years and 100 days —but he had been unable to write for the first 156 days because of the round-the-clock interrogation, and he had been unconscious or immobilized for 28 days after the wall of his ditch had collapsed, injuring him so gravely that he had been taken to the hospital in Peking.

When the accident happened, Christopher had already been in prison for more than three years. He had been using the mattock, chopping at the wall of his ditch. The earth had shaken itself like a wet dog—Christopher felt the muscular contortion of the soil through the soles of his canvas shoes—and dirt poured in, burying him. He could not possibly escape; the top of the ditch was four inches above his head. He slammed the mattock into the lip of the ditch and tried to pull himself out, but the cascading dirt seized his legs and then his throat, and the last thing he saw was the horrified face of one of his guards as he ran toward him, shouting in Mandarin for Christopher, who was being buried alive, to give him his hand.

When Christopher regained consciousness, he remembered nothing of this. He knew that he was not in his cell. He smelled antiseptic. He was in pain. When he opened his eyes and saw the bandages and the plaster casts on his body, he thought that he had been injured in the crash of Gus's plane on the runway in China, and that all that had happened to him in the three years since had been a dream.

Then he heard voices speaking in Chinese. When he understood what they were saying, he realized that he had been in China long enough to learn the language.

At the foot of his bed, a man and a woman were conversing in Mandarin. Christopher did not understand everything they said; the Chinese did not want him to learn Chinese. They hardly ever spoke to one another in his hearing, and when they talked to him, they invariably used English. Nevertheless, he listened closely to the Chinese as they talked. It had been more than a year since he had heard so many human voices speaking at the same time.

The woman was a doctor. The man wore a uniform. Evidently he held high rank: the doctor responded with great deference as he asked a series of questions about Christopher's injuries. Christopher learned that he had suffered a broken leg, a broken pelvis, cracked ribs, a punctured lung, concussion. He had been unconscious for eight days.

The man in the uniform asked more questions. He had a clear tenor voice. Currents of humor, detectable even by Christopher's foreign ear, swirled in his rapid sentences. He inquired, with anxiety, if Christopher was likely to suffer a permanent loss of memory as a result of the injury to his head. The doctor was not willing to commit herself on this point; her tone was sober and cautious. Clearly she realized that it was important to tell this man, whoever he was, the absolute truth.

Christopher thought that he recognized the man's voice. He could not place it among the voices of the Chinese who had interrogated him, prosecuted him, instructed and disciplined him in the time that he had been in captivity. Had he heard the voice outside of China? It resembled a voice Christopher had heard speaking in another language. But whose?

Christopher saw the female doctor in profile. She was young, with a bespectacled, serious face. The man seemed to sense that Christopher was awake and watching. He turned and looked directly into Christopher's eyes, and it was then that Christopher recognized him.

It was Gus, the pilot who had flown Christopher into China. He wore the mustard-colored uniform of the Chinese Army, with colonel's badges, but under the floppy service cap with its red star he had Gus's seamy, mobile face.

Even then, Christopher wondered if he was hallucinating. He tried to speak to Gus, but could not form words.

Gus covered his face with his hand and turned his back. He said something to the doctor, who threw a startled look toward Christopher in his bed.

Christopher coughed. His broken ribs sent a pain running through his body. When, at the end of the spasm, he opened his eyes again, Gus was gone. The doctor was at Christopher's side.

"How long have you been conscious?" she asked in slow English.

"Not long."

"What is your name?"

Christopher told her.

"What is your nationality? In what country are you now?"

As she asked these questions and as Christopher answered, she peered into his eyes with an examining light.

"Do you remember what happened?" she asked.

"No."

"Do you remember your work?"

"The digging? Yes."

"The ditch collapsed. You were buried. There was a minor earthquake in . . . in the place where you have been."

[260]

Christopher had never been told the name of the place where the Chinese kept him. He did not now ask where he was; it would have been discourteous. Besides, it did not matter. The doctor completed her examination.

"Are you hungry?"

"Thirsty."

The doctor produced an orange from the pocket of her coat and peeled it. Christopher's entire head filled with the pungent odor of the opened orange; it was the first orange he had seen in three years. Droplets of juice sprang from the fruit as the doctor broke it apart. She fed it to Christopher, a section at a time, with the sort of impersonal, efficient goodwill that the Victorian English called "loving kindness." This was a common quality among the people of the puritanical new China that held Christopher prisoner.

It was seeing Gus, or imagining that he had seen him, that started Christopher on the systematic recollection of his life. He had begun with an effort to remember the details of the accident in the ditch. In this he succeeded. Soon he was engaged in remembering every detail of everything that had ever happened to him, everyone he had ever known, everything he had ever said or heard. He recorded it all, a word a day, in the shorthand of his poem.

In the years of his imprisonment, he had passed through all but the last years of his life outside of China. He understood nearly everything.

But even after seven years of intensive thought, Christopher did not understand why Gus should have been in his hospital room, wearing the uniform of a Chinese colonel. Though Christopher had never had a hallucination, it was certainly possible that Gus had been a hallucination. However, the doctor had not been a hallucination, the pain had not been a hallucination, the orange had not been a hallucination: in his memory, Christopher could smell the orange and see the doctor's nimble fingers as she fed it to him. He could see the colonel's wrinkled face and hear his good-humored voice. These belonged to Gus.

Christopher pulled up the quilt and prepared to fall asleep. Though he had dreamed colorful and intricate dreams all his life, he no longer did so. He supposed this was because he exercised his mind so rigorously when he was awake. However, he still had unbidden thoughts, and as he began to doze, he remembered Molly: a gesture she had made, walking toward him through the Roman evening on the Ponte Sisto. For a moment, he let himself see her as she had been in the first days of their

[261]

love for one another. Then he stopped remembering. He never let memories of her run on; he still found it impossible to say good-bye to her.

— 2 —

Christopher had already been awake for some time when the reveille whistle blew: the season was changing from winter to spring and he could see the morning light beyond the frosted panes of the barred window set high in the wall. The weak bulb screwed into the ceiling fixture switched on, erasing the glow in the window. The peephole opened with a screech and the guard looked in.

Christopher rose at once and put on his clothes, a discarded army uniform of quilted cotton that he had patched himself. He then folded his pallet and quilt into the regulation triangles and waited, standing at attention. In a moment the peephole opened again. Then the door swung open and the guard, a man named Cheng, greeted Christopher with a brisk nod. He did not speak; the guards were not permitted to speak to this prisoner.

Christopher put on his padded cotton boots and walked ahead of Cheng down a narrow corridor. There were cells to each side, but they were empty. Christopher was the only prisoner in this installation. Like his school in Switzerland, the prison was a former monastery, built of greenish stone.

Outside, the country, as revealed in the thin morning light, was hilly and empty. Christopher's ditch, a perfect straight line, ran up and over the nearest hill, vanished, then reappeared on the flank of the hill beyond. Mist hung in the low places. Birds muttered in the eaves of his prison. The line of the roof was very beautiful. Cheng watched, his Chinese-model Kalashnikov with its bright yellow stock slung across his chest, while Christopher defecated into the concrete latrine, then sprinkled lime on the droppings.

Inside his cell again, Christopher washed in the two liters of cold water that he had drawn from the outside faucet on the way back from the latrine. When he was through, he wiped out the glazed pottery washbasin and dried the piece of Sunlight soap, replacing them neatly on their shelf. Then, spitting into the tar-lined slop bucket, he brushed his teeth with a toothbrush, wooden with pink bristles, and hung it up. He folded his towel into a triangle.

Because Christopher had no relatives in China and was too poor to buy his own necessities, all these items had been provided to him by the government; it was understood that he would return them at the end of his sentence.

He had two books: the Shorter Oxford English Dictionary, which he was permitted to keep, and a copy of *Wuthering Heights*, which was one of the twenty-two books in English that he was given at a rate of one book per month; when he got to the end of the list, he started over again with the first book. He had taught himself to read very slowly. The dictionary was the one material object he still loved. He read it every day like a breviary. The thought of losing it or having it taken away from him was almost unbearable.

This was Tuesday, the day of the week designated for shaving and for the clipping of nails. Cheng opened the door and gave Christopher a small pair of nail clippers. Christopher removed his beard with this instrument, one whisker at a time, a task that consumed about an hour. Then he clipped his fingernails and toenails, placing the parings in a small box provided for this purpose. Every two months, the clippings were collected for use in the manufacture of traditional Chinese medicine.

By now it was eight o'clock. Cheng brought Christopher the first of his two meals. The menu never varied: it consisted of two pieces of rough cornbread, each weighing 150 grams, a piece of salted turnip, and a bowl of gruel. Christopher ate every bit. He would have the same things again at four o'clock, along with a cup of tea.

Cheng marched Christopher to his ditch. Christopher descended a ladder and walked along the bottom. Cheng stayed up top, looking down on his prisoner. The ditch was Christopher's principal labor. He was required to dig 1.5 cubic meters of dirt every day. This advanced the ditch, which was 2 meters deep and 1.5 meters wide, a distance of one half meter. He enjoyed the work, which made the daylight hours pass swiftly, and took satisfaction in producing a ditch that was pleasing to the eye, with smooth perpendicular walls and a flat bottom.

The ditch was now about two kilometers in length; it seemed to have no purpose. When they reached the end, Cheng measured off the day's quota of soil, driving a peg into the ground to mark the place where Christopher would stop digging. Christopher picked up his mattock and his shovel in his callused hands and began to dig. He swung the mattock in a slow, steady rhythm; the blows he delivered to the loam were the only sound in this empty, windswept place.

Turning his back to the prison so that his moving lips could not be seen, Cheng began to talk to Christopher in Chinese. Christopher, hidden from surveillance in his ditch, replied. This was forbidden, but the two men had been together in the outdoors all day, every day, for more than ten years. Cheng had begun to speak to Christopher, even though he did not understand, merely to pass the time. Christopher replied, repeating words and phrases. Now he hardly sounded like a foreigner; when he spoke Mandarin, he sounded like someone who came from a remote part of China, there was the shadow of another dialect in his speech, but nothing that could be called an accent.

"Go on with the story of the old miser," Cheng said.

Patiently, grunting with each blow of the mattock, Christopher told the Chinese the story about Eleazer Stickles and his bride, Melody.

Cheng had never heard such stories as Christopher told him. He admired this American. He was an excellent worker. He was forty-nine years old. He had no gray hair. His face was weather-burned. He weighed 165 pounds. His broken bones had long since mended. He was in perfect health. If he felt the fear of death, Cheng had never seen any sign of it.

Christopher finished the story and began to sing in English. This was not permitted, but Cheng did not order him to stop; the two men, guard and prisoner, were used to each other.

That night, before he slept, Christopher, lying in the dark, worked on his poem. He wrote the 3,570th word. Once again, he glimpsed Molly on the Ponte Sisto; he always saw her there and she always made the same gesture, touching her heart with her fingertips. She was always twenty-four years old. He never remembered her unclothed, never (now that he had ceased to dream) saw her as she had looked in any of the hundreds of moments in which they had made love.

In the morning, after breakfast, Christopher had his weekly meeting with Ze, his interrogator. Every Wednesday, for ten years, Ze had spent the day with Christopher, who looked forward keenly to these encounters.

In the early days, Ze had been only one of a dozen men who had interrogated Christopher. The Chinese had crowded around him, shouting accusations and demanding his confession. For months, Christopher had worn manacles and leg irons connected by a heavy chain two meters long. He had been obliged to carry the chain looped in his arms at all times; it was forbidden to let it touch the floor. These sessions, called the Struggle, had lasted for hours at a time. Their purpose had been to exhaust the prisoner, to break down his resistance, to make him accept confession as a virtuous action.

All agents of the Outfit were under instructions to confess everything they knew if they fell into the hands of a hostile power. Though he was no longer an agent of the Outfit, Christopher had told the Chinese, in as much detail as they asked, everything that they seemed to want to know. It was useless to submit to torture; no human being could stand up under it. The Chinese had never tortured Christopher, unless standing in chains for ten hours at a time in a room full of screaming secret policemen can be called torture.

But he had never confessed to spying against the People's Republic of China. This refusal to submit to revolutionary justice and ask for mercy was the reason why Christopher was treated with exceptional harshness. Every week for ten years, Ze had reminded Christopher that his stubborn refusal to acknowledge his crime was a matter of the utmost seriousness. Now he reminded him again. The sessions with Ze always began with the same words.

"You have been given a great opportunity," Ze said. "Failure to confess, failure to make a clean breast of everything, can only mean that you remain in your heart a remorseless counterrevolutionary."

Ze wore a look of real sadness. Christopher felt a pang of sympathy. Ze had been severely tested by the years he had spent as Christopher's interrogator. He truly wished to save Christopher from execution at the end of his allotted twenty years, but Christopher would not help him. This was a great failure for Ze; had the interrogator been a Jesuit instead of a Communist he might have suspected that his own faith was not strong enough to be of real service to God. Perhaps he did suspect something of the kind. He had been given time to save Christopher's political soul, and it was slipping through his fingers. To be executed without having confessed was to Ze what dying without the last rites of the Church would have been to the Jesuit.

The conversations with Ze were held in a square, whitewashed room, very brightly lighted. There was a red star on the wall and a portrait of Mao. Ze wore the dark blue flannel uniform of a Communist Party functionary.

The two men always spoke in English. Ze's command of the language had improved markedly over the years; it was he who had given Christopher his dictionary; he kept the mate to it on his table and sometimes consulted it in the course of the interrogation.

"You understand," Ze said on this Wednesday morning, for the five hundredth time, "that the only chance of mitigating your sentence lies in your admitting your guilt?"

"I understand. But I did not commit the crime of espionage against the People's Republic of China."

"We know that you are guilty of that very crime. Why do you deny it?"

"Because to confess would be to lie. I cannot lie to you and live as I must live."

"Do you wish to die?"

"No."

"How old were you when you entered the People's Republic for criminal purposes?"

"I was thirty-nine years old when the pilot of my plane became lost and landed in this country by mistake."

"You are prepared to die in less than ten years' time, at the age of fifty-nine?"

"I am not prepared to make a false confession."

"I remind you," Ze said, "that the sentence can be executed sooner if the prisoner is deemed to be beyond rehabilitation. You could be executed at any time."

Ze had never before made this threat. He paused and gazed for a long moment at Christopher. He did not expect to see fear, but he had expected that his words, delivered in a harsh voice, would startle Christopher. However, the American wore his usual expression of mild good humor. He was seated on a low stool. A piece of chalk lay on the floor in front of him, between his bare feet.

"Pick up the chalk," Ze said.

Christopher did so.

"Write the word *espionage*."

Christopher wrote the English word across the scrubbed tiles of the floor.

"Write the definition of *espionage*," Ze said.

This was part of the ritual of interrogation. In the early days, Christopher had sometimes written for hours on this floor, wearing the chalk down to a brittle nub that could barely be gripped between the thumb and the fingers, and then starting again with a new stick. Christopher was surprised that Ze was asking him to write this particular word and definition; it had been a long time since he had asked him to do so. Ze was especially solemn today.

Christopher, who had long ago memorized the words, wrote: *The practice or employment of spies.* It was one of the briefest definitions in the Shorter Oxford Dictionary.

"Read aloud," Ze said.

Christopher did so. Ze searched Christopher's face with great thoroughness, as if there was something still hidden in it after all these years—or as if he did not expect to see it again. Christopher had never seen Ze behave in this way.

"You are not guilty of espionage?" Ze asked.

"Yes, a hundred times over," Christopher replied. "Against the Soviets, against the Vietnamese, against the Poles and the Czechs and the Germans and many others. But never against the People's Republic of China."

Ze sat bolt upright as usual on his own stool, behind his table. A very long silence developed. This had never happened before. Ze stared at his folded hands, a look of bleak disappointment on his face. Had he, after all these years, lost heart?

Under the rules of interrogation, Christopher could not speak except to answer a question. To do so was a sign of bad attitude and could lead to a loss of privileges: in Christopher's case, this usually meant being deprived of books for a month or longer. So he waited, quiet and immobile.

Finally Ze spoke. "You must make a choice today," he said. "You will not be given another opportunity to confess and reform."

Christopher remained as he was.

"For the last time, then," Ze said, and paused.

He looked down on Christopher, kneeling on the floor. Over the years, Ze had learned to read expression in his prisoner's strange gray eyes. He saw nothing there now except intelligence and calm curiosity —the same things he always saw. He repeated his words, which ought to have struck terror in his prisoner.

"For the last time," Ze said, "bearing in mind that your sentence can be carried out at any moment, bearing in mind that you can die today, will you admit that you are guilty of the crime of espionage against the People's Republic of China?"

"No," Christopher said.

He waited. Ze let several moments pass. The two men looked at each other; Ze realized that he knew Christopher's face better than any other—so well that it had long ago ceased to look blotched and coarse and un-Chinese.

Ze said, "Very well. I believe you."

He walked around the table and thrust out his hand. It took Christopher several seconds to realize that Ze was offering to shake hands. Christopher stood up and enclosed the soft fingers of the party functionary in his own curled, horny paw. He had not touched another human being in more than ten years.

— 4 —

In the morning, at the hour at which the reveille whistle ought to have blown, Christopher heard a strange noise. It was a knock on the door of his cell. The door opened and Cheng came in as usual. He carried a satchel. Christopher recognized it at once: it was the leather overnight bag he had carried aboard Gus's plane; he hadn't seen it since he left Saigon. Cheng handed it to him. The leather, once wonderfully supple, was now dry and a bit stiff.

Cheng picked up Christopher's padded uniform, which was folded as required on its shelf, then gathered up his bedding, his toilet articles, and all his other belongings.

"You will wear those clothes," Cheng said in Chinese, indicating the satchel. "Do you want to defecate?"

"Yes," Christopher said.

Cheng hesitated, then handed back the padded uniform and boots. Christopher put them on and walked as usual to the latrine. When he returned to his cell, he took off the uniform, folded it, and handed it back to Cheng. Cheng went out and the steel door rang behind him. Inside the leather satchel he found, freshly laundered and pressed, the change of clothes he had packed in Saigon for the trip to Hue. These consisted of a cord blazer, a pair of cotton trousers, a faded navy-blue polo shirt, socks, drawers, and shoes. He dressed. The clothes were large for him and they felt thin and insubstantial; when he pulled the nylon socks over his feet, they snagged on the roughened skin of his soles. The leather shoes seemed very heavy after sneakers and the quilted boots he had worn in winter.

He reached into the bag and brought out two Penguin novels and a copy of the airmail edition of *Newsweek* over ten years old. In a blue cloth bag, closed with a drawstring, he found his toilet articles: a Schick Injector razor with blades, nail scissors, a toothbrush and comb, tubes of shaving cream and toothpaste with Italian labels. He examined these, turning them over and reading the inscriptions; they looked and felt strange, yet they were familiar, as if they were artifacts he had seen many times in pictures and now actually held in his hands.

The door of the cell opened and a Chinese Christopher had never before seen came in. This man spoke to Christopher in Mandarin, the first time anyone in China, apart from Cheng, had addressed him in this language.

"Please follow me," the man said.

Christopher, who had been sitting cross-legged in the approved position on the floor, obediently got up and walked to the door of the cell. The corridor was empty; Cheng was nowhere about. Christopher stayed by the door. The Chinese came out with Christopher's leather satchel in his hand. He spread open its mouth and held it up to the light to show that Christopher's belongings were inside.

The Chinese handed Christopher the bag and walked briskly down the corridor. Christopher followed. At the end, the Chinese opened the door and they went outside, walking together across the deserted court-yard. A helicopter stood in an open space. The Chinese led Christopher under the drooping rotors and gestured him inside the cockpit.

The pilot started the engines and with a deafening stutter the machine rose into the air. Frightened by the noise, birds poured out of the eaves of the monastery, silvery in the morning sunlight like water spilling over a stone. Below him, his ditch, which had seemed so long and deep to him for so many years, grew smaller and thinner and then seemed to close like the lips of a healed cut.

The helicopter, with the rising sun on the left, crossed the Great Wall, and then the sulfurous cloud of pollution that hangs over Peking came into sight. According to the clock on the instrument panel, the machine had been airborne for an hour and forty minutes. Christopher knew at last approximately where he had spent one-fifth of his life: at a place in Mongolia less than two hundred miles northwest of Peking. The helicopter landed. Christopher's Chinese companion, again opening doors for him, ushered him into a windowless van. He closed the doors and they were in the dark. The van drove, very fast, across a smooth surface, then stopped with a screech of brakes.

The doors opened. The Chinese got out and gestured for Christopher to follow him. Outside, Christopher found himself at the base of a stairway. The steps led to the open door of an airplane. The plane was painted dull gray. It carried no markings.

As Christopher approached the airplane, its engines started with a whine. The Chinese handed Christopher a wrapped package, indicated the door of the plane with an outflung hand, and got back into the van.

The unmarked plane was parked at the far end of a runway. Apart from the van as it sped away, the airport was deserted; nothing moved. Smoke belched from the chimneys of Peking to join the deck of smog above the city; the smell of burning fuel was very strong.

Christopher walked up the stairway, ducked his head, and entered the plane. A young Chinese in Western clothes gestured him aboard, indicating without speaking that he should turn to the right and walk through a curtain into the fuselage.

Christopher drew the curtain aside and looked into the passenger compartment. It was laid out like a sitting room, with easy chairs and tables and a television screen.

Horace Hubbard, enormously tall, stood in the middle of the cabin, his long face with its bushy eyebrows illuminated by a joyful smile.

"Paul," he said.

"Hello, Horace," Christopher replied.

The door of the plane slammed shut and it began to taxi. The cousins sat down, side by side, as the jet made its takeoff run and climbed above the sun-drenched clouds. Christopher looked out the window.

The attendant brought orange juice. Christopher, who automatically consumed any food that was set before him, drank it off. Then, undoing the knots in the string with great patience, he opened the packet the Chinese had given him at the foot of the stairs to the aircraft.

It contained his watch, his passport, the keys to his apartment in Rome and to his car, the money he had had in his pockets, and a letter from Molly. Christopher supposed that she had hidden it somewhere in his leather bag so that he would find it when he had reached his destination, and was alone. He had not known of its existence until now.

He opened and read it. He had always been able to hear Molly's voice when he read her handwriting. He heard it now, and smiled at secret jokes that were more than ten years old. She would be thirty-four years old, he realized, still young enough to bear a child.

Christopher shook the watch, a self-winding Rolex. It began to run again.

— 5 —

Christopher had lost what little tendency he had ever had to ask questions. On the plane, he listened politely while Horace Hubbard told him the news of America: Elliott Hubbard was still alive; David Patchen was now Director of the Outfit. Horace himself had been in China for eighteen months, as chief of the Outfit's station in Peking. America and China were friends again. Especially, their intelligence services were friends.

"In a way, I owe my high post to you," Horace said. "Patchen was determined to get you out. I guess he thought the Chinese would listen more sympathetically to your cousin than to a stranger."

After several hours of flight, the plane landed at an American naval base in the Aleutian Islands. The aircraft remained sealed, doors shut and shades drawn over the windows, during the refueling. After the trucks had pulled away, the door opened and the cabin was flooded with arctic air. Horace had gone forward, beyond the curtain, and Christopher heard the murmur of voices as the engines began to whine.

When Horace returned, crouching slightly so that his head would not brush the overhead, he was followed by David Patchen.

Patchen wore his usual dark suit. His hair, which was now snow-white, had been feathered by the wind. He moved with even greater difficulty than Christopher remembered, but the scars on his face had faded as his skin had aged and lost pigment.

Patchen saw Christopher and paused. He seemed uncomfortable, as if he had walked into a house without knocking. Christopher's good manners came back after their long sleep and he stood up and smiled. "My friend," Patchen said in his cracked voice.

Christopher smiled at Patchen's emotion. Coming from him, these two dry words were a passionate declaration of brotherly love. The two men shook hands. The plane began to taxi and Patchen lost his balance. Christopher seized him by the arms to prevent his falling. Then Patchen sat down, reaching across his body to support his bad leg with his good hand, and fastened his seat belt. The engines howled; it was useless to speak. As the plane rolled faster down the runway and then began its steep climb, Patchen cleared his throat repeatedly. The jet leveled off and flew more quietly.

"You look well," Patchen said at last.

"I've been leading a healthy life," Christopher said.

The attendant brought drinks and a dish of salted nuts. Christopher ate the nuts. Patchen watched with disapproval.

"Too much salt," he said. "Salt is a villain to the middle-aged."

Christopher drank his orange juice, upending the glass as before. He put down the glass and waited for the other men to speak.

"Did the Chinese tell you why you were released?" Patchen asked.

"I didn't know that I was being released until I saw Horace," Christopher replied.

"What did you think was going on?"

"I didn't know. It seemed possible that they were going to execute me. They don't explain, they just do things."

Patchen's watchful face reminded Christopher of Ze. So did his way of speaking; Christopher had often imagined Ze speaking to his children, if he had any, in the same tone he used with him.

"You made an excellent impression on the Chinese," Patchen said, "and you should know that it is that, and not anything the Outfit or anyone else in the U.S. government did, which led to your release. You have nothing to thank your country for. You're under no obligation to tell us anything."

"I see."

"Good. I'm not going to let anyone from the Outfit anywhere near you. If you want to talk to me, or Horace, that's fine. But it's your decision."

Plunging into things in this way, Patchen seemed to take it for granted that Christopher was still the man he had always been. This puzzled Christopher, who did not himself know for certain if he had kept his sanity.

[272]

"You may not have much peace and quiet," Patchen said. "There was a lot of fuss when you turned up in China. That died away, of course, but when the media find out you've been released they'll be baying at your heels."

"The media?" Christopher said.

"You don't know that word? You will. It's what used to be called the press. It would be better to keep your homecoming quiet, but secrets have been banned in America. Patriotism is the new pornography. You'll notice great changes in our country."

The attendant brought food, an American airline dinner of salad, filet steak, and buttered vegetables. The tray looked exactly as it had looked in the past, but it smelled much stronger. Christopher ate the salad, holding the bowl under his chin and using his fingers. Then he consumed the bread. The attendant poured wine into stemmed glasses. Patchen examined the label; it was a good Pomerol. He drank it as he ate. Christopher finished in a matter of seconds and sat back, watching Patchen and Horace wield their knives and forks. He drank no wine.

Patchen ordered the table cleared.

"There's something else," he said. "It's not good news."

Looking into Patchen's face, Christopher knew what had happened. Patchen told him anyway.

"It's a death," he said. "Your Australian girl, Molly."

Christopher asked his first question: "When?"

"The night you left Paris. She followed you to the airport. She was hit by a car. Tom Webster saw it happen."

Christopher unbuckled his seat belt and got up. He went into the toilet and shut the door. The fluorescent bulb came on with a sound like a trapped insect. There were no shadows at all; everything in the little cubicle was made of plastic or metal.

'Looking into the mirror for the first time since the night of Molly's death—he remembered exactly the time and place where he had last seen himself in a glass: the men's room at Orly, Tom Webster standing beside him—Christopher recognized himself at once.

His hair was cropped short and it was darker than he remembered. His face, too, was darker, not in color, but in the loss of light, as if youth had been burned out of it by a disease. Still, he was the same man.

Christopher tried to remember Molly as he had seen her so many times on the Ponte Sisto. He could imagine the bridge, imagine the roofs and the trees of the city beyond it, imagine the brown Tiber flowing beneath it—imagine, even, the jovial noise of Rome and the way the city

[273]

smelled of dust and coffee. But, looking into his own eyes for the first time in all these years, he could not make Molly appear again in his memory. She was gone.

Silently, watching himself in the mirror, he began to cry. He tried to speak. For the first time in ten years, he had no control over his actions; his body was acting on its own, tears squeezing out of his eyes, words squeezing out of his larynx. He heard a noise deep in his throat, then a whisper, and finally a shout. Each time, he repeated the same word: "Good-bye."

As he wept, what he remembered best was the stinging pain he had felt on the day he had seen his mother for the last time, when the policeman had struck him with his truncheon.

Four

"Tell me about Paul Christopher," Patrick Graham said.

"I don't know anything about him," Stephanie Webster replied.

"But you *knew* him. You told me that he used to come to your parents' place in Paris."

"When did I tell you that?"

"In New York."

"Christ. Is there *anything* about New York that's slipped your mind?"

Just after college, Patrick and Stephanie had, for part of a summer, been fellow members of a revolutionary cell in the East Village. They had plotted kidnappings and assassinations and bombings; they had had sex with each other; they had taken Arab underground names as a demonstration of their solidarity with the Third World. They had never actually committed an act of violence or subversion; in the style of their generation, it was all a game.

In the end, most of the members of the underground cell went back to their families. Now Stephanie was a psychotherapist. Patrick Graham was a television reporter with star quality. She hadn't seen him for at least two years.

"Come on, Saffiyah," said Graham, calling Stephanie by her underground name. "It's too early in the morning to be coy."

It was seven-fifteen. Graham's face, on tape, flickered on the kitchen TV; he had turned it on when he came in, and now he held up a hand for silence as he listened to his own strong voice as it described the state of his latest investigation. Graham's speciality was the exposé.

Stephanie Webster opened the door of her refrigerator and poured herself a glass of juice. She had gone out at six-thirty as usual for her morning run through Georgetown, and when she returned she had found Graham waiting on her doorstep. She was still damp with sweat. Stephanie drank her apple juice and shivered; her body was cooling too quickly in the air-conditioned house.

Patrick Graham still watched himself on the tiny screen of the Sony. Stephanie did not like television; the set had been a gift from her father. She stripped off her sweatband and spoke in a piercing voice in order to be heard above the television set.

"I've got to shower and go to work," she said.

Graham followed her out of the kitchen and up the stairs. The chic house that she lived in, a narrow brick structure in what had once been a slum, would have sold for half a million dollars on the current market. Works of art worth more than that hung on the walls. Graham recognized a Seurat, a Cassatt, a Hicks. He knew about such things. He had studied art history at Yale.

"What the fuck are you doing in a place like this?" he said.

"House-sitting," Stephanie said.

"Who for?"

Graham never left a question unasked. Stephanie didn't answer. The house belonged to Horace Hubbard, but this was not a name she was going to speak in Graham's presence. She went into a bedroom and closed the door. Graham tried to follow, but Stephanie had locked the door. He put his ear to the panel and heard the shower running.

When Stephanie came back downstairs, dressed in the jeans and blouse and tweed hacking jacket that she wore to work, she found Graham looking at the pictures. He had turned on the track lights the better to see them. On his face, as he leaned toward the Seurat, was a look of lust.

"It's theft from the people, to own such paintings," he said.

"Unless you're the one who owns them. Look, I've got to go."

"Do you just leave this stuff in the house?"

"There's an alarm system. You can't get near them without bells going off and cops jumping out of the closets. Out, Patrick."

"Whose house is this?"

"No one you know."

Stephanie shook her key ring at Graham and jerked her head toward the front door.

"You haven't told me about Christopher," he said.

"I was a child the last time I saw him," Stephanie said, holding the front door open. "He was a nice man and he always seemed to have a beautiful woman with him. He used to drop in for a drink. Then the Chinese arrested him."

"Do you know why?"

"Espionage, the papers said."

"I mean *why*. What was his mission in China? If he was a friend of your father's you could have heard the real story. You used to play with your dolls and listen to spies while they talked about their dirty tricks, at least that's what you always said in New York."

"I never played with dolls."

"Nothing changes. Even in the cell you wouldn't tell any real secrets. It was just a lot of talk about how tough it was to be an Outfit brat. Never any details, just a bunch of Freudian junk."

"I don't know any real secrets."

Stephanie pushed Graham out the door, turned on the alarm system, and pulled the door shut. As she turned the key in the lock, Graham asked her another question.

"Who else from the Outfit was he close to, besides your father?"

"For all I know, Patrick, Paul Christopher sold ballpoint pens for a living. I don't know who he knew."

"Wolkowicz? Did he know Wolkowicz?"

Stephanie blew out an exasperated breath, waggled her fingers, and got into her Volkswagen. As the engine started, Graham rapped on the window.

"*Did* he know Wolkowicz?" he asked through glass. "By God, he did; I can see it in your eyes. That's *wonderful*, Steph."

"In your absence, Paul," Sebastian Laux said, "Elliott and I made a number of decisions about your property."

"Property?"

Sebastian refused coffee and waited until Elliott's servant left the room before he spoke again.

"We thought you'd want a place of your own when you came back," Sebastian said. "We guessed you'd prefer Washington. Your friends are there. It's a small house, but quite nice."

"A house?"

"On O Street," Sebastian said. "There's a small garden in the back. Horace lives in it when he's in Washington. While he's been in China, Tom Webster's daughter, Stephanie, has been house-sitting, but she's got a line on another place, so it's yours at any time."

"How? I had no money."

"But you did have money," Sebastian said. "Your father left an estate of $78,587."

"He left it to my mother, nearly thirty years ago."

Sebastian and Elliott exchanged smiles. They were selecting cigars and the conversation stopped while each rolled a Havana beside his ear, listening for the faint crackle of the tobacco leaf. Sebastian clipped the end off his cigar and handed the cutter to Elliott. He drew a candle toward him and began to speak again as he puffed energetically, releasing bluish smoke.

"Twenty-nine years ago," Sebastian said. "Precisely. You wouldn't touch it. You said it belonged to your mother."

Elliott spoke. "It's yours, Paul," he said. "It's always been yours. We took the liberty of making that legal, some years ago."

"You've had my mother declared legally dead?"

"Yes. I hope that doesn't disturb you."

"You found proof of her death?"

"No," Elliott said. "I don't think there'll ever be proof. But she's been missing since 1939. Can she have survived—the camps, the war, whatever came afterward?"

"People do survive," Christopher said. "There's no actual proof that she's dead."

For a moment, neither Elliott nor Sebastian said anything more. Sebastian held Christopher's eyes with his own bright gaze.

He chose not to ask a question. Christopher was finding that no one wanted to ask him questions. His relations and friends behaved as if there were no such place as China. His imprisonment was like a disfiguring war wound, seemingly invisible to everyone but the wounded man.

Sebastian produced a document from the inside pocket of his jacket.

"This is your balance sheet," he said. "There have been the inevitable taxes. But it's not a bad picture, overall. Thirty years is a long time to let a capital sum grow undisturbed. We've averaged a modest ten percent, compounded."

The balance sheet was a heavy yellow document covered with columns of figures handwritten in black ink.

"Just tell me, Sebastian," Christopher said. "How much of the seventy thousand dollars is left?"

"Seventy-*eight* thousand. Then there was an additional ten thousand that's been working for only ten years."

"An additional ten thousand?"

"Tom Webster found it in a bed in Paris. He said it belonged to you."

"In a bed?"

"Was there a young friend of yours, an Australian girl? Tom thought she'd left it behind."

"Molly," Christopher said. "It's the money I left for her."

"So, you see," said Sebastian, "it isn't a matter of how much is left, but of how much it has grown. Not counting the house in Washington, you are worth . . ."

Sebastian put on his glasses and peered at the balance sheet.

". . . One million, four hundred fifty-eight thousand, two hundred ninety-two dollars," Sebastian said.

' Elliott burst into laughter.

Sebastian leaned across the polished table, offering the balance sheet to Christopher. "Your family has always thought that money is comical," he said. "This time it *is* a joke, in a way. I often thought of it in the past ten years, Paul, as your fortune grew. The joke is on the Red Chinese. You must have been the biggest capitalist in captivity over there."

Christopher moved into the house in Washington at once. He still followed his prison schedule, rising at dawn, going to bed at dusk, eating little. Otherwise, he adjusted quickly to freedom: the house was full of books, his and Horace's, and he had hung up the drawing of Lori. He had begun to write out the poem he had composed in his head in prison. He worked very early in the morning at a desk by a window that looked out onto the street.

He was seated at his desk, copying out lines he had composed in the early days of his captivity, when he saw Barney Wolkowicz on the sidewalk in front of his house. It was just after first light, but Wolkowicz was already dressed in a suit and tie. He carried a battered pigskin attaché case. He looked into the window and grinned at Christopher with his crockery teeth.

Inside the house, he gripped Christopher's shoulders and shook him in his old gesture of affection, but said nothing. His eyes wandered. He went to the piano in the living room and struck a series of chords. Wolkowicz made a face; the piano was badly out of tune.

His eye fell on Zaentz's drawing of Lori. He ran a finger along the backs of Christopher's books; he went to the desk and squinted at the lines of poetry Christopher had written out on sheets of foolscap.

"Got any coffee?" he asked.

Christopher went into the kitchen and made coffee, using the elaborate machine that had come with the house. Wolkowicz sat down in a kitchen chair. When Christopher set his coffee before him, he heaved his attaché case onto the table, worked the combination lock, and opened it. From the jumble inside he extracted a pint bottle of Scotch. He poured whisky into his coffee cup and put the bottle back into the attaché case. There were two other pints inside. So that they would not rattle, Wolkowicz padded them with Outfit files marked *Secret.*

"Yeah," he said, "I'm still a fucking alcoholic. We all are, except Patchen. Have you seen any of the others?"

"Patchen and Horace, on the plane."

"No debriefers?"

"Patchen is protecting me from debriefers."

"Is he? It's great to be all-powerful."

Wolkowicz heaved himself to his feet and poured a second cup of coffee. This time he drank it without whisky.

"So," he said, "how did the Chinks treat you?"

"All right."

"They didn't cut off your dingus or anything like that?"

Christopher smiled. "Nope."

"No shit? They used to go in for that in a big way."

Wolkowicz blew his nose. He put his handkerchief away. "Just out of curiosity, kid," he said, "what were you doing in China in the first place?"

"The pilot got lost," Christopher said.

"Got *lost?* He must have been some pilot. What happened to him?"

"After we landed, he shot at some Chinese soldiers. They shot back."

"That must have been exciting. Where'd you get this guy?"

Christopher said, "It was your friend Gus."

A look of puzzlement flashed across Wolkowicz's face. "Gus?" he said. *"Gus?* How the fuck could it have been Gus?"

"It was Gus who answered the phone in Saigon when I called the number you gave me."

"I gave you his number?"

"In Zermatt."

Wolkowicz frowned. "You're right. I did." He shook his head in wonderment. "I'll be goddamned," he said. *"Gus.* That's unbelievable."

Wolkowicz poured a third cup of coffee. His hand was perfectly steady. He opened the attaché case again and mixed himself another toddy. Christopher had not smelled alcohol on another person's breath for a long time.

"It's terrific the way things turn out," Wolkowicz said. "I'm fifty-five years old. In my whole life, I've liked, actually *liked,* two people—you and your father. He was killed right in front of my eyes, and now it looks like I got you thrown into jail for what—ten years? eleven?—by recommending the wrong pilot."

He swallowed his coffee, drinking the hot liquid down as if it were a glass of water.

"You must have been pissed off at me," he said.

For the first time, he looked straight into Christopher's eyes. Wolkowicz had always looked at others as if he were a mind reader; in a sense, because he expected so little of human beings, and because they usually behaved as badly as he expected them to, he was.

"Why?" Christopher said. "You weren't flying the plane."

"No. Gus was. Were you really in solitary the whole time?"

"I was the only prisoner in a prison. I saw the guards, the interrogators. It wasn't exactly solitary."

"But no broads. Was that hard on you? Thinking about it, I thought that must be the worst part for you. You were a guy who loved women. Not just ass, like everybody else—you were a sucker for women, for themselves. Isn't that right?"

"I suppose it is. I missed Molly."

"I can understand that," Wolkowicz said. "Let me tell you something really funny, just to start you off in your new life. I see you're writing a poem, so you must still collect strange facts about the human heart."

Christopher smiled, recognizing Wolkowicz's old sarcastic tone. Wolkowicz was behaving as if there had been no interruption of their friendship, and so it seemed to Christopher, too.

"It's been twenty years since Ilse went bad on me," Wolkowicz said.

He paused to look out the window into the garden again, then leaned across the table and pointed a finger at Christopher. "In all that time," he said, "I've never banged another woman."

"Never?" Christopher said. "Why?"

Wolkowicz waved a hand as he drank coffee. "What difference does it make?" he asked. "But it's kind of funny—I haven't been getting any more nookie out here than you got in prison."

After years of isolation, Christopher's senses were very keen. Colors seemed brighter, voices louder, tastes stronger. Of all his senses, smell was the most powerful. For a whole decade, he had not come into contact with men who ate meat and drank whisky.

Wolkowicz's whisky breath, as he laughed, was overpowering, but Christopher smelled perfume on him, too, a rosy, girlish aroma. He wondered where that came from.

— 4 —

David Patchen had a new Doberman, a more playful animal than its predecessor. The dog scouted ahead of him and Christopher as they hiked across the Georgetown campus. Students, hurrying through the twilight, nodded to him as they passed. After twenty years of evening constitutionals, he was a familiar figure. An eccentric professor, generations of students had surmised, walking his dog before supper.

"I hope you don't mind being left alone," Patchen said.

"I don't mind. I'm surprised that the Outfit hasn't wanted to debrief me."

"I told you on the plane: if you want to say anything about the last eleven years, you can say it to me or to Horace." Limping along the path, Patchen coughed. "I hear Wolkowicz dropped in on you. Did he want to debrief you?"

"He asked me what the fuck I was doing in China."

"What did you tell him?"

"The same thing I told the Chinese, the truth. My pilot got lost."

"We must talk about that. Meanwhile, you may want to avoid Barney."

"Avoid him?"

"He's being hunted by the media. Some television man is working up an exposé. If he digs very far below the surface, your name will come into it."

"Dig below the surface? A journalist? Barney's life has been a secret."

Patchen laughed. "A secret?" he said. "There are no secrets. America these days runs on paranoia. It's the psychic fuel of the nation. You could say that Barney is the fossil from which the fuel is made. This television fellow is going to dig him up and burn him. Patrick Graham is the reporter's name: you should know that, in case he finds you."

Patchen, coughing again, a grating noise in the mellow spring evening, made a gesture that dismissed Wolkowicz and Patrick Graham as subjects for conversation and walked a little faster.

The Doberman twitched at its leash. Its ears went up and its muzzle pointed down the path, toward a patch of darker ground.

"He sees someone," Patchen said.

He gave the dog a signal. It walked ahead of them, alert and menacing. Patchen stopped talking, but he took no other precautions.

A man stood on the path, facing them. The dog, making no sound, led Patchen and Christopher to within a couple of paces of the waiting figure, then stopped.

The man seized the dog by the head and gave it an affectionate shake, then pounded the animal on its ribs. The Doberman panted happily and leaned against his legs. It was Wolkowicz.

"You've got yourself a real killer here," he said.

He pushed the dog away. Even in the open air, Wolkowicz smelled of whisky.

"You didn't return my calls, Patchen," he said.

They moved along the path into the glow of a streetlight. Wolkowicz seized Patchen's sleeve and pulled him to a stop. Patchen's glasses glittered. Always pale, his face seemed whiter than usual under the sodium light. He did not answer.

Wolkowicz paid no attention. "I just don't understand you," he said. "Why did you can my operation?"

"Because it was illegal."

"*Illegal?* What the fuck business do you think the Outfit is in? We *exist* to do illegal things."

"Not in this country, not to American citizens."

"Not to reporters, you mean. You're afraid of the bastards."

"No. I'm afraid of you, Barney. Who authorized you to bug Graham's phone, to mike his office and his bedroom, to follow him around and plant girls on him?"

"Not you, that's for fucking sure. You know what kind of girls he likes? Long black hair, size six. He likes to slap 'em around. You wanna see feelthy pictures?"

Patchen tried to draw away. Wolkowicz still held a fistful of Patchen's coat. He turned his wrist, tightening the cloth. The Doberman, silent, gathered itself, waiting for another signal.

"You're making a big mistake, pal," Wolkowicz said. "I'm *onto* that fucking Graham. Give me another week, one week, Patchen, that's how close I am. After that, you can ship me to New Zealand."

Patchen breathed steadily through his nose, emitting little clouds of moisture into the cold air.

"Barney," he said. "Not now."

"Not now? Then tell me when. On the day I get my gold watch? By that time the whole thing—*everything,* Patchen—will be down the drain, and you know it."

Wolkowicz moved a step closer to Patchen.

"Barney," Christopher said, "the dog."

Patchen turned his scarred face away from Wolkowicz's breath. He handed the leash to Christopher.

"Walk him back to the house, Paul, will you?" he said.

Christopher nodded and started back the way they had come. Wolkowicz's loud voice followed him.

"I've got that bastard wired," Wolkowicz was saying to Patchen. "We're right on top of him, Patchen. We're going to get Graham and some fucking Russian or some fucking Cuban on tape. We're going to have *pictures*. And you want to tear out the wires, God damn it! Why?"

The dog was reluctant to leave. Christopher twitched at the leash and spoke to him, but he wasn't trained to respond to ordinary commands. Patchen was speaking now. Christopher could not make out the words, only the flat, calm tone.

In the ghastly sodium light, Wolkowicz was gesticulating. His deeper, louder voice was easy to hear.

"Horseshit, Patchen," he bellowed. "That's horseshit. Who the fuck repealed the law of self-preservation?"

Patchen murmured and looked up the path toward Christopher.

"You're worried about *Christopher?*" Wolkowicz shouted. "He's been locked up in China for over ten years and he's got more sense than you. Let him hear the story. Let him judge. Come on, God damn it. We'll tell him."

He seized Patchen by the lapels, using both hands this time, and jerked. Patchen's long, thin body leaped into the air, black cloth and pallid face.

The Doberman attacked. Christopher had been holding the leash in his left hand. The force of the dog's charge pulled him off balance and dragged him, staggering, ten feet down the path. Regaining his balance, he seized the leash, a length of steel chain with a leather loop at the end, and set his feet. The dog, gagging and snarling, leaped against its choke collar. The chain sawed at Christopher's tough palms and waves of shock ran up his arms.

Patchen stepped away from Wolkowicz and gave a command. The Doberman subsided but continued to watch Wolkowicz, its ruff raised. The three men stood quiet, listening to the wheezing of the dog as it tried to breathe through its bruised windpipe.

Wolkowicz tightened his lips and shook his head. He lifted a hand. The dog growled.

"Relax," Wolkowicz said to the animal, "I'm not going to touch the crazy bastard."

Wolkowicz covered the ground between the Doberman and himself in two rapid strides. He pushed the dog aside with his knee and seized Christopher's shoulders. It did not occur to him that the dog, which seconds before had tried to kill him, might misunderstand his gesture and attack again. He had never believed in caution.

Wolkowicz pointed a thumb at Patchen. "Keep an eye on your roomie," he said. "He doesn't know which side he's on."

Breathing hard, he glowered at the Doberman.

"Graham's protected by the Constitution," he said. "He's trying to kill us, but we haven't got the right to bug his phone or follow him. We've lost the right of self-defense. That's what you've come back to, kid. Patchen will fill you in. He's our guru, where civil liberties are concerned."

He said nothing more to Patchen, but strode away into the darkness.

For his homecoming supper, Christopher went to the Websters'. His friends had changed very little. They were a little fatter and a little more drunken. Christopher, standing in the Websters' living room, drank Perrier.

"It costs a dollar a bottle," Sybille said. "Who but the French would ship it across an ocean, who but us would buy it? Do they have mineral water in China?"

"Not Perrier, as far as I know," Christopher replied.

Sybille saw Wolkowicz approaching and glided across the room to sit beside David Patchen on a sofa. Telling Patchen a story, Sybille was all animation. Patchen was as impassive as a mannequin.

Wolkowicz smiled, his old sardonic grin that narrowed his slanted eyes and lit up his shrewd muzhik face.

"Patchen is in a class by himself," he said. "Look at the son of a bitch in his black suit, he's a fucking undertaker. That's appropriate. Hear that hammering outside? They're building a coffin for the Outfit."

Christopher was amused; Wolkowicz had always amused him. His disgust, his impatience, his profanity were like the single-minded vitality of a child, except that Wolkowicz never wore himself out and went to sleep.

"Who's building the coffin?" Christopher asked.

"You'll meet 'em, thanks to Patchen."

At the drinks table, Wolkowicz mixed himself a Rob Roy in a water tumbler.

"That's a nice house you're living in," he said. "Are you okay? Got everything you need?"

"Yes, everything's fine."

"Glad to hear it. Let me ask you something. Why did the Chinks let you out?"

"I don't know."

"Didn't they tell you?"

"No. They just did it."

"Patchen must have made a deal with them."

"He says he didn't."

"That means he did," Wolkowicz said. "Patchen and the Chinks are asshole buddies these days. He thinks they love him because they hate the Russians. I tell him a Communist is a fucking Communist—Russian, Chinese, Fool Factory, they're all the same. He doesn't want to hear that."

Wolkowicz shook his head, as if to clear it, and studied Christopher. "You haven't missed a hell of a lot, being away," he said. "You'll see. I'm too drunk to talk to you tonight. Have you got a phone?"

"No. It's disconnected."

"I'll be around," Wolkowicz said. "We'll talk over old times. Does Patchen let you talk about China?"

"There's not much to tell, Barney."

"I want to hear it anyway. What *did* you do to pass the time?"

"Remembered you."

"Remembered me?"

"You and all the others."

"For ten years? It must have been pretty goddamned boring."

"No. It was very interesting."

Wolkowicz gave a contemptuous laugh. "There were a few interesting moments," he said. "A lot of it I never could figure out. But, shit, you're back from the dead, kid. You must know everything."

"No," Christopher said, "not everything. Not yet."

Something moved in Wolkowicz's eyes. Sybille called them to the table.

"Have you met up with Stephanie?" Sybille asked.

"Not yet."

"I hope you will. We're so proud of her. She's a psychotherapist. She treats disappointed radicals; Stephanie's practice is ideologically correct, nothing but members of the New Left. *Our* cultural revolution turned out badly, too, and all the hooligans are terribly sad. They have all these dunce caps and nobody wants to wear them anymore. Stephanie was living in your house on O Street, you know. Maybe she forgot something and will have to come back for it. No, not Stephanie. She has no middle-class wiles. But she does want to see you; you were always her favorite uncle when she was little."

Sybille was the only woman at the table. She sat next to Christopher and held his hand.

"I mustn't talk about my child," she said. "It isn't easy to find an interesting subject, though. Nothing has changed in your absence, nothing. Talking to David Patchen is the same delightful experience it always was. It's like bouncing a tennis ball off the wall of the barn—you throw an idea at him, you hear the thud, you catch it, you throw it back, aiming for a slightly different spot. It's absolutely hypnotic. I know! Stephanie can invite you to go running with her."

"Running? Why running?"

"Don't ask. Only a bourgeois fool doesn't know *instinctively* the deep spiritual meaning of running. Stephanie's very reverent about her running. It's tremendously ritualistic. You put on a sweat suit and tennis shoes with funny soles that cost a hundred dollars and are all wound around with dingy adhesive tape, and you run through the public streets, dripping with sweat. It gives you shin splints and snapped Achilles tendons and wobbly knees but in compensation you build up your state of grace and these marvelous muscles. Stephanie's whole body is like a drumskin. I know I shouldn't talk about my daughter in this way, but I really don't think she'll ever get married unless I list her good points to the bachelors she meets."

Christopher put back his head and laughed. He had not made this sound in years. His own voice escaping from his throat sounded delicious to him. Every face at the table turned toward him. They all smiled; even Patchen smiled. It seemed that they were not able to stop smiling.

Sybille lifted Christopher's hand to her lips and kissed it. "Oh, cookie," she said, "we've missed you so."

It was after midnight when they rose from the table. The others lingered for a moment, chatting. Wolkowicz had never believed in ceremonious good-byes; at the end of an evening, he simply got up and left. Now, crumpling his napkin and draining his wineglass, he nodded brusquely to the Websters and strode out of the dining room. He beckoned Christopher to follow him.

In the hall, he seized Christopher's arm. With all his old suspiciousness, he kept watch on the others over Christopher's shoulder while he spoke, and finally drew him outside onto the steps.

"You don't know everything yet?" he said. "What's that supposed to mean?"

"Just that I'm still thinking," Christopher replied.

"Some guys never learn," Wolkowicz said. "We'd better get together. Soon."

He gave Christopher's arm a final squeeze and hurried along the brick sidewalk—trotting almost—on his round short legs.

Car doors slammed, five or six of them one after the other. Then Christopher heard the sound of running feet scuffling on the pavement. Wolkowicz stopped where he was, beside a large tree. A blinding white light flooded his squat figure. He took a step or two backward, then turned as if to run. A second brilliant light came on. Wolkowicz leaped behind the tree. His P-38 fell out of its holster and clattered on the sidewalk. He went down on all fours to recover it. The men holding the lights began to stalk Wolkowicz, moving around the tree as he tried to escape them, trapping him in the glare.

Wolkowicz uttered a howl of rage and rushed one of the lights. He delivered a kick. The light fell to the ground with a clatter but kept on burning. Arms pumping, Wolkowicz ran back toward the Websters' door, pursued by the other light, his P-38 in his right hand. Someone was shouting at him, calling him by name.

Pursued by the panting television crew, Wolkowicz stumbled up the steps and turned, at bay.

Christopher stayed where he was, squinting into the blue-white strobe. Patrick Graham ran his hands over his thick hair and leaped onto the step beside Wolkowicz.

"Are you going to use that gun on me, Barney Wolkowicz?" he asked.

Wolkowicz stared at the P-38 in his hand, then shoved it into its holster. He turned his back to the camera. Wolkowicz's shirttail was out of his trousers. This made him look fat and defeated, but there was no expression at all on his face as he lunged up the steps.

Patrick Graham, excited and alert, thrust a microphone into Wolkowicz's face. "Why are you running away?" he said. "Don't you want to answer our questions?"

Graham spoke to the camera. "We want to ask Barney Wolkowicz, the most decorated secret agent in the history of the Outfit, why he's been following me, why he's been tapping my phones, what he's afraid of. Can you shed any light on this for us, Barney Wolkowicz?"

Wolkowicz, with a sudden twitch of his stout body, threw a hip into Graham. In a windmill of arms and legs, the newsman fell down the steps. Sprawled on the sidewalk, he rocked back and forth, gripping a bleeding knee with one hand and his microphone with the other.

Wolkowicz put a sweaty palm on Christopher's chest and pushed him into the hall. The camera and the lights followed them over the threshold.

Wolkowicz slammed the door. Seizing Christopher's arm, he hurried him down the hall. Christopher resisted.

"Come on, God damn it!" Wolkowicz said. "They saw you."

Christopher shook his head. Wolkowicz gave him a long scowling look. He plunged out the back door and disappeared into the darkness.

"Patchen?" Christopher said.

"He left long ago," Webster replied.

The doorbell rang insistently. Webster led Christopher up a back stairway and into a bedroom. They found Sybille there, standing in the dark, looking out the window.

Below them, on the front walk, Patrick Graham was on his feet again, gripping his microphone. A crowd of the Websters' neighbors had gathered and they stood in a circle with drinks in their hands, watching the filming.

Graham spoke in a strong voice that seemed to bite on words as if to crack them open and reveal the lies they concealed. Christopher could not make out what he was saying. The crowd applauded. As the camera lights went out, Graham lifted his microphone above his head in a gesture of triumph.

"Do you think they got pictures of you?" Webster asked Christopher.

"It's possible. Won't they chase Barney home?"

"Follow Barney? Besides, he doesn't have a home. He doesn't believe in it."

"He still disappears at night?"

"Vanishes. It drives Security crazy. If the Russians ever kidnap him, we won't know until morning."

"The Scarlet Pimpernel," said Sybille. "Where do you think Wolkowicz sleeps, in the bus station? In parked cars? What a figure of romance he is."

Tom Webster walked home with Christopher. It was now after midnight and most of the houses in this neighborhood were dark. The traffic had ceased. Christopher was astonished by the peacefulness of America. In prison, he had remembered only the noise of the world of free men. He stopped for a moment and listened as the wind rustled the leaves of the young trees that grew along the curb.

When they reached Christopher's house, Webster lingered.

"Want to come in?" Christopher asked.

"Yes, if that's all right."

Inside, Webster took off his glasses and rubbed his eyes again, a new mannerism.

"There's something I'd like to get over with," he said.

Christopher knew what this must be. "All right," he said.

Christopher invited Webster to sit down, but Webster, whose eyes were fixed on the carpet, did not seem to see his gesture.

"Did Patchen tell you about Molly?" Webster asked.

Christopher nodded.

"Did he give you any details?"

"He said that you saw it happen."

"That's why I'm here," Webster said. "I want to explain."

"There's no need to explain."

Webster shook his head impatiently and put his glasses back on. "Don't tell me that," he said. "It was my fault. I owe you an explanation."

Webster's round face was stretched tight by the strength of his feelings. He sat down on a sofa and ran his hand over the slipcover. He remained silent for several moments, chewing his lip.

"The fact is," he said at last, "I don't really have an explanation. All I have is details. I don't know why it happened. She got past us, that's all."

Webster looked upward at Christopher, who was still standing. Christopher sat down opposite on a matching sofa.

"Why don't you just tell me the details?" he said.

"Okay. Go back to the men's room at Orly on the night you left Paris. You're washing your hands. We're talking. A Frenchman comes in. You walk out. Are you with me so far?"

"Yes. I remember all that."

"I follow the Frenchman outside, just to make sure he isn't following you, right? He goes straight to the taxi stand. It's two-thirty in the morning. There are no taxis. Just then, a taxi pulls up across the street. The Frenchman's eyes light up. A girl is getting out of the taxi. It's Molly."

Webster stroked the slipcover. "I couldn't believe my eyes," he said. "Did you know she was coming to the airport?"

"No. She was asleep when I left the safe house."

"I was going to grab her, stuff her into the car, and send her home. She was walking across the driveway. She saw me and gave me a big smile."

Webster caught himself stroking the slipcover and stopped doing it.

"She took maybe six steps," he said. "And then this car, a green Peugeot, hit her. It was a professional job. It was over in less than a second, Paul. She couldn't have felt anything."

Webster watched Christopher's face for a long moment. "My fault," he said at last, "all my fault."

Christopher said, "What happened to the Frenchman?"

Webster frowned. He didn't understand why Christopher was asking this question. What he had feared, all these years, was that he would ask about Molly's injuries. Webster knew he hadn't the courage to describe the way she had looked in death.

"The Frenchman," Christopher said, "didn't stay after the car hit Molly?"

Webster lifted his eyes. "No," he said. "He must have grabbed a taxi and got out of there. He was signaling for a taxi when Molly was hit."

"Signaling? How was he signaling?"

"What do you mean, how?"

Webster snapped his right hand upward.

"Like that," he said. "He had a newspaper in his hand—a rolled-up copy of *France-Soir*."

Five

"I'm sure you don't remember me," Stephanie Webster said.

"Of course I do," Christopher replied. "You haven't changed so very much."

Firmly, Stephanie shook Christopher's hand. She was now a woman of twenty-five, but she had the same dark hair, the same wary face and watchful eyes that she had had as a child. She wore a leather headband across her wide forehead. It was very becoming. She had her mother's straight Grecian nose, but she had not grown up to be a belle like Sybille. This seemed to be the result of an act of the will. There was a determined plainness about Stephanie. She avoided unnecessary smiles. She wore no paint or jewelry; her hair fell down her back from a straight white center part.

"The amazing thing is," Stephanie said, "you haven't changed very much, either."

Christopher led her into his sitting room. In the soft spring evening, they could hear the sough of rush-hour traffic on Wisconsin Avenue. The sound came in through the open windows on a warm breeze that billowed the curtains.

A dozen pages of Christopher's manuscript blew off the desk and fluttered down the long, narrow room. Stephanie chased them and gathered them up. For a moment, she stood where she was, reading. Then, catching herself, she brought the pages to Christopher.

"Sorry," she said. "I'm a compulsive reader. I walk down the street reading the label inside my umbrella. Those are beautiful lines."

She read from his poem:

> "It was the beloved of summer, that island,
> with a little pool of winter at its heart. . . ."

Christopher put the sheets of his poem back on the desk, under a paperweight. When he turned around, he saw that Stephanie was biting her lip in embarrassment. Instantly, she turned the mannerism—he remembered it, too, from her childhood—into a smile.

"Well," she said. "I stopped by to see if you were able to find everything. I'm sorry just to barge in like this, but you don't seem to have a telephone yet. I should have called and had it connected. Would you like me to do that tomorrow?"

"Thank you, no. I don't think I'll need a telephone."

"No phone? What luxury. Is there anything you do need? The house is all right?"

"It's wonderful. Thank you for looking after it so well."

"Living with Horace's paintings gave me fits of anxiety. I worried about them all day at the office. What if I came home and they were gone?"

Stephanie looked around the room to reassure herself that the pictures were in their places. They hung in shadow. Christopher had not yet learned to remember that he could turn on the electric light whenever he wanted it.

Stephanie realized that Christopher was studying her. When she turned her head, intercepting his stare, his glance did not waver. His eyes were as calm as a child's. He seemed completely unselfconscious. The light was behind him as he stood by the tall windows that looked out onto O Street. He had a leathery look, as if he had been out in the weather for years. His neck and his bare arms were muscular and corded and his rough scarred hands hung inertly at his sides, as though he had forgotten how to gesture with them. His clothes, khaki pants and an old polo shirt, were faded and slightly large for him.

Suddenly Stephanie felt that she was disturbing Christopher, as one might disturb the atmosphere around a ghost.

"Well," she said, "I'll be going. If you need anything . . ."

Christopher lifted his hands. Stephanie saw the thick pad of yellow calluses, two rows of them on each palm. She was greatly moved; his roughened hands with their twisted fingers somehow made his suffering real to her. There was nothing more real to Stephanie than physical labor, hard labor that changed the very shape of the body, because in all her life she had never known, never been so close to, someone who had worked in this way. She had only imagined it. Christopher saw the emotion in her eyes.

"Do you have to go?" he said. "Stay. Have something to drink. I'm sorry; I was surprised to see a visitor. My manners haven't really come back to me yet. What would you like?"

"Apple juice, unless the gallon I left in your refrigerator is all gone."

When Christopher returned with two glasses on a tray, he found that Stephanie had switched on the track lights that illuminated the pictures.

Christopher had hung Zaentz's drawing of Lori on the wall near his desk.

She went closer. "My God, that's wonderful," she said. "Do you know who the model was?"

"My mother. She was about nineteen when the original drawing was made. This is a copy."

"That explains why Horace didn't hang it. He was very careful of your privacy. They all were."

Stephanie looked sidelong at Christopher. He drank his apple juice and for the first time smiled at her.

"Do you like it here?" she asked.

"Oh, yes. It's a very good place to be for now."

"For now? You're not going to stay here?"

"I don't know if that will be possible."

"You mean Patrick Graham? He has a very short attention span."

"You know him?"

Stephanie hesitated. "Yes. He came here looking for you, just before you moved in. I should have warned you. He's not a danger to anyone, just an embarrassment."

"Do you know him well?"

"As well as you can know a man who has Patrick's problems. One summer after college, we were revolutionaries together."

In a calm voice, keeping nothing back, she told Christopher about the cell in the East Village.

"You didn't enjoy the experiment?" Christopher asked.

"Not much. It was so stupid, so false, renting rooms in the slums and playing Third World."

"What about Graham?"

"Oh, *Patrick*. Those were the happiest days of his life. All that meaningless sex, all that synthetic fear of Big Brother. Just the environment for a paranoid with a narcissistic personality disorder."

"Are those his problems?"

"Problems? They're the reasons for his success. He's a merchant of paranoia. His audience loves it."

"You sound like Patchen."

"Do I? Good God."

Stephanie changed the subject.

"Did you learn Chinese?" she asked.

"A little, enough to understand what was being said."

"Were you able to work?"

"Every day, from breakfast to supper."

"That's wonderful. And they let you bring it out with you?"

"Bring it out?"

Stephanie pointed to the pages of his poem on the desk. Christopher smiled for the second time.

"Writing poetry wasn't the sort of work I did in China," he said, "I dug up the earth with a pick and shovel."

Stephanie closed her eyes in embarrassment. "I'm sorry," she said. "It's difficult, making small talk with a man who's been in prison since I was fourteen years old."

"That's all right. The digging was very satisfying work. I miss the exercise now."

"Maybe you'd like to run with me, then. It's not honest labor, exactly, but it's what Americans have as a substitute. I could stop by for you in the morning. Six-thirty. I do two miles."

In spite of her effort to control it, emotion flickered in her face again. Christopher realized that she felt sorry for him. He did not want to embarrass her again by refusing. Besides, time hung heavy on his hands in the morning. He still rose at sunup, just as he had done in China, but now he had nothing useful to do, no reason to go outside.

"Why not?" he said.

Stephanie ran with stiff concentration, striding over the brick sidewalks of Georgetown with her head thrown back and her dark ponytail bouncing. The back of her shirt was soaked with sweat and her legs shone with perspiration. She was not a natural athlete, but it was clear that she had studied the technique of running as she might have studied a foreign language. She earnestly applied the grammar and vocabulary of the sport, wearing the proper equipment, doing stretching exercises before she set out, placing her feet in just the right way, carrying her head and arms correctly, breathing deeply. But she didn't have the accent quite right. It was a charming weakness. She reminded Christopher of the earnest hikers in the forests of Rügen. She reminded him constantly of herself as a child. There was something endearing about her solemnity.

Christopher moved along easily behind her. He was in excellent condition, though his muscles were heavy and tense, better suited to digging than to loping. Stephanie wore a pedometer on her belt and as they approached O Street she consulted it, holding up two fingers to signify that they had covered the scheduled two miles. She had expected Christopher to be exhausted and stiff after this long a run, but he wasn't breathing hard.

"You're in really good shape," she said, when they reached the door of his house. This realization pleased her, and her serious face relaxed for an instant, though still she did not smile.

"It was enjoyable," Christopher said.

"Do you want to come with me again tomorrow? You've got a lot invested in the gear, after all."

The evening before, Stephanie had driven Christopher to a shop and he had bought shorts, a sweat shirt and socks, and a pair of running shoes. Stephanie and the clerk had fussed over the shoes, which were every bit as expensive as Sybille had said they were.

"Sure," Christopher said. "It's nice to be outside at this time of day."

"Good. The only thing is, you'll have to let me shower and dress here afterward. I live over on Connecticut now and I won't be able to run with you, then fight the traffic to my place, shower and dress, and get to work on time."

"All right. Will you be late for work today?"

"Not if I go upstairs now and take a shower. My things are in the car."

She opened the trunk of her Volkswagen and got her clothes.

When she came downstairs, dressed for the office in her jeans and blazer, she found Christopher already at his desk, writing with a fountain pen. He wrote without hesitation, never revising, effortlessly putting one word after another, black ink on heavy white paper.

Stephanie, making no effort to hide what she was doing, read the lines over his shoulder. She shook her head as if she could not quite comprehend the beauty of what she had read.

"Don't get up," she said. "Write."

A luminous, womanly smile spread over her face, which was glowing from her exercise, and the child Christopher kept seeing in her disappeared.

— 2 —

The friendship between Stephanie and Christopher developed very swiftly. They ran together every morning. Soon she began stopping by in the evening and they ate together, simple plain food that she prepared. Stephanie put limits on the relationship. She would not leave clothes at the house, or even her bottle of shampoo. Except for her work, they were almost constantly together. They exchanged books and talked about them. They went to films. Stephanie searched the newspapers for quiet events: chamber music in the National Gallery, exhibitions of new pictures.

Of all the people he had seen since returning home, only Stephanie asked Christopher about his life in China. She was intensely interested in him. She watched him eat, she watched his face as he read, she listened with close attention to everything he said. In her soft, serious voice, she asked any question that came into her head. In her dogged honesty, she felt that she had to explain this.

"You're the only person I've ever known personally who has suffered," she told him.

"That can't be true."

"Can't it? You should spend a day with my patients. They think they're Third World persons, like starving Africans and tortured Iranians, because they can't achieve orgasm. Have you thought about—really thought about—the implications of living in a society in which a million people will pay fifteen dollars for a *diet* book?"

At the end of a month, she knew all the surface details of his life in China. Nothing shocked her. There was no question she was not willing to ask. She was, of course, a psychotherapist, but her way of looking at the world went beyond professional training. She hated hypocrisy. She would no more soften a question or use a weak word when a strong one would do than she would wear perfume or a silk dress. She was determined to see things as they were, to live life as it was.

One summer night, they were sitting in the garden, beside a Roman fountain that some dead Hubbard uncle, an amateur archaeologist, had excavated in Cappadocia. It was dark. Stephanie launched a new line of questioning.

"In China," she said, "what did you do for sex?"

"Very little," Christopher replied. Her bluntness amused him. She made him think of Rosalind Wilmot, of Molly. He had nearly forgotten how relentless young women could be when their interest was aroused.

"But what exactly?" she persisted. "Did you use other men?"

"There were no other men. I had myself, but that only lasted for the first few years."

"Why?"

"I could no longer remember what a woman's body looked and felt like."

"You needed to visualize a woman's body in order to have an orgasm?"

"Yes."

For some reason this nonplussed Stephanie. She rose from her chair and went inside. Through the window, Christopher saw her moving about in the lighted kitchen, unloading the dishwasher and putting the plates away. He expected her to come back outside to say good night —that was her usual routine—but she switched off the kitchen light and remained in the house.

When he went inside, Christopher found her in the sitting room, reading his poem. Absorbed in her reading, she was startled when he came into the room. But she didn't stop.

"I know I should have asked," she said. "It was lying on the desk and my eye fell on it. I don't think I can stop now."

The poem had interested her from the first day. She knew that it was a record of everything that Christopher had remembered in prison. He had never invited her to read it, and it was the only thing in his life that made her shy.

"I read your other poems," she said now. "You gave me a copy in Paris. I used to read them when you were first in China. It helped me to visualize you. They're so full of emotion and you're so . . ."

"Go ahead."

"Empty, Paul. As if all the feelings have run out of you through a wound. You seemed so alive to me in Paris, when you used to come to the house with those beautiful women. Molly especially."

When she spoke of their earlier friendship in Paris, she never said, "When I was a child." She did not seem to want Christopher to remember that he had seen her as a child.

"Are the women from Paris in this poem?"

"Everything's in it," Christopher said. "You can read all of it if you like."

"What I've already read is so plain and true," she said. "You really have forgotten how to lie, haven't you?"

Christopher didn't know what to say to that.

Stephanie sat down at the desk. "It's eleven o'clock already," she said. "Go to bed. I'll sit here and let myself out when I'm finished."

Christopher went upstairs. In his bedroom, he took off his clothes and folded them neatly, as Cheng had taught him. Then he lay down and went immediately to sleep.

Even before he woke, Christopher knew that Stephanie was with him. When he opened his eyes he found himself looking into hers. The whites glistened against the tawny skin of her face. He started to speak. Stephanie laid a finger on his lips.

"Don't," she said. "Let me."

She was expert, studied, earnest, as in her running. Finally, Christopher reached for her. When his rough coolie hands touched her own smooth skin, she shuddered and murmured.

Christopher closed his eyes and, as Molly had promised him all those years ago in the snow on the Jura, he believed for an instant that it was her joyful young body that he held in his arms. For the first time in years, his mind opened completely to let her in. While the lovemaking lasted, he saw Molly as she had been and remembered how it had felt to love her with all his heart.

When Stephanie looked at him again, Christopher's face was wet with tears. He spoke. Stephanie didn't hear him.

"What did you say?"

As on the airplane, he spoke without thinking.

"Love," he said.

Stephanie bit her lip, then smiled with happiness. Christopher, who had not altogether forgotten how to lie, smiled back and kissed her with the utmost gentleness.

Six

— 1 —

Patrick Graham continued to hound Wolkowicz. On his Sunday night
show, Graham ran dramatic snippets from the encounter on the Websters' front steps. In a slow-motion montage, viewers saw Wolkowicz's
snarling face, his P-38 gripped in his hand, his attack on Graham, and
Graham's fall to the sidewalk.

"This man is the greatest secret agent in American history," Graham told the camera. "Barney Wolkowicz, the Red-slayer. What are the
secrets of his success, the secrets of his life? They are the Outfit's most
closely guarded secrets, and we hope to reveal some of them on an
upcoming broadcast."

"I'm sending Wolkowicz to Berlin," Patchen said. "He'll have to fly over
on an air force transport. He can't carry his P-38 on commercial flights
anymore."

Patchen and Christopher sat in the garden by the plashing fountain, the Doberman at Patchen's feet.

"Sometimes it seems to me that I've spent half my life getting Barney out of the country," Patchen said. "This won't solve the problem, of course. Barney will be on television in the end. Graham will scour the globe for him."

"Then why send Wolkowicz away? What's the point?"

"I thought perhaps getting Barney out of Washington would have an effect on Graham's . . . enthusiasm."

"His enthusiasm?"

"His fixation, then. You saw Wolkowicz, waving his gun for the camera. *That's* what Graham is after. He thinks that the Outfit is a collection of storm troopers. Barney's such a drunk, such a thug. Everything about him confirms the delusions that Patrick Graham lives by."

On an evening in June, with rain in the air, Patchen wore a light woolen cardigan.

"It's all very strange," he said. "The media seem to operate on some sort of insect intelligence. They all get the same delusion at the same time. Then they swarm out of the hive and sting something to death. I hope it's not going to be you this time."

"Why should it be me?"

Patchen coughed. "You may well ask. Wolkowicz thinks the answer to that is simple: it's a Communist conspiracy. Graham is a Soviet agent. Another Soviet agent inside the Outfit is feeding him scandal."

"You don't think that's the case?"

"It's a very simple answer to the problem. Simplicity is Barney's specialty, of course. In Graham's case, I wish it *were* that simple. If he were an agent, it would be less disturbing than the truth about him and his colleagues. These people are tetched in the head."

Patchen studied the stone of the fountain, worn by the waters of centuries. His one eye, when he turned back to Christopher, was unfocused. Christopher realized that he hadn't really seen the fountain; Patchen had never taken much notice of beauty.

"I wish Graham hadn't seen you and Wolkowicz together. I feared that, you'll remember. I'd hoped you could live in peace, but that's hard to manage nowadays."

Patchen paused. "Barney should retire," he said. "God knows what harm he'll do in Berlin."

Patrick Graham, who loved conspiracy, enjoyed the tradecraft that his source insisted upon. He would receive a phone call and a whispery voice that sounded like a robot from a science fiction show on black-and-white TV would give him a time and a place. He researched the voice and concluded that his source was speaking through an electronic device called a voice-changer, to baffle attempts to identify him. It was a wonderful touch of cheap melodrama, and Graham had recorded the calls, for use on the air.

Graham, with his famous face, could do nothing in secret; he was recognized wherever he went. It was intelligent, then, to meet in a busy place.

He never met the source himself. The material—amazing material, marked with the red *Secret* stamp of the Outfit on every page—was given to him by a young girl. She had long hair, so black that it shimmered with blue lights. After passing Graham the material, she vanished. Because she was so elusive, and because Graham was an incurable romantic, he called her Rima, after the bird girl in W. H. Hudson's *Green Mansions,* the favorite novel of his adolescence.

Today Graham, still in his running clothes, strolled through the Georgetown Safeway. People who came to the market early in the morning were too busy comparing produce and prices to pay attention even to a famous stranger.

He looked for the girl and at first he could not find her in the crowd. He was late. Usually she wouldn't wait if he didn't come on time. Then he saw her. She was standing beyond the checkout with her back turned, her shawl of blue-black hair hanging down her back.

In her hand, she carried a string bag filled with oranges. She waved to him as if they were college sweethearts—she was amazingly good at all the roles—and took his arm. As they strolled away from the market, she reached into her bag and handed him an orange. Graham had learned that it was useless to ask her questions. When he tried, she looked at him as if she didn't understand English. He had developed a fancy for her. Wolkowicz's information was correct—Graham did have a weakness for small, slim, black-haired girls. On a whim, he kissed her, a hard kiss on the mouth. She tasted of peppermint. He had expected something more exotic.

"Good cover, right?" he said, grinning down into her face.

There was disgust in her eyes, but only Graham could see it. For the benefit of any surveillance, she smiled and walked away across the parking lot, running a little and looking at her watch, as if this sweet, hurried rendezvous had made her late for a class. She made you imagine that she had a stern father who would not approve of this lover, who so obviously came from another world.

In his car, Graham examined the orange. A neat circle of skin had been cut around the navel. Graham pried it out with the manicured nail of his index finger. A tube slid out of the orange. Inside the tube, as usual, he found a strip of film, photographs of Outfit documents.

Graham ran the film through a battery-powered viewer. When he realized what he had, he put his car in gear and drove toward Georgetown.

— 3 —

As she ran, leading the way down a quiet street, Stephanie saw something. Her pace, which had been so strong, became tentative. She slowed down and looked over her shoulder at Christopher.

"Shit," she said.

Patrick Graham, dressed in running clothes, waited for them a few yards away, in the dappled light beneath a maple tree.

As they approached, Graham smiled warmly, a flash of white in a tanned face. Stephanie ran on. Christopher stopped.

Graham spread his arms as if he were inviting a body search. "No camera," he said, "no recorders. I didn't come to your house, Paul. You've earned a little privacy."

Graham's voice was the same in life as it was on television. He spoke slowly and clearly, enunciating every syllable, as if he were addressing a slow-witted child.

"I want to talk to you," he said. "Informally. Just for a moment."

Christopher waited. Graham examined him, a quick professional reading that missed nothing. Graham had a smooth, handsome face. But an expression of suspicion, mixed with hostility, overlay his healthy good looks like a membrane.

"You're a fascinating character," Graham said. "All that talent, all that misfortune. I've read your poetry; I used to admire your journalism when I was at Yale."

Christopher didn't answer. Graham smiled; his teeth were capped. He was as well tended as a millionaire's young wife: hair, skin, teeth, nails—everything about him betrayed signs of professional attention. Christopher had never seen a male who took such care of his appearance.

"Frankly," Graham said, his voice even more controlled, "I was a little surprised to see you at the Websters' the other evening, especially in Barney Wolkowicz's company."

Far down the block, Stephanie had stopped. She was running in place, to keep her muscles loose. She looked back anxiously at Christopher and Graham.

"I understand now that you and Wolkowicz are old friends. That was news to me," Graham said. "I knew about Tom Webster's background, I knew that you and Dave Patchen were roommates at Harvard. I know now that you've been seeing these people—walking across the Georgetown campus with Dave. But I didn't know about Barney."

Christopher had never heard anyone call Patchen "Dave." Graham seemed to use nicknames as talismans, as if they gave him some intimate connection with the people he was talking about.

"The thing is, Paul," he said, "I want to be fair. I'm working on a major piece on your old Outfit. Barney is the figure I'm focusing on. I never dreamed you'd come into it. But now you have. There are so many connections. I think you've earned peace and quiet; no reporter in this town would have bothered you after all you've been through. But now you've stumbled into my story. I can't ignore that. But I'm not out to embarrass you in any way. Obviously, you're a victim, capital *V.*"

Stephanie was coming back, running very slowly. Her dark eyes under her white sweatband glittered with emotion.

"After all you've been through, nobody wants to dump on you," Graham said. "What I want to suggest, Paul, is that you come over to the studio and talk to me in front of the cameras."

"Why would I want to do that?" Christopher asked.

"In the interests of truth. I'd like to talk about Wolkowicz a little. You can talk about anything you want to get off your chest—China, your feelings about what's happened to you."

Graham examined Christopher's face. "It's disconcerting," he said, "talking to someone who doesn't bother to respond. You do understand the options here?"

"Options?"

"This is a story that could run wild. Look at it from the viewer's standpoint. You're in a Chinese prison, convicted of espionage, for more than ten years. You come back in secret, you're seen with nobody but Outfit people. You refuse to be interviewed. It's hard to understand."

Stephanie arrived, sweat shining on her face. She had an early suntan. Under the tan, her cheeks were flushed, two angry spots of red. Graham ignored her, as if she were a stranger.

"They've sent Barney to Berlin, you know," he said. "You can tell Patchen it won't work. I'm going after him."

"I'll be late to work if we don't get moving," Stephanie said to Christopher.

She didn't look at Graham. She turned and broke into a run. Christopher followed her. Stephanie moved slowly until, hearing Christopher's footfall, she looked over her shoulder and saw him. Then she began to pick up the pace.

Graham called to Christopher in his powerful trained voice.

"Paul," he shouted. "Why? What do you owe those creeps?"

— 4 —

As the fall television season began, "The Patrick Graham Show" devoted a half-hour segment to the death of Hubbard Christopher, which had taken place nearly thirty years before.

In film shot in Berlin, Graham reenacted the murder, returning on the same sort of pallid August morning, at the exact hour of the crime, to the exact scene in the Wilmersdorf Wood. Actors played the roles of Hubbard, Wolkowicz, and Horst Bülow. Once again Bülow got off the streetcar, once again Hubbard started across the street, once again the death car headed straight for him, once again Wolkowicz slew Hubbard's murderer and Bülow ran away through the woods.

In a veterans' hospital in Massachusetts, Graham had found Jimmy Jo Mitchell, the army sergeant who had driven Hubbard's car. He had flown Mitchell to Berlin and interviewed him at the scene of the crime. The sergeant was an old man now, ravaged by drink. When he described Hubbard Christopher, his voice broke.

"Colonel Christopher was one hell of a man," he said; "he gave his life for his country. Those were rough days in Berlin. It was a war, it was fought in secret, but it was a war, all right."

"What was Hubbard Christopher doing out here that morning?"

Graham intoned. "Why did he come to this lonely place in the Wilmers-dorf Wood?"

This repetition of names—names of dead men, names of foreign places—achieved a dramatic effect. Graham could do a lot with tones of voice, gestures, the merest tug of a facial expression.

Mitchell said, "He came here to meet that agent. They all had code names. I know he was a Kraut. He came over from the Russian Zone. He had something Colonel Christopher wanted."

"What was that?"

"I don't know. It had to be important or the colonel wouldn't have come himself. He was the C.O."

"The agent, a German, nameless, was bringing something out of the Soviet Zone that was so important that Hubbard Christopher risked his life and the lives of Wolkowicz and you, his sergeant. Was he close to Wolkowicz?"

"Nobody was close to Wolkowicz. He was a hard-nosed son of a bitch, but he was good. They worked together fine."

"This German agent, this nameless man from the Soviet Zone, did Hubbard Christopher know him?"

"No, Wolkowicz made him for the colonel."

" 'Made' him? You mean he pointed out the German agent, identified him for Hubbard Christopher?"

"Right."

"And, moments later, Colonel Hubbard Christopher, chief of American intelligence in Berlin, was struck by a speeding car and killed. Then Wolkowicz killed the driver of the death car, then you shot at the fleeing German agent, the nameless agent from the Soviet Zone. Why did you do that?"

"Because he was getting away."

Graham's crew had chalked the outline of Hubbard's dead body on the pavement. With the sergeant, Graham stood over this drawing.

"Then what happened?"

"Wolkowicz put the colonel and the dead Kraut—the guy who was driving the car that killed Colonel Christopher—in the staff car and drove away."

"What did you do then?"

"I policed the area."

"Policed the area?"

"Looked for any evidence and cleaned it up."

"What did you find?"

[308]

"The brass—the empty shells, right?—from Wolkowicz's P-38 and my .45. The Kraut agent dropped his briefcase. There was nothing in it but a sandwich but I took it anyway, in case there were fingerprints. And then there was the envelope I told you about."

Graham's voice grew more urgent.

"There was an envelope. Let's talk about that envelope."

"Colonel Christopher was carrying it. It flew out of his hand when the car hit him. I found it over there, in the grass. It was busted open and the pages were blowing around. Otherwise I would have missed it."

"Pages? It was a file, a secret file."

"Everything was secret in our Outfit. It was all in German."

"You couldn't read it?"

"Only the name on it."

"What name was that?"

"Christopher, like the colonel. The first name was a German girl's name, I can't remember it. There was a photograph."

Patrick Graham turned to the camera. "Even after thirty years, Sergeant Mitchell remembers the face in the photograph. Using a police artist, we've reconstructed that face."

Lori's face, coarsened by its long stay in the memory of the alcoholic sergeant, flashed onto the screen and over the network.

"This woman was the wife of Hubbard Christopher, an American spy who was killed in Berlin just after the war," Graham said to the cameras. "She was also the mother of Paul Christopher, an American spy who has just been released after spending ten years in a Chinese prison. She herself disappeared in 1939, suspected by the Nazis of treason and espionage. What are the connections of this family to Barney Wolkowicz? We'll explore that subject in a future broadcast."

— 5 —

On the day he returned from Berlin, Wolkowicz called Stephanie Webster at work and told her that he wanted to see Christopher. He gave detailed instructions as to the time and place of the meeting.

When the two men met, in the Hirschhorn Sculpture Garden, Wolkowicz did not waste time explaining how he knew that Stephanie saw Christopher every day. This was the sort of information Wolkowicz always possessed.

"You're the first person I'm seeing in Washington," Wolkowicz said. "After that TV show, I suppose you think I lied to you about your mother."

"No, I don't think that. But if Graham had the facts, you left something out of the story you told me."

"That's right. I thought the whole thing had gone far enough. Your father had this obsession that your mother was alive. Why should you inherit it?"

Wolkowicz was agitated. Words rushed out of him. He seemed eager to tell Christopher these secrets. It was a startling change. To the old Wolkowicz, even the smallest secret was something to be jealously guarded, and never to be shared. Christopher had never before seen him in such a state.

Wolkowicz sensed his puzzlement. He put an arm around Christopher's shoulders and walked him among the sculptures.

"This has bothered me for years," he said. "Then to have you see it on TV. Jesus."

"*Was* my mother alive?" Christopher asked.

"Your father hoped so. He got hold of part of her Gestapo file."

"How?"

"It just turned up in some stuff an agent handed over. But it was just the first pages of the file. Photograph, date of birth, color of eyes, suspicious associations. I never read the whole file."

"What happened to it?"

"I don't know that, either. Jimmy Jo Mitchell said on the Graham show that he picked it up. That was the first I knew about that. He must have turned it in. If he'd kept it, Graham would have had it on TV in living color."

They walked among the abstract sculpture, misshapen chunks of stone and metal, gouged by the chisel and burned by the torch.

"I don't know how anyone can like this shit," Wolkowicz said. "Look at it. Nothing's *finished,* for Christ's sake. What happened? Did all these sculptors die right after they got started?"

It was early in the day and it had been raining. There were few people in the sculpture garden—a group of schoolchildren, a young woman with a sad face speaking urgently to a man who carried a briefcase. Beneath a glistening form of stainless steel, Wolkowicz paused and looked around to be certain that he would not be overheard.

"I don't want you to think bad things of me," he said. "That day at the Harbor, after your father's funeral, I couldn't tell you all the facts.

You were still an outsider, you weren't cleared. Then, when we got the medals, you heard what happened."

"But not that my mother was involved."

"Paul, listen. She was only involved in your father's mind. His dying had nothing to do with her."

"What *did* his dying have to do with, then?"

"The Russians. Everybody in Berlin was crazy then. They were flyswatting people right and left."

"So they baited a trap with my mother and flyswatted my father?"

Wolkowicz's slanted eyes, bloodshot and rheumy, examined Christopher. He blinked rapidly. He shook his head, got out his handkerchief, and blew his nose and wiped his eyes. For a long time, he did not reply.

Then he said, "No. I was the one who gave him the file, it was my agent we were going to meet. The Russians just saw an opportunity and grabbed it. Hubbard was too good; he was hurting them."

"How could that happen? What about your security? How could the Russians do that, see an opportunity, know exactly where to be and when to be there?"

Wolkowicz tried to speak but couldn't. He coughed violently and spat on the ground. Finally he was able to speak again.

"I used Ilse to set up the meeting," he said.

Wolkowicz was hungry. They took a taxi across the river to Alexandria. Wolkowicz ordered the cab to stop at an intersection near the old part of the town. From there he and Christopher walked for several blocks, ending at the door of a restaurant called the Thai Pagoda.

Wolkowicz pounded on the door. A young girl grinned delightedly through the glass at Wolkowicz. She let them in, twittering in Thai, and locked the door behind them. Bowing and smiling, she led them inside. She had been setting the tables for lunch. She seated them at one of the tables and trotted to the bar.

She returned with two Rob Roys on a tray. Wolkowicz spoke to her in Thai. She left the two drinks in front of Wolkowicz and went away again. In a moment she was back with a club soda for Christopher, then disappeared into the kitchen again. Christopher heard other female voices and smelled the aroma of cooking.

"We can talk here," Wolkowicz said. "It'll be a couple of hours before the lunch crowd arrives."

But, waiting for his food, he lapsed into silence. When the meal came, a breakfast of fried eggs and rice, he broke the yolks and mixed them with the rice and condiments and ate the mixture, sprawling over the plate and shoveling with chopsticks.

Wolkowicz had not mentioned Hubbard or Lori since he had had his fit of coughing in the sculpture garden, an hour before. But now he picked up the subject as if only seconds had passed.

"Your father was the smartest man I ever knew," Wolkowicz said, "but on this one subject he was irrational. He must really have loved your mother."

Christopher waited.

"It was tough, watching him," Wolkowicz said. "He just couldn't accept that she was dead."

"Was that it? If he had seen proof, he would have accepted it. There was never any proof."

"No proof?" Wolkowicz stared hard at Christopher. "You don't think she was alive, do you?"

"I don't think anyone can know. Did you know that I was alive in China?"

Wolkowicz shook his head, as if to clear it of a hallucination, and stared at Christopher.

"No," he said. "To answer your question, no—I didn't know for a fact that you were alive in China." He laughed his rough barroom laugh. "You know what they all said about you? They said, 'Poor Christopher, he'll come out completely changed, the Chinks will destroy his mind.' I said, 'Horseshit.' *Nothing* changes you. You're just like your old man, a fucking genius. It isn't just brains. It's persistence. You never give up. You're the only two I've ever known. It must run in the family."

Wolkowicz looked at his watch.

"Gotta go," he said.

He left no money on the table and when the Thai girl let them out, no bill was offered. The girl twittered again and laughed at Wolkowicz's jokes. She went outside and looked up and down the street, shaking her apron to cover the activity, before smiling at Wolkowicz to signal that the street was clear.

"Old friends run this place," Wolkowicz said. "It's a good place to leave messages for me. Sterile paper, sign it *Max* if it's urgent and I'll meet you the next morning at ten and every third hour after that on the hour, in the zoo, by the elephant cage. You remember how to do it."

"What about your house? I don't have the address."

"I'm never home," Wolkowicz said brusquely.

He led the way outside to a bus stop.

[312]

"We're going different ways," Wolkowicz said. "I'm sorry all this shit is coming out. There'll be more, you know. We were in on a lot of things together, you and I. The Sewer, Darby, all that crazy shit in Vietnam. Nothing's sacred. Fucking Graham's got a direct line into the Outfit."

"I don't understand it."

"Neither do I. Maybe Patchen does. Ask him, the next time you're out walking the dog together."

Wolkowicz's bus pulled up to the opposite curb. Without another gesture, he dashed across the street, puffing and holding on to his gun through the wrinkled cloth of his checked polyester jacket.

He leaped aboard his bus at the last moment. As it pulled away, Christopher saw Wolkowicz in the bluish brightness of its interior, glaring suspiciously at his fellow passengers, one after the other.

— 6 —

"Does my mother's file exist?" Christopher asked. "Have you been able to find it?"

They were walking in the cool of the evening. Patchen, less eager to blurt the truth than Wolkowicz, did not answer Christopher's question at once.

"I'd like to see the file," Christopher said.

Patchen paused on the path. The Doberman stopped too. They were under the same streetlight where, in the early summer, they had encountered Wolkowicz.

With a sudden movement, strange for Patchen, who was never spontaneous, he gripped Christopher's shoulder with his good hand. The pressure was painful: Patchen was tremendously strong in the unwounded parts of his body.

"The answer is no," he said. "You're out. Stay out."

"We're not talking about the Outfit, David. Graham has found a trace of my mother."

"He's found no such thing. There is no trace."

"Then what is there?"

"Paul, I know how your father felt, I may even know how you feel. But thirty years have passed."

"And somebody named Patrick Graham knows more about what

happened to my mother than I do, than my father did? If he knows, David, it's because the Outfit has always known."

Patchen turned a haggard face to his friend.

"How could I have forgotten how you are?" he said. "You're a Jeremiah, you always have been. Everything you've ever touched, every mystery you've ever solved, has caused unbelievable trouble. You're a truth junkie. Leave it alone, Paul. Go running with Stephanie. Write poetry. But don't look for answers. There are no answers."

For Patchen, this was a very long speech. Disturbed by his loss of self-control, he turned his back on Christopher and looked up at the streetlamp. Its saffron glow deepened the scars on his face and brightened the color of his white hair.

Christopher realized that he had, once before, seen Patchen give way to emotion. When they were still in the Marine Corps, recovering from their wounds in a naval hospital, Christopher had pushed his friend in his wheelchair to a ceremony. An admiral had awarded Patchen the Silver Star—a very high decoration for a marine in the Second World War—and the Purple Heart for his wounds. His scars were fresh then; his ruined eye was covered by a patch; he expected to lose the sight in his other eye, the doctors had told him that it would go blind in sympathy.

On the way back to his bed, Patchen ripped the medals off his bathrobe and threw them into the shrubbery, as if they were insulting small coins that had been left as a tip.

There had been emotion on his face then. Patchen had hated his life, hated his country, hated Christopher, whose own wounds, a bullet through the leg, were so clean, so trivial. In years to come, women would touch Christopher's wounds in bed, neatly healed punctures on an otherwise perfect body, and murmur in admiration. No female would ever caress Patchen's scars.

Beneath the streetlight in Georgetown, Patchen's emotion passed.

"I'm sorry, Paul," he said. "You reminded me of the past. Too much has happened to you. No matter how much I tell myself it was all your own fault, I feel responsible. Stay out, just this once. Give me a little time and I'll tell you anything. But not now."

"Sorry," Christopher said. "I've waited long enough."

Seven

— 1 —

When Christopher told Stephanie that he was going to Massachusetts,
she rescheduled her Monday appointments so that they could spend a
long weekend together. She had a secret present for him.

After the long drive in Friday night traffic, they arrived at the
Harbor in the dark and slept in the narrow bed in Christopher's old
room. Stephanie woke first. When Christopher opened his eyes, he
found her sitting cross-legged at the foot of the bed, watching him like
a cat.

She gave him a package. Inside, bound in leather and printed in
handset type on heavy rag paper, was his prison poem.

"There are only two copies," Stephanie said.

Christopher smiled. "Who's the other copy for?" he asked.

"Not who you think."

She lay down beside him and kissed him in her measured way, as
if each caress were a means of gathering a small new fact about her
lover. Usually Stephanie recovered almost at once from sex, but on this

morning, lying in Christopher's room—a boy's room with the photographs of his family all around—she seemed reluctant to let it end.

"I've wanted to give you something from the start," she said.

"The book's a wonderful present."

She shook her head and sat up so that she could look into his face.

"Not just the book," she said. "Something more. The other book
is for your child, when it's grown."

"My child?"

"That's what I want to give you."

"Stephanie, I'm old enough—"

"Don't. I know our ages. I'm not speaking of marriage. If you want
a child, we can start one. I'm saying that."

She looked around at the pictures.

"It's a way for all these people to live a little longer," she said. "It's
wrong to let what you love die out, Paul, if you can keep it alive. You
owe something to the future."

Stephanie nodded briskly. The question was settled. Smiling in
satisfaction, she turned her head to one side and began to braid her hair
for their morning run.

— 2 —

It wasn't a long drive to the veterans' hospital, about an hour over back
roads through the hills that Christopher remembered from his boyhood.

He found Sergeant Jimmy Jo Mitchell sitting on a log bench in a
grove of pine trees on the hospital grounds. He wore a baseball cap with
the logo of Patrick Graham's television network stitched on the front.
Candy wrappers and empty whisky bottles lay among the unpruned
canes of dead rose bushes.

"I wished I could've got in touch with you," Mitchell said, "but I
figured somebody had probably done that or they wouldn't have let me
go on the air. I didn't want to do a thing to hurt anybody belonging to
Colonel Christopher."

"You haven't hurt anyone."

"That's good, but I knew it was okay," Mitchell said. "When the
TV got in touch with me and started asking about Berlin, I said I'd have
to check it out. So I called the Outfit and told 'em what I was being
asked."

"What did the Outfit say?"

"They said sure, go ahead."

"Who said that?"

"The guy who called me back. When I called, I left a message. It had to go up through channels. It took a couple of days for them to get back in touch."

"What was his name?"

"He didn't give a name, just said it was the Outfit calling."

"You remember his voice?"

"Very hoarse. What's the matter, you think he was a phony?"

"No."

"Good, because there's no way he could have been a phony. He called me Dogpatch over the phone. That's my old code name from Berlin. Nobody but the Outfit could know that."

Christopher asked about Lori's file. Mitchell had turned it in to the duty officer at headquarters. He'd never seen it again.

"It wasn't the originals, not the typed pages, you know? It was photographs, enlargements."

"You could see the face of the woman, even though it was a photograph of a photograph?"

"It was blurred, but I could see it." He laughed. "I *guess* I could see it. At first I couldn't. I drew a blank, nothing. But then they hypnotized me."

"Hypnotized you?"

"The TV people came up with the idea. It's a new technique, even the cops are using it. Everything registers on the subconscious, see, but you gotta bring it up to the surface. That's where the hypnotism works. I remembered the face under hypnotism and that's when they drew the sketch. The artist talked to me while I was under. When I woke up, there was the face. I remembered it then, clear as a bell."

"What else did you remember?"

"A lot of stuff, it surprised even me. They let me listen to the tape after I came to, and then later on I remembered more stuff, after I came back here. It just popped into my head."

"Things that happened that day in Berlin just popped into your head after thirty years?"

"Right. Little details, like I was watching the Kraut agent, and I remembered why I shot at him. On the show I couldn't answer that question. I was going to say Wolkowicz was shooting the shit out of the car, why not me? But that wasn't it. It was what the Kraut did."

[317]

"What did he do?"

"The son of a bitch signaled the driver of the hit car. I didn't even realize it at the time, it was only just now, after the hypnotism, that I knew what he was doing."

"What did he do, exactly?"

"He had this rolled-up newspaper, see?"

Mitchell got to his feet and demonstrated, gesturing.

"This is the newspaper, see? He signaled, jerked up his arm like he was calling a cab. *That's* when the hit car headed straight for your father. The newspaper was the signal to kill him."

— 3 —

When Christopher turned around and she saw his ravaged face, Stephanie said, "Good God, Paul, what is it?"

He hadn't come into the house on his return to the Harbor. Working by the window in the kitchen, Stephanie had heard the car door slam, and then, through the open sash, she had seen Christopher climbing through the steep pasture. When he hadn't answered her call, she had followed him up the hillside. There had been something odd, even frightening, about the way he plunged up the mountain, as if he had lost his sight and his hearing.

Stephanie found him in the Hubbard graveyard, staring down at an adder that was sunning itself on Indian Joe's boulder headstone.

"Why did you come here?" she asked.

"To think," Christopher said.

Stephanie teased him. "About what? The child? We could conceive it here. The time is right."

She put a hand against his chest as she spoke to him. His body was rigid and cold. Empty-eyed, he stared at the torpid snake. She realized that he hadn't heard what she had said to him.

"Paul, what is it?"

"I know what happened," Christopher said.

"What happened? To you? You mean in China?"

"To me, to my father, to Molly. All of it. I understand it. Jimmy Jo Mitchell lifted his hand, like this, and I understood it."

Stephanie let her own hand fall. Christopher began to tremble. He closed his eyes and clenched his fists, trying to control the shaking, but he could not make his body obey his will.

Stephanie seized his face with both her hands. She had to reach high to do this and her body pressed against his.

"Paul, don't try to control it," she said. "Don't."

"Oh," he said. "Oh, Steph. Oh, Jesus. I loved them so."

He began to sob, but no tears came.

"Paul, open your eyes," Stephanie said.

He obeyed. She had never seen so much intelligence, or so much pain, in anyone's eyes.

"Now your fists," she said. "Open your hands."

Stephanie rubbed her body against his. With her thumbs, she pressed his cheekbones, as if to force the tears to flow. Christopher was still trembling violently.

'How did you know?" Stephanie asked.

"I just saw the connections, the whole thing."

"What are you feeling, Paul? Tell me."

He shook his head.

'Tell me."

"I can't."

"Yes you can. Everyone you love is dead. Are you telling me you know who killed them?"

"Yes."

"Go on. Tell me more. *Who* killed them?"

"Fools. They were murdered by fools."

Suddenly, and for the first time in his life, Christopher broke. He put his arms around Stephanie and crushed her against him. He was enormously strong after his long labors in China. His hands were still as hard as weapons. Stephanie could scarcely breathe. She thought that he might be breaking her bones. She murmured his name. Christopher had no idea that he was hurting her.

"I want to kill them," he said. "I want them to die. I've been so lonely, Steph. First my mother. Then my father, then Molly. Will they let you live? Can a child of mine live in this world? I'm alone, absolutely alone. The loss! Prison was nothing to me. I went in alone and I came out alone. And now that I know, I want to kill a man I've always loved. That's the final aloneness, that will make it complete. I hate them, I didn't know I could do that, Steph."

He cried at last.

"Jesus, I've been so lonely," Christopher said. "So fucking lonely. I'm going to make them pay. I'm going to get them for what they've done. I am, Steph. I can't help it."

"Good," Stephanie said, as his tears wet both their faces. "Good. Good. Good."

Eight

"I always thought," Alice Hubbard said, "that if I were going to take a lover, I would have chosen David Patchen; he's so utterly intelligent, so utterly sane. Or a woman—Waddy always advised a woman."

Alice had kept up her friendship with Patchen. After leaving the Harbor, Christopher invited himself to Sunday lunch in New York, and when he arrived, he found Patchen already there, drinking sherry in front of an open fire. Alice amused him. As she chattered, something like a smile brightened his tired face.

"If Waddy was right, maybe I should have seduced the Hubbard abstractionist," Alice said. "Talk about revenge."

Soon after her divorce from Elliott Hubbard she had moved to Paris, coming home to New York only after the early death, from cancer, of Emily, Elliott's second wife, the painter.

"In the end I did nothing—well, almost nothing—because in my heart I believe in telegony. You're not familiar with the theory of telegony? It holds that an earlier mate will impart his characteristics to the offspring of subsequent ones. The Hubbards breed so true—look at your father and Elliott, Paul, look at Horace and his half brother what's-his-name. Elliott had his way with me for years. Who knows what little bushwackers he may have left lurking in my unsuspecting body?"

Alice was an old woman with the manners of a madcap debutante. As a girl she had discovered that speaking the truth made people laugh. She still said whatever came into her head.

She lived in the same apartment on Central Park where Paul had visited her after the divorce. Her shrewd eyes, brimming with laughter, still leaped from face to face as she talked. Her skin, as it had aged, had grown leathery, and her hair, cut short, was white, but her gaunt figure, like a model's, was the same. She wore her jeans and silk shirt as well as Stephanie wore hers.

"I hear you've acquired another delicious girl," Alice said to Christopher. "The Websters' daughter, is it? That must mean you're all right after your experience."

"You know the Websters?" Christopher was surprised.

"We met them on the *France*, Waddy and I, years ago, a very dreary crossing in February. We were trapped in the salon. The Duke of Windsor was aboard, playing the piano, a little wrinkled man with a little wrinkled wife. It was right after your disappearance. The Websters could talk of nothing else."

Alice gave Christopher a Perrier with a slice of lemon in the glass and sat on the sofa beside Patchen.

"Now you're back," she said to Christopher. "Can you talk about your adventures? Are you writing a book? That's what everybody does now; they tell all and make millions."

"No book," Christopher said.

"No? Surely David here has pumped you out, he and his spooks? Don't they want to know every detail, no matter how trivial, no matter how seemingly insignificant?"

"No. They haven't been interested at all."

"Really? Is that true, David? I call that odd—very odd."

She was sitting on Patchen's blind side, so he had to turn his head all the way around in order to look into her face.

"Paul wasn't working for us when he went into China, we did nothing to get him out," he said. "What right would we have to question him?"

"I thought you had a right to do anything you liked. That's what that man on television, the one who's after that muzhik who jailed Waddy, says."

"Patrick Graham."

"Yes. I thought that program about Hubbard and Lori was awful. Really, David, you should have stopped that. The muzhik is one thing, but Paul's parents are another. Funny about the muzhik . . ."

"Barney Wolkowicz," Patchen said.

"Thank you, David. David," she said to Christopher, "is my namer; he supplies the names I can't remember. The muzhik was such an ape and still he played the spinet so beautifully, that Christmas at the Harbor in the middle of the war. That was when it all began, wasn't it? Everyone in uniform, everyone covered in mystery. It had the smell of disaster even then, grown men jumping out of airplanes and swearing secret oaths. Were you there, David?"

"No."

"When *did* you join up with the Hubbards?"

"I came with Paul."

"To Hubbard Christopher's funeral. Yes. You were shocked by the Hubbard merriment, I remember. The muzhik played that day, too— Bach. Such a delicate touch—tinkle, tinkle. You'd have thought he'd smash the keyboard; he had hands like hams."

The doorbell rang. Alice rose to answer it, then heard a key in the lock and sat back down.

"Waddy," she said, comfortably. "He'll be delighted to see you, Paul, he's been dying to. I didn't tell him you'd be here, or David, either; he's skittish about Outfit people, as well he might be. Waddy lives up in the Berkshires now, you know, eating natural foods and dwelling in a solar house; Waddy's tremendously in tune with the environment."

She broke off and smiled at the door through which her brother must come. As he entered, Waddy was puffing a bit. He wore a small orange rucksack and carried a bushel basket full of McIntosh apples. When he saw Patchen, he stopped short and half a dozen apples tumbled out of the basket and rolled over the carpet. Waddy got down on his hands and knees and recovered them, searching under the coffee table.

He polished the apples on his jacket. It was a faded denim jacket, the kind that farmers once wore, but embroidered all over with flowers. He gave one apple to Alice and one to Patchen.

"Straight from my own trees in Ashfield," he said. "No sprays, no preservatives." He smiled his boyish smile. Like his sister, Waddy had brought his manners with him from an earlier stage of life. *"Unpoisoned* apples," he said.

Still on his knees, he turned around to offer Christopher an apple and, because Christopher was seated with his back to the door, saw his face for the first time.

"My God," he said. "Paul."

"Paul wanted to surprise you," Alice said.

Waddy's arms dropped helplessly to his sides and he gave his whinnying laugh.

The luncheon menu was the same as it had been twenty years before: cold asparagus in vinaigrette, an omelet, cheese, and a German wine.

This time Waddy did not drink too much Riesling. He had given up alcohol. Also ordinary food; in his rucksack, he had brought his own lunch—millet, bean curd, raw vegetables. He swallowed several vitamin and mineral capsules from a row of bottles that he set out in front of his plate, washing them down with spring water that he had transported from the Berkshires in an antique green jug.

Waddy's discomfort with Patchen and Christopher did not last long. Soon he was chattering away about himself and his life. Waddy taught a course in political science at an experimental college in Massachusetts, he reviewed books about the witch-hunting era for a magazine for intellectuals, he tilled the soil of his upland farm. Mostly, he traveled from campus to campus, lecturing on his life as a victim of anti-Communist hysteria in the 1950s.

"Waddy is a culture hero," Alice said. "He gets two thousand dollars a talk, plus disciples."

Waddy patted Alice's hand and gave a self-mocking smile. "Do you remember the last time we had lunch with Alice?" he asked Christopher. "The sky was falling down. But it didn't fall after all. Everything really is for the best, Paul, in this best of all possible worlds—or don't you think so?"

"Maybe not quite everything."

"No, not absolutely everything, but we're a couple of jailbirds, you and I, and we know things these innocent folks can't possibly know, don't we? Prison does focus the mind wonderfully, didn't you find?"

"Yes."

Waddy shot Patchen a keen look. "You should try it, David," he said. "The way things are going, maybe you will. *I* know that you know not what you do, you and Horace and all the rest. But my audiences can't believe that; they're idealists. They come up to me on campus, these young people, after my lectures, and say, 'How can you be so forgiving, how can you be so calm?' They think all you people ought to be hung, like the Nazis at Nuremberg. First we have to win the war, I tell them. *Then* we'll try the war criminals."

"Are you winning the war?" asked Patchen.

"Yes, of course. It's always been an inch-by-inch proposition. Look at my life. That's what I tell the kids: look at my life and take heart. History was with me, history is with them. The witch-hunters threw me in jail, they took away my living, they drove me into the wilderness. And here I am, still fighting."

"Isn't it admirable?" Alice said. "Even when they turned out to be mass murderers, even when they strangled art, through thick and thin, Waddy stuck by his Russians. No wonder he's a culture hero."

"Alice scoffs," Waddy said, "but I never for a single moment ceased to be a revolutionary."

"Really?" Alice said. "I thought you were innocent of the charges. That's what you said when they were hauling you off to prison."

Waddy's eyes, twinkling with the wry amusement of a sage who understands all, looked across the table at Christopher.

"Of course I was innocent of the charges against me," he said. "Paul knows how that is. The more obvious it is that you can't possibly have committed a crime, the less possible it is for your accusers to believe you. But I've found peace, years afterward; I see that there was a purpose, and what the purpose was. You will, too, Paul—that's why I hoped to see you, to tell you that. You may not see it now. But you will."

"See?" Alice said. "What will Paul see?"

"The exact nature of the purpose in this insane thing that's happened to him. He knows there *is* a purpose. He must; I did. You can't get through it otherwise. What bothered me was not knowing just what the purpose *was*—the details. In time, it all comes clear, you see the light. You just wake up and see it, whammo."

Patchen cleared his throat. Waddy continued to smile round the table. He was now totally bald and this hairlessness, the scrubbed glossy scalp above the wide blue eyes, intensified his look of childish eagerness.

Patchen coughed. Alice poured more wine and tapped his glass, instructing him to drink and cure this trouble in his throat.

"I'm not sure I follow you," Patchen said to Waddy. "You mean you were literally innocent of the crimes you went to jail for?"

"Of course I was," Waddy said. "How can you, of all people, ask such a question, David? I mean, you're Director of the Outfit, aren't you?"

"I still don't follow."

"No?" Waddy said. "It was all such a joke. What was the charge against me? That I'd committed espionage as a member of Mordecai Bashian's spy ring. What was the evidence? Bashian said from the start he didn't even know me. Nobody in the Addressees Spy Ring knew me. *Naturally* they'd say that, correct? Communists lie."

Waddy turned to Christopher again. "Did the Chinese ever believe *you* when you told the truth?"

"In the end, they said they did."

"Did you believe them when they said they believed you?"

"No."

"*Voilà.* Mordecai Bashian used to dog my footsteps in prison. 'Why?' he would ask. 'What diabolical purpose do the capitalists have?' He thought I was an FBI spy, that my conviction was all a trick, that I was in jail to weasel into his confidence. He actually spread that story. For a while, I lost all my friends in and out of prison. Only Elliott never believed it. Elliott was one of *you.* If he didn't believe it, how could you believe it? How could anyone believe it?"

"Believe that you were a Communist spy?" Patchen said. "Why would that have been so hard to believe? There was your background, there were witnesses."

Waddy held up a forefinger. "One witness," he said. "The slave of love. Jocelyn Frick. She testified that I had had sex with her. She wept on the stand, describing an unnatural act she performed upon me. I've never had sex with a woman in my life."

Alice burst into laughter. "It reminds me of the *France,*" she said. "Paul, you must ask your Stephanie about the *France* and Waddy."

A puzzled look came over Waddy's face.

"The velvet suit, the German woman, the brig," Alice reminded him.

Waddy laughed at himself. "The velvet *suit,*" he said. "I'd forgotten."

Alice gave Waddy a broad smile; they knew a joke the others didn't know. Christopher began to ask a question. Alice shushed him.

"No," she said, "we can't tell, it would be wrong. You must ask the Webster girl. Go on, Waddy."

"I just couldn't understand it at first," Waddy said. "When I found out that Wolkowicz was involved, I thought it was a personal vendetta. He's hated me ever since Burma."

As Waddy spoke, he watched Christopher. He saw that he wanted to ask a question, and he paused.

"He hated you?" Christopher said. "What happened in Burma?"

"We got separated during a firefight. I got away on an elephant."

"On an elephant?"

"You must know the story about Waddy's magic elephant," Alice said.

"It's a boring story," Waddy said. "Paul doesn't want to hear it. The long and short of it is, I escaped and Wolkowicz didn't and the Japs gouged out his teeth with a bayonet. Naturally he was upset, anyone would be. But it was the fortunes of war. Back to the spy ring. After all, the Outfit *knew* I was queer—I was thrown out after I failed the lie detector test. I *passed* the questions about being a Russian spy. Those questions didn't bother me; I was innocent. It was *Have you ever had a blow job from a queer?* that did me in."

Patchen, very still and upright in his chair, asked a question: "Do you still think it was a personal vendetta?"

"God, no. Wolkowicz is too efficient for that. The truth dawned on me when I was still in prison. If I *had* been an FBI spy, I would have been invaluable to the capitalists. I won the confidence of all the members of Mordecai Bashian's spy ring. We talked about our cases. Every one of them told me the same thing: they knew Jocelyn all right; they had all enjoyed her favors; Mordecai Bashian had been her pimp and they knew Mordecai as a friend and a progressive. Furthermore, they were all Party members or fellow travelers and they all were working for communism in any way they could. They were very keen politically. All that was true, nobody denied it. But this is the vital point, David: *Every single one of them was accused and convicted of the wrong crime.* They had entirely different assignments, entirely different targets, entirely different superiors from the ones they were convicted of having. The Addressees Spy Ring didn't exist, it was a figment of the imagination."

Alice whooped. "Waddy, why haven't you ever told before?"

"I was waiting for the right audience."

"What did Mordecai Bashian say about all this?"

"Well, of course he acted out the part of spy master. What would you expect him to do? It was his hour of glory."

"Mordecai claimed that the ring was real?"

"To me, yes. I told you, he thought I was an FBI spy. He thought I'd fricked poor Jocelyn, penetrated his operation. 'Stupid bourgeois cow!' he'd say. But back to the point. It was all for the best. There *was* a purpose."

Waddy looked alertly at Patchen, fondly at Christopher, triumphantly at Alice. He had surprised his sister into real laughter; she wiped the tears from her eyes.

"Look how wonderfully it turned out for everyone," said Waddy. "Wolkowicz got decorated again, the congressional committee was happy, the press was ecstatic. Happiest of all was the international Communist conspiracy, me included. Think about it. All Wolkowicz and the committee got were little fish, me and that ass Mordecai Bashian. The really big fish got away and went right on being Russian spies. David knows who they were, I'll bet. They wouldn't *believe* the names, would they, David? What a diversion!"

Waddy reached across the table and gripped Christopher's hand. "You never know," he said. "That's the message, that's the meaning. I thought my life meant nothing, for years the truth was hidden from me, Paul. But if I'm right—and I think I'm right, don't you?—then I've been pretty useful in my way. That's the test of belief, the test of commitment—to submit when you don't understand, to let yourself be used."

"Like Jocelyn Frick," Alice said.

— 2 —

Stephanie remembered her meeting with Waddy aboard the *France*. On the second night out, someone had organized a passageway party. The doors of all the first-class staterooms had been thrown open, everyone had put out bottles and canapés, and passengers in evening dress had wandered from cabin to cabin, chattering and drinking.

"I had just turned fourteen then," Stephanie said, "a skinny little kid. Pants suits had just come in in Paris, they'd hardly been seen in public. Mommy had bought me one: it was velvet, dark blue, it came with a ruffled shirt. My hair was cut very short then, I'd had it chopped off. Daddy called me Steve, for a joke."

"I remember," Christopher said.

By now, Stephanie was not surprised by Christopher's memory.

"I wore my velvet pants suit to the party," she continued. "It stormed all the way across the Atlantic on that trip. The ship was heaving, things were falling off the tables. Half the people there got sick and rushed into the bathrooms, so there were a lot of stray husbands and wives all mixed up together. The air was thick with adultery."

"You observed all this at the age of fourteen?"

"I was a spy, Mommy always said so. Anyway, I wandered off by myself and was sitting in a strange cabin when Waddy came in. I had a vague idea of who he was. He'd been talking to my parents and I knew he and his sister were some sort of ex-relatives of yours. He was wearing a velvet dinner jacket like mine.

" 'We match,' he said. 'Bored by the party?'

"I said I was very bored.

" 'Me, too. My name is Waddy. What's yours?'

"I said, I don't know why, 'Steve.'

"Waddy offered me a cigarette out of a gold case, as though I'd been smoking for years. This won my confidence completely. I remember giggling a lot as I puffed away. Waddy was a terrific gossip. He'd noticed the ridiculous thing—a mannerism, a nose, a voice, clothes, whatever—about every single person at the party. He was like a child, very observant, funny-malicious. He never once asked me where I went to school or any of the other stupid questions adults usually lay on kids. He gave me sips of his champagne: he'd brought a bottle with him.

"He asked me if I liked velvet. I said sure. He said his sister couldn't stand it, couldn't touch it without shuddering. He stroked my jacket, just the sleeve, and invited me to stroke his. 'Imagine shuddering! Women are strange,' he said. He closed the door, turned around, and started stroking me, as if it were a game. I knew it was no game. I wasn't at all shocked or frightened—a little scared of getting caught, of course, but not afraid of him."

Stephanie laughed. In the last light of evening, they were sitting in the garden behind the house on O Street.

"I haven't thought about this for years," she said. "I've never told anyone except my therapist about it. The fact is, I *do* think about it. It was my first real sexual arousal. Waddy was really quite sweet. He was holding me on his lap. Waddy was panting a bit and that tickled me, it made him seem vulnerable. All of a sudden, to my amazement, Waddy put his hand between my legs."

Stephanie giggled. "He leaped as if he'd been shot.

" 'You're a bloody *girl!*' Waddy cried.

"My hair was cut like a boy's, I was wearing what could have been boy's clothes, I had given him a boy's name. Naturally he'd thought I was a boy.

"At this moment, the door opened and in came the owner of the cabin in a cloud of perfume. She was a German. I remember that this woman was wearing a silver evening gown. Waddy's face was still distorted by surprise and, I suppose, disgust. He looked at the woman. She looked at Waddy, who in his shock had not removed his right hand from its resting place.

" '*Vot* are you doing in my cabin?' the woman said. She had a German accent—her English was perfect, but she said *v* for *w* and expectorated her consonants.

" 'Just chatting,' Waddy replied.

" '*Chatting? Chatting?* You call this *chatting?* I'm going to call for the captain and have you put in the brrrrig!' the woman said.

"She was outraged. She made a hell of a scene. It made a much greater impression on me than Waddy's stroking. She was a Valkyrie, this woman, busty and fierce. She sent for Waddy's sister and threatened them both with the brig. The sister was tougher than Waddy. She not only saved him from the brig by calming the woman down, but also got me to say that it was all a mistake."

Stephanie laughed again. "Of course it *was* all a mistake. Poor Waddy. It was years before I understood what had happened."

"Is that all that happened?" Christopher asked.

"All?" Stephanie's good humor was still bright in her face. "There are people who'd pay a shrink twenty thousand dollars to dig out a story like that."

Stephanie took Christopher's glass out of his hand and stood up. "It's getting too cold to sit out here," she said.

"What happened?" Christopher asked. "Did they tell your parents, was there trouble between Waddy and your father?"

Stephanie bit her lip. "No, thank God. I was in trouble enough with my conscience for being a spy."

"For being a spy?"

Stephanie bit her lip, deep in a thought of the past.

"That's interesting," she said. "It must have been the perfume and the German accent that triggered *that*. I haven't thought about the Baroness for years."

"The Baroness?"

"That's just what I called her. I used to tail her around Paris. She was a woman of mystery. I'd see her in the Parc Monceau, always by herself. She came to watch the children. She had this terrifically melancholy look. So I tailed her."

"You followed her?"

"All over Paris, for weeks. It was what I did after school. Then one day I caught up to her, in Aux Trois Quartiers. She was trying on dresses. I hid behind a rack, observing her. She grabbed me."

"Grabbed you?"

Stephanie nodded. "She pulled me into a changing booth. She was in her underwear—no slip, just pants and bra and a garter belt. It was terrifying. *'Vhy* are you following me?' she hissed. She shook me like a Raggedy Ann. I thought I was a goner. I've been frightened of garter belts ever since."

Stephanie started to leave. Christopher took her hand. His palm, months after his release, was still unyielding and rough, like a slab of raw lumber.

"Finish the story."

"I was rescued. Wolkowicz rescued me."

"Wolkowicz?"

"He burst into the changing cubicle and grabbed me away from the murderess. Barney was in Paris for some reason; he'd been to the house a lot. He must have been tailing somebody himself. He just happened to be there."

"What about the woman?"

"She smelled of perfume, clouds of it. That's why I've never been able to wear it, I guess. Ah, analysis!"

"But what happened to her?"

"I don't know; I never saw her in the Parc Monceau again. Wolkowicz hurried me out of there and took me home. He got the whole story out of me. 'You need your little ass paddled,' Barney said. But he never told on me. Mommy would have done worse than paddle."

"Do you remember what the woman looked like?"

"Just the underwear. It was that sleazy pink stuff, with lace."

Christopher asked Stephanie if she objected to being hypnotized.

[331]

"Hypnotized?" Stephanie said. "Whatever for?"

He told her about Sergeant Jimmy Jo Mitchell.

"I'm not sure I *want* to see the Baroness again," Stephanie said.

"But I do," Christopher said. "I want to be sure she wasn't somebody I knew."

Christopher had never before asked Stephanie to do anything that was not absolutely sane. She didn't know how to refuse to do this for him.

"All right," she said lightly. "If I can choose the hypnotist."

— 3 —

"It looks like her," Patchen said. "Anything is possible."

He slid the drawing back into its envelope and handed it to Christopher.

"And what if it *is* her, after all these years?" he said. "What would that tell us?"

"That she's alive, that she's in the West."

"I guess that's interesting. Obviously it's interesting to you." Patchen looked at a still life on the wall of his living room, as if it contained a more tantalizing face than the one Christopher had just shown him. "Tell me," he said, "how do you find a hypnotist? Do you look in the Yellow Pages?"

Patchen, who had no small talk, seemed ready to drift away into chitchat. As he spoke, he was busy at a side table. He took the stopper out of a decanter of port, poured two glasses of wine, replaced the stopper, put the glasses on a tray, offered the tray to Christopher. Because he had to do everything one-handed, this took a long time.

Christopher took the port even though he did not want it and held it in his hand. Patchen, who had such an orderly mind, could not seem to remember that Christopher did not drink wine. He offered him nuts from a bowl. Christopher took a walnut and cracked it in his bare hands.

"You seem to be on a trail," Patchen said. "Alcoholic sergeants, Waddy Jessup, hypnotists. What are you trying to find?"

"Explanations."

Patchen shrugged, the most passionate gesture in his repertoire. "So many people are dead," he said. "Mordecai Bashian and that woman, Jocelyn Frick, are dead. Your father, all those people in Vietnam. Did you know about them? Nguyên Kim, the Truong toc—murdered about the time you were captured. A car bomb for the Truong toc; Kim was strangled. There were those who thought you'd killed them. Clearly that was impossible. Not you. In any case, everyone is dead. But then, interviewing the dead was always one of your specialties, wasn't it?"

Patchen examined his still life again. It was unlike him, this wandering gaze.

"Do you have a theory?" he asked. "Do you know what it all means?"

"Were you listening to Waddy? He called the Addressees Spy Ring a diversion. Maybe everything, all along, was diversion—just one diversion after another."

Patchen sipped some port. He was having trouble with his voice. He had become less and less audible, and now spoke in a croaking whisper.

"It's as good a theory as any," he said. "If dead women can float up from Stephanie Webster's mind wearing garter belts, why should anything be impossible?"

Patchen cleared his throat repeatedly. He couldn't speak. Christopher handed Patchen his own port and the other man drank it. It opened his throat and he came back to the original subject.

"Are you going to show this to Wolkowicz?" he asked.

"I don't know. Should I?"

"Do as you like. Do you have some way of finding him? I don't. As far as I know, Barney sleeps under bridges. His apartment is never used. Where does he go at night? It's a mystery."

Patchen smiled his agonized smile, as if even he, at times, was amused by Wolkowicz's unrelenting suspicion of everyone and everything.

— 4 —

To Christopher's surprise, Stephanie liked the food at the Thai Pagoda.

"It's my radical principles," she said, eating highly seasoned pork and canned pineapple off a skewer. "If it comes from the Third World, it has to be good for you."

Christopher wrote something on a scrap of paper and gave it to the waitress as she cleared away the plates. It was late; Stephanie and Christopher were the last customers. The lights dimmed.

"I think they want us to leave," Stephanie said.

"Not yet," Christopher replied.

Firm footsteps crossed the empty room. The proprietor, his muscular torso stretching the thin material of a white silk shirt, stood beside their table.

"Hello, Pong," Christopher said. "How have you been?"

"Alive and well," Pong said. "I thought it was you when you came in the other day with our friend, but it's been a long time."

Pong shook hands, first with Stephanie, who flinched at his strength, then with Christopher. His English had improved since his days in Saigon as Wolkowicz's driver, and he had a new ease of manner. He wore designer clothes and jeweled rings on his powerful hands. He drew up a chair and sat down.

He snapped his fingers, a detonating sound in the empty restaurant, and the pretty little waitress brought three extra desserts and a bottle of cognac. She bowed to Pong and went away. Pong poured the liqueur himself.

"Is that your daughter, the waitress?" Stephanie asked.

"Right," Pong said. "She's in medical school, Georgetown. Off duty, she's a real American girl. The whole family are citizens. We had a special bill in Congress."

"How did you manage that?" Stephanie asked.

"Friends," he said. He lifted his glass to Christopher.

Christopher wet his lips with the cognac. Pong drained his glass, then folded his hands in his lap, out of sight.

In Vietnamese, Christopher said, "Is Barney a partner, or did he just help you out when you started this place?"

"Barney never wants anything for himself," Pong said in the same language. He jerked his head toward Stephanie. "She doesn't understand?"

Christopher shook his head. Stephanie got up and went to the ladies' room.

"English is better," Pong said. "I never liked Vietnamese. Now, less. You want to contact Barney?"

"Yes, but it's not urgent. Do you know where he is?"

"I can take a message. Maybe Barney told you I still do him some favors."

Pong and Christopher smiled at one another, two old friends of Wolkowicz's who understood what friendship with him entailed.

"I'm always glad to help Barney out," Pong said. "It really has been a long time. You retired now? Everybody's retiring."

"Yes."

"I don't miss the life," Pong said.

But he did. He poured himself another brandy, rings flashing, and offered more to Christopher. Like other old agents Christopher had known, Pong enjoyed a good gossip. He mentioned two or three other names, Outfit people from his days in Vietnam.

"Everybody on the Vietnamese side was mixed up with the Cong —*everybody*. Barney knew that," Pong said. "Nobody else would believe it. Not even you, my friend. There were Vietnamese you actually loved. Remember?"

"I remember."

"You had a lot of enemies out there, too. It was because you were good. Barney always said you were the best."

"Barney said that?"

Pong tossed down his brandy. His eyes watered and a deep flush crept up under the brown skin of his unlined, youthful face.

"You know Barney. He'd never *say* anything like that. But he didn't like your enemies. He took care of you."

"Took care of me?"

"Took care of your enemies. You'd better ask Barney." Pong laughed. "Hell of a lot of good that'll do you. *He* won't tell you what he did for you. It was a lot, though, no shit."

Stephanie came out of the toilet. Pong stopped speaking. But instead of returning to the table, she strolled through the shadowy restaurant, looking at the decor, travel posters of Thai scenes. Pong's daughter joined her and they chatted. Pong looked on with approval. Stephanie, with her neat body and her tawny coloring, looked something like the Thai girl. Her black hair was less beautiful.

"Your wife?" Pong asked.

"No."

"Maybe you should marry her. At least she's quiet. American woman talk so fucking much. *They* answer all the questions, *they* choose the food. I say to my daughters: 'Not you, baby.' I'd send them back to Thailand if they pull that shit. They don't want to go, they want to be American girls—college, boyfriends, music all the time, crazy ideas. But not around me."

Pong poured himself a third cognac, then put the cork back in the bottle, slapping it home with his horny palm. In his day, he had been a killer, skilled with his bare hands, good with weapons. In Vietnam, when he worked for Wolkowicz, he had carried a box of sand with him in the car; waiting for Barney, he would pound the edge of his hands into the sand, hundreds of blows every day. His hands had been like two stone axes. Obviously he remembered his youth with pleasure.

"You missed the worst parts in Vietnam," he said. "There was a lot of mess to clean up. I helped, right up until I came to the States."

"Working for Barney even after he left?"

"Sometimes, odd jobs. He always keeps in touch."

"How about you, Pong? Do you keep in touch?"

"The guys come in here for a meal. I see some of them. I remember them all. Barney taught me how to remember faces—you divide them in three, right? I knew you right away."

"There's one guy from Saigon I've been trying to remember," Christopher said.

"Yeah? Who's that?"

"A pilot. His first name was Gus."

"Gus Kimber," Pong said without hesitation.

"Kimber? Was that his name?"

"Skinny guy, used dope, didn't give a shit for anything. He did a lot of stuff for Barney. That was the only Gus I knew."

"I heard he was killed."

"Gus? Killed?" Pong chortled. "Not this Gus. He'd get himself beat up in bars, but that was it. He was in here last year, drunk as a skunk. He's giving flying lessons out West somewhere. Shit, wait—he left a card."

Pong snapped his fingers. His daughter brought him a cigar box. It was full of business cards. Pong put on a pair of half-moon reading glasses and went through them. He found a Polaroid snapshot of himself, standing in front of a moored cabin cruiser. In the snapshot, he wore a yachting cap.

"My boat," he said. "Chesapeake power squadron."

Peering over the tops of the half moons, Pong watched for Christopher's reaction to this evidence of his affluence. Despite his gray hair, despite his history, the glasses, perched on his round face, made him look like a child playing with a grown-up's things. At last he found Gus Kimber's card and gave it to Christopher.

Christopher read it and handed it back.

"Blythe, California," Pong said, peering through his lenses. "That's in the desert, near the Arizona line, according to Gus. No trees as far as the eye can see. Gus liked that. He didn't enjoy having the Cong shooting at his ass whenever he'd have to fly over the jungle, I remember that."

Pong closed his cigar box and took off his glasses. He rested his hands on the lid of the box and, unable to stop himself after his long day at work, yawned.

He covered his mouth with one hand and lifted the other in apology to Christopher. On his index fingers he wore Nguyên Kim's ruby rings.

Nine

— 1 —

"You want to see the intaglios?" the woman asked, when Christopher called Gus Kimber's number in Blythe. She had a stripped American voice, loud and free of accent. Christopher didn't know what the intaglios were; he didn't ask. The woman didn't wait for his answer.

"The best time to see them is sunup," she said. "The charge is fifty dollars for a half-hour flight. Gus'll meet you out at the airport at five-thirty. You'll see the sign: *Kimber Flying Service.*"

Christopher flew to Phoenix and rented a car. It was after midnight. Driving westward through the desert, he realized that he was truly alone for the first time since he had left China. He stopped the car and got out. The moon had set and the black sky above this empty country was filled with stars. A gust of wind brought him the parched smell of dust, like the dust he had inhaled during the firefight after Gus's plane had crashed in China.

He drove on. It was not yet five o'clock when Christopher arrived at the Blythe airport. In the starlight he could see small planes parked on the apron. A dog barked furiously behind a chain-link fence, then wriggled through a gap in the wire and leaped onto the hood of Christopher's car. The animal, a mongrel with a lot of Alsatian blood, snarled at him through the windshield, scratching the paint as it scrambled for a foothold on the smooth body of the car.

Headlights approached, jouncing on the rough dirt track that led in from the highway. An old Jeep pulled in beside Christopher's parked car and its driver, a man wearing a high-crowned Stetson, leaped out. The dog barked at him. He seized it by the collar and the tail and flung it, like a sack of garbage, into the darkness. The animal hit the ground, yelping, twenty feet away, and scuttled off.

The man in the Stetson looked through the windshield. Christopher lowered the window.

"Sorry about the dog," the man said. "It belongs to the night watchman—he turns it loose if he sees a strange car. Hard on the paint."

The rising sun, its disk still invisible beyond the eastern ridgeline, sent a shaft of light through a cleft in the rocks.

"Might as well crank her up," the man said. "The sun'll be up by the time we get up in the air. You know the price?"

Christopher got out of the car and handed him a fifty-dollar bill. There was just enough light for them to see each other. The man unsnapped the breast pocket of his western shirt and put away the money without looking at it. He wore a stainless-steel Rolex watch on his left wrist.

"Couldn't Gus make it?" Christopher asked.

"What?"

"I was expecting Gus."

"I'm Gus," the man said, in a strong Texas accent.

He was lanky, an inch or two taller than Christopher, with a lean, weatherbeaten western face, unmistakably a Texan.

His aircraft was a Piper Super Cub, a slow, reliable machine. Once they were airborne, scorched air blew into the cockpit from the heater. The mountains to the east were still purple with night, but the sun made little ponds of light on the barren flanks of the hills to the west. Below them the Colorado River, shining in the morning light, wound through squares of irrigated land, green and placid as paddy in Asia.

The plane climbed, bucking a little as it crossed the water, and flew over the bleak desert. Gus banked and pointed downward. On the flat

[339]

top of a high mesa, directly below, Christopher saw the outline of an enormous human figure. It was at least a hundred feet in length. Gus nudged Christopher and pointed again: the figure had large pendulous testicles. Nearby was the outline of a deer.

"Those are the Blythe intaglios," Gus shouted. "You know the history?"

Christopher shook his head.

"Some lost pilot found 'em in 1932," Gus said. "Just flew over and there they were. Nobody'd ever seen 'em before. You can't see from the ground. Whoever made 'em, made 'em by turning over stones that are dark on one side and light on the other, so the light side is up."

Gus flew to another mesa. There were more intaglios below, winged objects like flying machines, concentric circles that looked like targets, Maltese crosses, and other abstract designs.

"They're all over the place," Gus said. "Nobody knows who put 'em here, or why, or what they mean."

"Can you land on the mesa?"

"Sure, this thing'll land anywhere. But you can't see anything from the ground."

Gus landed the Super Cub on a tiny patch of rough ground, littered with sharp stones, among huge rocks. The two men walked together to the intaglio. Gus crouched down, a long-shanked figure in his jeans and boots, and turned over a stone.

"See?" he said. "Black on the bottom, light on the top. This is the guy with the testicles. The Indians who made these—if it was the Indians—never did get to see 'em. You've got to be at least five hundred feet above the deck."

Gus replaced the stone carefully, in the exact spot from which he had taken it, and stood up. It was full daylight now. The wind took Gus's hat; he caught it deftly in midair.

Christopher told him who he was.

"No shit?" Gus said. "The guy who was in China all that time?"

"Yes."

"Glad you made it back. How long ago did they get you?"

"Ten years ago last January. You were in Saigon about that time, weren't you?"

Gus nodded and pulled his hat down tighter on his forehead. The wind was growing stronger. Gus shot an anxious glance at his plane, which was rocking in the wind only a few feet from the edge of the mesa.

"That was a bad year for me," he said. "It started out bad. I got the shit beat out of me in Saigon on New Year's Eve. Busted my face, ruptured my guts, I was a mess."

"You were in the hospital?"

"For a solid month. They had to take out my spleen and I had this fucking cast on from my neck to my knees."

"Bad luck."

"It was only the beginning. While I was in the hospital, some son of a bitch stole my airplane. A brand-new Piper Apache."

"Did you get it back?"

Gus shook his head. "No, that mother was long gone. I had another plane for a while, but shit, I got tired of that scene out there and came on back after about a year."

Gus's eyes were on his Super Cub. Holding on to his hat, he started to walk fast over the carpet of stones in the direction of the parked machine. Christopher followed him.

"Did you see the fellows who beat you up?" Christopher asked.

"No, I don't know who the fuck they were. I walked out of Rosie's —that's where it happened—turned right, and got cold-conked. D'you ever hit Rosie's? They had a girl in there who smoked cigarettes with her pussy."

"I was there once."

"I imagine the Communists closed it down. I wonder what Rosie's doing for a living."

"Was it a fight you were in, or what?" Christopher asked.

"It wasn't much of a fight. Some son of a bitch popped me on the back of the neck. He damn near killed me; separated vertebrae and I don't know what all. He must have kicked the shit out of me while I was out, lying on the ground. Took everything, my watch, five hundred dollars, my stash—I used a little dope out there, like everybody. Gave it up when I got home, though: the love of a good woman."

Gus hurried toward the plane. Light as a kite, it rocked in the wind that swept like a draft in a chimney up the sheer face of the mesa.

"Did you ever meet a Chinese pilot out there?" Christopher asked. "Little fellow, spoke with a cockney accent?"

Gus seized a strut and put his weight on it, to anchor the plane.

"A Chink pilot with a cockney accent? No. All the pilots I knew out there were cowboys. Help me turn this sucker around."

They turned the plane into the wind. Gus started the engine and took off, flying off the edge of the mesa. The plane dropped, then soared above the intaglios.

"Christ knows there *could* have been a Chink like the one you're talking about," Gus shouted above the stammer of the engine. "They had everything in Nam."

— 2 —

In Christopher's absence, another episode of "The Patrick Graham Show" went on the air. This time, Graham told his audience about the Sewer.

"You and Wolkowicz were the stars again," Patchen said to Christopher. "Deep beneath Vienna, Graham showed us the actual spot where you crouched with your machine gun, mowing down the Red dogs. He knew all about the code machines, all about Wolkowicz's medal."

"He seems to know everything."

"Not quite everything. There was no mention of Darby, no mention of Ilse Wolkowicz. Graham's source is being very selective; he's not giving him everything. You'd think that would make Wolkowicz happy —he comes off as a hero every time. But no."

They were walking, in a light mist, down the familiar path through the Georgetown campus. Patchen took off his glasses and wiped them: economically, one lens only. There was no need to polish the glass that covered his blind eye.

"You've seen Barney?" Christopher asked.

"We talked on the telephone. He won't show himself at all. Even Graham can't find him."

"He's disturbed?"

"You could say that. He wants me to turn the Outfit inside out, find Graham's source, cut off his dingus."

Patchen, swinging his bad leg, took a dozen steps before he spoke again.

"To be honest with you," he said, "I'm not so sure that the Outfit is the right place to look for Graham's man."

Patchen's tone was even and controlled, as if he had always been perfectly willing to talk to Christopher on this subject.

"You think an outsider could have access to this kind of information?"

"I didn't say an outsider. For example, Darby is still alive. So far, everything Graham has learned is something Darby knew. And there's been no mention of Darby on the air. Why?"

"Has Graham been to Moscow, to interview Darby?"

"I don't think so, but of course we don't have him under surveillance. Anyway, it doesn't have to be Moscow. For that matter, it doesn't have to be Darby. Others are also alive."

"It could be me," Christopher said.

Patchen stopped and his dog came bounding back to him, its wet coat opalescent under the sodium lights.

"Yes, it could be you," Patchen said. "It could be anyone. It could be Wolkowicz, or me, or somebody with a multiple personality."

He set off down the path, walking rapidly again. Christopher kept pace in silence.

"I don't think Wolkowicz is pointing in the right direction," Patchen said. "All this material of Graham's is old. It all has something to do with you. The timing—right after the Chinese let you out. . . ." Patchen slowed down again. "You don't think *that's* strange?"

Patchen sighed, a deep, exasperated sound. The Doberman froze, confused by this unfamiliar signal from his master.

"You think you know, don't you?" he said.

"Not all the details, not yet. I think I understand the reason."

"Tout comprendre est tout pardonner," Patchen said in his dreadful French. He rubbed his face, as if after all these years he could wake up the feeling in it. "Or is it?" he said.

He spun around and set off in the opposite direction, leaving Christopher alone on the path.

— 3 —

"Patchen wants to believe it's an outsider?" Wolkowicz said. "Sure he does. They always want to believe that. The Outfit has never been penetrated, right? It's fucking unthinkable. They all went to the Fool Factory together and sang 'The Whiffenpoof Song.' *They* wouldn't let themselves be recruited by some peasant of a Russian in a J. C. Penney suit."

"That's not really what I wanted to talk to you about," Christopher said.

A cold wind filled with rain whipped down the low canyon formed by the buildings in the zoo. They hurried around the elephant house to the entrance; it was too wintry for the animals to be outside. Wolkowicz wore no topcoat, not even an undershirt; the curly black hair on his chest was visible beneath the transparent fabric of his soaked drip-dry shirt. Inside, he didn't bother to wipe the water from his hair and face. The keepers were cleaning the cages. The atmosphere smelled strongly of ammonia. Wolkowicz inhaled. His mind leaped to another subject.

"When I was a little kid in Youngstown, Ohio," he said, "my father always used to get me out of bed in the middle of the night to see the circus load and unload. He was a circus freak. One night, about two o'clock in the morning, as I'm sitting up on my old man's shoulders, watching them put the animals on board, along comes this Barnum & Bailey midget. The midget is drunk. He's all dressed up in a suit with a checked vest and a watch chain and he's wearing a derby hat. He's with his buddy, the Strong Man, also drunk; they're singing dirty songs. There's a cop on duty and he walks up to the midget, swinging his nightstick, and gives him a dirty look. 'Better get on the train, pal,' the cop says. 'We don't want no drunk midgets in Youngstown, Ohio.' The crowd is with the cop, local pride is aroused. 'Yeah,' says the crowd, 'yeah.' 'Hold my hat,' says the midget to the Strong Man, handing him his derby. The midget walks up to the cop. 'There are those among us,' says the midget to the cop, 'that have rubbed the likes of you plumb into the elephant shit.'"

Wolkowicz got out his peanuts and fed the elephants. His voice reverberated against the bare walls of the concrete building. He didn't seem to care if the keepers heard what he had to say next.

"If fucking Patchen had left me alone," he said, "Graham would be rubbed into the elephant shit by now. I'd have it on film, I'd have it on tape, there'd be no mystery. Just remember that. You were there when he pulled me off Graham. You saw him, kissing the fucking Constitution."

Wolkowicz turned his back on the elephants and grinned as their trunks searched for the fresh bag of peanuts in his pocket. He had heard what Christopher had said to him five minutes before. Now he was willing to acknowledge that fact.

"You said you wanted to ask me something," he said. "What?"

"I wanted to ask you about Gus Kimber. I went out to see him in California."

"You still think it was him who flew you into China?"

"No, but it may have been his plane. He says it was stolen."

Wolkowicz frowned in concentration. It took him only seconds to remember.

"That's right," he said. "Gus got busted up in a fight, too. I had to sneak him into the army hospital under fake ID; he was just a contract type, like all the fliers. The Outfit would never give those guys medical benefits; they were too low-class."

"Was the stolen plane ever found?"

"Are you kidding? It's probably hauling opium out of Laos right now. If Gus wasn't your pilot, who was?"

"Whoever stole his plane. When I went into China, did anybody run a check on the pilots in Saigon?"

Wolkowicz watched the keepers for a moment. Their shovels rang against the concrete floor.

He said, "Patchen polygraphed them all."

"Himself?"

"I don't know. It happened after I left Saigon."

"What were his conclusions?"

Wolkowicz let another moment pass before he answered. "Patchen wouldn't say," he said. "He wouldn't let anybody near your case."

"Not even you?"

"Especially not me. I thought we should go in after you. We had all those helicopters. We could have got you if we'd have gone right in, while you were still on Hainan Island."

"Is that where I was?"

"Two hours from Da Nang, right? Where did you think you were? Patchen thought my plan was incautious. He always thinks I'm incautious. He handled every little thing, right from the start. I imagine *he* was very cautious. He went out himself to talk to the Chinks after you were sentenced. He went out to get you on the airplane when you got out."

Wolkowicz bared his false teeth.

"Just a perfect friendship," he said.

Ten

— 1 —

In his London club, Sir Richard Shaw-Condon smiled in genuine pleasure.

"It's marvelous to meet you at last, my dear fellow," he said. "I can't think why it's taken so long. I knew your father well, you know. And we have masses of friends in common. Of course, you've been away, haven't you?"

Christopher smiled in return. Sir Richard sipped Riesling from a green-stemmed glass.

"You ought to have some of this hock," he said. "We're rather proud of it. It's a '71, best year of the century, they say; tastes of hyacinths and honey. That's from your father's poem about German wine. Do you know if your father actually ate hyacinths, ha-ha?"

Sir Richard had been delighted to hear from Christopher; he had fond memories of Hubbard.

"At my age," he had shouted into the phone when Christopher called him from America the day before, "one lives rather in the past. Very glad to see ghosts—even the sons of ghosts, ha-ha."

Across the table from Christopher, Sir Richard ate smoked salmon, using two forks; he had been raised to believe that it was a sign of low birth to cut fish with a knife. Sir Richard, now retired, had never quite reached the top in his intelligence service, but he had become very senior. Every day of his life, he had taken two hot baths and at the age of seventy he had the pink soft skin of an infant. He still had his mirthful schoolboy face. His flaxen eyebrows and mustache had turned snow-white. Beneath his coat he wore his school cricket sweater, with the rampant lion of Worksop College stitched in blue on the breast.

Christopher looked around the dining room. This was a club for men who had fought behind enemy lines in the Second World War. Half a dozen members, most of them older than Sir Richard, ate alone at small tables. The club offered only a cold lunch: with his noble Rhine wine, Sir Richard, after finishing his salmon, ate a Scotch egg, pale pink ham-and-chicken pie with a soggy crust, and a mound of cold sliced beets. His glance followed Christopher's.

"This place had its great days, but I'm afraid they're past," he said. "Everyone's dying off. Their war dies with them, you know. Sad, really."

On the walls, smudged by forty years of tobacco smoke, hung group photographs of underground fighters—Frenchmen and Belgians in berets, Greeks in tassels, Yugoslavians in peasant boots, Burmese in sarongs. At the center of each group, in thick woolen battle dress or in khaki shorts and rolled-up sleeves according to the climate, stood a young British officer, the team leader.

"Strange, isn't it, to think of old parties like these leaping out of Mosquitoes and Dakotas by the light of the moon?" Sir Richard said. "Still, they had a good war."

Sir Richard took the dripping bottle out of its ice bucket. Christopher's wine was untouched. He filled his own glass.

"You asked about Rosalind Wilmot," he said. "She's round and about. I'm sure I have a number for her in my book."

"Maybe you can give it to me. I'd like to see her."

Sir Richard got out his address book and read off Rosalind's telephone number.

"You two were great friends in Vienna days, I know," he said, going back to his Scotch egg. "Marvelous woman, Rosalind. I always thought she'd make a useful wife—mine, by preference. But it just wasn't on. She's awfully attached to that young brother of hers, Clive. He got his leg blown off in Ulster."

"What news is there of Robin Darby?" Christopher asked, abruptly.

Sir Richard looked up from his food. A quick smile twitched at his lips: so *that* was what Christopher was up to!

"Very little, you know," Sir Richard said. "The Russians gave Darby the Order of Lenin and a sumptuous flat in Moscow and I suppose he's advising or translating or doing whatever it is that heroes of the Soviet Union do after they get caught."

"He's still living?"

"Rotting away, you mean. We don't inquire, really. Have you come to London to reopen the Darby case?"

"Nothing so dramatic as that."

"Good. I should have thought you chaps would have drama enough at home these days, starring on television. Amazing, the things your press is permitted to do, amazing. Do taste that hock."

Christopher tried the Riesling. Because of his ancestry, strangers had always assumed that he liked German wines but, in fact, he had always found them too sweet. Christopher put down the glass and nodded in appreciation.

"What I would like to do, if you'd introduce me to the right man," he said, "is look through the club's collection of photographs."

"Photographs?"

"Of the special operations teams from World War II. They still maintain the archives?"

"I believe so," Sir Richard said. "But you won't find any pictures of your father, you know. One didn't pose with one's agents in Hitler's Germany."

"It's not my father I'm looking for. There's a face I can't place."

"Whose face is that?"

Christopher smiled. "That's what I hope to discover. In prison, I tried to sort out the names and faces of everyone I ever knew. . . ."

"Whatever for?"

"To pass the time. I got them all but one. There's one face I can't put a name to."

"British?"

"I think he must have worked with you during the war, in the East."

Sir Richard gave Christopher a keen glance from under his theatrical eyebrows. They were so symmetrical that Christopher realized that Sir Richard must have them trimmed, like his mustache.

"It must have been hell," Sir Richard said, "lying in a cell, not able to place the chap."

"Exactly."

"Worth a trip to London, I should think."

"Yes."

"Your father was like that, you know," Sir Richard said. "A bear for detail. Nothing escaped him, nothing. Of course you may look at the family albums. I'll fix you up after lunch."

The aged waiter took away their plates and came back with two squares of pastry, glazed with some sort of syrup.

"Treacle tart," Sir Richard said. "You hardly ever see it in England nowadays, thank heaven."

Christopher spent the afternoon in the club library, studying yellowing photographs. Using a large magnifying glass provided by the club secretary, he examined each likely face.

Finally, in a photograph made in 1944, he found the face he was looking for, in the second row of a group of half-naked young Asians, posed before a pagoda in the jungle. They were armed to the teeth with rifles and pistols, knives and swords and grenades. The team leader, a tall bearded youngster with knobby knees and a face full of intelligence, was seated in an armchair. He wore a sarong and a British officer's cap and held a blossoming frond of some kind in his hand instead of a weapon. What a joke, he seemed to be saying with his drooping flower, what a *prank* it all is: the war, death, the jungle, these earnest brown and yellow killers having their picture taken.

Receiving this droll message across the decades, Christopher smiled.

According to the indexing information, the officer's name was Captain R. Dirzinskaite, D.S.O., M.C.: a strange name for an Englishman.

— 2 —

"A *very* strange name," Rosalind Wilmot said. "That's why Robin changed it to Darby after the war; Lithuanians always seem to call themselves after horse races when they decide to anglicize."

Rosalind and Christopher had her flat in Onslow Gardens to themselves. She had sent her brother out for the evening. Clive Wilmot's artificial leg hung by its straps from a coat rack in the front hall.

"Someone gave Clive a peg leg, he prefers that," Rosalind explained. "It's a pity you missed him. He was dressed as a Tsarist dragoon. He and Charlotte Grestain—you remember her, she drinks Scotch and milk and looks like a cheetah—are going to a costume party."

But Rosalind was worried about her brother. Rain sluiced down the windowpanes and from time to time she looked anxiously into the street, thinking about Clive skittering over the slippery pavement on his peg leg. Framed photographs of the two of them, smiling into the camera in front of the Blue Mosque in Istanbul, before the Pyramid of Cheops, on the Promenade des Anglais in Nice, stood on tables all around the room. Clive was younger than Rosalind, and even prettier. The photographs formed a strangely sentimental motif in a room decorated by the Rosalind whom Christopher had known in Vienna.

"I don't often think about Vienna," Rosalind said, "but when I do, I think of that fight in the snow, and all that blood. Wolkowicz was such a primitive. Robin thought it was so dreadfully funny. I always wondered why."

"Darby—Dirzinskaite, should I say?"

"Should you? Your Lithuanian seems a bit rusty. What about him?"

"He had a very active sense of humor. When Wolkowicz called on him in prison, to gloat, he even made a joke of that. He gave Barney one of his Persian carpets."

"I suppose he knew he was going to get away and couldn't take it with him. Robin was a great one for having the last laugh. It was dreadful, the way he taunted Wolkowicz when he was having Ilse."

"Taunted him?"

"Robin knew that Wolkowicz was following the two of them. He'd kiss Ilse on the street and fondle her while the jealous husband was secretly watching—you remember how pneumatic, how like a fragrant rose she was," Rosalind said. "Barney simply writhed. The odd thing is, I think Darby and Wolkowicz liked each other, at heart."

"I never saw much evidence of that."

"All the same, they were fellow proles, you know. They made a joke of that. They talked Russian to each other at first."

"Talked Russian?"

"The passwords were in Russian at first, before they changed to Kachin. They were tickled pink with themselves."

"Why did they stop?"

"I don't know. It may have been your presence. You were so tremendously not a prole. Ilse always went on about how your mother had been a baroness. 'A *Prussian* baroness,' she would chortle, with Hun superiority."

Although Rosalind's black hair was long, like a young girl's, it was streaked with gray. She wore ribbed woolen stockings and a pleated skirt and blazer, like a school uniform. But when she held out her ringless hands to the electric fire, the blue veins of middle age showed on the backs. There was a little less light than formerly in her clear violet eyes.

"Well," she said, "Vienna brought none of us happiness, did it? You slew all those Russians, Wolkowicz slew his wife, Robin slew himself. The hell with Vienna. Tell me about China."

Christopher told her. Like Stephanie, she was interested and listened in silence, her eyes wide open and fixed on his.

"Surely," she said, "it *couldn't* have just been an accident? You weren't sentenced to death for pilot error? How could you bear the thought?"

"What difference did it make?"

"To die for stupidity? A great deal of difference, I should have thought. To you especially. You were quite eerie, you know, the way you never did a stupid thing. Not even on the female body. That's awfully rare in a member of your sex, to know where everything is."

Rosalind warmed her hands again. She hadn't intended to speak about their life in bed; there had never been anything between them but sex and jokes. But as Christopher described his years in prison, alone and silent, she had had a sudden sharp sensation that it had somehow been her own body that had lain on his pallet in China. She shook her head in annoyance at this romantic fantasy. Christopher was watching her. She supposed he could read signs as well as ever and knew that she had been thinking of the past.

"Did Robin ever talk about the past?" Christopher asked.

Rosalind was startled, but she was glad of another subject. She surprised herself with the length of her answer. "Robin? Not much. If you asked, he'd just recite his *curriculum vitae*. His parents hiked out of Lithuania before he was born, 'with little packs on their backs,' he always said. They went first to South Africa. They were heroes to Robin, heroes. I don't know if they walked all the way, over the water I mean, but Robin made it sound as if they had. Then they came to

London, just at the end of the First World War; Mrs. D. was pregnant with Robin and they wanted him to be born in England. He went to grammar school in London, Highgate, I believe, and won all the prizes and a scholarship in oriental studies at London University. He got a commission in the Special Forces on the strength of his languages— Chinese, Japanese, strange Burmese dialects. And Russian, of course."

"Did he ever talk about Burma?"

"No, never. Of course everyone knew that he was practically the T. E. Lawrence of the jungle. He was such a god to the headhunters that they had to give him the D.S.O. even though he had crawled out from under a rock somewhere south of the Thames and was called Dirzin- skaite. Even after he came over onto the permanent strength of the service, he insisted on talking like a fish porter, cocking a snook at the old Etonians. They detested him, they always kept him in the field, but they couldn't do without him."

"Do the files on his Burma days still exist?"

Rosalind displayed no surprise at this improper question, no cau- tion. "I suppose they must," she said.

"I'd like to know something about his team out there."

Rosalind listened to Christopher's list of requirements. It was short: a picture, a name, a certain dispatch.

"Am I to understand," Rosalind said, "that you want me to steal this information out of our Registry, for old times' sake?"

"Yes."

"Very well," she said.

Christopher handed her a theater ticket, for a performance of *King Lear.* Rosalind put on her glasses and examined the ticket.

"Tomorrow night?" she said. "Very impetuous, you Ameddicans."

Rosalind arrived late at the play, just as the third act was beginning. When the lights went down, she pressed a hat-check token into Chris- topher's hand. She had left the things he wanted in an envelope in the cloakroom of the theater.

"It's all there, just as you guessed," she whispered, as Lear's voice and the noise of a wind machine filled the theater. "What sly dogs they were. Poor Paul, to know it all along, and be locked up in China."

Eleven

— 1 —

On the eleventh anniversary of his capture, Christopher called on Pong's daughter, the medical student, and asked her to deliver a message for him.

She shook her shining cape of black hair, a gesture of disgust. "I don't know about going to his office, he's always coming on to me," she said. "All the other meetings were outdoors."

"This would be the last time you'd have to see him."

"You say that. What will Barney say?"

"He'll agree."

"All right, but if there's trouble, you'll have to explain to my father."

"I'll explain," Christopher said. "To Barney, too. I'll be seeing him tonight."

That night, Christopher's friends gave him supper at the club. Horace Hubbard had come home from China for the holidays. He told Christopher about the annual suppers attended by Patchen, Webster, Wolkowicz, and himself.

"You mean the four of you met every January for this ritual?"

"The *five* of us. Everybody except Wolkowicz believed that you were there in spirit, at your empty place at the table. We ate soup and roast beef, drank sentimental toasts, and exchanged information about you. Only there was never any information. The Chinese just wouldn't talk about you. Even after we opened a station in Peking and Patchen sent me to China, there was no information."

"None at all?"

"Every January, Patchen would report that you were still alive. He had some means of knowing that."

The cousins were walking together down H Street in the direction of the club. A light snow, the first of the year, had dusted the sidewalks, and Horace looked over his shoulder at their footprints. He threw his long arm around Christopher's shoulders and gave him an impulsive hug.

"Snow," he said. "I was thinking of those sled rides at the Harbor."

Tom Webster had arrived at the club before them. They found him upstairs in the private dining room, drinking Scotch. In his emotion, he breathed audibly through his nose.

"I gave up on this," he said, grasping Christopher's hand. "I never thought it would happen, that you'd walk in here. I really thought you were gone." He blinked. "Ten years of these suppers."

Webster was on the point of tears. When the door opened, it was too late to hide his feelings. Wolkowicz looked him up and down and snorted.

"I hope this is the last crying jag I have to be in on because of you, kid," he said to Christopher. "Webster usually gives us the holy water a little later, after the wine."

Wolkowicz punched Webster on the arm, a hard jab that shifted the other man's weight.

"This is the last supper, buddy," he said. "Cheer up. He is risen."

Guffawing, Wolkowicz put an arm around Christopher and gave him an affectionate shake. In the overheated room, Wolkowicz's frayed tweed jacket smelled of wet wool; evidently he had walked some distance in the falling snow without a topcoat. The thick rubber soles of his soaked shoes left a pattern on the hardwood floor, like the mark of a soccer shoe on skinned turf.

The waiter brought a tray. Wolkowicz lifted his Rob Roy into the air.

"Absent friends," he said, with a flash of teeth. "That's the toast of Patchen's Merry Men. I'm glad we got one back, at least."

Webster drank, but turned away afterward. Patchen came late. He made no apologies. Other waiters put the soup tureen on the table.

Wolkowicz ladled his bowl full, broke a piece of bread in half, and put his face into the dish. As he spooned pea soup with his right hand and dipped bread with his left, his eyes were fixed on Patchen. Midway through the soup, a double Rob Roy, his third, was brought to him in a water tumbler.

While the food was consumed, there was no conversation. Patchen finished eating his tiny portions very quickly.

"Somehow," he said, "I'd imagined that this would be a happier occasion."

These were his first words. In the black suit he wore in winter, he looked paler and lamer than usual. Wolkowicz, on the other hand, was pink-faced after his walk in the open air and jovial, in his brutal way, after the Rob Roys he had drunk. He splashed wine into his glass, filling it to the rim.

"We're happy," he said. "No shit. Christopher especially. What's ten years? Look at him, surrounded by the friends who never forgot him. He's rich, he's a TV star. He's even tight with Webster's daughter." He pinched Webster's cheek. "Isn't that right, buddy?"

Wolkowicz was not interested in Webster's reply. He raised his wineglass. "All's well that ends well, kid," he said to Christopher. "Everybody says so." Wolkowicz snapped his fingers for another Rob Roy.

Like Christopher, like Hubbard before him, Horace was amused by Wolkowicz. He smiled fondly at him, but Wolkowicz didn't see this; he had gone back to his food. Patchen laid his knife and fork across his plate, saying nothing, looking at no one. He, too, wore a faint smile, as if everything was happening just as he had expected.

When the table was cleared, a decanter of port and nuts in a battered, paper-thin silver bowl were brought. When the decanter reached Wolkowicz, he slid it along to Horace without pouring any for himself. In a moment, the waiter brought him his fifth double Rob Roy.

"One more," Wolkowicz rasped as the servant shuffled away. He drank from the tumbler just as thirstily as he had done at the beginning of the evening.

"Let me have your attention," Patchen said, rapping on the tabletop with a walnut. "There's something I want to say. I'm sorry, Paul, that this hasn't been a jollier evening, but these suppers don't have a jolly history. There's been very little to talk about. We had no facts. We knew that you were in prison, under sentence of death. We didn't know if we'd see you again. Some of us may have thought that you were gone forever. We didn't know what had happened to you, or why it happened."

Patchen's throat went dry. He paused for a sip of port. Wolkowicz, sprawled in his pushed-back chair with one bulging leg crossed over the other, sipped at his drink. His eyes were closed. As Patchen's silence persisted, he opened his eyes.

"What a crock of shit," Wolkowicz said.

Patchen cleared his throat. "A crock of shit, Barney?"

" 'We didn't know what happened to Paul, or why it happened.' *Who* didn't know? He went off to get himself killed because the fucking Outfit had hung him out to dry, and he didn't succeed. *That's* what happened, and why."

Wolkowicz reached across the table into the silver bowl and found another walnut. He held it, grasped delicately in the tips of his meaty fingers, beneath Patchen's nose, as if Patchen had never before seen a walnut. Patchen took the nut. Wolkowicz turned to Christopher.

"Tell 'em, kid," he said. "Your roomie here is so fucking sensitive he can't bear to ask."

Christopher smiled at his old friend and protector. "You tell them, Barney," he said.

Patchen seemed to be looking for the nutcracker. There was none. Wolkowicz took the walnut out of his hand, laid it on the table, and slammed it with the edge of his hand, crushing the shell. Then he spoke to Christopher again.

"You thought they were going to kill your girl, kid, and it was all your fault? Isn't that right?"

Wolkowicz waited for Christopher's answer, his palm upturned in encouragement. Christopher merely waited for him to go on.

"He won't answer," Wolkowicz said. "He'd never answer a simple question. Why should he? But that's what he thought—that's what we all thought. They didn't give a shit about the girl. They just wanted to hurt Christopher because he'd hurt them. So he decided to go out to Vietnam and let them kill *him*. He was going to die for love—I saw it in his fucking eyes when I said good-bye to him in Zermatt. Tell me that isn't right, Paul."

Wolkowicz had almost never called Christopher by his Christian name. Now he underwent another change. The tone of his voice changed. He stopped cursing. He leaned forward and looked at each of the others in turn, as if to make sure that they saw the transformation he had undergone.

"What *happened* is that we all let Christopher down," Wolkowicz said in a voice that was hardly louder than a whisper. "He was cut off, he was out of the Outfit, none of us was supposed to help him or even go near him. But we were his friends. Never mind the Outfit, we said to each other, never mind the risks, we're going to help him. So we helped him. Patchen helped him get out of Washington after he came back here and told the folks who *really* killed Cock Robin. I helped him to get back to Vietnam. Webster guarded his girl in Paris. Patchen got money out of the safe in Washington and gave it to him, so he could afford to travel. Otherwise, how was he going to find the people who wanted to kill him? Horace was supposed to watch his back in Saigon, but he lost him—let him get away. We made it all possible."

Wolkowicz paused. Patchen, watching intently, picked the walnut meat out of the litter of shell before him and ate it. Wolkowicz waited until he was done. Then, with a sigh, he gripped Christopher's forearm where it lay on the table.

"You didn't have to do it, kid," he said. "It was all wasted."

"Didn't have to do it?" Christopher said.

"You didn't have to save your lady love, you didn't have to be the sacrificial lamb."

Wolkowicz seemed unable to go on. It was almost impossible for him to reveal a secret. He uttered a grunt, as if he were trying to force words out of his head or force memories back inside. Abruptly, he reverted to his old self. He grinned contemptuously at Patchen and smashed another walnut on the table.

"Have another walnut," he said. "I'm going to give you a treat, Patchen. I'm going to confirm something for you. I'm going to put myself in your power. This shit has gone on long enough."

Wolkowicz gave Christopher's forearm a little shake; his elbow thumped on the table. "You were supposed to hear about it when you got to Saigon," he said. "Horace was supposed to tell you. Horace, tell him now."

Horace was puzzled. "Tell him what?"

"Tell him who died the night he flew into China."

"Molly," Webster said.

"Tom, shut up," Wolkowicz said.

"Not only Molly," Horace said. "The Truong toc. Nguyên Kim."

"Christopher's enemies," Wolkowicz said. "The guys who wanted to kill Molly. Kill the girl with the beautiful legs first, so you'd suffer for a while, then you, kid. That was the plan. I changed their horoscopes before I left Saigon."

"You killed them?" Christopher said. There was a smile in his eyes. Wolkowicz thought it was gratitude and the old amused affection.

"Let's just say I told my man Pong where he could get a couple of ruby rings real cheap." Wolkowicz pointed a warning finger at Patchen. "Remember, Horace never knew this," he said, protecting his former subordinate. "It was me, on my own."

"On your own?" Horace was truly horrified—not because of the murders, but because Wolkowicz had killed for personal reasons. "Why?"

Wolkowicz touched the silver bowl, saw that he had left a finger-print, and automatically smudged it. He drank the rest of his Rob Roy.

"What do you mean, why? I'm the guy who saw his father die, right in front of my eyes. I'm the guy Christopher dragged out of that fucking Sewer when Russians were coming through the wall like rats."

Webster closed his hand on his glass and snapped the stem.

"Then why did they kill Molly?" he said.

"Because you let her get by you, you asshole," Wolkowicz said. "And because maybe I wasted the wrong people."

Wolkowicz, who never did anything unplanned, turned his head and vomited, a yellow jet that smelled to him like C rations and the fecaloid rot of the rain forest.

— 2 —

When they came out the door of the club, all five of them together, Patrick Graham was waiting with a camera crew. A female assistant held an umbrella over Graham's head so that he would not be wetted by the falling snow. As he advanced on Wolkowicz with his microphone, the girl lowered the umbrella and Graham assumed his on-camera expression, a mixture of charm and skepticism.

In brilliant white light that turned his ruddy skin blue, Wolkowicz snarled and backed away. He whirled, looking for someone behind him.

There was no one there except Christopher. The other three men had darted back inside.

"Patchen!" he shouted. "You—"

Beyond the glass doors, Patchen hurried away into the cavernous old building that housed the club. A porter locked the door, stranding Wolkowicz and Christopher outside. The camera was very close to Wolkowicz. Patrick Graham was speaking to him in his powerful voice. Wolkowicz walked away. Graham followed. The cameraman scuttled along backward, keeping the camera focused on Wolkowicz's face.

Wolkowicz broke into a run and moved away with remarkable speed. Christopher turned and ran, too, his eyes fixed on Wolkowicz's squat figure. Far ahead, bent over, knees pumping, running like a full-back, Wolkowicz turned and crossed the street against the light.

For a few steps, Graham ran along beside Christopher, trying to talk but gasping for breath. "All I want is the truth," he said. At the end of the block, he fell against the stones of a building, chest heaving, hair disheveled.

Lafayette Park lay ahead. Christopher had lost sight of Wolkowicz. Near Steuben's statue at the corner of the park, he saw the hobnail print of Wolkowicz's peculiar shoe in a patch of undisturbed snow. Farther on, he saw another print, then part of another. Christopher, traveling at a lope, followed them. In the center of the park, he found him. Wolkowicz was breathing deeply; his clothes were twisted. For once, he didn't touch Christopher. Instead, he sank to the ground, picked up a handful of snow, and washed his face with it.

Wolkowicz held out his hand, cold and wet from the snow, and Christopher pulled him to his feet. Police cars, blue lights flashing and sirens hooting, sped west on Pennsylvania Avenue. Wolkowicz paid no attention to them.

Wolkowicz shivered. In the club, after he was sick, he had been covered with sweat. Now he was soaked and chilled. Christopher took off his raincoat and held it out to him. There had been a time when Wolkowicz would have refused such a gesture of human sympathy. Tonight, he did not argue or resist; he put his arms in the sleeves of his friend's coat and buttoned it up. For a moment, he gazed at the floodlit White House, a few hundred feet away beyond the edge of the park.

"After what happened tonight, you know what Patchen is, don't you?" he said.

Christopher didn't respond.

"I know you don't *want* to know," Wolkowicz said. "But think. Who knew everything? Who knew what you found out in Vietnam? Who knew where Molly was hiding in Paris? Who pulled me out of Saigon? Who knew what time you were arriving in Saigon and who you wanted to see? Who talked to the Chinese about you after you were taken? Who was there to hold your hand when you got out? Webster knew some of those things. Horace knew some. I knew some. But only Patchen knew them all."

Wolkowicz was shuddering violently now. His teeth chattered.

"You don't believe it," he said, hugging himself. "There's no fucking hope. The first guy I had to deal with in this business was Waddy Jessup. The last is Patchen. Nobody believes in Communists anymore, if you even suggest somebody might be a Communist, you're a mental case. I'm whipped. You can't fight the Fool Factory."

Wolkowicz seized Christopher by the ears and kissed him on the cheek. Then, without a word of farewell, he left, as Christopher had seen him do hundreds of times before. His borrowed raincoat was too long for him. Burly and short, plodding through the snow like a muzhik with the long skirt of Christopher's coat flapping around his ankles, he looked, ironically, like a Russian soldier.

It was useless to attempt to follow him. It was only through luck, or Wolkowicz's own design, that Christopher had been able to stay with him even for a couple of blocks. At the primitive, cunning tricks of spying, Wolkowicz remained the master.

Christopher waited until he was out of sight, then he walked up Sixteenth Street until he found a public telephone. He dialed Patchen's number and when he heard the other man's dry voice at the other end of the line he said, "Are you ready?"

"Oh, yes," Patchen said, through the blockage in his throat.

— 3 —

In his troubled sleep, Wolkowicz had thrown off the blankets. Toothless, he lay on his back, wearing raveled Jockey shorts, his broad fleecy chest rising and falling. His P-38 lay in its holster on the table by his head. His clothes were strewn over the floor, except for Christopher's raincoat, which hung, still dripping, above the tub in the bathroom, beyond the foot of the bed.

The phone rang. Wolkowicz's eyes flew open and the first thing he saw in the gray light of the winter dawn was the raincoat. It moved. He sat bolt upright and put his hand on his gun before he realized that what he saw was only an empty garment, turning in a current from the hot-air register.

The woman on the other side of the bed answered the telephone. She said, "Yes, immediately," into the mouthpiece, then hung up.

Wolkowicz watched her get out of bed. She wore a silvery blue nightgown with lace at the neck, her best color because it matched her eyes. He reached out and slid his hand under her gown. She was no longer young. The skin on her buttocks was thick now, pebbled like the skin of a fowl, and when she bent over, her breasts were like pears, small at the top and bell-shaped at the bottom, but she still excited him. She paused, looking at him over her shoulder like a mare, and let him stroke her. "I'll be back," she whispered, running a stiffened index finger down the bulge in his shorts and giving the head of his penis a hard pinch.

She went into the bathroom. Wolkowicz closed his eyes. His bones ached. It was not yet six o'clock; he had got into bed, after a longer run than usual to shake off surveillance, only an hour before. He went back to sleep and slid into a complicated dream. It seemed to him that he had been asleep for hours when a sharp little sound awakened him, but in fact he had been unconscious for less than five minutes.

The sound he had heard was the click of the clasp on the woman's purse. She stood by the chair, dressed for the street in a trench coat, with her hand in the pocket of his trousers. She held up a fan of paper money and smiled at him.

"Cab fare," she said, whispering again. "They want me."

"What the fuck for?"

The woman shrugged. She had covered her hair with a scarf. She wore no makeup. Without mascara and eye shadow, her pale eyes looked like the eyes of a blinded person, but she had a lovely smile.

Wolkowicz rolled over and closed his eyes. He opened them again and looked at the telephone. He realized that she had spoken German to the caller. The telephone had wakened her while they were in bed together a hundred times before, but she had never before spoken German.

Wolkowicz heaved himself out of bed and called the woman's

name, but she had gone. He looked out the window, through the slats of a venetian blind, but there was nothing to see. He had rented this apartment because it did not have a front exposure; all the windows looked out on air shafts and blank walls.

He pulled on his trousers and tried to put on his wet shoes. The soaked leather resisted and he bent over and forced the shoes onto his thick feet. Measuring time in his head, he knew that his struggle with the shoes had lost him the moments he needed to put on a shirt, so he snatched Christopher's raincoat off the hanger and put that on as he ran through the apartment and out into the hall, holding the P-38 in its holster under his armpit, beneath the coat.

The elevator carrying the woman was still in the shaft. It was slow. The whole building had been made on the cheap. Wolkowicz could heard Muzak, tinny strains of "The Merry Widow Waltz," as the door opened ten floors below. The service elevator was already on his floor; the woman had pushed both buttons and both cars had responded. As he went down, listening to Franz Lehár, Wolkowicz saw himself in the convex mirror in the corner of the car and realized that he had not put in his false teeth. The snout of a television camera, part of the building's security system, pointed at him. He turned his back and buttoned up the raincoat.

Through the plate-glass wall that formed the front of the lobby, Wolkowicz saw that the woman had gone outside. She was looking up and down the wide thoroughfare for a cruising taxi. She spotted one, a miracle at this hour of the day, and went up on tiptoe and waved to it. The cab stopped on the other side of the street. She was wearing a belted raincoat—a Burberry, she was as conscious of style as Wolkowicz was oblivious to it—and from the back, as she ran into the street, she seemed as slim and as supple as a girl of twenty.

As she ran through the slush, mincingly on her high heels, a man on the other side of the street watched her. Wolkowicz had not seen him at once; he couldn't understand how he had missed him. Wolkowicz went outside, to get a better look at the stranger. It was six o'clock in the morning—too early for anyone to be there for an honest purpose.

Now the woman was halfway across the street. With a brisk gesture, the man raised a rolled newspaper, as if he himself were signaling for a taxi. Fifty feet down the street, a car pulled away from the curb and accelerated through the wet snow, skidding and swerving.

"*No!*" Wolkowicz shouted, saliva flying out of his toothless mouth. "No! God damn it, no!"

He leaped down the steps, drawing his P-38. He called the woman's name. She heard him and turned. In the same instant, she saw the car bearing down on her. She covered her eyes like a frightened child.

Wolkowicz fell to his knees and leveled his pistol at the car. Before he could fire, the driver hit the brakes and the car skidded sideways, sending up a huge sheet of slush. The car spun completely around and came to a stop. A man leaped out and leveled a machine pistol at Wolkowicz's head. Wolkowicz, who automatically identified the weapon as a Kulspruta, and the man as Horace Hubbard, laid down his P-38.

Two more cars pulled up, forming a pen around the woman, who lay on the pavement. She was unhurt, but in her fright she crawled a foot or two through the melting dingy snow, then stopped where she was, on her hands and knees. Her eyes were fixed on the man with the newspaper, who had stepped off the curb and was walking toward her.

He dropped the newspaper and helped her to her feet. Her wonderful slow smile melted her ice-blue eyes. He had always been so good-looking, so quiet, so clever. She had always liked him, always admired him. Though she knew he was her mortal enemy, and that a kinder man would have killed her, would have killed Wolkowicz, rather than humiliate them in this way, she was glad to see him, glad that he had lived through everything.

"Paul!" said Ilse Wolkowicz. "It's true what Barney told me: you haven't changed at all. No one but you could have done this. My German boy!"

She leaned her head on Christopher's shoulder. He breathed in the refreshing scent of her rose perfume.

Twelve

The safe house in the Virginia woods was fitted out to resemble a gracious home: chintz slipcovers on the furniture, racing prints and watercolor landscapes on the walls. A log fire burned cheerily in the fireplace.

Wolkowicz sat on a sofa, huddled inside Christopher's raincoat. On a facing sofa, Patchen sat motionless, chalky with fatigue. He put his head back and closed his good eye. Wolkowicz cleared his throat, loudly. Patchen opened his eye and looked with distaste on the steaming cup of coffee on the low table between the sofas.

"I'm overcome with curiosity," Wolkowicz said. "How did you tail me?"

He glared at Patchen, as if he, Wolkowicz, were the captor and Patchen the prisoner, brought here for interrogation. Patchen did not respond. Ilse pointed a finger, immaculately manicured, at Christopher. Comprehension dawned in Wolkowicz's watchful eyes. He snapped his fingers.

"The raincoat," he said. "It was the fucking raincoat."

Wolkowicz leaped to his feet and took off the coat. This left him naked to the waist. There were many white hairs in the black mat on his chest and back and many puckered scars, mementos of the wounds he had suffered in Burma, where the hair did not grow at all. He ran his hands over the material of the coat. He felt something in the hem and, with a wringing motion of his powerful hands, ripped out the threads. A transmitter, no larger than a cuff button, fell onto the table. Wolkowicz didn't bother to examine it: it was, to him, a familiar object.

"I'm proud of you," he said to Christopher.

Without his teeth, Wolkowicz's voice was different—thinner, less sure.

Patchen said, "Would you just like to tell us everything, Barney? It would save time."

Wolkowicz put on the raincoat and buttoned it up. He ignored Patchen.

"Are you cold, darling?" Ilse asked.

"Naw—I've got my best friend's coat on," Wolkowicz replied. He grinned. His empty mouth looked like an exit wound, clotted with dried black blood. "I'll tell you what I'm going to tell you, Patchen," he said. "Nothing. Not a fucking thing."

Patchen nodded and stood up. "Then I'll leave you to say good-bye to Paul," he said. "Take all the time you need."

He went out. Two men, armed with machine pistols, stood guard outside the door. It was the only exit; there were no windows. They were in a cellar.

"I wish I had my fucking teeth," Wolkowicz said to Christopher. He drank Patchen's coffee and stared into the bottom of the upturned cup. Christopher had never seen these mannerisms before.

"Now," Wolkowicz said, "besides catching me in bed with my wife, what do you and One-Eye think you've got on me?"

Christopher had been holding a manila envelope on his lap. He opened it, removed the photograph he had brought back from London, and handed it to Wolkowicz. Holding it at arm's length, Wolkowicz examined it. He snorted and shook his head.

"There we are," he said, "the sweet girl graduates."

He handed the photograph to Ilse.

"That's you and Robin," she said. "You were both so *skinny*. Was this your pagoda in Burma?"

"And some of our friends. Notice the Jap, third from the left," Wolkowicz said in a conversational tone.

The severed head of a Japanese, driven onto a stake, stood in the second row between two grinning Chinese guerrillas. The decapitated Japanese wore round spectacles over his wide-open dead eyes.

"That's a flower from the bamboo Darby's got in his hand," Wolkowicz said. "He couldn't believe his luck. It only blooms every forty years, and Darby, the world's greatest flower lover, was there when it happened."

With a grease pencil, Christopher drew a ring around Gus's head. Carelessly, Wolkowicz looked at it.

"Gus," Christopher said.

The guerrilla standing to the right of the severed head was unmistakably Gus; even as a young man he had had the wrinkled wry face of second childhood.

For the space of six breaths, Wolkowicz lifted his eyes and looked straight at Christopher. Finally he said, "He hasn't changed a hell of a lot, has he?"

"True name?"

"He never told me," Wolkowicz said. "By 1944 he was already using a funny name. Wang is what we called him in the jungle. I don't know what they call him in China these days."

"You kept in touch with him all these years?"

"We were good buddies."

"Darby taught him English?"

"Darby was a great one for improving the working class. His Chinks all sounded like him, cockneys. I suppose you noticed Gus's accent. Is that what blew everything?"

"Darby recruited you in Burma."

Wolkowicz waved a hand in dismissal. The answer was so obvious, he seemed to be saying, that it was a waste of time to reply. He leaped to a more interesting subject.

"Darby's Chinks were really something," he said. "After we killed some Japs, they'd cut off all the heads and chop off all the balls. Then they'd slit 'em open and rip out the livers. It was like the Seven Dwarfs —'Whistle While You Work.' They'd put the heads on stakes, fling the bodies into the brush, light fires, and have a barbecue on Jap liver—"

Christopher interrupted. "What was the reason, Barney?" he asked.

"What reason?" Wolkowicz looked at him without guilt or remorse. He remembered his reason for becoming a traitor exactly, and forty years afterward it made him smile.

"Waddy Jessup shot an elephant," he said. "That pissed me off."

Even though Christopher gave no sign that he was going to speak, Wolkowicz held up a hand for silence.

"You don't believe a fucking thing I tell you, do you?" he asked.

Christopher did not answer. Wolkowicz closed his eyes. Ilse, stumbling over the low table and Christopher's feet, moved onto the sofa beside him and took his hand. She gazed anxiously into Wolkowicz's face.

Wolkowicz opened his eyes and stared at Christopher. Tugging hard, he took his hand away from Ilse, and when she fumbled for it, put it out of reach between his crossed thighs.

"Okay," he said to Christopher. "You finally know everything. You tell me."

"This is what I think happened," Christopher said. "Waddy Jessup ran away in Burma and left you to the Japanese. Darby rescued you and while your wounds healed, the two of you talked. Did you speak to each other in Russian?"

Wolkowicz snorted, pleased, as always, with Christopher's intuition. "I couldn't have described what happened in English," he said.

"You wanted to get Waddy. Darby showed you a way to do that."

Wolkowicz sat up and shrugged inside the raincoat. He was intensely interested. "Go on," he said.

"You blackmailed Waddy into recommending you for a permanent job as a civilian and he gave you a letter to my father. In Berlin, the Soviets picked you up. They fed you information, they gave you agents. They wanted to establish a reputation for you, fast. The agents were always unwitting. Horst Bülow thought that he really was working for U.S. intelligence. My father admired you, but something made him suspicious. What was it?"

"Zechmann."

"Friedrich Zechmann was a German, always and only a German," Ilse interrupted. "Hubbard didn't mind if Friedrich worked for Germany as long as he shared with America; working for Germany frightened the Russians."

Wolkowicz shushed her. "The Russians wanted to make Hubbard suspicious of Zechmann. They wanted to make him think Zechmann was a Soviet asset. It was hopeless. Your father saw through it."

"But he trusted you."

Wolkowicz grunted and slumped. "You didn't know your father. He smelled it on me right from the start."

"So you killed him."

Startled by the hatred in Christopher's face, Ilse took Wolkowicz's hand again. He submitted to her sympathy, but his eyes never left Christopher's.

"No," he said. "It wasn't me. But we can come back to that."

Christopher nodded and went on.

"After Berlin, you asked for duty in Washington. You told the Director that you thought the Outfit might be penetrated. With the help of the Russians, you worked up the Addressees spy case. There was no espionage ring led by Mordecai Bashian, even though Bashian himself thought there was. The Russians set him up, had him circulate garbage and run fake agents. In order to do it, in order to hold up under questioning when he was caught, he had to believe that he was a master spy. Jocelyn Frick was just frosting on the cake: the usual Russian love of dirty pictures for blackmail purposes. The purpose of the operation was to throw some American romantics, Party members and fellow travelers, to the witch-hunters and let them burn in public. The smoke hid the Soviets' real assets in the United States. Is that substantially correct?"

Wolkowicz nodded. He was smiling in admiration.

"Did you jail Waddy just for revenge, for what happened in Burma?" Christopher asked.

Wolkowicz nodded pleasantly. As Christopher guessed his secrets, he felt at peace, like a man surrendering to an anesthetic. It was no surprise to him that Christopher knew so much. The facts of his betrayal had been lying around in plain sight for years. He had been living among blind men; it was a relief to be in the company of someone who could see.

"Go on," he said.

"Vienna."

"Ah, Vienna," Ilse said, lowering her eyes.

"It was a disinformation operation," Christopher said. "The Russians didn't just know about it, they set it up. It succeeded beyond their wildest dreams. They couldn't believe that the Americans and the British could be so stupid as to believe that the Russians wouldn't *know* that there were fifty people and ten code machines in an abandoned sewer, twenty-five feet below the soles of their boots. It went so well, the Outfit and the Brits fell for it so completely, that the Russians thought it was an American operation against them—that we were just *pretending* to believe all that crap they were feeding us."

Wolkowicz was enjoying himself. He looked at the ceiling for a moment, savoring a hilarious memory.

"You're right," he said. "They *couldn't* believe it. But that wasn't the main reason. They couldn't stand the expense. They had to invent a lot of lies for us to bug, and that took more and more personnel. They had half the fucking KGB in Vienna, staying up all night, writing fictitious cables for us to intercept. It busted their disinformation budget. 'What the fuck do you guys think you're doing with all those rubles?' Moscow kept saying. Also, they were scared shitless, because a certain amount of the traffic had to be genuine. They were smart enough to check that in Washington—just barely. Somebody had to decide every day which real Russian secrets to send out over the bugged lines. Nothing important was ever transmitted, but you can get your goddamned head blown off in Russia twenty years after you've made a mistake. It gave them the shits."

Wolkowicz, in his contempt for bureaucrats, did not discriminate between Russians and Americans. In his experience, one was as stupid and as blind as the other.

"The Outfit and the Brits wanted to believe the Sewer was for real. *Wanted* to? Shit, they had to. It made them look so fucking good they couldn't resist it. 'What a coup!' That's what they said around the Fool Factory."

He searched Christopher's face for a sign that he agreed with him on this point.

But Christopher wanted to stick to the subject. "So the Russians decided to terminate *our* operation and didn't know how to do it," he said. "They thought up the affair between Ilse and Darby."

Ilse blushed. "Even though it was a fake, I was scandalized," she said. "It was such a charade. Do you remember Darby and me kissing in St. Anton where you and Rosalind could see us? *So* disgusting. You were so shocked, Paul! What a good friend to Barney you were. But you didn't tell him. My God, the trouble that caused!"

Ilse's hands fluttered as if to cover another blush, but her face was dead white. Without her makeup, she resembled an actress who, after giving the performance of her life, takes off her greasepaint and is, at last, free to be herself.

"It wasn't the Russians who pulled off the fake kidnapping in Vienna," Christopher said. "Barney wasn't going to give them Ilse as a hostage. He used his own men. Afterward, Ilse went fictitious. The two of you lived together in secret. Ilse went everywhere, in secret, on false papers."

"Berlin, Saigon, Paris, always hiding, always a new place. It was so expensive, even the Russians complained. But I liked being invisible to everyone except Barney. It's kept our marriage alive."

She gave Wolkowicz her lovely smile. With curious gentleness, he put a hand on her head and stroked her hair. It was dyed golden blond, blonder even than its color in Ilse's youth. It was very odd to see his tenderness. It lasted only for an instant. He let go of her and crooked a finger at Christopher, beckoning the next words out of his mouth.

"Darby," Christopher said.

Wolkowicz looked into the fireplace. A broad smile formed on his face.

"Tell me what you think happened," he said.

Even Ilse was grinning, her mistake with Stephanie forgotten; she was happy again.

"Darby was blown anyway, finished," Christopher said. "The Brits were after him. Even Patchen told me at the time he knew about him. The Russians decided to let you catch a big Soviet spy. It was an operation, one more thing to build up your reputation as a Communist killer. To make you even more trustworthy."

Wolkowicz laughed in pure delight at the cleverness of Christopher's mind.

"You really *did* have time to think in China," he said. "The Russians panicked again. Some defector—a real one, not one of their plants —knew about Darby. Robin was tired. He wanted to retire and work on his botany, so he said—*Darby* said, not the Russians—let Wolkowicz catch me. Why not turn a bad situation into a gain for our side?"

"The Russians didn't mind the publicity?"

"They were going to get publicity anyway. The Brits were right behind Darby. So was Patchen. It was a hell of a job, beating them to it. Patchen didn't want to let me do it—the Brits complained to him that I was trying to embarrass them. That's why I had to use Foley."

"He didn't know about the Brits?"

"Foley? Who'd tell Foley anything? Everybody was happy in the end except the Brits. The Russians had outsmarted the capitalists, Foley had made political points, I got another decoration, and so did you. And Darby got to cultivate his orchids in the Crimea."

"You gave him the poison to kill his guards?"

Wolkowicz hesitated, then shrugged. What did it matter?

"You were there when I did it," he said.

"It was concealed in the book?"

The Manchurian Candidate. Two needles, in the binding. The Russians are big on poison and books that shoot people and all that crap. It made Darby laugh, but it got him out of jail."

"You liked Darby?"

Wolkowicz was genuinely astonished by the question. *"Liked* him?" he said. "Yeah, I liked him. Darby and your father and you—those are the people I've liked in my life. Until today, Darby was the only one who knew me. That was a problem for me. Stop talking, Paul. You don't need to know anything else about my career. I want to explain two things, then we'd better call Patchen."

Ilse looked anxiously into Wolkowicz's face and took his hand again, massaging the hairy back, the swollen knuckles.

"I set up your father," Wolkowicz said. "You know that. You knew it as soon as Graham put that shit about the way he died on the air. The file on your mother was a fake. The Russians put it together. It was the one sure way to hook Hubbard. He was so goddamned smart it was almost impossible to neutralize him. There was only one subject on which he was not intelligent—your mother. He wouldn't believe that she was dead. I'm sorry, Paul, but that's the way it was. I planted the file on him, I set up the meeting with Bülow; he was supposed to bring the rest of the Gestapo file on your mother. We said the file had turned up in stuff the Russians had captured. That was the bait."

Wolkowicz talked in a steady, clear voice, without hesitation. He was reciting facts, setting the case in order.

"I didn't know they were going to kill him," Wolkowicz said. "I thought it was going to be a snatch, that he'd spend a few years in Russia and then they'd swap him for somebody. When I said I didn't kill your father, that was a lot of shit. You can bet your ass I killed him. I killed him by being too dumb to see what was coming. I never made that mistake again."

Wolkowicz was suffering. Suddenly he couldn't bear to be touched and, after another little tug-of-war, he made Ilse let go of his hand. There were tears in her eyes. She kissed Wolkowicz on the face. He did not resist or respond or even move.

"Now, about you," Wolkowicz said, forcing himself onward. "At first, in Vienna and then on the Darby case, I wanted you around because of what I'd done to Hubbard. I figured I could make it up, protect you. Then I saw you were just like him, a fucking genius. You and Hubbard and Darby are the only geniuses I've ever met. Do you know what makes a man a genius? The ability to see the obvious. Practically nobody can do that. Your father could, most of the time. Darby could, some of the time. I think you do it all the time. I don't know how you've stayed alive."

Wolkowicz's throat was dry. He coughed harshly into his fist, then wiped his palm on the sofa. To the empty air he said, "We could use some water in here." He knew that the room was equipped with hidden television cameras and microphones, and that somewhere Patchen was watching and listening.

"As soon as I realized what kind of a mind you had," Wolkowicz said to Christopher, "I wanted you inside on my ops so I could control the information that got to you. If you'd been outside, Christ knows what you would have found out. I was so right. You got away from me and look what happened. You started sniffing around the fucking assassination, you got the Vietnamese all stirred up, you scared the Russians shitless. Just before you went to China, you were close to something that *terrified* them."

"What was I close to?"

"I don't know. Whatever it was, the Russians didn't want to be blamed for it. Maybe they knocked off the President, maybe not. I don't know. I didn't give a shit. They wanted to kill you. I couldn't let that happen again. China was the only place on earth where nobody—not even the Russians—could get at you. Anything is better than dying, Paul."

"Anything?"

Wolkowicz made a gruff gesture of dismissal, as if Christopher's question were an insect to be batted away.

"I got in touch with Chinese Gus," Wolkowicz said, rushing on. "I told him what a red-hot agent you were. I had Pong break Gus Kimber's neck and Chinese Gus stole his airplane. You thought I was lying to you about the Truong toc and Kim, but I did kill the bastards to protect you; I thought the Russians might be running them somehow. Even if they weren't, why the fuck should they live to kill *you?* I did it all."

Wolkowicz stopped, to give Christopher an opportunity to speak. But he said nothing.

"Let me tell you something else," Wolkowicz said. "I'd do it again. You're sitting here instead of lying under the ground, a fucking heap of bones."

"Molly, too?" Christopher asked. "Would you do that again?"

Wolkowicz shook his head. For an instant, he was impatient, his old rude self. Then he seemed to realize that his answer was important to Christopher and he did the best he could. "I should have known they'd hit her after they set up the operation. They're stubborn bastards, the Russians," he said. "I thought Webster was smart enough to keep Molly inside, where they couldn't get at her. I was wrong. It was my fault. And the answer is yes: I'd do it again if it would keep you alive."

For once, Wolkowicz's face showed what he felt. It glowed with affection and relief. He hugged Ilse again. Christopher had never seen Wolkowicz in such a mood, with words tumbling out of him. He seemed sure that Christopher could understand anything, forgive anything, if he could only see him as he really was.

Wolkowicz's confession had freed him of a terrible burden. He actually said, "I feel better."

He slumped on the sofa, exhausted. Ilse looked from Wolkowicz to Christopher with joy in her pale eyes. She was happy. So was Wolkowicz.

Christopher asked another question. Like all the others, it wasn't really a question. "You weren't working for the Russians at all, were you, Barney?" he said. "You were working for yourself."

Wolkowicz and Ilse looked, smiling, into each other's eyes.

"Don't tell the Russians that," Ilse said, "they'd be so disappointed. Do you know why *I* did it?"

"Yes. Because Barney asked you to."

Nodding, Ilse took both of Christopher's hands in hers. "I *love* this ape," she said. "Isn't that funny, a girl like me?"

Christopher looked at Wolkowicz. "You did all this," he said, "turned yourselves into this, *to get Waddy Jessup?*"

"To get *all* the fucking Waddys," Wolkowicz said. Abruptly, he laughed his snorting laugh which was so full of ridicule and contempt. "Jesus," he said. "I never realized it. It was the class struggle—me against the Fool Factory. I'm a fucking Red!"

Overcome with mirth, Wolkowicz and Ilse held hands and shared this delicious joke with Christopher.

Christopher, grieving for his dead parents and his dead Molly and his deadened life, realized that this was his true homecoming. He covered his face and made a sound deep in his throat.

Ilse flew to him and pried his fingers away from his eyes.

"I know it's hard, Paul," she said. "But what Barney is talking about here is operations, not feelings. We've always loved you. Always."

The chief interrogator for the Outfit had a theory. He believed that a man like Wolkowicz, who had once held up under torture, would break if he was threatened with torture a second time, because he would know too well what to expect. Patchen would not let him try it.

"If you make the threat, you may have to carry it out," he said.

"That's all right with me."

The interrogator hated Wolkowicz, who had made it impossible, forever, for the Outfit to trust its own men and women. Outfitters had always been outcasts, but they had lived happily enough because they trusted each other absolutely. They had believed that the Outfit could not be penetrated: its people were too patriotic, too bright, too idealistic. Now the greatest of all the Outfit agents had turned out to be an enemy; had turned out always to have been an enemy. Why? How? The interrogator was willing to use anything to get the truth out of him: clubs, electricity, water, surgical instruments.

"No," Patchen said. "Leave his ego alone. Wolkowicz has always believed that we were too civilized. It will upset everything if he suspects he's been wrong."

Before the interrogation started, Wolkowicz asked to see Patchen. He wanted to ask him to be civilized about Pong.

"I just want you to realize that Pong is clean," Wolkowicz said. "He was just doing favors for me, passing the stuff to Graham. He didn't know what he was passing. Pong is a patriotic American."

"I know that."

"Okay. Just don't fuck around with him."

He glared at Patchen as if he had the power to make him pay if he dared to harm Pong, Wolkowicz's loyal agent. Wolkowicz had always expected to be captured in the end. His status as a prisoner did not change his personality.

The interrogators used sleeplessness, drugs, the polygraph, and endless relays of questioners. Wolkowicz made no attempt to evade the questions they asked him. The interrogators were not always satisfied with his answers. Wolkowicz had survived dozens of lie detector tests in the past, and still the needles traced normal lines. They only jumped when he was asked about the Christophers. Any question about Ilse produced wildly erratic tracings.

"I've never seen anything like it," the polygraph operator said. "He must be a pathological liar."

Patchen studied the tracings. "No," he said. "He just doesn't feel any guilt." He ran a finger over the nervous peaks marked with Ilse's name and Christopher's. "Love, yes," Patchen said.

Once a week, Wolkowicz was shown a documentary film about a state mental institution in Arkansas. The hopelessly insane were confined there in conditions of unbelievable filth and squalor. Wolkowicz watched them fight, copulate, defecate and smear themselves with the feces. No one was ever released from this place. He watched the film, time after time, in fearless contempt. It had no effect on him. He supposed it was some sort of brainwashing technique devised by academics. It was not, he thought, nearly so effective as a bayonet and a block of wood.

After the first three months of interrogation, Wolkowicz asked for a piano and, on Patchen's authorization, a spinet model was moved into his room for an hour each day. His guards, lithe young men in blue jeans who carried their Kulsprutas carelessly, like boys walking across a campus with lacrosse sticks, were as astonished as everyone else always had been by the delicacy of his touch on the keyboard. Each note, as it came over the earphones they used to monitor his every sound, was pure and free and separate from all the others. Sometimes, if the door was opened for a moment while Wolkowicz happened to be playing, a few strains of Bach or Mozart would drift through the soundproofed house. The chief interrogator had objected to the piano. Hearing the piano, Ilse would know that Wolkowicz was alive and in the house with her, and that would reduce the psychological pressure on her.

"It's one of Wolkowicz's tricks," the interrogator said.

"Let him outwit us just one more time, then," Patchen replied. "That will mean a lot to him."

Wolkowicz himself had been surprised when they had given him his piano. He had nothing else, not even a book or newspaper, in his room. He had no blankets or sheets; the room was kept at a temperature that made them unnecessary. He wore coveralls with the sleeves and legs cut off so that there was no piece of cloth long enough to be used as a hangman's noose or a strangling cord. Because he was not allowed to use a razor, his beard had grown long.

He knew that the interrogation had been completed when the guards came into his room with barbering tools. They shaved his grizzled whiskers and trimmed his hair.

That day, Patchen came to see him. It was the first time they had met since the morning Wolkowicz had been caught.

The youthful guard had brought a folding chair. He opened it and Patchen sat down. Patchen was wearing a lightweight suit. This meant that the seasons had changed. Shut away from windows, from noises and smells, Wolkowicz had become an even more avid reader of clues. For months, he had had virtually no clues to read. He had no idea what was going to happen to him. He was sure that Patchen had some plan for him. He waited for him to reveal it.

"Thanks for the piano," Wolkowicz said.

In his cut-off coveralls, hairy Wolkowicz looked like an ape in rompers. Patchen had been ignoring his appearance for years. He paid no special attention to it now.

"I'm glad you're comfortable," Patchen said. "You seem a little thinner. It must have something to do with giving up liquor. There are a lot of calories in Rob Roys."

Wolkowicz scratched himself, some sort of signal that he had not changed, that he could still repay a pleasantry with an insult.

"What," Patchen asked, "are you going to do now?"

Wolkowicz cupped a hand behind his ear, as if he hadn't heard, but Patchen did not repeat himself. Wolkowicz did not reply, not even with a joke.

"You'll want to see Ilse before you go," Patchen said. "A conjugal visit."

Another man might have smiled or betrayed something by the movement of a hand, but Patchen sat still and expressionless.

"Before I go?" Wolkowicz said. "What the fuck are you talking about?"

"You're all pumped out, they say. You may as well leave."

Patchen stood up to go.

"Just a minute," Wolkowicz said. "What about a trial?"

"Trial? I'm afraid not, Barney. No grand finale for you. You're not going to be exposed as a Soviet agent. It would destroy the Outfit. Sorry."

Wolkowicz, sprawled on his cot, glowered at Patchen.

"You think that's going to save the Outfit, not trying me?" Wolkowicz said. "If you let me go, I can go right back to Graham and blow the whole fucking story."

Patchen shrugged. "If you think he'd believe you, go to him. What are you going to say? That *you* passed him all that stuff through Pong? That you set out to destroy yourself, the best agent the Russians have ever had, as a way of ruining the Outfit?"

"It's true."

"Yes," Patchen said. "But it's insane."

"You don't think I can do it? Assholes like Graham will believe anything, as long as it's what they want to hear. He'll be enthralled to think that the Russians have been running the Outfit for thirty years. It'll explain everything. You're an even bigger bunch of assholes than he thought."

"You may be right, Barney."

Wolkowicz had to lean forward and cup his ear to hear Patchen.

"One last thing," Patchen said. "I know why you did it. But why did the Russians do it? Why you? What was there about you?"

Wolkowicz snorted. Patchen's question broke through to him in a way that months of drugs and sleeplessness had never done.

"Who the fuck did you *think* they were going to recruit?" he said. "Waddy Jessup?" He waved a hand in dismissal.

"No, don't stop now," Patchen said. "I want to know your opinion."

Thirty years of exasperation with Patchen and his kind spilled over in Wolkowicz. "Out in Burma, before he ran away from the Japs, Waddy told me that I was the son of a worker," he said. "That, asshole, is the key. I'm a member of the lower classes. So was Darby. We were the KGB's aces, baby. The Russians are out to kill people like you. They'll use you, but you don't count. Look at the Brits. Philby, Burgess, MacLean, Blunt—all members of the bourgeoisie. All sacrificial lambs. The Russians didn't give a shit for them, they didn't give a shit for British intelligence. The Outfit was the target because the United States is the target."

Patchen nodded. He had no more time for this interview. To the television camera in the corner of the bare, overlighted room, he said, "Come in now, please."

The guards brought Wolkowicz his clothes—one of his checked polyester jackets, a pair of slacks, a drip-dry shirt, and a necktie, all freshly cleaned and pressed. They handed him an envelope containing his watch and his wallet.

"Good luck," Patchen said, ready to leave.

Automatically, Wolkowicz counted his cash, seventy-six dollars— fifteen dollars less than he had had when he was taken. Then he remembered Ilse, waving the fan of bills at him in the bedroom: her taxi fare.

"Wait a minute," Wolkowicz said. "What about Ilse?"

Patchen seemed surprised that he would ask.

"Oh," he said. "She'll stay with us. You'll want to know she's all right. You can write to her, she can write to you. We'll give you a post office box number for yourself and one for Ilse. You can make two telephone calls a year, on your birthdays. You'll have to give her a number to call in your letters. Is that reassurance enough?"

Wolkowicz understood Patchen's plan.

"If you open your mouth, if one word of what you've been for the last thirty years appears in print, even if the Russians do it for you against your will, we'll move her."

"Where to?"

"An asylum. In Arkansas, say. If she tells them the truth about herself, she'll never get out."

"She could live for thirty years," Wolkowicz said.

"I don't see why not," Patchen replied.

He turned around and walked out of the room.

Thirteen

— 1 —

Wolkowicz had been blindfolded in the car and in the small plane that carried him away from the house in Virginia. He had no idea where it was. He knew that it was beyond his resources to find it. Because of Patchen, he had to run from the Russians. What he would get from them was more months of interrogation, more drugs, and, in the end, Russia for himself and the asylum for Ilse.

Still, he was not without hope, not without resources.

Patchen's men let Wolkowicz out of the car at Fourteenth Street and Constitution Avenue. Without looking back, he walked purposefully up the street, past the gray government buildings that had always reminded him of a city of the dead. Hurrying up the hill past the National Press Club, Wolkowicz puffed a little. He was out of shape after his months of confinement. He sweated. It was spring—people were eating sandwiches in the parks among beds of jonquils and tulips. Wolkowicz looked automatically into the windows of the shops in order to see the reflections of the people behind him. The street teemed with the lunch-hour crowd; they had let him out into it deliberately, he knew, to make it harder for him to spot his surveillance.

At a cash machine, he used his bank card to withdraw money. He went into a cheap clothing store on F Street and bought a pair of pants with the bottoms already cuffed, a jacket, a shirt, a tie, underwear, shoes, and socks. He left the clothes the Outfit had given him, along with any transmitters that might have been sewn into the seams, in the dressing room and went out into the street again. He walked north, stopping at a public phone. He dialed a number and got a stranger. He said, "This is the Same-Day Shirt Laundry. If you don't pick up your shirts before the end of business today we'll have to give them to the Goodwill." The astonished person at the other end of the line said, "What?"

Wolkowicz hung up. A man in a seersucker jacket and a rep tie hurried closer, so that he could hear what Wolkowicz said if he made another phone call. At another telephone, a block or two farther on, Wolkowicz dialed another number at random and said the same thing, word for word, to a second stranger.

Now Wolkowicz could see all the men behind him—six of them, two teams on foot. There were no crowds here to hide them. He had walked his pursuers into a stretch of Fourteenth Street that belonged to drug pushers, muggers, and prostitutes. Rioters had burned this part of town once, and some of the stores were still boarded up. The girls and men who loitered in front of the massage parlors and the porno shops and the bars paid little attention to Wolkowicz. Fat middle-aged men in cheap clothes were their clientele. But they turned wary faces down the street, like animals sniffing the wind, as they spotted the men who were following Wolkowicz. They didn't belong here. They were too young, too good-looking. They all wore the same clothes.

In a shop, Wolkowicz bought a cheap switchblade knife. Back on the sidewalk, he looked into the faces of the whores until he saw what he was looking for. The girl he chose was young, no more than sixteen. Her skin was dull, as if it were in the process of changing, a shade each day, to the color of ashes. Her eyes were dreamy with the deep amusement of the perpetually drugged. She pulled Wolkowicz into a doorway and told him a schoolyard joke. Wolkowicz laughed.

"I want to play a joke on a buddy," he said. "You see that guy looking in the window behind me, the one that looks like he don't know whether to shit or wind his watch?"

The girl's dreamy gaze fastened on the man in a seersucker jacket. "That one?"

Wolkowicz nodded. He told her what he wanted her to do.

"Shit, man," the girl said. "You're crazy."

Wolkowicz gave her a fifty-dollar bill.

"You're still crazy."

He gave her another fifty.

"You girls do it all the time," he said. "The cops aren't going to bother about it."

He gave her the switchblade knife, wrapped in a hundred-dollar bill. "I'll be right behind you," he said. "You'd better hurry."

The girl rolled her two hundred dollars into a cylinder, like a cigarette, and tucked it underneath her platinum wig. The man in the seersucker jacket had been replaced on the point by another man who had crossed the street to take his place, and now he waited obediently at a crosswalk for a *Don't Walk* signal to change so that he could take up his station on the opposite sidewalk.

The girl spoke to him. She was wearing gold hip boots, a garter belt, and a miniskirt. She lifted the skirt to show him the heart on her bikini panties. The man in the seersucker jacket smiled at her and shook his head. He stepped off the curb, anxious for the light to change, then stepped back on. Some of the other members of the surveillance team smiled in amusement. Had they been Wolkowicz's men he would have fired them for revealing themselves. He started back the way he came. The driver of a car waiting at the light looked around frantically to see if he was able to make a U-turn.

The girl persisted, whispering into the ear of the man in the seersucker jacket. He tried to move away. She fondled the front of his trousers. Shocked, he pushed her away. She reached under her wig for Wolkowicz's switchblade knife and, with a dreamy smile, stabbed him in the thigh. Then she ran, leaving the knife in the wound.

Wolkowicz jumped into a taxi that had stopped for the light and as it pulled away he saw the girl running across the street against the light. Nobody was following her.

For the next two minutes, nobody would be following Wolkowicz. That was all the time he needed.

[381]

Walking down to the waterfront across the spongy lawn of Pong's summer cottage on Chesapeake Bay, Wolkowicz smelled forsythia and magnolia. In the light of the full moon, he could make out the pale colors of the flowering trees—like damsels in ball gowns, out for a stroll in the garden, as Jocelyn Frick might have said. A whippoorwill sang down from a willow tree and the dappled waters of the bay lapped against the shore.

Wolkowicz was oblivious to the beauty of the night; he looked for Patchen's men behind the drooping trees. He knew the snows of Russia and the heat of Burma, and he regarded nature as a mindless, implacable enemy. He had never, from choice, walked in the country, he had never been on a picnic, he did not know the name of a single songbird or wildflower, he had never been to the beach for pleasure.

The Outfit had taught him to swim. Waddy Jessup had been his instructor. *"Doucement,* Barnabas, easy does it," Waddy had advised, as young WOJG Wolkowicz thrashed in the pool, pitting his strength against the water. "Remember the teaching of Lao-tzu," Waddy had said; "weakness will always overcome strength." Waddy turned on his face and, with effortless strokes, slid away through the quivering green light beneath the surface.

At the dock, Pong's cabin cruiser gleamed in the moonlight, all teak and chrome, flying the Thai ensign. Wolkowicz went aboard. The keys were hidden in a little magnetic box at the stern. He found them and opened the cabin hatch. Inside, in its hiding place under the deck, Wolkowicz found Pong's loaded pistol, well greased and sealed inside six layers of plastic bags. It was a four-barreled .357 magnum derringer called a COP—an executioner's weapon, powerful enough to blow off the top of a skull, but inaccurate beyond the width of a rug. There was a "survival knife"—a killing knife, really, razor sharp—in the hiding place too; it had a bright orange cork handle so that it would float if it fell in the water. Wolkowicz tucked both weapons into his waistband, then started the engine and cast off.

The boat moved out into the bay, leaving a bubbly phosphorescent wake. There were no other craft in sight, but along both shores Wolkowicz could see the clustered yellow lights of sleeping towns. He headed south until he could see no more lights. The bay was broader here, and the path of light thrown down by the moon seemed wider, too.

Wolkowicz hardly noticed these things. They were irrelevant; but that was not the only reason he ignored them. Wolkowicz was remembering scenes from his childhood.

This surprised him. Since the interrogation in Virginia, his memory had been none too good. All the details of his life, or nearly all, had been dragged up to the surface. The act of recalling everything had, in an odd way, caused him to forget everything. He could not remember the names of people he had known all his life, he could not recall the minutiae of operations. More and more, as if he had become a very old man, he found himself remembering things from the deep past that he had thought forgotten. Now, as he sailed down Chesapeake Bay at the end of a spring night, his memory was filled with his long childhood walk across Asia on his father's shoulders. Oddly, what he remembered about this was sleeping—sleeping deliciously with his head against the rough wool of his father's coat, and in his sleep hearing the scuffling sound of his father's felt boots mile after endless mile, hearing the barking of dogs far away, hearing the beating of wings as a flight of ducks rose from a pond, hearing voices shouting in Russian in a wood. All his life, Wolkowicz realized, he had heard these sounds in his sleep. He had smelled snow and barnyards and food in his sleep. Even now, when he dreamed, he dreamed the aroma of moldy black bread or the scent of a turnip pulled from the chilly wet earth of Siberia. He remembered, also, everything that had happened in the jungle with Waddy. These were the things he hadn't talked about under interrogation. Everything else, every detail, he had willingly confessed. He had been glad to get rid of it.

Wolkowicz turned off the motor and the running lights. Pong's boat drifted on the dazzling surface of the bay. Wolkowicz climbed onto the roof of the cabin and looked, first with the naked eye, then with binoculars, at all 360 degrees of the horizon, to be sure that he was absolutely alone. Nothing moved. Onshore, a navigational strobe light blinked on a hillside and he could hear cars on a highway, farther inland.

Working methodically, he got a rubber raft out of its locker and inflated it. He put it overboard and secured it to the boat with a line. Then he dragged the anchor, which was attached to a heavy chain, across the deck and loaded it—first the anchor, then the chain, a bit at a time, into the raft. The raft buckled under the weight.

Wolkowicz started the engines again and drove the boat toward the head of the bay, dead slow. He lashed the wheel and went astern, pulling the raft alongside. Holding on to the line, which was doubled around a stanchion but untied, he got into the raft. It nearly capsized under the extra burden of his two hundred pounds, but then it floated, its bottom slapping heavily on the wash from the boat. Wolkowicz let go of the line and the boat, lights burning and engines gurgling, cruised away toward the shore.

Wolkowicz wrapped the anchor chain around his body, standing up in the bobbing raft in order to pass it over his shoulders and around his waist. When it was secured, he sat down again and got out the survival knife and the blunt executioner's pistol. He fired the pistol once into the air, a test shot. It kicked hard against his palm, bruising the fleshy base of his thumb. He cocked the gun and clasped it under his left armpit.

Wolkowicz took the knife out of its sheath and threw the sheath overboard. It drifted away in the strong current. Then, working clumsily because he was wrapped in the anchor chain, he slashed the raft, one air chamber after the other, with rapid, sure strokes. As the air hissed out, he heard Waddy Jessup say, "Is your father a worker, Barnabas? Then we're dying for him."

"Fuck it," Wolkowicz said.

The raft was already sinking. He only had a moment to act. He threw the knife into the water, seized the gun, and placed his thumb on the trigger. With a last smile for this final act of cunning, Wolkowicz reached behind him, pressed the muzzle of the derringer against the back of his skull, and pulled the trigger.

The recoil tore the pistol out of his dead hand and it splashed into the sea. The raft capsized and floated away after the bobbing orange handle of the survival knife. Together, Wolkowicz and the pistol fluttered downward. The gun sank into the silt. The anchor bit into the bottom and held.

The chain was not heavy enough to overcome the buoyancy of Wolkowicz's stout body. The current took him to the end of the anchor chain, and there he floated, arms outstretched, a nimbus of blood and brains around his shattered skull, in the splinters of moonlight that penetrated the surface of the water.

EPILOGUE

Lori

Pulling the Flexible Flyer behind him, Christopher climbed the mountain above the Harbor. David Patchen, higher on the path, paused at the Hubbard graveyard. It had been a hard, early winter, and deep drifts lay among the headstones.

Patchen went inside, walking on the places that had been swept bare by the wind so as not to leave footprints, and read the inscriptions on the markers. Wolkowicz had been dead for five years.

"Odd about Wolkowicz," he said. "Ilse wanted to cremate him. She had some Teutonic idea of scattering his ashes over Berlin, the birthplace of their love. But we didn't dare destroy the body. It would have created another conspiracy theory."

As Wolkowicz had foreseen, the discovery of his body had given birth to a storm of investigations and publicity. It was a classic spy-thriller homicide. Patrick Graham was eager to believe that the Outfit had silenced its most heroic agent with a bullet. Who knew what foul secrets it wished to protect?

Wolkowicz had been buried in Arlington National Cemetery, with a flag on his coffin and all his medals pinned to his corpse. After all, Patchen said, he had been an authentic American hero. The funeral had been covered by all the networks, but to the end it was Patrick Graham's story.

"This is Barney Wolkowicz's last secret," Graham had intoned in his on-camera voice, as Taps and the clash of rifle fire resounded in the background. "He is being buried with full military honors, and we can only wonder if his mourners are, perhaps, also his murderers. Barney Wolkowicz, you may be sure, would not want us to know the truth. He kept his oath of secrecy until the end."

Patchen brushed off Indian Joe's stone, then blew away the powdery snow that stuck in the grooves of the letters that the second Aaron had chiseled into the granite.

"Have you told her about Indian Joe?" he asked.

Christopher looked down at the small child who sat on the sled. "Not yet," he said.

The little girl rolled off the Flexible Flyer and, tugging it along behind her by its rope, started up the path by herself. She trudged along with a determined stride, taking deep breaths, pausing now and again in childish curiosity to study some object along the way—a rock covered with icicles, a flight of crows. Christopher followed, and Patchen, floundering through billowing snowdrifts, joined him again on the path. He did not hurry; he was content to walk behind the child. He seemed to take pleasure in watching her.

"To the extent that it can ever be over," Patchen said, "the Wolkowicz affair is over. How he'd bitch if he could hear me calling it 'the Wolkowicz affair,' as if it were . . . a fucking love story. But that's what it was. Did you believe him when he said he had you kidnapped into China in order to save your life?"

"Yes. Of course. Everything he did, he did for personal reasons."

"He was never anybody's agent. How could we, how could the Russians have spent so many years thinking that he'd work for us? It wasn't in his nature."

It was Christmas Eve. Patchen paused and looked over the valley. The wind lifted a puff of snow; it hung for an instant against the hemlock-blue mountaintop, then vanished.

Like Hubbard's ashes.

Patchen looked at Christopher, to see if once again they were having the same thought. Christopher smiled. They both smiled. They had known each other for such a long time; they had known the real truth about so many things. Yet they knew almost nothing. That was what made them smile.

The child had reached the top of the hill. She turned the sled around and got on. Christopher called out a warning. She was too small to go down alone. Patchen called out, too. There was terrible danger here. Without a moment's hesitation, the child pushed off and started down the mountainside. The sled dipped and gathered speed.

"Watch out!" Patchen said.

Runners singing, the sled hurtled down the steep path, plunging among the rocks and the stone walls, flying (as Christopher knew it seemed to the little girl) down into the bare branches of the trees below. The two men were unable to stop it as it went by.

They ran down the mountainside after it, Christopher covering the slippery ground in long thumping strides, Patchen slithering and falling on his bad leg. At the bottom, the sled ran into a snowdrift and turned over. The child was thrown clear. Stephanie, her mother, had been watching from the window. She ran out of the house, black hair flying, and floundered into the snowdrift.

The child was unhurt. Christopher took her out of Stephanie's arms. His daughter looked at him out of enormous, clear gray eyes. She was just beginning to speak in sentences.

"I wasn't afraid," she said.

"Yes, Lori, I know," Christopher replied, his heart overflowing with love, his voice trembling with fear.

Author's Note

The characters and events in this book are wholly imaginary and are not intended to resemble anyone who ever lived or anything that ever happened. For details of life inside a Chinese prison during the regime of Mao Zedong I consulted the excellent *Prisoner of Mao*, by Bao Ruo-Wang (Jean Pasqualini) and Rudolph Chelminski (Penguin Books, 1976), and other sources, but Christopher's experiences are invented. In an earlier novel, Christopher was said to have an older brother, his parents' favorite child. Readers of *The Last Supper* will recognize that this was unfounded gossip.

C. McC.